WOODCOCK FLIGHT

A Novel

ANTHONY MCDONALD

Anchor Mill Publishing

Anchor Mill Publishing

4/04 Anchor Mill

7 Thread Street

Paisley PA1 1JR

SCOTLAND

anchormillpublishing@gmail.com

For Tony Linford, in memoriam, and for Nigel Fothergill.

Acknowledgements:

The author would like to thank Lindy Seton-Winton, James Simpson, Will Tatters, and Joachim Vieritz.

Part One

Autumn 2012

Anthony McDonald

ONE

He went to Seville. There were other places he would have to go eventually, but none appealed. None came bounding into his mind, tail wagging, with a label round its neck that said home. Seville, even if it no longer answered to the name of home, was different.

He took the morning train south to Madrid. It took a couple of hours. Then the AVE, the high-speed service, up and running between Seville and the capital for some fifteen years now but new to him. It delivered him to the Santa Justa station, also new to him, just as the afternoon heat was leaving the streets.

The Giralda, the Moors' old minaret, was comfortingly in view, and he threaded his way towards it, backpack and guitar on back, until he found a *hostal* and checked into it, behind the cathedral, in one of Seville's mazes within mazes of tiny streets. A search for an early evening beer took him inevitably to the Bodegón that long ago had been the centre of his social life. It was much changed: reduced to half its old character and size. Castrated, Karsten thought. But peering out of the window across Calle Santander and upwards he could see the windows of the apartment where he'd lived, and that was reassuringly the same. Except for the apartment's occupant of course. The current one, visible through the window, appeared to be an artist, standing working at her easel, palette and brushes in her hands. Behind her back a television set was on, in Karsten's full view. A woman was being interviewed; it must be the *Telediario*. Karsten recognised her. A British lawyer who had been in the Spanish news during the last few days, criticising the government for something, he didn't remember what, on behalf of the European Court of

Human Rights. He could see her face now, in the aquarium light of any TV viewed through two sets of windows as you peered into someone else's flat. He couldn't hear the lawyer's words of course, but her name came to mind, remembered from last night's news. Philippa Brookes.

A great disturbance erupted in the street. The urgent huff of powerful air-brakes, yells and shouts. Karsten didn't pause to think. He ran out of the door, alongside one of the waiters from behind the bar. People with phones against their ears were shouting, *'Ambulancia. Urgencia.'* Others were shouting indiscriminately at each other. A medium-sized truck had mounted the narrow pavement a metre or two away as it turned the sharp corner out of Calle Temprado opposite. Pinned between its flank and the wall of the Bodegón Torre del Oro, where Karsten's beer waited for him on the other side, was a bicycle and, astride the bicycle, though collapsed like a thing of red-soaked rags, was the body of a young woman.

Among the voices that urged others to call an ambulance one or two shouted, 'A priest. Get a priest.' Karsten, right there at the centre of the scene, bizarrely remembering an accident with a lorry and a piano at the exact same spot, said automatically, 'I am a priest,' and knelt among the blood and the wreckage of the bike. 'Go in,' he said to someone, anyone. 'Get water. Olive oil.'

It was surely too late for any doctor to be of use, or for any ambulance. Reaching into the gap between truck and wall where the bicycle and its rider were tightly wedged, Karsten was able to touch the woman's head. He felt for a pulse at the temple but didn't find one. And breathing seemed to have ceased. In case she could hear him, though Karsten doubted this, he said to her in Spanish, 'My daughter, in God's name I absolve you from your sins. Go in peace to Him and to eternal joy.' Water arrived from inside the Bodegón, and olive oil from a table-top cruet set. Karsten blessed the water, dippcd a finger in it and moistened the woman's lips, though blood was beginning to seep between them from inside her mouth. He poured a little of the oil onto his fingers and touched the bit of her forehead that he could reach, while reciting the prayer of the sacrament of the dying. After he had finished he felt once more for a pulse at the temple, but without success. He couldn't see if her eyes were closed: he would have had to lie on the ground among the still flowing blood and look up, and he didn't want to do that. He got to his feet. 'An ambulance is coming?' he asked the crowd. 'But I think she's gone.' He wanted to be gone himself, a middle-aged man in jeans and T-shirt who had just attracted unwanted attention by announcing that he was a priest. He hadn't practised as one for several weeks now. Not since the day he'd decided quite suddenly that he no longer believed in God. He was uncomfortable now: in the wrong time and place.

The police arrived then; their headquarters were only a block or two away. Karsten seized the moment to flee the scene. He went up to the nearest of the approaching officers and said, 'I'm not a witness. I gave her the last rites because I used to be a priest. I'm sure she's dead.' Then he walked quickly away in the direction of the Rio Guadalquivir and its palm-spiked waterfront. 'Wait!' the policeman called after him, but Karsten didn't break his stride, turning the corner a moment later by the ancient Tower of Gold.

He had no real idea why he'd wanted to come to Seville, nor of what he was going to do now he'd got here. He spent the next couple of days striding round the streets of the city centre, trying to find a purpose in simply absorbing the beauty of the place. It was not greatly changed since he had lived here as a young man. A labyrinth of small streets, few more than a hundred yards long and barely wide enough to drive a car down, that offered you a multiple choice of other alleyways at the end of each. The labyrinth was cut through occasionally by wider roads that even so weren't all that large. Any that could boast two-way traffic and pavements had orange trees growing along them, in rows down each side. Closely spaced so that their canopies almost touched they were loaded at this time of year with dark green but full-grown fruit. The houses behind the trees were painted mostly icing-sugar white with egg-yolk yellow trim. The unchanging colours of Seville that warmed the heart.

He took his guitar into one of the most charming of the *plazas* in the Barrio Santa Cruz: the one named Donna Elvira. He knew that he was no longer the cute and tousle-headed youth of the old days, and calculated that the stage set offered by the Donna Elvira plaza, with its blue and yellow tiled benches, its hedges of box, its floor of miniature cobbles in eye-beguiling patterns and its canopy of orange trees, would compensate for age-related deficiencies in the matter of his looks. His strategy paid off. The tourists who sat eating outside the restaurants or were simply absorbing the beauty of the place on the seats in the centre of the tiny square rewarded him decently after he had played, when he walked among them with his guitar turned upside down, inviting them to place coins on its chestnut-shiny back.

This activity, practised thrice daily, brought him enough to eat. At least for now. He lived mainly on fruit, and on sandwiches made from bread and *chorizo* and other fillings which he bought in the small shops he passed.

Walking along Calle Linares one morning, near the back of the ochre-walled El Salvador church, he saw an extraordinary sight. Ahead of him a youngish man leaned towards the plate-glass window of a shop in which his reflection now appeared, leaning out and towards him. The man's lips touched the glass and he gave his reflection a kiss. Or that was how it appeared to an astonished Karsten. But a second later, as he reached the spot, he saw what had really happened. One section of plate glass had been slid open. Inside the shop a young woman stood, the hose attachment of a vacuum-cleaner in her hands. It was she the young man had kissed. Now they stood talking together, he in the street, she inside the open window of the shop, as Karsten passed on his way.

Things were not always as they first appeared, of course. It hadn't needed that extraordinary illusion in the shop window to remind Karsten of that. It was possible, he thought at that moment, that the purpose of his return to Seville had already been achieved. In giving to a dying girl the sacrament – a consolation in whose efficacy he no longer believed – he had perhaps fulfilled the city's requirement for his presence here. As he turned this over in his mind he remembered that he had not paid for his interrupted beer in the Bodegón Torre del Oro. He'd had no intention of returning there again, now that he had revisited, and been disappointed by, the place. But, though no longer a priest, he had not lost his belief in a man's obligation to honour his debts. Later that day he went back to Calle Santander to pay the two euros or whatever it was for that unfinished drink.

He didn't know if the staff would remember his earlier visit, or even if the same staff would be on duty. It would be easier if they didn't remember him, he thought. He would just put the money on the counter, say that he'd forgotten to pay for a beer a couple of days before and walk straight out. But they did remember him. A barman whom he recognised, and another man who was probably the manager of the place. There was no question of his paying for the unfinished beer, they told him. They insisted he have another one, now, on the house. They had something to tell him, one of them said. The family of the dead girl had come to the place, or some of them had, the day after her death. They had heard about the jeans-clad priest who had helped prepare her for her ultimate journey and they wanted to meet him, to thank him face to face.

'I'd really rather not,' said Karsten. He found himself feeling very awkward about this. The manager gave him a suddenly doubtful look and he realised he would have to explain. 'I am a priest,' he reassured the man. 'They need have no doubt about that. But I'm a priest in the sense that a priest is always a priest, no matter what happens to him in life, or what happens to his belief. He cannot be unordained. But priests do sometimes leave the Church. Their faith sometimes leaves them. That is in fact my case.' Karsten stopped, unsure how this had gone down with his interlocutors, unsure if they would even have understood. He was relieved to see that he had been understood perfectly. The two men, who were probably not believers themselves or else drifted in and out of belief as occasions in life demanded, nodded, and the one whom Karsten had guessed was the manager said that he entirely understood Karsten's difficulty, the delicacy of his situation.

On the other hand, he didn't seem ready to let go of the matter just yet. 'Perhaps,' he suggested, 'if just one of the family was to meet you – one was her uncle and seemed a reasonable sort of man – just for a few minutes, perhaps in here... Maybe that would be possible?'

Karsten thought he might just manage that. Just one uncle, though. Not a great big Catholic family crowd.

How crazy all this was, Karsten thought. Never go back. Wise people all over the world said that. But Karsten had come back, foolishly perhaps, to the street in which he had once lived, to the bar in which he'd drunk. And this tragedy had occurred as soon as he'd reached the spot. It was something he couldn't have imagined happening however hard he'd tried. Years ago he had comforted the relatives of people who'd died in a crash – a plane crash that time, in which he himself had been slightly injured – and as a direct result of that he had discovered his faith; in the aftermath become a priest. Now, no sooner had he lost that faith than the thing had happened again. He said suddenly to the two men, whose attention was still focused on nobody but him, 'I used to live here when I was twenty-four or - five.' He gestured through the window to the houses across the street. 'Right opposite. And this was our local bar.' He'd said *our* bar. His and Borja's. Theirs and all their friends'.

The manager smiled for the first time. *'Hijo de la casa,'* he greeted him. Son of the house.

'I came back, just passing through, to see how things looked after so long. To see if things had changed. Some have, of course, and others not. The trams are a bit of a shock.' He paused for a second. 'I didn't expect to get mixed up in a tragedy.'

'You're not Spanish,' the younger bar tender said to him. 'You have an accent. Only very slight, of course,' he added emolliently.

'I'm German,' Karsten told him. 'I've lived all my adult life in Spain but,' he half smiled, half grimaced, 'I'm as German as Angela Merkel, I'm afraid.'

TWO

An uncle is a person of some age and gravitas and so Karsten was surprised to see that the dead girl's relative was a decade or more younger than himself. Surprised for only a second or so. Of course uncles, like policemen, had to grow younger as your own age increased. Anyway, Karsten was in no doubt as to the man's identity. He was one of a small number of customers seated at tables in the Bodegón when Karsten entered at five in the afternoon. Dressed in an immaculate suit and with tinted glasses he radiated such an air of tense expectancy that it was quite unnecessary for the barman to step forward, as he politely did, to indicate to each of them who the other was.

He rose to his feet to shake Karsten's hand. When he invited him to take a drink Karsten read his cue in the glass of coffee that sat in front of him and ordered the same for himself. Despite the early hour he found himself wishing the man had been drinking something a bit stronger and that he could then have reasonably asked for something alcoholic himself. He felt as wrong-footed by the younger man's suit and tie (Karsten was in T-shirt and jeans) as he was by the delicate awkwardness of the whole situation. They introduced themselves – the man was called Eduardo – and they sat down.

Eduardo looked closely at Karsten for a second – through his tinted glasses he could see more deeply into Karsten's eyes than Karsten could into his – and then said, 'Please don't look so worried. I came only to thank you and, on behalf of Elena's family – Elena was the name of my niece – to see you face to face. I have no other agenda: nothing to ask for, nothing to explain.' He waited for Karsten's reply.

It came of course in Spanish, the language in which Eduardo had addressed him. Over the past thirty years it had more or less replaced Karsten's native German as his language number one. 'Sorry if I looked apprehensive. It had nothing to do with anything you might do or say. But there are things, which I have to be honest about, that might make you less than happy about the priest who gave the last rites to Elena being me.'

Unsurprisingly this made Eduardo look less than happy at once. 'What things?'

'I no longer work as a priest,' Karsten said. He looked down at himself and made an involuntary gesture with his arms. 'As the clothes I'm wearing may indicate.'

Eduardo leaned back in his chair a little. 'Have you been … what is the expression … unfrocked?'

This made Karsten smile. It was a moment of slight relief. He thought he knew what was going through Eduardo's mind and set about dispelling that particular worry at once. 'No. I am not a molester of children, if that was your anxiety. My departure from my job was my own choice, unconnected with anything of a sexual nature.'

'Then how...?' Eduardo's interest seemed sincere. Karsten was surprised by that, and found quite unexpectedly that he wanted him to hear the truth.

'I lost my faith. Quite simply. Over a period of no more than a few days. Within the last few weeks.'

Karsten's coffee arrived. Eduardo said, 'Would you like a *coñac* with that?' Karsten said a grateful yes, and Eduardo asked the waiter to bring one for them both. 'Do you want to tell me?' Eduardo asked.

'Perhaps I do,' Karsten said, feeling the tug of conflicting impulses familiar to anyone who has ever been invited to confide in a stranger. 'I made a promise to a friend that I was finding hard to keep.' He stopped at that point, unsure in what order to arrange his thoughts.

Mistaking the reason for his hesitation Eduardo said, 'Before you continue, let me tell you I know how things work in the Catholic Church. That a priest remains a priest whether he loses faith or not. The sacrament you offered Elena was as valid as if given by any practising priest.'

Karsten was glad that he thought that, or said he did, but did not reply to Eduardo's point. 'This friend said to me, on the day I told him I was planning to become a priest, 'Will people like me have to suffer you in ten years' time denouncing them from the pulpit for the sin that cries to heaven for vengeance?' I promised him that I would not.' Karsten peered carefully in through Eduardo's glasses.

Eduardo peered equally carefully out. 'Are you *maricón*?'

'No,' said Karsten. 'I'm not. And I know that I'm not. But you're in the right area. My friend was. And if he's still alive, no doubt he still is.'

'I am not gay either,' Eduardo said. 'I'm married and have children – which proves nothing, I grant you – but take my word for it, I'm not.' He sipped at the brandy which had opportunely arrived. 'There is someone in my family who is.'

'It was the Pope,' Karsten said seriously, ignoring what Eduardo had just said. 'Writing letters to politicians and world leaders, then having letters read in churches, telling people which way to tell their parliaments to vote... Especially in England, where my friend lives. He's Spanish but his partner is an Englishman.'

'My uncle's partner was an English guy,' Eduardo said. 'A younger man. They lived very happily here, between Seville and Jerez. The family never got used to it. The Englishman died.' He shrugged and sighed. 'Water under the bridge.'

'The final thing was,' Karsten needed to get this out, 'the Cardinal of Scotland refusing to speak to the government because of it...'

'To the Scottish government? I didn't know they had one. Or to the British...?' Eduardo seemed to want to have the details right.

'I forget which. One or the other. It was just four weeks ago. But I remembered then the promise I'd made. The whole thing … the faith thing … like a house of cards.' Karsten took a sip from his own *coñac*. He was rather red in the face.

'I understand,' said Eduardo.

'Do you still have faith?' Karsten asked him a bit sharply.

'My family does. My wife... We bring the children up as good Catholics. My sister, Elena's mother, she is very religious. Her husband even more than she. For me... well, it's an intermittent thing. Sometimes it's very strong in my heart; sometimes I'm like you, and I don't believe at all.'

Karsten – these days – thought that was fair enough. The same had gone for most of his parishioners and schoolchildren in Gijón.

Eduardo leaned forward again. 'Forgive me – it isn't my business – but your situation interests me. If you have lost your faith and cannot practise as a priest, how are you living? What do you do now? Were you a priest here in Seville?'

'In Gijón.'

'Then what has brought you six hundred – seven hundred? – kilometres south?'

'The weather, for a start,' Karsten said, attempting to lighten things a bit. Automatically they both glanced through the window: the September heat and brightness still cheered the street in the late afternoon.

'Seville was my first home in Spain,' Karsten went on more seriously. He then announced the fact that he was German – something which, to judge from his lack of reaction, Eduardo had already guessed – and that for part of his time in Seville he had lived precisely across the street from where they sat.

'People say you should never go back.'

'Everybody says that people say that,' answered Karsten evenly. 'But surely an exception should be made for Seville. *Non?*' They both chuckled a bit at that. For the first time since they'd met. 'This was my bar back then. Mine and a little crowd of friends'.'

Eduardo was granted an insight at that moment: one that had not yet come to Karsten himself. 'You have come back to find your friends. Of course. But after so long they will not be here.'

'Perhaps you're right,' Karsten said. 'Thank you for explaining my behaviour to me.' He smiled. 'I hadn't quite realised I had come here for that.'

'And where are they now, your friends? Do you know? Did you keep in touch?'

Karsten thought. 'Perhaps a letter or two during the first few years. I don't remember well. I think I probably thought it was best to let the contacts lapse. My world had become so very different from theirs.'

'But now, once again, it is not?'

'Maybe,' Karsten said.

They met again the following day. In a different bar, this time. It was Eduardo who suggested the Casa Morales, a couple of blocks away on Calle Vinuesa. Of all the bars in the city it was the one that would probably have changed least since Karsten had frequented these streets, and Eduardo thought, correctly as it happened, that Karsten would like that. The place was much cleaner than it had been, it was true, and offered tapas for sale – which it hadn't done in the past. In the old days you brought in your fried fish from the *frituria* opposite and unwrapped the brown paper package on the bar counter in front of you as you consumed your drink. But in most respects the Casa Morales was the same: earthenware jars ten feet high receded reassuringly to infinity in the dark end of the cavernous room; the same advertisements for brandy hung on the walls as had hung there when Karsten knew the place, and had hung there before he was even born.

Karsten had not been overjoyed when Eduardo proposed a second meeting. They had already talked about the dead girl, and about her boyfriend who worked in a bank, about the parents and brothers she had left behind. He was very afraid of them all turning up, this very religious family – exactly what he had dreaded when the manager of the Bodegón had suggested a contact in the first place. Especially as, apparently, they all lived in Seville. Karsten knew how hard it would be for them to stay away. He'd explained this to Eduardo. But Eduardo had promised he would come on his own. 'I have to go now, you see,' he'd explained, after a nervous glance at the sleeve under which his wristwatch lay, though without looking at the watch itself. 'But I feel our conversation hasn't finished yet.' Which gave Karsten new uncertainties about the benefits of a second encounter. Yet he had felt unable to say no. So now here he was, and he was discovering, a little to his relief, that Eduardo wanted to pursue a thread from their earlier discussion that had nothing to do with his niece and the mixed fortunes of his family's religious faith.

'Tell me their names again.' Eduardo said. They were standing by the familiar counter, in front of each of them a copita of fino de Jerez, and Eduardo took a gizmo from his pocket, an iPhone or something similar. Karsten hadn't thought of that. There had been a desk-top computer in the priest's house where Karsten had lived and worked. It had been sufficient for his needs. He hadn't given much thought to how he was going to function without it in the brave new world into which he was setting out.

'There were Pippa and Mark,' Karsten began. 'I'm afraid I don't remember their family names. Also, just before I left Seville they split up.'

'Ah,' said Eduardo. 'That might not be so easy. Unless one of them became famous under a single name. Like ... oh, Madonna, or I don't know who.' But to demonstrate his thoroughness he typed in Pippa and Mark anyway. He was rewarded with a wedding photo of a beautiful young couple who had married the week before. He showed his finding to Karsten.

'Very lovely,' Karsten said. 'But unfortunately far too young. By about thirty years I should think. Anyway it's unlikely that any of my old crowd are famous in the least.'

'They needn't be,' Eduardo said. 'Anyone who gets a mention in a newspaper, however provincial, turns up if you look hard enough. Anyone who signs off a press release for the company they work for... Tell me the others.' His fingers hovered, quivered, over the little screen.

'I had an English girlfriend,' Karsten said a bit shyly. 'Well, a sort of girlfriend. Alexa. Alexa Soares. She was a brilliant guitarist. She made quite a career in Spain. Which was astonishing, since she was female. Although her name helped. In England Soares was pronounced with one syllable but the Spanish were able to make it sound Spanish by pronouncing it as three.'

'I remember the name,' Eduardo said. 'Fantastic red hair she had. I remember that. But it was years ago.' He tapped the name. 'Here we are. Things are coming up. Concert notices from years ago. Nothing recent.'

'I suppose she got married,' Karsten said, unable to mask the disappointment in his voice. 'Had children. Career over. *Sic transit gloria mundi.*'

Eduardo shot him a rather arch look. 'Are not children some of the world's glories too?'

Karsten grimaced. 'You put me to shame,' he said. He went on, 'Then, Borja and James. The gay Spanish man I made a promise to, and his English other half.'

'And would you remember their surnames by any chance?'

Very seriously Karsten said, 'Borja Alcorlo Silva and James Miller.'

'There'd be a lot of James Millers, I imagine. The other guy might give us a better chance.' But they tried James Miller first. One site announced cheerfully that there were over two hundred James Millers in the UK alone. One worked in the philosophy department at Durham University, another was a TV cameraman and one was a paraplegic athlete. Karsten didn't think the James he'd known would be any of those.

'Well, OK,' said Eduardo, 'here's another one. He's being interviewed in the press about the closure of a theatre in the English Midlands. Or its imminent closure. He's the … art-istic director. That's what it says. Lack of government funding... etcetera, etcetera...'

Karsten peered at the words and frowned. 'That doesn't sound like the one either. He worked teaching English when I knew him. I never heard him talk about the theatre much. On the other hand, he did like quoting Shakespeare rather a lot. Or misquoting him. It was a game that he and Borja used to play between themselves. I shared that flat with both of them for a bit. Before that, with Borja only. During a period when he and James... Well, that's not important now.'

'Let's try the Borja one, shall we?' Eduardo said. 'After all, he's the one you really want to find. Am I right?' Eduardo didn't wait for an answer to that but keyed in the name. 'Not many of those,' he said. 'Let's see... *commended for his quick thinking...* Go with that one ... *Senior Captain Alcorlo diverted the plane on its approach to Gatwick, landing at Southampton where medical assistance...* My God.' He passed the thing to Karsten. 'Is your English better than mine? Have I understood this right?'

Karsten peered at the miniature account of an emergency on board an airliner en route to England from the Algarve. The call had gone out for a doctor – Karsten couldn't not think of his own urgent summons just days earlier – a passenger had choked on something. 'The doctor operated with a knife, opened the wind-pipe and kept the hole open with the tube of a ball-point pen.'

'That's what I thought it said,' said Eduardo. He couldn't hide his satisfaction that his comprehension of English had been up to the task. 'And the quick-thinking pilot...' He looked at Karsten. 'Was your friend a pilot?'

'He was a clerk in the tourist office. But he did talk about wanting to be a pilot during the last few weeks I spent with him. I don't think anyone took him seriously. He was still very young... He'd had a bit of a thing with an airline steward.' *The* airline steward, Karsten thought. Rafael, who died in the crash that I was in... 'It was a very long time ago.' He thought for a moment. 'He *might* have become a pilot, I suppose. Some people do achieve their dreams.'

'There's another one,' Eduardo announced. 'He's writing to a local newspaper in England. He doesn't want his local theatre closed. This one's just three weeks ago. Of course it could be a different Borja Alcorlo Silva.'

'I don't think so,' said Karsten. 'Or if it is, then this one's the right one. It ties up too closely with the James Miller whose theatre's about to shut down. Where is it exactly?' With a bit of darting about they extracted the name of the place: it was a market town or small city in the English Midlands, whose name Karsten didn't know. Karsten asked the barman for a scrap of paper and wrote the names and places down.

'You'll contact him, of course,' said Eduardo.

'Will I? I'm not sure what I'd have to say.'

'I kept my promise to you,' suggested Eduardo. 'I gave up my career on your account and now I need a place to stay and a job.'

'I'm not sure how well that would go down,' Karsten said, deadpan.

Eduardo shared his surname, Ybarra, with a very well-known brand of olive oil. That might have been a coincidence, of course. But the suit he was wearing, and the one he had worn the day before – a different one – indicated that he was quite comfortably off, whether because of olive oil or not. 'I talked to my uncle about you,' he told Karsten. 'To the uncle who is *maricón*. We spoke on the phone. He was very interested in your story.'

'Because of the English boyfriend thing, I suppose.' Karsten wanted to show Eduardo that he'd remembered that.

Eduardo frowned. 'Not only. Because he had conflict with his family – my family, my very Catholic family – about being the way he was. As many of his generation did.'

'How old is he?' Karsten asked.

'A year or two past seventy, I think. He imagines you will travel all the way to England to meet your friend face to face.' Eduardo smiled. 'He is a dreamer, Tio Paco. But I thought I'd mention it. He quoted a Greek poem. Thankfully he quoted it in Spanish. It's called Ithaca. Have you heard of it?'

'I think I have. If you voyage to Ithaca, pray that your journey be long... Or something like that.'

'I have to voyage to Madrid tomorrow night,' Eduardo said, 'and I'm praying that my journey be short. 'Can we meet one more time before I go?'

'Er... yes,' said Karsten, a bit surprised. He'd met Eduardo twice now, as a courtesy. He'd been surprised at the interest Eduardo had shown in him, and grateful for his help this time in looking up his old contacts on the net. He wasn't expecting a friendship to develop, nor thinking he particularly wanted one. Again the anxiety surfaced that the whole family would turn up, though again Eduardo reassured him that would not be the case. In the end, thinking it was perhaps as well that Eduardo was leaving for Madrid and also that it might be time he left Seville himself before he got sucked into the dead girl's family tragedy as into an inescapable quagmire, he accepted Eduardo's suggestion that they meet again here at Morales, for an early evening beer the following day, before Eduardo's train went.

There was an envelope of course. Karsten watched with a sinking feeling as Eduardo drew it from his pocket while they stood at the bar. 'You know I can't possibly accept money from you,' he said as Eduardo opened his mouth to speak.

'You don't know how much or little is in the envelope,' Eduardo said. 'It's from all of Elena's family, not from me. It's a sum that's very easy for them to give.'

'All the same...'

'Listen.' Eduardo waved the envelope between them, politely though, not actually in Karsten's face. 'You gave my niece a gift which was easy for you to give. All the easier for the fact that you no longer believed in what it meant. It was a gift she couldn't refuse, yet which put her in no sense in your power. Our family's gift in return, though infinitely less important, is offered in the same spirit. Perhaps I don't believe any longer in the value of this money of ours. As a German, you must be more aware than most of money's ability to disappear like smoke. The Weimar Republic... To say nothing of what's happening to the euro now. All those billions given to Greece... The way things are going the contents of this envelope might not buy you coffee and *tostadas* in six months' time.' He grinned. 'Alternatively, the British pound might fall through the floor and, if you do go to England, you might be able to buy a whole airline for yourself.'

Karsten had to laugh. 'I am thinking of going to England now, it's true.' Since yesterday the idea had become as much about escaping from this family he had never met as about finding Borja.

'I thought you'd say that. You'll need money to get there. Busking won't do.' Eduardo had heard from Karsten how he was precariously earning his bread these days in Seville. 'And I know there's no redundancy packages for ex-priests. Out on your ear, that's the Church's way with those who don't toe the line.'

'There's always my father,' Karsten said a bit huffily.

'The lender of last resort,' Eduardo said, smiling. 'Talk about being in someone else's power then.'

With a shrug Karsten picked up the envelope that now lay on the counter between them. 'I'll pay it back to you when I can.'

'No hurry for that,' Eduardo said. 'One last thing. If you're back here looking for work in a few months, we'd find something – something clerical and liveable-on – in one of the companies we have. You can depend on that.'

'I'm sure it won't be necessary,' Karsten said, thinking that in picking up his envelope he had said goodbye to his dignity for a bit. 'But thank you for the thought.' The two men shook hands and this time Eduardo did look at his watch. He had a train to catch.

THREE

'Tell me again, who that woman is?' A tiny exclamation mark of a frown appeared above Andy's nose as his head turned from the TV towards Nick. It was as close to a real frown as Andy's face ever got.

'Philippa Brookes. James and Borja used to know her in Spain. You used to know that.'

'I know I did,' Andy said. 'That's why I asked you.' The exclamation mark disappeared among the new punctuation lines of a smile.

'She was a teacher where James used to work. When he taught there. He liked her a lot. So did Alexa. And … Mark.' A thought surfaced, and it was Nick's turn to frown. A frown whose fluid lines got entangled in the less yielding ones of his spectacles. 'I think she used to be Mark's girlfriend, fiancée even. I think one of them told me that.'

Andy nodded faintly – the stirring of a memory that wasn't very important anyway.

'She's a big-shot lawyer now.' Nick's interest in Andy's question began to kindle just as Andy's own faded. 'She's very high up in Europe.'

'Like the Pope,' suggested Andy.

'Not quite.' Nick thought for a second. 'European Court of Human Rights? Something like that.' He jerked his head towards the screen where the lawyer was now in full tirade against something. She had a way of delivering her words, and a way of addressing the camera, which hinted that not least among the targets of her righteous anger were the viewers themselves. 'Back then they all knew her as simply Pippa.'

'Simply Pipper! How spiffing!' Andy hooted a Bertie Woosterish celebration of the sound of the words that was the more startling for the fact that his own accent was Edinburgh Scots. 'Anyway,' he returned to his more usual tones, 'she certainly knows how to twist the knife when it comes to the government.'

'She was the same with the last government, remember. And the Spanish government, whichever one it happens to be. America too...'

Before the list could grow longer Andy intervened. 'Mark was American.'

'Still is,' Nick said. 'I spoke to him on the phone earlier.' The frown came back for a moment. 'Though his mother was Spanish.'

'Which would have cut no ice with Pippa, from what you say.' Then the exclamation mark reappeared between Andy's blond eyebrows as he realised that something else Nick had said might have an impact closer to home. 'You spoke to Mark today?'

'Just by chance,' Nick said. 'I called Alexa and he answered. He always seems a bit bemused when it's me on the phone. Like he doesn't know what he's supposed to do. It's not that he forgets who I am. It's just that the standard things like, *I'll just get her*, or *Can I give her a message?* or *Shall I get her to call back?* seem to elude him. Perhaps it's part of being a poet.'

'Being someone who used to say he was a poet,' Andy amended. 'He never had anything published.'

'So?' Nick challenged. 'You've never had any poetry published either.'

'That's because I'm not a poet,' Andy explained in a patient tone. 'I never went round saying I was. I've never written a poem in my life. Well, not since I was about ten, I suppose.'

Nick could have corrected him there. At the age of rather more than ten – rather more than thirty, actually –

Andy had written a love poem to Nick. It had been excruciatingly bad, yet at the time it had worked its magic. Nick chose not to remind Andy of this. Instead he said, 'I don't think there's going to be any more work coming my way from the Trust. That's the news I took from Alexa anyway.'

Andy looked carefully at Nick. 'Is that such a bad thing? It brings you – what – a couple of hundred pounds a year, and keeps you anchored to the computer for hours at a stretch.'

'A bit more than a couple of hundred,' Nick objected without much conviction. 'It's just that...'

Andy continued Nick's thought for him, speaking very gently, 'It's just that it's your last remaining contact with the world of professional music.'

Nick looked down. 'Something like that. You've got your flying and so on...' But the weather forecast had come on and for a minute or two they both turned their attention to that. Then Nick roused himself and said it was time he went and got into his kitchen whites. He got up from the sofa and went into the bedroom.

Left on his own Andy switched off the television. He would be on duty soon himself, as mine host, behind the bar. A moment's anxiety about Nick caused the exclamation-mark mini-frown to reappear. He supposed that doing his minute amount of admin for the Eulogio Pérez Memorial Trust had helped to keep Nick from getting bored or frustrated, or whatever it was that was supposed to happen to younger life partners when they found themselves in a bit of a rut. Now Nick wouldn't have that. At least he still had his grand piano. Though it wasn't actually his grand piano. It was James and Borja's grand piano. Though not exactly theirs even. It simply lived in the building on the other side of the garden from the house in which they lived. For a moment Andy tried to think whose piano it actually was, but then stopped bothering.

Perhaps James could find some work for Nick again, Andy wondered vaguely. But he doubted that Nick, now turned forty, would want to return to stage management again – or that James would want to employ him in that capacity now. Maybe James could find him something else.

It wasn't that things were going badly between Andy and Nick. For years they had been going astonishingly well. Astonishingly because they were not just living together, but working in harness, day after day – in the admittedly picturesque setting of a country pub. But Andy's was every twelve-years-older man's fear that such a state of affairs, like a bike-ride without hills or punctures, couldn't possibly last.

Nick emerged from the bedroom in his kitchen things, smiled at Andy and said, 'See you down there,' then pattered down the stairs. Andy thought Nick looked lovely in his chef's whites. He always did. But he tried to limit the number of times he told him so to twice a week.

In the morning Nick made his way up to Sevenscore. As it was fine – it was more than that, it was a blue-skied jewel of a September morning – he walked across the fields rather than drive the longer way round by the lane. Across the road from the Rose and Castle, alongside the graveyard and the village church, a gate conveniently opened onto to the old carriage drive that had once brought trade vehicles to the back entrances of the mansion, Sevenscore House. Now the drive was just a grassy piece of pasture: the only clear sign of its route – actually unmistakeable – was a double line of Lombardy poplars that ran all the way up the slight incline of two fields, through the farmyard at the top, finally ending where it met the modern driveway by the kitchen door of the Court House, where James and Borja lived.

The pasture through which Nick and the old carriage drive made their way had a fluted appearance, as if sculpted by a giant moulding-plane. Long ridges ran in parallel away from the drive in both directions, each one about ten feet wide, cambered gently like a roadway, rising to no more than six inches in the centre, then falling away to a faint concavity, from which the next ridge began gently to rise at once. They could be seen most easily at sunrise or sunset, when they actually cast shadows in the horizontal light. At other times you could miss them altogether. But once spotted they were hard to forget, those last traces of medieval field strips that had first been ploughed more than a millennium ago.

When Nick was about halfway along between the poplar trees, he spotted Sancho Panza a little way off towards his left. He was engaged in one of his favourite pastimes: the pursuit of voles. He never ate his captures, but occasionally would bite the head off one, or the tail, as a symbolic ritual closure to the incident. Seeing Nick now, Sancho Panza abandoned his quest and began to accompany him up towards the farm. He did not want it to appear that he was accompanying Nick. He followed his own path, parallel to Nick's, about twenty yards away, and made a point of not looking in Nick's direction once. When their routes had to converge, as they did at the gateway to the farm, Sancho hung back, still keeping his distance as he followed Nick through. After the farmyard was crossed the old drive became a cart-track, made up with flints, but with grass growing down its centre line. Then it dived into a small spinney (through which Sancho followed at a distance, like a spy), to emerge and open out into a broader space where there was parking room, and the garages of Sevenscore, and the back wall and kitchen door of the Court House itself.

Sancho made his way indoors through his own private flap in the bottom of the kitchen door, but Nick went on round the corner of the house and opened the double gates there that gave onto the lawn. A very big lawn it was. At the far end a balustrade divided it from the miles of countryside that unfolded below and beyond. Nearer at hand a rectangular stone fish-pond – the *bassin* it had always been called – claimed the centre ground. The view was framed on either side by two identical buildings, believed to have been designed by Inigo Jones, each of them strongly resembling the Banqueting House in Whitehall, if on a slightly smaller scale. Scattered around were cypress trees, an orchard, and herbaceous borders brilliant today in the early autumn sun. Had you been told you had been transported to a Renaissance garden somewhere among the Florentine hills, you might be tempted to believe. And there in the middle of the lawn, seated at a garden table, with mugs of tea or coffee in front of them, were the tenants of the illusion and the panorama, tenants of all they surveyed, in shirt-sleeves and jeans.

Although they were half turned away from him, they quickly became aware of Nick's arrival: peripheral vision perhaps, the faint rumble and click of the gate, or the minute sound of footfalls on grass and barely perceptible rub of clothes. Both men looked up towards Nick, bottoms swivelling slightly on chairs. 'Hallo the kid,' said Borja, and his teeth shone in a smile. James, whose smile was always a quieter affair than Borja's, raised a hand an inch or two and said, 'Morning.'

Nick greeted them both from a yard or two away and then diverted towards the garden door of the Court House, which stood open behind them. Reaching inside he picked up the massive seventeenth-century key to the

West Pavilion and then retraced his steps towards his hosts. 'No work today?' he asked as he arrived beside the table at which they sat. He had been surprised to find them both at home, though he was not surprised to find that, being here, they were taking advantage of the sun and a garden full of flowers, enjoying morning coffee on the lawn.

'I'm going in this afternoon,' said James. 'And there's a board meeting tonight. I didn't feel like burning the mid-morning oil as well.' There were other reasons for James's rather laid-back approach to his job these days, which Nick well knew, but they weren't going to be aired right now.

All around them dewdrops still lay on the grass and bushes, sparkling like tiny lights, though lights which were already being extinguished one by one as the sun dried them out. Beyond the lawn the borders flamed with the colours of the season: waves of golden rod, tall Japanese anemones mauve and white, and rudbeckia, with giant daisy petals the rich yellow of yolk of egg, and button-dark centres that drew the eye.

'I'm off to Gatwick later,' said Borja. 'Early start tomorrow. Thought I'd told you.' He said this in the most easy-going way, with no suggestion that Nick, having been told, ought to have remembered. 'Flying to Athens like an owl.'

'Like an owl?' Nick showed slight puzzlement on his face. 'Why like an owl?'

'It's a German saying,' Borja said, leaning back on his chair so that the front two legs lifted an inch from the ground. 'Sending owls to Athens is their way of saying coals to Newcastle.'

Nick was momentarily surprised that Borja, still Spanish despite living thirty years in England, should be so ready with German idioms, but then remembered Borja telling him that he'd once shared a flat with a

German lad in Seville. That probably accounted for it. All the same he asked immediately, 'Why don't they just say coals to Newcastle, though?' and then regretted, not for the first time in his life, not having thought before he spoke.

James didn't pass up the opportunity to tease him gently. 'They don't have Newcastle in Germany.'

'They don't have Athens either,' Nick retorted, and then realised that he should have thought before saying that too. He had heard the radio news that morning. Another hand-out required by Greece. Another pound of something exacted in return.

Not bothering to beg to differ, Borja skipped ahead. 'Some would say the same goes for Spain. Mrs Merkel didn't get a very warm welcome in Madrid last month.' Then feeling that the conversation was getting rather serious for such a relaxed moment and such a beautiful day, asked, 'Do you want a coffee? Just instant.'

Nick said no thank you, he was going to crack on with Mozart and Schumann, and he'd see them later – or James at any rate. Probably in the pub when the board meeting was done? He turned away and set off across the grass, around the curving, flower-bordered colonnade to the West Pavilion, which had been the ballroom in the days of the vanished great house. He let himself in with the massive key he was carrying and vanished from James and Borja's sight. A moment later they heard the opening phrases of Schumann's Scenes From Childhood ricocheting around the lofty space inside the ballroom, and then winging their zigzag way, like a flight of birds, out into the garden through the door, which Nick had left open.

Nick asked himself constantly why he continued to keep up an activity that was so time-consuming and so demanding of effort, both mental and physical. It was twenty years since he'd collected his music degree and in all that time the possession of it had done nothing to enhance his professional status or improve his bank balance, nor to influence his choice of job. He had worked backstage in the theatre, then briefly at the National Library, then he'd become co-owner of a village pub. He'd done nothing else. He could hardly call himself a professional pianist. He didn't give concerts – he'd never kidded himself he could be as good as that – nor had he ever taught: neither piano nor music in a more general sense.

And yet practising the piano was something he'd just always done. If nobody ever heard the end result? Well, actually, people did. It was not unusual for people to come into the pub, after walking along the canal-side path, or after arriving on a boat and say, 'We heard the most wonderful sound of a piano being played, drifting across the fields.' That happened in summer, when the pavilion windows would be open, but as the pavilions lay over half a mile from the route of the canal, it was a testament not only to Nick's playing but to the carrying power of the old Broadwood, boosted by the reverberant acoustic of the ballroom. Then Andy would say nonchalantly, 'Oh, that would be my partner Nick you heard,' his throwaway tone belied by a just perceptible upturn of his mouth at the corners and a gleam of something in his eyes that he could never manage to hide.

Sometimes Nick's playing was listened to more deliberately, too. James and Borja would often overhear his practising, as they were doing now, for as long as their coffee lasted them on the lawn. When he had worked up a couple of pieces to a reasonably presentable state he would drag Andy along to hear them, together with Borja and James as well as anyone else, dinner-guests, neighbours, other friends, who happened to be around.

There was an upright piano in the 'new' bar of the pub, on which he could practise on cold winter mornings when the prospect of walking up through the snow-blanketed fields and unlocking the ice-cold ballroom did not appeal. On this little upright he would also, very occasionally, entertain customers with a bit of Scott Joplin if the moment, the mood – and the customers themselves – were right or, even more rarely, accompany some brave soul among the clientèle who wanted to sing a song. But that instrument was hardly to be compared to the eight-foot Broadwood in the ballroom pavilion, nor was the joy of playing it. It was certainly one of the things that motivated Nick to go on with his musical pursuit: the instrument itself, with its lovely tone, its beautiful setting in the double-cube room created by Inigo Jones, and the melting acoustic created by that volume and shape of space.

Another factor had to be the couple who had charge of the Broadwood and, up to a point, the building that housed it: Borja and James themselves. It was nice that Borja had just called him the kid, Nick thought in a moment's pause in his work on the Schumann Kinderscenen, nice that he still did that. Because even at a little over forty that was still how Nick saw himself in relation to the other three. Borja and James, like Andy, were a dozen years older than he was; it was a fact that none of them could change or very easily ignore. And his visits here were among the many threads that bound them all, that kept the two couples, who were scrupulously separate when it came to sex and the more possessive emotions, somehow together.

During the months in which Nick had got to know James and Borja, living here with them at Sevenscore, their lodger in the Chinese bedroom of the Court House, he had managed to fall briefly and lightly in love with them both. First of all as a couple, which had done no harm, then, one at a time, with each of them separately. And each of them in turn had briefly and in a smallish way, fallen for him. In the end those episodes had done no harm to anyone either. But though it was easy to see this in hindsight; it had been less easy to see which way things might be heading at the time. Curiously, though perhaps unsurprisingly, this piano had been involved both times. A moment of Schubert had led to a rash kiss between himself and James, and in Borja's case it had been a slow movement of Bach's that had nearly undone a beautiful evening. In a way those things had been tributes to the power and charm of Nick's playing, but Nick also knew that the music on those occasions had become the lightning rod for something else.

Then Andy. Andy had opened the door and walked into this room twenty years before, bringing Nick to a stop as he crashed through the glittering darkness of Beethoven's last sonata. And asked him to share his life with him. Andy's voice and even his body had shaken as he'd uttered that irretrievable invitation. Andy, who had at the time been an airline captain, like Borja. Andy, who had not long before faced danger and the nearness of death, had been afraid of Nick's power to say no thanks.

Today Nick was working on another piece besides the Schumann. It was Mozart's K339 Fantasy in C minor. It shared its key with that final Beethoven sonata, and had perhaps to some degree inspired it. It too was full of jewelled darkness, of landscapes lightning-lit. It had once invaded Nick's dreams, turning out to be the programme music for Blake's painting of The Fall of Lucifer. In his dream Nick had seen the lightning bolt of the doomed angel's endless descent into the abyss, while his former fellows danced on the points of pins, impossibly high, on pinnacles of rock. Nick had supposed this dream to be the result of drinking brandy late at night: it was something he'd avoided doing since.

Nick worked for a further half hour on Mozart's iridescent trills and heart-melting cadences, polishing gravity-defying leaps and runs. Then he closed the piano, locked the pavilion and crossed back across the lawn to the Court House. The table was still on the lawn, still in the full end-of-summer sun, although James and Borja and their coffee cups were gone. But the front door of the Court House still stood open, between two small bright patches of nasturtium flowers. Nick deposited the ballroom key on the little mahogany table just inside. He remembered what he'd meant to tell Borja and James: that he and Andy had seen their old friend Pippa Brookes on TV once again. He called into the house but there was no answer. James might have left for work by now, while Borja might well be in the loo or shower. Nick didn't intrude further. He made his way back round the corner of the house, shutting the gate behind him, to return the way he had come, down to the farm and along the carriage drive through the medieval fields towards the pub, where he was due to start work in half an hour. Sancho Panza did not join him on his march.

FOUR

The Greek baggage handlers were going on strike. Borja's homebound flight from Athens was scheduled for a take-off slot thirty minutes before the strike began, but a delay to their departure from Gatwick that morning had made this impossible. Their new slot was forty-five minutes later. The baggage had made it as far as the aircraft stand, in two tractor-hauled trains of trucks, but then the drivers and loaders had departed towards the terminal building on foot. One of them had had the grace to turn and look up at the cockpit window with a smile, a shrug and a wide-armed gesture that was meant to say, no bad feelings, mate, but this is life.

'I'll call ground,' said Borja. 'Tell them we'll load it ourselves.'

'And hang on to the slot?' his first officer queried. 'We'll be pushing it. Can't you get them to let us go ten minutes late?' Missed slots usually resulted in delays of half an hour or more. 'Give them an earful like you did in Madrid. That worked a treat.'

'That was because I'm Spanish,' Borja said. 'I'm not Greek as well. We'll rope the cabin crew in. Charlie's pretty willing.' Borja wasn't sure if he'd phrased that very well. Charlie was the purser, or director of cabin services as you were supposed to call them now. He had an engaging personality, and on stopovers his body-language had more than once suggested, although not too blatantly, that he might be happy to have sex with Borja, had Borja wanted it. Borja had wanted it, but had managed to resist the implied invitation. Just. But Ryan, Borja's co-pilot today, would not have known any of that. Nor, as a cosily married man whose wife was expecting their third child in just a week's time, would he have been interested.

Borja spoke to ground control in English, and learned from a not very sympathetic voice that if they failed to capture their slot they wouldn't be able to get another one until the morning. It was now not only the baggage handlers who were going on strike. The ground controllers would be joining them in half an hour's time.

Two minutes later the two pilots, along with Charlie and another young man whom Borja didn't know but who was the other male member of cabin crew, were working at a Keystone Cops pace, unloading the baggage from the lines of trucks in remorselessly hot sunshine and stowing the cases in the hold. At least the flight was not full, for which they were grateful: the quantity of baggage was not as vast as all that, and Borja did find himself feeling pleased that it was a Boeing 737 he was flying, rather than something with three times the capacity of that. Even so, all four of them were visibly perspiring by the time they re-boarded the jet: there were beads of moisture on foreheads and wet patches under arms, the latter something that cabin crew at any rate were expected not to display. Borja remembered to say a breathless, 'Thanks, boys,' to Charlie and his right-hand man as they hurriedly parted at the top of the steps. 'We'll have a drink sometime.'

Still at double-quick tempo the two pilots completed their preparations for departure, agreed the paperwork with the dispatcher, despatching him also very rapidly, and calling for the doors to be set to automatic. They were cleared for engine-start ten minutes before ground control was due to shut down. Ryan, the handling pilot for the homeward leg, his breathing still audible to his captain sitting at his side, taxied towards the runway threshold slightly faster than regulations permitted. Borja, who hadn't got his breath back either and could still feel his heart knocking in his chest from his exertions, pretended not to notice the speed they were

bouncing along at; he hoped that nobody in the tower –
he imagined them all reaching for their jackets, ready for
going home – would notice either. Once on the runway
itself the only thing they needed to cross their fingers for
would be the actual clearance to take off. Once that was
given, no power in the world could call them back.

Again they felt a sense of relief and good fortune: they
were cleared as soon as they turned onto the runway:
those jackets must be on by now, their wearers already
standing up. Borja, checking engine gauges, called,
'Power set,' and Ryan released the brakes. As the plane
rose smoothly into the air forty seconds later Borja had
the feeling that he was in an adventure film, escaping
some threat with seconds to spare as below them Athens
International, at three in the afternoon, effectively closed
for the night.

Athens Air Traffic Control was still operating,
although there could be no guarantee how long this
might last. At least their route had already been cleared
as far as Zagreb. Borja asked for this to be reconfirmed
and relaxed a little further once it was. As soon as they
had crossed out of Greek airspace he would contact the
next ATC along the route, which happened to be
Albania, where no strikes were to be expected, at least
for today.

Borja hoped for an uneventful return journey to
England. He felt he was owed that. Not only had they
been delayed departing Gatwick, and then had to deal
with the baggage emergency; they had experienced a
mildly alarming malfunction on the journey out. While
crossing the Alps an alarm had sounded: the landing-
gear configuration horn. It was supposed to sound a little
time before touch-down in the unlikely event that you
had forgotten to lower the wheels. At thirty-two
thousand feet, more than twice the height of the
mountains that were passing, cloud-wreathed, below

them, there was no question of needing the gear lowered, and no need for the warning horn to sound. Both pilots looked at the displays in front of them in an attempt to find the source of the anomaly. Borja spotted it: it was on his side. 'My radio altimeter's showing twenty-eight feet,' he announced.

Glancing out at the snowy caps fifteen to twenty thousand feet below, Ryan grunted a kind of small laugh. 'Let's not pay too much attention to it, then,' he said. Borja switched off the nerve-rasping horn.

There were four other altimeters to work with, after all. Two remaining radio altimeters, and two barometric ones. The radio altimeters were used mainly in the vicinity of airports because, bouncing radio waves vertically below them, they recorded the exact distance between the plane and the ground, including, during the last moments of landing, the runway itself. The barometric altimeters were less useful at this juncture. Few runways in the world, if any, could lie at mean sea level. On the other hand, once safely clear of the terrain below, those altimeters were used as a means of maintaining level flight. Responding to the pressure of the air outside, and adjusted according to local atmospheric conditions as the flight progressed, they offered heights above sea level for the use of pilots and autopilot alike. Feed radio altimeter information, on the other hand, into the autopilot during the cruise and you'd be hopping up and down over every hill and valley that you crossed.

For the final stages of descent towards Athens they had used the two radio altimeters that were still working perfectly, although, when Borja glanced out of curiosity at the malfunctioning one, he noticed that it had returned to normal, its readings agreeing with the other two. Nevertheless, Borja logged the incident once they had landed, and would report it at Gatwick on their return.

Shortly after they reached the top of their climb out from Athens – on this route it usually happened in the vicinity of Mount Parnassus, which Borja thought was rather sweetly appropriate – Charlie knocked at the cockpit door. These days, post nine-eleven, getting onto the flight deck was not as easy as in the past. Planes built since that time were equipped with cameras for identifying the person who wanted to enter, or else with a spy-hole in the door. The latter was a bit of a nuisance for the pilots as one of them would have to remove his harness and get out of his seat to see who was there. Borja was quite glad that his airline used older planes, and a simple system of coded knocks. He had only to reach forward to press a button, which unlocked the door and let Charlie in. 'You both OK?' he asked, once he had re-locked the door behind him. 'That was all a bit hairy, wasn't it? At least we got away. Coffee? Whisky?' The second offer was, of course, a joke.

'Coffee would be nice,' Borja said, and Ryan said, 'Yes please.'

'There's another thing I wanted to ask,' Charlie said. He had a rather round, cherubic face which lit up charmingly when he grinned. This happened now. 'Would it be OK if I came in a bit later and videoed a bit?'

Borja knew what Charlie was after. He had wanted for some time to film a landing from the cockpit window and put it on YouTube: it was something that many people did. Making video films in the cockpit was not allowed by the company they worked for, and Charlie knew this. But he also knew that this was the best possible moment to ask Borja to let him break the rules: he had just lent him his muscles and got himself into a sweat dealing with the baggage alongside the two pilots, and Borja had acknowledged his debt to him and his junior steward by offering to buy them a drink. Borja was aware of all of this. He smiled, though Charlie, standing behind him, could not see that. He said, 'Provided you forget we had this conversation, and that you stand behind me so that I don't see what's going on... OK?'

'Thanks mate,' Charlie said. Borja found himself wondering how it was that two such short words could convey so much gratitude and delight. 'It's just that it's such a clear day. Perfect.' Charlie leaned forward between the two pilots' heads and peered appreciatively at the mountainscape around them and the silvered inlets of the Ionian Sea in the distance beyond.

'Clear all the way to London,' Ryan volunteered, cheerfully adding his tuppence-worth to the sudden jollity of the moment.

After Charlie had left the cockpit to go and fetch the pilots' coffees, Borja thought about him for a moment, and about himself. Before becoming a pilot, but already wanting to be up here and doing this, he had decided that if he didn't pass his pilot's exams he'd settle for working as cabin crew. Rafael, of course, whose example had inspired Borja in the first place, had failed to get on a flying course. It was only because Rafael had ended up as a steward that Borja had run into him again. With major consequences for them both. Had Charlie also set out with dreams of becoming a pilot? He'd never volunteered that information, and Borja had never asked him although he knew him well enough. Next time they were alone together he would.

The cruise was reassuringly uneventful, the kind of flight that passengers and crew all like. Charlie arrived a couple of times on various pretexts, though really to film the landscape below and ahead, occasionally shifting the camera's attention to the instrument displays and controls, while Borja and Ryan studiously kept their backs turned to his activity. Charlie was in the cockpit when they passed Lake Balaton on their right. Hungary's inward-facing coast. He filmed that too. Ryan said that he'd used to drink a wine that came from there. 'When I was at college,' he said. 'Long time ago. Bull's Blood, it was called. Ever try it?'

Charlie said that he didn't go back that far, while Borja explained, 'You're forgetting where I come from. We had enough cheap *tinto* in Spain to put hairs on the chest. Even some called Sangre de Toro. We didn't have to travel east.'

Later, Charlie filmed the Alps as they tracked across Austria towards Munich on the other side. It was, as he had said, a perfect day. The afternoon sun was drawing the snowy caps into meringue-like points, while hurling blue-black shadows into dizzying whirlpools of valley mist below. Eventually the mountains subsided like a sea growing calm after a storm. White peaks gave way to biscuit brown, and then to the undulating green of the German countryside. They threaded the maze of air corridors over Germany and Belgium to the Channel coast, which they crossed overhead the Costa beacon, near Zeebrugge. Charlie had left the pilots to it after the Alps, though they were both fairly certain he would reappear during the landing approach if he possibly could. That was the footage that he'd be wanting most of all.

They headed out to sea on a bearing that would take them to Clacton if they followed it long enough, though this happened rarely. Usually, after a very few minutes London ATC would instruct them to turn left, westward across the Kent coast, and give them a 'straight-in' approach to Gatwick's runway 26 Left. But today there was different news for them. 'Severe congestion in Gatwick approaches. Maintain flight level three three zero and Clacton heading.'

'We're very late already,' Borja told the controller. 'Try and find us a gap we can slide into if you possibly can.' Years ago he wouldn't have dreamed of chatting back to a controller like this, but age and increasing seniority had surprised him with the number of things he was now prepared to do and say.

'See what I can do,' the controller said, 'but I doubt it.'

'If they're not going to descend us till we reach Clacton,' Borja observed to Ryan, 'it means...'

'Yep.' Ryan finished the sentence for him. 'They're going to hit us with a really long approach.'

As Borja had predicted, Charlie arrived a minute or two later, heralded by his coded knock, to ask about the route. He had noticed that the plane, already in mid-Channel, was still in level flight. Descent into Gatwick usually began within moments of crossing the Belgian coast. 'Stick around,' Ryan told him. 'It looks like being a scenic ride home.'

They really did get close to Clacton. The town, its beaches and the pier were clearly visible just ahead, which pleased Charlie if no-one else. Then at the last minute ATC instructed them to turn left, along the Essex coast on a heading to Rochford, near Southend. And they were at last cleared to start their descent. As it would take about a hundred miles – and about twenty-five minutes – to get down from their present height in any degree of comfort, and as Gatwick was no more than sixty miles distant in a straight line, it was clear that ATC still had a few more twists and turns for them to follow on the way down. So it was no surprise that on reaching Rochford their next instruction was to head fifty miles south to the Timba holding point, which was situated a good way past Gatwick on the other side.

The Timba hold was a vast invisible edifice in the sky, constructed of nothing more substantial than radio beams. It had the shape of a giant paper-clip that had been pulled out and extended downwards like a coil spring. It towered twelve thousand feet into the clouds and, some seven miles long and three across, lay roughly between Burwash in the Sussex Weald and Battle, towards the Hastings coast. It was what most of us call a stack. At busy times aircraft making for Gatwick from the east would make race-track shaped circuits around Timba until approach control allowed them to track northward via the Mayfield beacon, to join the queue of arriving planes on the final straight-line approach to the runway. They would turn left onto this line just west of Tonbridge, about a dozen miles from touchdown.

Borja sighed a bit theatrically after he'd acknowledged his order to go to Timba, and fed the new heading into the autopilot, causing the plane to bank steeply as it turned left to head back across the Thames towards the south. 'Back to the Sussex coast. Why couldn't they have just sent us there in the first place? Up north. Down south. A real woodcock flight this is turning out to be.'

'Why woodcock?' Charlie wanted to know. He wasn't minding too much. He'd found another moment to leave the passenger cabin, and was filming the Thames estuary, the twisting waterways that encircled the Isles of Sheppey and Grain, and the long straight stretch of Roman Watling Street as it sliced like a cheese-wire through the Medway towns.

'They fly zigzag,' Ryan told him before Borja could assemble his own words. 'Avoid predators. Makes them difficult to shoot.'

'Hope the same's true of us,' Charlie said lightly. It was a remark that he'd remember later, and then never forget for the rest of his life. Then he returned to his domain to oversee the securing of all moveable objects in cabin and galley and prepare the passengers for landing. He wasn't in the cockpit to film the sprawl of Maidstone as they passed just east of the town, nor to point his camera in the direction of Gatwick, thirty miles away as they crossed the invisible line that extended eastward from runway 26 Left. Not that it would have been easy to turn directly onto the glide-slope right now. They were still at 18,000 feet and to go straight down to the threshold from here would necessitate a very steep descent – the sort of thing that passengers generally didn't like.

But ten miles further on, with the sparkling Channel and Beachy Head now visible in front of them they received news from ATC. 'Gatwick approach have a slot for you if you can take it. You can call them now.' Borja thanked the controller, while Ryan confirmed his willingness to accept the unexpected offer. Borja changed radio frequency, called Gatwick approach control, and was told to turn immediately right: 'Heading 295.' This would put them on course to capture the glide-slope six miles from touchdown in about four minutes' time. But at 13,000 feet they were still much too high, and the approach controller knew this. 'Descend at pilot's discretion to capture glide-slope at two thousand.' It was going to be the sort of descent that passengers didn't like, after all. But it was either that or going on to the hold at Timba and flying circuits there. The new, suddenly offered straight-in would at least reduce the lateness of their arrival by ten minutes and the passengers would appreciate that. So there it was. The new heading and descent profile were keyed into the automatic pilot and the jet started to plunge downwards like the most unsettling sort of fairground ride.

Charlie entered the cockpit again a minute later with the news that the cabin was prepared for landing. This was his not very subtle way of announcing that there was nothing left for him to do except to take his seat when told to, and it was understood as a tacit request to stay in the cockpit and film the final approach and landing. Then he noticed something, and although it wasn't any of his business he pointed it out anyway. Partly because he was on easy terms with both pilots and partly because it might be important. 'Radio altimeter's reading twenty-five feet,' he said in a rather affronted-sounding voice.

'It's OK,' Borja told him calmly. 'It did that for a while on the way out. We're not taking any notice of it. The others are all fine.' They were passing Tunbridge Wells now, Gatwick clearly visible fifteen miles ahead, a little to the left of their present track. They would turn towards it when they intercepted the glide-slope in a couple of minutes' time. They were still too high, though. 'Lose another thousand now,' Borja told Ryan. 'With as little pain as possible. But it can't be helped.' Over-riding the autopilot Ryan pushed forward on the control column and the plane swooped even more steeply down.

They would intercept the glide-slope from above. Quite a common procedure at some airports where the approaches were cramped, like London City or Amsterdam, but not the usual thing at Gatwick in the Sussex countryside. Now, with the nose pitched steeply downwards, Charlie's viewfinder gave the disconcerting impression that they were diving straight into the centre of Lingfield race course a mile or so ahead.

The two pilots had rather forgotten Charlie by this stage. They were busy calling off yet another list of checks; they were keyed-up and waiting for the instruments in front of them to tell them they had captured the localiser beam of the glide-slope. That happened a second or so later, and they turned smoothly left, while Lingfield disappeared beneath the banking plane's up-tilted right wing.

'Localiser captured,' Borja reported to approach control, then took his leave, changing frequency to liaise with tower, which would monitor the final arrival of the flight along the ILS beams and onto the tarmac. Notwithstanding Ryan's brief intervention a minute or two earlier, the autopilot was still flying the plane. It could deal with the minor buffets and other effects of low-altitude turbulence that you met in the last stages of descent better than human pilots could. It would be disengaged for the last minute of flight only, when the pilots' visual awareness of the nearing runway would give them the edge over the computers and gyros that went together to make up 'George'.

Having made their final left turn they were perfectly positioned in the horizontal plane – the instruments and the view they now had of the runway and its approach light bars directly in front of them agreed about this. But they were still at two and a half thousand feet: five hundred above the glide-slope at that point. Borja entered the numbers that would tell the autopilot to lock on to it at the correct height. This would mean another moment or two of precipitate descent, but it couldn't be helped.

'Gear down, flap forty, landing check,' Ryan called. They heard the whine of the undercarriage doors opening and then the thud of the landing-gear locking into place. Borja brought up the final check-list on the screen in front of him, calling off the items as he and Ryan checked them, Ryan voicing his agreement in each case.

'Glide-slope active,' Ryan announced, as their descent converged with the glide-slope at last. Borja spoke into the cabin microphone. 'Cabin crew, seats for landing.' There remained about a minute of flight to go. Suddenly he caught sight of Charlie out of the corner of his eye, still standing at his shoulder. 'Charlie! What the fuck... Jump-seat, man. Now!'

And Ryan, cutting across his protest, said, his voice raised and urgent with surprise, 'We're not locked on. Glide-slope not captured. We're falling short.'

'Mierda,' Borja said. 'Pull up.' The command was hardly necessary. Ryan was already pulling back on the column to raise the aircraft's nose. The plane's nose did pitch up, but they were still heading remorselessly down. The auto-throttle had reduced engine power to idling speed during their rapid descent, but now they had reached glide-slope height, should have powered the engines up again. But that hadn't happened. On their present path they were heading for the half mile of green fields that lay between the M23 on its way from London to Brighton and the railway line that made the same journey in parallel. The airport perimeter was immediately beyond the railway tracks.

This was the second time in his life that Borja had seen those railway tracks from far too close and found himself in mortal terror that his aircraft wouldn't clear them. The first time he had been on the other side of the railway line, hurtling down the runway towards it in a plane that nearly didn't take off. He had still been a first officer then, the captain beside him, Andy. The situation now was the exact opposite of that one but the result, if something couldn't be done to remedy things in the next few seconds, would be dire. As for the grass fields that lay so prettily between the motorway and the railway, they offered no comfort. They were hummocky and small, and divided by hedges from which sprang full-grown trees. There were houses and barns. All pilots knew that a plane had tumbled down there in 1969, demolishing a house and killing those within as well as all on board. That patchwork of green fields promised no cosy ending.

Thinking took seconds, or bits of seconds, when all that was left was seconds, even if they seemed to expand extraordinarily in time, while your thought processes accelerated to a degree previously unimaginable. Each second was a window of opportunity that was smashing into shards, each shard another opportunity that you picked up in desperation, your thoughts cutting themselves on them as you did so. Borja checked that the speed-brakes were not, for some unknown reason, extended and slowing them down. Automatic warnings sounded in the cockpit. 'Air-speed low.' The master caution warning beeped and flashed its amber light at them. 'Disconnect autopilot,' Borja called to Ryan, but the first officer was already doing that.

'I can't get power,' Ryan said, pushing at the throttles, puzzlement and desperation colliding in his voice. The aircraft was driving ever more remorselessly towards the ground.

The next bit of the emergency drill rushed into Borja's speeding consciousness. 'Auto-throttle, then. Toga switches.' Take-off / go-around. The hands of both pilots scrabbled at those last-ditch escape switches on the thrust levers. Another memory exploded into Borja's mental whirlwind. 'Captain Burkill,' he said, but there was no time to explain to Ryan what he meant. He reached for the flap lever and reduced the wing-flaps' angle by five degrees. Just as a BA captain had done when his aircraft had inexplicably lost power while approaching the perimeter fence of Heathrow a couple of years before.

He called 'Mayday, mayday,' on the radio to tower – the first time in his life he'd heard his shaking voice utter those words in earnest, and as he did so he felt the plane ride up a little in response to the extra lift offered by the reduced flaps. It rose over the motorway like a racehorse clearing a fence. It was only a temporary respite, though. The engines were beginning to spool up at last, in response to the go-around command, but not quickly enough. The stick-shaker, last-chance warning of an impending stall, was now making the columns clatter back and forth, while yet one more alarm began to buzz. They were skimming the fields at two hundred feet and falling, and the railway line lay just ahead. The occupants of the cockpit wondered how high the fence on the far side of it might be. Twenty feet? Thirty? They could hear one another's intakes of breath as they skimmed the railway yards and tracks. The good altimeters were reading forty feet. Their bodies tensed to feel, and their ears waited to hear, the tearing of the undercarriage into the fence below them but they cleared it – who knew how, or by how much. Borja called into the cabin mike, 'Brace for impact. Brace, brace.' He should have dinged the cabin bell twice to alert the cabin crew to a crash-landing, but there'd been no time for that. Ahead of them runway 26L, that alphanumeric painted huge and white upon its threshold, was flattening out to the point of nearly disappearing, the way it normally did only after you had touched down. And then they landed, inside the airport boundary but well short of the runway, on the grass, with an almighty bang and jolt. The cockpit door broke free from its hinges and crashed to the floor. Borja and Ryan simultaneously reached over, their hands meeting, to close the throttles, and shut the engines down.

And now both pilots realised that the time for action was past. Nothing they did in the next few seconds could make any difference to the fact that they'd crash-landed, were careering erratically across grass, and could only wait and watch, in awed close-up, what was going to happen to them next. Their thundering progress became noisier yet as they skidded off the grass and onto the hard runway surface: it sounded as if a twelve-blade plough were being dragged along a road. But the increased friction slowed their progress too. They slewed sideways, as happens when you hit the brakes in a dodgem car, and juddered to a stop.

At once Charlie unclasped his harness and, with a loud exhalation that might have been, 'OK?' leaped out of the jump-seat, trampling the cockpit door as he floundered back into the passenger cabin to deal with his new responsibilities there. For Borja and Ryan, once they'd made eye-contact and exchanged a quiet, are you OK? you too?, there remained a new check-list – as there seemed to be for every conceivable eventuality – that had to be gone through, with thudding hearts and voices that struggled to get the words out, before they could legitimately leave their posts. Whether everyone else was OK – the buggers in the back, as Andy had liked to call them sometimes – that was Charlie's job to establish just now, not yet theirs. They saw fire engines racing towards them. The red vehicles drew up alongside. Borja was surprised at how tall they seemed. And that gave him a piece of information that hadn't quite had time to register before: the undercarriage had collapsed and sheared off when they hit the ground; they had slithered here, the aircraft on its belly, like the serpent after the Garden of Eden débâcle.

FIVE

James's mobile was switched off. He was watching the dress rehearsal of Romeo and Juliet, sitting in the second row of the dress circle next to the director and the head of design. It was just as the lights began to come up at the beginning of the interval – there were audible shuffles of relief from various parts of the auditorium – that the wardrobe mistress came along the row of tipped-back seats towards him. 'I just heard on the news – it's nothing bad, but it's Borja's airline. There's been a crash at Gatwick.' Seeing James rear up from his seat with an expression of the utmost terror on his face, she touched his forearm, saying quickly, 'No-one's hurt. But you had to know.'

'Thank you,' James said. He didn't wait to say or hear more, but squeezed past her, running through doors, down stairs, backstage, into the green room, reawakening his mobile and pressing the button that would dial Borja's number as he went. In the green room the television was on, unwatched, showing an ancient episode of Only Fools and Horses with the sound turned down. He grabbed the remote and flicked urgently through the channels. Meanwhile his phone was telling him that Borja was calling someone: he hoped, him. None of the channels was showing scenes of a plane accident. James found a wisp of comfort in that. The lack of casualties, of carnage, had meant that the accident had not been deemed serious enough for programmes to be interrupted with footage of the crash. He would have to wait for that till the news at six o'clock.

There was a voice message on his phone now. Their attempts to call each other had collided in mid-air. 'We've had a crash-landing at Gatwick.' Borja sounded a bit breathless but otherwise calm. 'By some miracle no-one's badly hurt. I'm standing outside the plane with everyone, waiting for transport to the... But I am OK. Talk very soon.' There was a pause, then Borja's voice said quietly, and this time there was the beginning of a crack in it, 'Christmases and birthdays, you know.'

James sank into the nearest seat, an armchair with stuffing coming out of it, that had sat in this spot for over twenty years, his physical composure ripped apart by an explosion of wrenching tears and sobs.

Borja's managers first insisted, then implored, that he spend the night, along with Ryan, in a hotel. But he didn't. Neither did Ryan, whose wife was expected to go into labour within a day or two, if not in the next few hours. Charlie alone had dared to risk making the obvious joke; that it was as well that Ryan rather than his wife had been flying the plane. There had been a lengthy debriefing, as well as a searching interview with the police. Both Borja and Ryan had been breathalysed: they were assured this was purely routine. Pilots who crashed their planes were breathalysed as automatically as motorists who crashed their cars. A medical once-over had resulted in their being declared in good physical shape, and Borja, reassured at being told there was nothing wrong with him, announced to his manager and union representative that there certainly would be something wrong with him if he didn't get back to James that night. So he drove off, on his own, round the M25, then forty miles up the M1, and at last down the lane through the time-warp wood – as they still called it after all these years – to the Court House, where James waited up for him, just a little drunk by the time Borja got there shortly after eleven o'clock. They had soup from a packet and sardines on toast.

In the morning Andy and Nick arrived, tumbling out of the car from opposite sides, outside the kitchen door at eight o'clock. Andy pushed at the door and went in. Like Nick he was not expected to knock, and certainly not today. Borja was making toast, in a green silk dressing-gown and white socks; his neat trim calves on partial display between them. James was elsewhere, getting dressed for work. Andy threw his arms round Borja, quickly and hard. 'You're safe, mate. You're safe,' he said, head on Borja's shoulder as he clasped him tight. Nick hung back for a second but then James came into the kitchen, fully clothed and Nick bestowed the embrace he was all primed to give to Borja on James instead: a sort of proxy hug. 'I got him back,' James said.

A minute later the two pilots went into the living-room together, where the morning sun was slanting in as if to reassure everyone that there was nothing at all wrong with the world. They carried a mug of coffee each and held slices of toast in their other hand, transporting them at an odd angle, like just-arrived postcards. They began at once an urgent rapid conversation about the events of the previous day in an idiolect that encompassed speed-brakes and landing checks, altimeter settings and engine power. It was a conversation that neither James nor Nick was competent to understand, even though they knew how profoundly necessary it was to the other two.

'Step into the yard,' James said. And Nick and he retreated through the kitchen door onto the cobbled court where the cars were parked, surrounded at a little distance by outbuildings and overhanging trees. High up, the leaves of the poplars, rustling in the morning chill, were just beginning to turn from green to gold. James, for a moment finding it difficult to speak, gestured imprecisely around him. Then, 'All this,' he said.

'I know,' Nick said. 'But you'll keep it.' He tried to express conviction in his tone, but his voice still sounded, as always, like the kid. 'You won't lose this.' There came back to him the memory of standing on this exact spot alone with James, so many years before, in a midsummer dawn with the birds just starting up their songs. He'd burbled stupidly about woodcocks and James had smiled and quietly called him crazy kid, and that he hadn't found his home yet, or something like that. Now they looked at each other, exactly as they had done back then, standing on this very spot. And this time, for a moment, there was a desperation in James's eyes that he couldn't at first hide, though after a second he did. There was a moment when they jointly considered a second hug and another when together they decided against it. 'I'm OK,' James said, shaking his head and slightly smiling. 'I am OK.' They went back indoors to rejoin the others.

Over the next few days Borja's needs pushed all other concerns out of James's head. Taking care of Borja, not that he showed any physical or other signs that he required wrapping in cotton-wool, occupied all James's waking thoughts and not a few of his night-time dreams. The opening night of Romeo and Juliet, for which he was ultimately responsible although with not much hands-on involvement, came and went as if that too was happening in a dream. Its teething troubles, the minor clashes of artistic egos, the backstage dramas and inter-departmental tiffs followed their natural courses as the planets followed theirs. During this time James felt the world of the theatre, which he had inhabited for half his lifetime, beginning to slip away from him. Its lives were lived and its undercurrents flowed, but as if in a rockpool: they were things half-glimpsed through the shiny dividing surface, while your more important concerns flew above.

Of course James attended the first night. And he made sure Borja accompanied him, as he usually did if he wasn't flying that day. James didn't want him brooding alone at Sevenscore, deep in the autumn countryside, for all those hours. Nor did he particularly like the idea of him propping up the bar of the Rose and Castle, at the mercy of every neighbour and pub-goer, whom James imagined as eager as vampires to have the gory details of the crash from the most authentic of possible sources. Against that he would at least be in the comforting company of their two best friends, one a fellow pilot himself, but even so James was happier with the idea of Borja by his side. In fact, the way he was feeling about Borja right now, he didn't ever want him to be anywhere else.

The Romeo and the Juliet were youngsters fresh from drama school. But in their final year at their different colleges each had already done the play and played their leading role. It was a neat piece of casting strategy, an attempt to solve that eternal conundrum: that when you were old enough to play Romeo or Juliet you were too old to play them.

Borja was able to focus on the play sufficiently to notice that both young people turned in good performances. It helped that they were both beautiful of form and face. Borja made those observations to James in the interval, drinking a glass of wine amidst the crush and compliments of the circle bar. He also asked James if the pretend romance on-stage had overflowed into the two young people's private lives, or whether it was likely to. James so no, that was quite unlikely. The Juliet had a boyfriend in London – he was actually here somewhere in the audience tonight – while the Romeo was in fact gay. James lowered his voice as he said this, adding that, because of the particular role he was playing, that wasn't something he'd chosen to share too widely during the four weeks he'd been at the theatre. James spelled all this out to Borja carefully, all the time aware, though, that he had given the same answer when Borja had asked him the same question just a week before. And the answer being what it was, it was not something that a man of Borja's sexual orientation would have forgotten in the normal course of events. James interpreted this as an indication of Borja's seriously preoccupied state.

Borja was trying to work out what had happened on the approach to Gatwick, worrying at the pieces like someone doing a jigsaw puzzle. Of course the investigators were doing that too, working with real pieces of evidence: the computer systems and mechanical parts of the plane, the cockpit voice recorder and the black box. They would publish a report, which would have the shocking power either to exonerate Borja from blame or else find him culpable, or partly culpable, in the expensive write-off of a Boeing 737. The report would appear 'in due course'. That might mean just a few weeks, though more usually it took months, and in some cases even a couple of years. Borja, going through it with James, not just once but time and time again, was unable to think of a single thing that either Ryan or he had done wrong on the approach and let-down. He could think of no remedy they had not tried during those seconds between the plane's failure to capture the glide-slope and their hard landing on the Gatwick grass. He would tell James again and again, 'The auto-throttle just decided to fly us into the ground. We disconnected it as quickly as anyone could and tried to power up, but there simply wasn't any more time.'

'It's a bit unlucky that you had Charlie whatever his name is up on the flight-deck during landing,' James said. 'It was a bit irregular, you must admit.'

'He wasn't on the flight-deck during landing,' Borja said emphatically, deliberately missing James's point. 'When the time came for us to land he'd have been back in the cabin.' Borja didn't know this for a fact. He almost knew that the opposite was true: Charlie would have stayed where he was, strapped himself into the jump-seat at the last second and filmed the whole landing, while Borja and Ryan turned a blind eye. But he wasn't going to say this to the enquiry, and, in order to get himself in practice, wasn't going to say it to James now. 'Because, if you remember, we didn't actually land. We crashed about ten seconds before we were due to touch. And seconds after that he was back in the cabin, at his post and behaving like a hero. He evacuated every single passenger and flight attendant before...'

'You all behaved like heroes,' James reminded him gently. It wasn't the first time since he'd said this either. 'Never lose sight of that.'

Borja pretended not to take any notice of this. He went on, 'His being on the flight deck had nothing whatever to do with the crash. It was a malfunction of the auto-pilot, or the auto-throttle or both. Just, nobody yet knows why or how or what.'

Borja was suspended from flying for an indefinite period. Suspension automatically followed any serious incident; it was routine; no hint of possible culpability was implied by it. It occurred to James that Borja might decide he wanted to come and work backstage at the theatre again, as he had done twenty years before: the last time, the only other time, he'd been suspended from operations following an incident. If Borja wanted to propose that, well, let him do so, and James would decide how to deal with the question then. He wasn't going to raise the possibility himself. He couldn't see Borja submitting so easily now to the indignities of erecting flattage and checking prop lists in the easy way he had done when he was a gung-ho thirty-year-old. Although one never knew. He had spent the last half of his life working for the same holiday airline, but not without grumbling from time to time that he really wanted to give it all up and keep chickens. This might be his chance to do that too.

James was not too happy to find that Borja spent much of the first two days of his suspension combing the internet for stories of planes that had crashed in similar circumstances to his own. He delved with mole-like absorption into the story of the crash-landing of a 777 at Heathrow a couple of years before. It was his memory of that case, of Captain Burkill's presence of mind in changing the wing-flap settings at the last moment, that had inspired Borja to do the same and – Borja believed – prevent the disaster from turning into a catastrophe involving massive loss of life.

He reacquainted himself with the experience of Captain Moody, whose 747 had lost power to all four engines because of ingestion of volcanic ash at high altitude. Moody had glided his aircraft calmly downhill until the engines restarted again, eventually landing his passengers safely on the island of Java. Of course, there had been no significant volcanic ash in the air above East Grinstead two days earlier...

'Captain Moody got in touch with all the passengers and crew who were on that flight. He set up a special social network. Maybe when this is all over I'll do the same.'

'Yes, maybe,' James said. 'And, like you say, when it's all over. In the meantime, can't you just leave it alone for a bit?'

Borja didn't take the point. In his gruffest and most Spanish tones, which his voice always fell into when he felt himself pressured by James, he said, 'I need to know what happened. Whatever the report says or doesn't say. Can't you see how important this is for me?' James knew when a tactical withdrawal was called for and for the moment left Borja alone with the computer. But the information about Captain Moody's social network had given him an idea, although one on a smaller scale. Although he didn't want Borja stressing himself by driving down to London to meet the colleagues who had shared his traumatic experience, he would have no objection if Borja wanted to invite them up to Sevenscore: he thought it might even be the best thing for him. Sevenscore was a perfect place for entertaining people who needed to de-stress themselves, and it had six bedrooms after all. Sometimes James and Borja rented these out to actors and directors who were working at the Regent: their address was on the theatre's digs list. But nobody from the theatre was staying with them just now.

Even as he thought about the possibilities James realised that they couldn't invite Ryan. His wife had gone into labour the morning after the crash and had given birth later that day. Borja had spoken to Ryan on the phone as soon after that as he reasonably could, and conveyed his congratulations. He'd learned that the baby was a boy, and they would call him Merlin. Borja and Ryan had also enquired about each other's state of health and mind and been mutually reassured. Borja had said that it would be good to meet up some time, when things were calmer at Ryan's end, and Ryan had agreed. Though for anyone who had just become a father, *when things were calmer* might well be some time after Merlin had started his first job.

James thought he would have preferred to have the happily married Ryan, whom he had met, as a visitor rather than Charlie, about whom he knew only that he was gay and that Borja liked him. But he reminded himself it was Borja's welfare that he was concerned about rather than any micro-jealousies of his own. Borja and Charlie had in any case exchanged a couple of emails since the crash. So James suggested that Borja might like to ask Charlie up for a few days, if Charlie were free.

Charlie was free, and would love to come. He had heard of Sevenscore and was delighted at the idea of seeing a place that only a couple of senior captains at the airline had ever visited, and that the rest of the company knew about from hearsay only. The rumour went that Borja lived in a sort of baronial hall in the country, probably with suits of armour displayed on the walls around the ancestral dining-table, sharing both house and his life with a high-flying something in the world of theatre. Or possibly film. But who was in any case male. They were a high-profile gay couple in their part of rural England. Wherever that part was.

'It's up the M1,' Borja told him on the phone. 'Come off after Milton Keynes.' He went on to give full directions from there to the Court House's kitchen door. Borja was impressed by the recent adoption of satellite navigation as a back-up system for guiding planes. He was less convinced of its helpfulness in getting the drivers of cars to where they needed to be.

Charlie drove up the next day, threading his way along the country roads that Borja had instructed him to use. He found himself crossing the Grand Union canal by a hump-back bridge, with an attractive thatch-roofed, stone-walled pub beside it, then, after following the lane up the hill, was startled to see the address he was seeking actually spelled out on the sign-post at the top. Next to the open gateway to the drive or track a notice read: 'Sevenscore Pavilions. Open Sat. Sun. 2-5 pm. April-Sept.' He turned onto the drive and saw it disappear in front of him, a field or two away, into dark thick woods with no sign of habitation in sight.

But once inside the wood he was quickly out of it again, and then a group of buildings did appear, among trees, another field away. A moment later the drive had opened out into a cobbled yard, from which he glimpsed through big shut gates a building that might have looked at home in Tuscany, while from the door of the more modest red-brick building to which the gate was attached, Borja emerged as he drew up.

Entering the house via the kitchen, which almost every visitor did, you got a back-to-front series of impressions of the place. The kitchen was big, very big, but it was by no means up to date, its principal features being a splendid but not very level floor of polished red bricks, and a large deal table of the kind that people's grannies had once had. Two doors opened off it: the one next to the cooker was half open and Charlie saw that it led directly into a bedroom. But Borja led Charlie through the other door, into a short passageway from which more doors led off, then down a step into a large living- and dining-room. There was a huge fireplace in one wall, a sizeable mullioned window in the opposite one and a collection of furniture whose credentials as antique were clear even to a non-expert. There was much inlaid walnut, and French and Dutch marquetry, that glowed in a variety of rich light browns and golds. Borja didn't comment on this, and Charlie suppressed the whistle that might easily have risen to his lips, as he was led without pausing, through the room into a small hall and from there into the garden.

'You see, the front is really the back,' Borja pointed out what was already becoming clear to Charlie, 'and vice versa.' It was late afternoon but still sunny, and Borja allowed his guest to take in his surroundings without, for the moment, explaining to him what he saw. Which was not just one Renaissance pavilion that looked like the Banqueting House but two – one on either side of the square lawn on which they stood. Plus all the rest of it: gardens, tall trees, the fountain and the *bassin*, and in the distance the view beyond the balustrade of countryside that rolled on serenely till it met the sky. Then Charlie did say what everyone said to Borja, or James, at this point. 'And you own all of this?'

And Borja turned back to him, laughing, and said, as he always did, and as James always did, 'None of it. Not a single brick or stone. We rent.' He made Charlie turn round and look back at the red brick building they'd come out of. 'And only that bit, the Court House, even then. The rest of it we get to look at, and walk in and sit in, free.'

'Some people do seem to have all the luck,' Charlie said, in a tone of voice that was difficult to read.

'Come back again in January,' Borja told him. 'You might not think so then.' They hadn't really greeted each other yet. Borja had told Charlie to leave his car just where it was, by the kitchen door, and had then ushered him inside, indicating with a hand gesture that he should just dump his backpack on the polished table in the living-room, on the way to the place where they now stood. But now that Charlie had had a few seconds to grasp the scale and nature of the unlikely home he'd been invited into, Borja suddenly took hold of both of Charlie's hands, looked into his eyes and said, 'It's great to see you.'

Then Charlie took the initiative in morphing the handclasp into a firm hug, at which moment the garden door they had just come out of, and which still stood open behind them, disgorged another male figure, a little taller than Borja and Charlie were, and with a remarkably full head of curly hair. James's car must have almost followed Charlie's down the drive. He held out his hand as he approached the other two, while they unhurriedly but a little awkwardly disengaged themselves. James flashed a smile that looked a little surprised or bashful and said, with Stanley-esque logic, 'Charlie, I presume.'

SIX

In the evening they drove to the Rose and Castle. The dark was coming early now and a walk down the old carriage drive between the poplar trees was not the attractive prospect it would have been a month before. It was more practical for Andy and Nick to dine with friends in their own pub than to turn out for an away fixture. James and Borja often dined at the Rose and Castle as paying customers. Sometimes they went as guests: social variations they all handled with relaxed sensitivity. Tonight, with their own guest in tow, Borja and James had been invited to join their hosts at a table for five in the restaurant area of the 'new' bar.

Andy was very much in charge. It was he who held the wine list in his hand, consulting with the others but in the end using his casting vote, courteously asking the waitress to fetch the bottle of Fleurie 2009 that would kick the evening off. Occasionally he would rise from the table in an unfussed sort of way and walk over to the bar counter to deal with some detail, but mostly he let his staff do what they were being paid for.

Nick was the dutiful younger boyfriend, deferring to Andy most of the time, though – Charlie was pleased to notice – not all of it. Nick, the same age as Charlie, was the tallest of the party, an inch or so taller than James. Yet Nick was clearly conscious of his relative youth and so, when he did take issue with something Andy said, or felt obliged to point out some imprecision of fact, he was careful to do it in a licensed jester sort of way at which neither Andy nor anyone else could possibly take offence. Charlie had never gone in for the idea of a life partner, but he thought that if you did want one, you could do much worse than Nick.

Charlie had heard the story of Andy's airline career from James and Borja. It had been told by both of them separately in little bits. Andy had been the rising star in the airline for which Borja and he had worked. Back then Borja had been a first officer. They had only flown together once: it had been a memorable flight for all concerned, not just Borja and Andy; it had been a real domino-tumble of mishaps. They had ended up landing at the wrong airport in Morocco, and there had been all hell to pay for that. Andy's career, rising like a rocket, had crashed in flames. He'd been promoted sideways, still captain, but on cargo, no longer passenger, flights. While Borja, co-pilot on that now infamous flight from Gatwick to Tangier and Casablanca, had been promoted to captain and effectively replaced Andy as the airline's *Man Most Likely To* overnight. But far from creating enmity between the two men the events of that day had turned them into lifelong friends. Charlie, not unusually naïve for a man of forty, had to suppose that there was more to it than that; and to realise that he was unlikely ever to know exactly what that was.

A few years after his sideways move Andy had been given the chance to take voluntary redundancy. That had coincided with the Rose and Castle's coming onto the market. Andy had seized the opportunity, and seized Nick too, dragging him away from his mole-like existence at the London Library to join him in this new venture, as landlords of a country pub.

Now Andy had another string to his bow. He worked on the glider aerodrome a couple of miles away as a tug pilot. He piloted one of the small single-engined aircraft that towed the gliders along the runway and pulled them into the air. Andy's was not a career path about which the younger Charlie could comfortably question him. On the other hand, Andy had a question for Charlie. Leaning across the table, his blue eyes open wide in a way that indicated that frankness was to be expected between them, Andy asked, 'What are you going to do with the famous cockpit video? Did you manage to save the camera?'

'I did save the camera,' Charlie said. 'I didn't give it a thought, what with the emergency and the evacuation, but it was hanging round my neck anyway, and when I finally got off the plane and we all began to check that we were in one piece, there it still was. It had filmed the whole thing, right up to the end, skidding along the grass. I hadn't been heroic with it or anything, not like a reporter in a war zone. I just didn't think to switch it off.'

'Do you think you'll be able to put it on YouTube?' Andy had heard about Charlie's intention.

'I don't know,' Charlie said. 'It'd be quite a treasure trove if I did. Or if I sold it to a TV company. But I might be in trouble. I wasn't supposed to be where I was, I wasn't supposed to be filming, according to company regulations. And it may be... What's the word?'

'Sub judice?' suggested Nick.

'That's what I meant. Maybe they'll want it as evidence at the enquiry.'

'Will they?' James asked. 'If they don't know it exists?'

'I don't know if they know it exists,' Charlie said uncomfortably. 'Was it mentioned in the cockpit in the last thirty minutes? I don't know.' He turned to Borja. 'Do you remember?'

Borja said, 'You mean will they pick up a clue from the CVR?' The cockpit voice recorder was a thirty-minute tape-loop, from which much evidence would be garnered by the investigators into the crash. Who said what to whom. Extraneous sounds. General mood and ambience in the cockpit in the minutes before the crash. Borja shook his head fractionally. 'I don't remember, honestly. I know we were trying – I mean Ryan and I were trying – not to notice what you were doing. So the chances are that we didn't say anything about it during that time. But I can't swear to that. I was preoccupied by other things. Ryan too. You could ask him.'

'Though, talking of preoccupied...' James began.

'I know,' Charlie cut him off. 'He's just had a baby.'

'I'm not going to bring it up out of the blue when they interview me,' Borja said. 'But if they know already, and then they ask me...'

'Well, there'd be no point denying it,' Charlie accepted.

'Sounds a bit Catch-22,' Andy said. 'You've got something that everyone would want, YouTube viewers, crash investigators, the media, but you can't profit from it without risking getting fired.' Involuntarily his lips tightened for an instant. 'They were never a company to see the human side of things.' He glanced towards Borja for a moment; perhaps that too was an involuntary thing.

Borja said, 'I think you'll just have to sit this out, Charlie. Till after the enquiry anyway. Once that's out of the way you could probably pitch your own idea for a TV documentary, use your own footage, and laugh all the way to the bank.' Everyone looked at everyone else, trying to read clues in other faces as to how serious Borja was being. It was hard to tell sometimes. Even for James.

Charlie had been given the Chinese bedroom. It led off the little hallway inside the garden door and was the nicest of the available five. It had silk wall coverings, scenes of bamboo and birds on a silvery yellow background, a bed-cover also of patterned silk and, in the morning, when the curtains were pulled back, a south-facing view of lawn and gardens, of the two pavilions and of the open country beyond. This morning the sun was already brilliant in the sky and was making the dew on the lawn sparkle with what seemed arbitrary colours: a red point of light here, a green one there, another a radiant diamond white. The flamelike flowers of late summer still stood tall and bright in the borders, but there was a tense look about them now, their beauty a precarious one, pushed to the edge by the imminence, any morning now, of the first frost. For all the beauty of the scene that confronted him when he opened his curtains, Charlie was gripped by a sense of something painful and poignant, a feeling partly induced by the fact that his bedroom, like most bedrooms in the depth of the countryside, was, despite a radiator below the window-sill, freezing cold.

Borja walked with Charlie around the gardens, mugs of coffee still in their hands. Borja explained about the vanished mansion that, '...stood on the spot where our little shack now stands.'

'And what happened to it?' Charlie asked.

'Usual story,' said Borja. 'Someone in the nineteenth century drops a candle and...'

'Yep,' said Charlie, and Borja saw his face harden. They looked into each other's eyes for a moment and saw that they were both thinking the same thing. Thinking about accidents that happened in the blink of an eye. And Borja, who mostly spoke to Charlie when Charlie was standing behind his head, or else late at night in some foreign hotel bar, found himself studying his face in bright sunlight, and thinking what a nice one it was, still youthful at forty or whatever Charlie was, with a puckishly turned-up nose, and helpfully framed by hair that had started neither to thin nor to turn grey.

Charlie turned back towards the Court House. It didn't look like a shack to him. Tall, its brickwork glowing in the morning light, its windows were outlined in yellow stone, while its gable ends rose in Dutch-style steps towards mock-Tudor chimney twists. 'What's on the upper floor?' Charlie asked.

'Believe it or not, it's a sort of barn. Storage space, though mostly empty now. You could turn it into bedrooms, I suppose, but there's already six, and there's no plans to make it into a school or a hotel.'

'How … how did you come by it?' Charlie had to ask. He owned a one-bedroom flat on the outskirts of Croydon, and struggled manfully to meet the mortgage repayment every month.

'It was owned by a local playwright when James first came to work up here. He lived in the East Pavilion there, and was happy to rent the Court House to us for peanuts. He died a few years ago. I'm afraid the drink got him.' Borja stopped for a moment as images of Neville coursed through his mind. Neville shaving in the garden because his lights had blown, Neville standing right here, taking the phone-call that would put him on stage that night, replacing an actor who had fallen sick... 'Of course he was an actor too,' Borja said, though the information didn't interest Charlie very much. 'The place was inherited by distant cousins when he died, but they don't interfere with us a lot. The East Pavilion's let to a banker... He's perfectly nice. But we hardly see him either. He's only here at weekends. And we still get away with the peppercorn rent. We're kind of unpaid caretakers if you like. There's a gardener called Stuart.' He pointed through the orchard to a distant wall. 'Lives in a bungalow behind there. Does all this.' He waved an arm at everything in sight. 'On summer weekends we take turns to go on the gate.'

'Blimey,' said Charlie. 'Talk about living the dream.' But he remembered what Borja had said about the winter, and remembered the temperature of his own bedroom just an hour earlier, and his face became a thoughtful frown.

'At least we got out of Athens when we did,' Charlie said as they parked the car at the bottom of Pembridge Street. 'What we heard on the news this morning. Armed guard for Mrs Merkel and police with tear-gas. Mind you, the news was very short.'

'That's why James insists on Radio 3,' Borja said. They were climbing the hill towards the Regent. 'We used to listen to the Today programme, but James said it made him feel unable to face the day ahead. As if he'd done a day's work already, and went in to the office with the world's cares on his shoulders as well as the Regent's and his own.'

Arrived at the theatre's foyer doors Borja pushed at the bright brass bar on one of them in the confident manner of a person on home territory and it swung open. 'Oh wow,' Charlie said as they walked inside.

'I'm to give you the front of house tour,' Borja said. 'James will join us when we go back. I mean backstage'

The Regent was a pretty place to show off. The jewel at its centre was the intimate space of the dress circle, with its wrap-around horseshoe shape, red plush and elaborate ormolu mirrors and lamps. 'It's so cosy you could eat crumpets up here,' Charlie said.

'I'm sure even that's been done,' said Borja, thinking that pretty well everything else had been done here by one person or another, or even two together, in the years he'd known the place. 'I'll get James and he'll take us back.' He said, as if afraid that Charlie might doubt this, 'I'm perfectly capable of giving you the backstage tour, but James did want to show it off to you himself.' To demonstrate his familiarity with the place and its ways he picked up the house manager's intercom that was on the wall beside him, and told James, who was in the office upstairs, where they were to be found.

James joined them a few seconds later. They trooped down into the stalls and from there through the iron pass-door, whose code – C245XZ – hadn't changed in all the years since Borja had worked in this place. They stood on the stage, behind the plain beige back of the massive safety curtain, which cut them off now from the auditorium where they had just been. The front of the 'iron' as theatre people called it was handsomely painted with theatre scenes, and cameos of the famous faces whose owners' feet had trodden these particular boards during the previous century and a half. Borja remembered that the reverse side of the safety curtain had had SNAFU scrawled on it (it had been explained to the Spanish guy that this meant *situation normal: all fucked up*) but there was no sign of the acronym now. Someone must have got hold of some bleach and scrubbed it off. James moved into the prompt corner and pressed the red button there, causing the iron to rise steadily to an accompanying electric whine. As it lifted it revealed yard by yard the tiers of seats in which Borja and Charlie had just sat, the elaborately carved dress- and upper-circle-fronts with their bracket-lights, and finally the high domed ceiling above the gods, painted with Commedia dell'Arte figures beneath an Italian sky, and the chandelier that showered light all around it, suspended from the rose at the apex of it all. When they'd had enough of admiring all this James pulled the release lever and the iron slid slowly back down again, sighing as it settled on its pneumatic cushions of air.

Borja felt the sensation he'd had several times a day since the crash: the feeling of physically falling down through space, a fall to which there seemed there could be no end. Each time he would come to with a jolt. He did so now, just as he'd done at Gatwick, as the air-brakes tightened and the iron's bottom edge hit the deck with a grunt and hiss.

James pointed up above their heads to where festoons of hemp-lines like church bell ropes ran aloft into the gloom, disappearing forty feet above their heads between the closely spaced oak beams of the fly-tower grid. No-one suggested they climb the series of ladders to get right up there, though Borja's memory did: climbing up close on Nick's heels – not to mention his calves, thighs and buttocks – rung after rung, ladder after ladder, cleat after cleat. And then what had happened when they got to the top and peered out over the town at sunset through the louvred slats of the smoke-vent cowl. All right, it had only been a kiss, if a rather potent one. Borja hastily packed the memory away, as if by allowing it to remain too near the surface of his consciousness he might expose it to James's view. After thirty years or so a pair of lovers could reach and read into each other's thoughts. Decades of intimacy wore your personal mindshield down to a transparent state. That kiss had been one of the harmless details of those few days when Borja had been alone with Nick. James hadn't known about it at the time. There was no point in revisiting the moment now.

The stage lay below road level – the dress circle was in the same plane as the street – and they moved through to the backstage area by means of a tunnel under the road. Proudly James showed off the carpenters' workshop and the costume store as if he'd invented them himself, and introduced Charlie to their denizens as if he'd created them too. With slightly more justification: he had at least given them all their jobs.

They climbed narrow wood stairs above the dressing-rooms. Here the old paint-shop stood, or rather towered, its proportions those of a cigar-box on its side. The hundred-year-old paint frames lined the long side walls: like the safety curtain they could be pulled up and down, disappearing into slots at the floor's edge, at the touch of

an electric switch. The whole room, if you could call it
such, was surreally spattered with paint, even up to the
skylight that formed most of the roof high above: It was
like a three-dimensional painter's palette, about 150
metres square and very used.

'Why do I keep thinking I'm smelling horse?' Charlie
asked.

'Because you are,' James told him, pointing to a sack,
one of many in a pile on the floor. 'Glue size. For
treating canvas before it's painted.' He let Charlie sniff
the sack at close quarters and work out the horse
connection for himself.

A little later, following sociable instant coffee in the
general office, Borja and Charlie left James and returned
to the street. 'Short tour of the city?' Borja offered. 'Not
that there's much to see. It's not Seville or Salamanca.
But it's a bit early for the pub.'

'It must be wonderful for James,' Charlie said,
pursuing his own line of thought. 'I mean, to have you
back again. He must have thought how close he came to
losing you in the crash.' He stopped and though a
second. 'I'm sorry if I've jumped in somewhere private.
It's just that I can't help noticing the way he looks, at you
I mean, when you're around. So… It's just, I noticed.
Sorry.'

'Don't be,' Borja said. Then, because he could think of
no reason not to say this, 'Is there someone somewhere
feeling wonderful because you've been resurrected from
the crash?'

Charlie shook his head, and smiled a tight little smile.
'No. Not really. Parents, I suppose, but that's not the
same. I've always been … well, I suppose, flying from
flower to flower. That's me.'

How different from me, Borja couldn't help thinking.
All his life he had wanted to belong to one person only,
even if, when he was very young, he hadn't known that.

But it had turned out that that was the way he'd been made. It had caused some heartache at various moments long ago but he didn't regret it now. He pointed out the Victorian Guildhall, and the eighteenth-century cathedral, promoted from homely parish church a mere thirty years before. 'And now there's this,' he said. They had stopped under the awning at the front of a newish-looking building made of reinforced concrete and glass. The Barraclough Centre was its name. 'We call it the Barracks,' Borja said.

'Oh yeah,' Charlie said. 'I've seen it on telly of course. Snooker comes from there.'

Then Borja said, speaking rather intensely for a conversation in the street, 'James clings to his job by his fingertips. He's been director at the Regent for five years now. He was general manager before that. But it's only a matter of time before the theatre company's wound up and the city council claims the building back. At least, that's what I think. They'll amalgamate it with this place – the stage doors of the two buildings are in the same street – and the whole lot will be run by the department of recreation and arts. So, you talk about living the dream, but for James it's not all husky dory.' You could listen to Borja for hours without anything happening to remind you that English was his second language. Only occasionally did something come out that gave you a bit of a jolt.

'Sounds like bad news,' said Charlie. He'd met James less than twenty-four hours earlier but was automatically at one with him in his struggles against the world, and concerned by any concern that was his.

'Well, there's nothing to be done about it,' Borja said, his more usual philosophical self again. 'It'll either happen or it won't, and we'll deal with the outfall when it does.' (Sometimes two came along at once.) Neither of them suggested going inside the Barraclough Centre to have a look round. They went to the Seven Stars instead.

The following night found the five of them at the theatre watching Romeo and Juliet. Borja already understood the pleasure of seeing the same production more than once. He enjoyed seeing the actors' performances develop as their involvement with the characters deepened and their understanding grew. He enjoyed watching them relax into the piece, inhabiting it more fully as they grew less preoccupied with moving around the scenery, with handling props, suiting their voices to the acoustic and to the moment, finding their light. If the play was by Shakespeare, so much the better, Borja thought. You could watch or read his work as many times as you liked and find something new in it on each occasion, find in Shakespeare's words and images an almost unfathomable, hologram-like depth.

It was during the interval, while James was handing back pre-ordered drinks to the others through the crush of the circle bar, that Nick remembered something he'd been meaning to tell James and Borja the day before the Gatwick incident. He'd been reminded of it while watching the news at six o'clock. 'We saw that woman friend of yours on TV again. A few days ago. Then this afternoon.'

'Which woman friend?' James asked, turning towards him and, with a snakelike twist of his arm, drawing his own gin and tonic towards him without making contact with a tall be-suited man, who was pressed by the crush against the Regency-striped wall at his back.

'The lawyer one. Philippa Somebody. The one who's always defending the indefensible. Hi-jackers, car-bombers... This time a Somalian pirate who got shot by a British serviceman.'

James laughed, though not at the death of the unfortunate pirate. 'Pippa. She's good value. Did me a great favour once. She and her boyfriend Mark.' He turned towards Charlie as he said this, wanting to explain to him who Pippa was. But then he realised he couldn't go on with what he was going to say with Borja standing at his side, his hand and the drink that he held in it practically brushing against James's chest. For it was when James and Borja had temporarily split up that Pippa and Mark had given him house-room when he had nowhere else. He cut to, 'I had reason to be grateful to her,' and left it at that, though he went on, 'She was an old friend of ours when we lived in Spain,' at which Borja nodded slightly, then modified his agreement with a bit of a snort. James continued, 'Very high powered now. Human rights law and that kind of thing. You'll have seen her on TV, Charlie. That extraordinary fringe.' He looked around him at the throng of people, themselves included, that were wedged into the small space. 'We should have gone into the office. Bit late now. I should have thought.'

When Borja and he had first known Pippa she'd been a highly attractive twenty-one-year-old. She had remained attractive throughout the early years of her public career – her TV appearances by now the only contact with her that they had. But following her divorce she'd had the front of her hair cut in a fringe that was both severe and long. It had come down hard across her forehead like an iron pelmet. It seemed to announce that she no longer wanted to be thought of in physically attractive terms, it looked also as if it were meant to serve as a warning sign to men. Keep Out.

Suddenly Borja spoke up. He said with great feeling, with so much feeling that his voice actually shook, 'I find it difficult to understand how someone can come to hate their country quite so much.'

James answered quickly, glancing at the others as he spoke. 'I don't think she actually hates her country.' He said this in a cautious, diplomatic tone of voice. Since the crash Borja had taken to making very forthright statements about things; it had not been his usual way of expressing himself before that. But it was only to be expected. James wanted to be careful with him. He continued in a moderate way, 'It's just that somebody has to stick up for the underdog. That's the way the law is. It's a good principle. Even the indefensible must be offered a chance to make its defence. Then the law decides.'

Borja didn't try to dispute that. 'She was so nice when we knew her,' he said. 'Naïve, if you like, but nice. Well-intentioned...' He stopped and shook his head.

Nick stepped in, supporting James by the tried and tested method of paraphrasing exactly what he'd just said. 'It's perfectly well-intentioned to allow someone their right to a robust defence, surely? Especially if that's your profession. Hardly naïve.' At which Andy gave his elbow a tiny nudge with his own; a private reproof for being tactless that nobody noticed – except Nick.

It was Charlie who realised most keenly that James and Nick's reasonable words were not going down too well with Borja. Although he knew Borja less well than the others, he was the only one of the party who had survived a plane crash with him. He alone had slid down an escape chute with him, landing on their bottoms on English soil with a bump. He knew, because he'd shared the moment, that Borja had never been so ecstatically happy to feel the solid turf of England beneath him. It was not surprising that Borja should have a heightened sense of his connection with his adopted homeland. Hardly surprising if Borja thought of England as a place that needed protecting from whomever this person was, this lawyer the mention of whose name had caused him to speak out. Charlie decided to change the subject. He turned to Andy and said, 'Is the actor playing Romeo gay, do you think?'

Charlie had heard Benjamin Franklin's aphorism about house guests, like fish, beginning to smell after the first three days. He in fact stayed four and would probably have been welcome for a day or two more, but he also knew the expression about quitting when ahead, so, pleading that he had things to do back at home – which was a fib: nothing of any importance awaited him when he got back to Croydon – he eventually drove off, calling in to say goodbye at the Rose and Castle on his way.

The day after Charlie's departure James returned home early from work. The theatre was increasingly becoming 'somewhere else' while his own place became more and more importantly – he often framed these words in his mind now – at Borja's side. Wherever Borja was. James was in time to watch the six o'clock news, sitting literally at Borja's side on the sofa, while the last of the afternoon sun streamed through the mullions on the slant. And there in front of them Pippa was. In order to attract maximum attention to the dead Somalian and engender sympathy with his cause she had raised funds to bring his bereaved family all the way to Britain. Now here they all were, standing beside her in front of the cameras, with real tears in their eyes, indicting the British justice system for its barbarity. Though to be fair to them, most of the talking was done by Pippa herself. Suddenly Borja startled James by banging the flat of his hand on the coffee-table beside him and saying loudly, 'I've had enough of this. Can we just go for a walk?'

'Yes of course,' said James, picking up the remote very smartly and turning the set off. The sun would be setting in twenty minutes and it would be pitch dark thirty minutes after that, but if Borja wanted a walk then a walk he should have, and James would be with him all the way. As they exited the kitchen door James picked up the torch that stood handy on the kitchen windowsill, just in case.

They walked up the drive and into the time-warp wood, where the long tree shadows already flooded the road with dark. James was relieved that Borja didn't want to talk about Pippa, but allowed James to lead the conversation into calmer waters; they talked about what a good mushroom season this was turning out to be. In the previous days, with Charlie, they'd foraged wood blewitts and ceps and cooked them in omelettes and on toast. From time to time one of them would take the other's hand and clasp it lightly for a few seconds before letting it go again equally lightly.

'Oh!' Borja suddenly said.

'Oh, what?' But somehow James was already about six steps ahead.

'Just – nothing. Just a pain. That's all.'

'Deep breaths,' James said. 'Walk slowly. Deep breaths. It'll go.' He realised he hadn't needed to ask where the pain was.

Borja clutched James's arm very tightly, pulling down on it. 'It hurts.'

James stopped walking, turned to face Borja, held both his arms. 'Can you stand? We'll turn round. Go back. But very slowly. OK to do that?'

Borja nodded, saying nothing. Unless his eyes were speaking. Looking apprehensive, James thought, and very big and shiny in the gloom of the twilit wood. Slowly they began to walk back the way they'd come. The last of the daylight a little way ahead of them was a cheering sight; at least they hadn't gone very far into the time-warp wood. James put one arm right round Borja's back, and felt Borja's arm come round his. 'Hey,' James said. 'Let's do this. See if we can remember it...' He began. *'Shall I compare thee to a summer's day?'* and paused.

Sure enough Borja took it up, speaking in quite a normal, strong voice. *'Thou art more lovely and more temperate.'*

'Rough winds do shake the darling buds of May ...' James ran on rather fast, *'And summer's lease hath all too short a date.'* He was pleased to hear Borja's voice, still firm, deliver the next couplet.

'Sometimes too hot the eye of heaven shines, And often is his gold complexion dimmed...'

'And every fair from fair sometime declines.... Oh what is it now?...' The line eluding him, James hesitated, but Borja did not.

'By chance or nature's changing course untrimmed.'

'But thy eternal summer shall not fade.' James put the accent strongly on the *not*.

'Nor lose possession of that fair thou ow'st,' Borja continued.

'Nor shall...' James was suddenly aware of what was coming next. He began again valiantly. *'Nor shall death ... brag ... thou wander'st in his shade...'*

'Stop. I need to sit.'

James tossed the torch to the ground and with both his arms lowered Borja to the leaf-strewn edge of the drive. He tried to remember what you did. The First Aid mnemonic, Dr ABC. But even if he remembered what all the letters stood for, he didn't think it would apply in this case. At least his phone was in his pocket. He dialled 999, praying they were near enough to the wood's edge to receive a signal. He'd never before tried to phone anyone from inside the time-warp wood. To hear a voice answer dispassionately, 'Which service...?' gave him an unexpected degree of relief.

'Suspected heart attack,' he heard himself saying, though he hadn't allowed the thought to crystallise in his mind before this moment. He gave the postcode. 'But we're out in the lane – the driveway before you reach the house.' He looked down at Borja, lying on the ground now: James was kneeling astride him, as if they'd just been having sex. 'It's all OK,' he said to him, seeing only Borja's eyes, terror-struck, reaching like drowning fingers into his. They'd seen a film – somebody placed something under someone's tongue – an aspirin, was it? – but there wasn't one of those out here...

'And you are?'

'His next of king,' James told the voice on the phone, realising that that hadn't come out quite right, and yet in a way it had.

The expression on Borja's face had changed. A degree of serenity had replaced the terror in his eyes, but his skin, which had no recognisable colour of any description in the speckling dusk, now had a wet sheen on it.

'Kiss me,' Borja said very quietly.

James leaned the last few inches down to him and did. He tried to say, 'Christmases and birthdays,' but the words would not come out.

SEVEN

Karsten returned to the priests' residence in Gijón only to make a few adjustments to the contents of his backpack, and to arrange for the rest of his things – they were not that many after all – to be sent to his parents' house near Düsseldorf. Then he took the bus along the winding north coast road to Santander, finally making his way on foot towards the docks and the ticket office of the ferry company that plied between there and Portsmouth. He asked the price of a one-way ticket and was astonished at the amount. He realised now what everyone who had led a less sheltered life than he had over the last twenty years already knew: that it would have been much cheaper to fly to England direct from Seville. But he was here now. Anyway, his trip was in no sense an urgent one. He was not sure why he was making it, why he had suddenly come to the decision that he wanted to see Borja. But perhaps it was better to travel hopefully than to arrive. Eduardo had reminded him about the poem Ithaca. *When you set sail for Ithaca*, Cavafy had written, *ask that your way be long*. He had no idea what would happen when he and Borja did at last meet, though it didn't seem to matter. He had the rest of his life in which to find out.

'Hey, we could do with you!' A woman's voice was calling to him from a little way behind his left shoulder. Karsten, fishing in his wallet for his payment card, looked round. The woman was on the move, and hadn't stopped walking to call out. She was young, rather pretty, wore some sort of uniform and was making for a doorway behind the check-in desks. But now that Karsten looked in her direction she did stop. She pointed towards the guitar that jostled with his backpack and said, 'A guitar player is just what we could use.' Karsten thought he saw what she meant. A ferry that took twenty-four hours to reach its destination presumably offered some kind of on-board entertainment, like a cruise ship, like a hotel.

'Are you serious?' he asked, serious himself. He was someone to whom seriousness came a little too easily. 'Because...'

'Well, I wasn't being,' the young woman said, her face falling slightly. 'Or perhaps I partly was. It's true that we're short of a jazz band on this particular trip. A group's just pulled out at the last moment.'

'Well, I'm serious,' Karsten said, and sounded it. 'If it means the difference between paying for the crossing and not having to...'

Her body gave signs of wanting to back away from such intensity. 'I really don't know,' she said. She looked around, as if for a way of escape. She spotted one, in the form of another person in uniform arriving on the scene. 'Oh, here's Mike,' she said, facing Karsten again. 'He's our entertainments officer. You could always have a word with him, I suppose.' She called to the hurrying man, 'Mike, here a minute.'

Obediently but with a frown Mike changed course and headed towards them. 'This young man with a guitar here would like a word about music on board. Offering his services.' She left it at that and walked on towards the Crew Only door at the check-in. But just before she reached it she turned back just long enough to give Karsten a wink. Which Karsten thought was rather nice.

'If you're not requiring a ticket...' Karsten said sorry to the lady behind the ticket desk and stood aside, out of the small queue. He had been cheered to hear the other woman refer to him as a young man, even if her tongue had been well inside her cheek, but the phrase seemed to have had the opposite effect on Mike, who really was a young man. His frown darkened as he faced Karsten, probably thinking that he looked a bit on the mature side to be a ship's entertainer, and said, 'So what was it you wanted to know?'

'I heard you'd been let down by your on-board musicians today,' Karsten said, trying to sound nonchalant. He'd realised that the young woman found him a bit intense, and remembered that it was something the English weren't too comfortable with. He reached over his shoulder and tapped the neck of his guitar case. 'I'm offering to work my passage if you like.'

Mike was startled but had the grace to laugh. 'Gosh.' It was a word he'd learned to use with passengers. 'I wish it was so simple. But our musicians are all booked through head office, which is in Paris. *Auditions*.' He enunciated the word carefully in case Karsten hadn't come across the idea before. 'And so on and so forth.'

Karsten held tight. He was fairly sure that someone like himself who had been able to sell the Catholic faith in the twenty-first century could probably sell pretty well any idea to no matter whom. 'I understand that,' he said, smiling encouragingly. 'But you're in an exceptional situation, are you not? And here am I, a classical guitarist, a former professional, with... Look, I'll prove it to you.' He unwound the guitar from around his neck and placed it on the floor. He opened the case, picked up the instrument and, without checking the tuning, as that might have given Mike time to walk away, launched into a breezy Bach gavotte. After half a dozen bars, during which Mike looked at him in astonishment, he stopped and said, 'You could phone the Paris office and let them hear me down the phone.'

Mike waved a hand. 'That won't be necessary.' The frown had disappeared. 'How much of that stuff have you got? Repertoire, I mean. We have two forty-minute slots to fill each evening, and a short one after lunch. Have you got eighty minutes-worth in your memory bank?'

'Yes,' said Karsten, half doing the calculation, half whistling in the dark. 'Yes, I do have.'

'OK,' said Mike, waving his hand again, though in a different way this time. 'Can you bear with me a sec? I am actually going to phone Paris now. Just in case.' He fished in an inside pocket for a phone.

Karsten stood and waited, guitar neck still in his hand, resting the body of it back in its case. He watched the curious spectacle of someone he'd never met before trying to contact his superior in very inadequate French to determine whether Karsten would or would not be entertaining the passengers aboard the Portsmouth ferry that night. Rather to Karsten's surprise Mike actually got through to the right person almost at once. He came back to Karsten a moment later. 'They'd only be interested if you'd be prepared to do it for a whole week. That's the way the contracts work. Would you be up for that?'

Karsten thought for a second. 'I could do it,' he found himself saying. His availability was pretty open-ended, after all. It encompassed the rest of his life. And Cavafy's poem about Ithaca had talked up the experience of seeing new and unknown ports, arriving with the rising sun. 'The only thing is, I'd need to end up in Britain at the end of the contract. Not back here.'

Mike spoke again to the person at the other end and then turned back to Karsten. 'That's OK then,' he said. He named the fee, and spelt out the terms for the week, adding, 'Take it or leave it,' with a shrug.

Karsten said, 'I'll take it.' Then, 'You're sure they don't want to hear me along the phone?'

Mike smiled briefly, then looked serious again. 'It won't be necessary. I've heard enough to be convinced. If you don't come up to scratch the passengers can always pitch you overboard. That's what they did to the last guitarist we had.' He jerked his head towards the pass-door behind the check-in. 'You'd better come this way.'

He had a four-berth cabin to himself. That was as well, he thought, as the space was minuscule. It was cramped enough with just him. What it would be like with four musicians sharing – especially if they needed to practise in here – he was appalled to think. It was below the waterline, he supposed, as it was beneath the car-decks, though there was no port-hole through which he could check. And, to judge from the room's triangular shape, it was situated right in the bow. If they were to collide with anything head-first Karsten thought it unlikely he'd survive. But he had staggered away from a plane crash nearly thirty years before, sustaining no injury more severe than a broken meta-tarsal, and he allowed himself to be cautiously optimistic about the unlikelihood of something similar happening again.

He unpacked his music and thought quickly about what he could play and what order the pieces could go in, writing a draft running order on the back of one of the information sheets that lay on one of the bunks. The programmes were dictated by the fact that he could play some of his repertoire from memory still, but some he could not – at least, not tonight. He decided to do the first recital without music in front of him, saving the items he would need to read from the score for the second recital, in the bar, late at night. He reasoned that by that stage nobody, not even Mike, would be caring, even if they noticed, whether he was playing from the music or not. He'd have to ask for a music stand of course, but decided to wait till the first recital was over before tackling Mike about that. For now there was nothing for it except to sit on a bunk, guitar on knee, and run through the pieces he was going to play. He was pretty sure that, situated where he was, he would not be overheard.

At the agreed time he put on the suit that Mike had lent him, emerged from his cabin, and threaded his way up steps and through corridors to the dining-room. He looked at his large, eating audience and tried to assess their mood. Then he took his place and, announcing each piece as it came along, and beginning with Albeniz's Sevilla, got on with his new job.

He was welcome to eat with the passengers, he'd been told, but would have to pay the price. The same food exactly was served to the crew in the mess, free of charge, and there was a crew-only bar there, where the drinks were offered at a reduced rate. When his first recital was over – he was pleasantly surprised by the warmth of his applause – he made his way to the mess. He'd be eating with strangers wherever he went, and he decided he might as well do so without cost. Somebody told him there had been news of a plane crash at Gatwick earlier that afternoon but, preoccupied with the thought of that looming second recital in the bar, barely took the information in. He made no connection with the fact that he was on his way to England to track down a pilot.

In the morning his way to breakfast took him past the door to one of the promenade decks. He stopped and opened the heavy door with a hearty shove. A stinging breeze greeted him, and a horizon that was limitless and grey. For half a second there seemed to be silence. Then came a deep long swishing sound, as if a cliff-sized horse were swinging its slow tail. Karsten went to the rail and looked down. A long wedge of white water was peeling back across the grey, as the ship bore down into the sea with an action that was part plough, part rocking-chair, to carve its furrow, parting the waters with the sonorous rustle of the deep. The bows rode up again and the noise all but ceased. A few seconds later the cycle began anew as the bows dropped again to create the next mighty unhurried swish. The sound took Karsten suddenly back in time, though he couldn't imagine to what point or where. He'd never spent a night on a ship before, or slept beside a beach. It was smells that were supposed to do that to you anyway, not sounds, he thought, remembering a Madeleine he'd heard about in a famous book he'd never read. But this, the early morning sound of the sea... He wondered if his memory was tapping into some deep source, a spring of experience that went back in time to long before his own insignificant birth.

'Must be about abreast of Brest,' said a voice near him. Another passenger was leaning over the rail. He made his little joke with the air of someone who has done so many times before and has no more expectation of raising a laugh this time round than on the others. It took Karsten a few seconds to work out what he meant: he was a bit hazy about the geography anyway, and the preposition was one that, when speaking English, he never used himself. But when he'd put it all together he realised what it meant. They were some way off the westernmost point in Brittany – there were seagulls around the ship to prove the point, even if the ship was too far from the coast for its passengers actually to see it – and had put the fabled Bay of Biscay behind them in the night. That fearsome beast of sailors' tales had turned out, this time round, to be a pussy-cat.

Someone else came out on deck just as Karsten turned back from the rail. It was Mike. 'Didn't really have a chance to say so last night but you played brilliantly.' There was real enthusiasm in his face. 'Keep that up all week and five gold stars for you. You evidently survived the night.'

'I haven't really played like that for twenty years, I think,' Karsten said, wondering a little at himself and his unlikely success.

'What were you doing in the meantime?' Mike asked.

'Teaching. Running a primary school in Gijón.' Karsten didn't want to add the *I used to be a priest* bit. That could keep for another day, if Mike and he found themselves getting to know each other better.

Mike started to say that that was an unusual thing for a German guy to be doing in one of the rougher corners of Spain but was interrupted by the arrival out on deck of a woman, well-dressed and well-coiffed, who came up to

Karsten and said, 'I heard you play last night. I thought you were simply great.'

Mike said to her, 'Yes, isn't he good?' Then, rather archly, 'My discovery,' before turning away towards the door that led to less blowy areas of the ship.

'Can we talk a minute?' the woman asked. Her eyes were lively, alert. She inclined her head towards the door. 'Perhaps inside?'

Karsten followed her into the calmer atmosphere of a lounge. They sat in an otherwise empty row of armchairs that lined the port-holed wall. 'The Bach and Handel especially,' the woman resumed. 'Though the Spanish and Latin American pieces too. A real feel for them. Where did you train?'

Karsten told her he'd studied under Manuel Lozón in Córdoba, and watched her face carefully to see whether that meant anything to her or if she was simply making polite conversation and wanted to keep him from his breakfast by making more.

'Oh yes,' she said with warmth. 'And Lozón was a pupil of Yepes himself – correct me if I'm wrong.' Karsten did not. 'It must be rather wonderful for you to come from such a lineage.' Karsten was acutely conscious of a minute rustling of her dress. 'I'm sorry. My name's Jo Lance.'

Karsten said, 'Karsten Bäcker,' and they shook hands.

'I knew your name,' Jo said. 'The gentleman who was with you just now introduced you before you played last night.' She gave a smile that was both understanding and mischievous. 'Though you probably don't remember that.' She went on, 'But I hadn't heard your name before. What kind of dates do you usually play? I mean, when you're not on board ship.'

A bit taken aback, Karsten answered, 'I don't normally do 'dates' at all. I haven't played in a professional kind of way for many years now.'

'Well, I wouldn't have guessed.'

Jo's surprise seemed genuine. Karsten wondered what made him so interesting to this forty-something Englishwoman who still showed clear signs of the beauty she'd had in youth. He knew from long experience that a dog-collar acted as a homing beacon for many women of her age, and had learned over the years to spot the signs – the hand that would remove imaginary bits of fluff from your shoulder, the half-veiled chat-up lines – and knew all the standard avoidance routines by heart. But he was not wearing a dog-collar now, and had said nothing to Jo that would lead her to think he ever had.

'Are you travelling by yourself?' Jo asked. Karsten guessed she was more interested in the implications of his yes or no answer than in the answer itself. Karsten answered with a simple yes. 'I wonder if you'd be free to join my husband and me for something to eat at lunchtime? If you have any thoughts about rebuilding a concert career I might have some thoughts of my own to add.'

'That sounds interesting,' said Karsten, trying not to let his face or voice indicate how startled he was. 'I'd like that.'

'And perhaps we'll get to hear what brought you all the way from Germany to the Bay of Biscay.' Jo began to stand up. The preliminary interview was coming to an end. 'Though I have to warn you that George, my husband, has a tin ear when it comes to music.' Jo smiled, then turned and left.

Karsten stayed where he was for a moment, still dazed with surprise. The encounter with Jo had been mystifying, though pleasantly so. Was she, as she seemed to hint, a high-powered agent or promoter of some sort, with a new career for him in her gift? A gift that could be bestowed easily over a light lunch on a ferry in mid-crossing? It was unlikely, Karsten had to tell himself. Or was her interest in him a more personal one? In a way that would be more flattering. Karsten did not think of himself as any kind of a catch; he didn't think he'd thought that even way back in his youth. The woman was married, of course. Karsten might gain a clearer picture of how things stood when he saw the husband she had mentioned. For now, without any evidence, Karsten pictured him as elderly and rich. Jo had said he had a tin ear. He might have a tin leg as well, or a wooden one, acquired in Venezuela. Other infirmities of age perhaps.

Karsten could not deny to himself that he had been very attracted by Jo. That discovery had come to him as something of a shock. As a young man his sexuality had been an elusive thing. He'd been attracted to women certainly, but he had never followed the matter to its logical end. He hadn't pursued women very energetically in a romantic or sexual way. And they hadn't tended to come on to him: until, that was, in one of life's heavier-handed ironies, he was safely a priest.

Before that, there had been Alexa, of course. The vision of that head of pre-Raphaelite hair cascading over a café table in Seville remained with him as vividly as ever. But romance hadn't entered the scene even with Alexa. He had become her guitar teacher instead – with extraordinary results. She had eventually moved to Córdoba to study with Manuel Lozón, and later had married his American friend Mark.

Thinking about Alexa and her move to Cordoba drew Karsten inevitably to memories of what had happened immediately after that. He'd found himself suddenly and shockingly attracted to Borja, with whom he was briefly sharing, almost care-taking, Alexa's Seville flat. Then almost within a matter of days had come the Valencia crash. That had caused him to become a priest. Which involved pushing the genies of sexual attraction and romantic yearning back into their bottles. With a degree of success that those who had never tried it still tended to think was impossible for anyone to achieve. Now the bottles seemed to be coming uncorked again, and unexpectedly soon. On an impulse he was seeking Borja out after thirty years, and now he'd met a woman whose effect on him was like an electric shock. He made an effort to change the focus of his thoughts; he got up and went in search of his free breakfast in the crew mess.

EIGHT

It was a day that became a night: then a night that wasn't a night, in the timeless world of hospital waiting rooms and hospital wards, places where life may die but never sleep. James spent much of the time just a foot or two from Borja, reluctant to leave his side. Borja wired up to every kind of apparatus. Borja unconscious but breathing fiercely, determinedly, an oxygen cylinder attached. But often James was left on his own as Borja was wheeled away for yet another test.

'How much did he smoke?' was a question that was repeatedly asked of James by men and women with appealingly bare forearms and stethoscopes worn around the neck like powerful amulets.

'He didn't smoke at all,' James said, wondering why he and his interlocutors were all automatically using the past tense. But then he thought back. 'He used to smoke the odd cigar when I first knew him. In his twenties.' But the more he thought, the more there was. 'Well, occasionally cigarettes at that time too. More recently? Well, only occasionally. Social events, weddings... But just the odd cigar again. Small ones,' he added in mitigation, trying to reduce those elegantly rolled items from mortal to merely venial things.

During the times they were together James, sitting close to the bed, would gently squeeze one of Borja's finger-ends, in emulation of the ECG clip that was squeezing another one. Then he would run a finger up his bare, hair-striated forearm with a new sense of wonder, joy even, at the fact that he still could.

At last one of the stethoscope-necklaced doctors, a graceful young woman who had invited James to call her Kate, told him that Borja was out of immediate danger. His rhythms had stabilised. No longer was his state to be labelled unconscious: he could be described more cheerfully as peacefully sleeping his experience off. They would need to keep him in for a day or two, for observation and further tests. Meanwhile it would probably be a good idea for James to go home now, to get some rest, and come back later in the day.

Which day would that be now? James wondered. He saw that it was after six o'clock in the morning, and as he waited outside the hospital entrance for the taxi that he'd ordered to come and take him home the fresh sun was lighting the still green trees almost horizontally, while squirrels unhurriedly crossed the paved area near his feet and climbed into the daytime foliage.

Back at Sevenscore James phoned his own office, leaving a message that explained the situation and said that he would be in late. Then he phoned the Rose and Castle, considerately leaving his message on the office phone, whose early morning ringing wouldn't wake Nick and Andy, rather than trying their private number or their mobiles, which would. He made and drank an instant coffee, then went into his and Borja's bedroom, unprepared for the experience of how changed it would feel and look. Without taking even his shoes off he lay down on the bed.

The next thing he knew, he was looking up at Andy, who looked somehow taller than usual, standing beside his bed and looking down at him with a concerned look on his face. 'The kitchen door was open,' Andy said. 'I'm glad he's out of danger. Are *you* all right?' James rolled round to look at the bedside clock. 'I wasn't sure whether to wake you,' Andy said. 'It's just gone eleven.'

When James saw Borja again, in the afternoon, he was awake though groggy, and sitting in a chair beside a bed in one of the observation wards. He was wearing pyjamas and a dressing-gown that had belonged to someone else. James tried not to think about the circumstances in which those garments had come to belong to the hospital. They said hallo, James leant down to Borja and they kissed. James saw that Borja's feet were bare and he reached at once into the hold-all he'd brought, pulled out slippers that he'd brought from home and, kneeling, slid them onto Borja's feet. He noticed more clearly than he'd done for some time the tiny rosettes of hair that sprang between the knuckles of both his second toes. 'Hobbit feet' he'd sometimes said in tender moments thirty years before, and realised that it was something he no longer said. As if to remedy that long-time lapse he said it to Borja now. 'Hobbit feet.' He was pleased to hear Borja's surprised though muted laugh.

In the hold-all James had also brought authentic Borja pyjamas and dressing-gown, a book, a bottle of Lucozade and two bananas plucked at the last moment from the fruit bowl on the dining-table at the Court House. He hoped that would be enough to be going on with – at least for overnight. That, James hoped, might be the limit of Borja's stay in here, with any luck.

As he jostled his feet a little more firmly into the slippers Borja asked, 'What news from the theatre, then?' Which James found touching, but it unnerved him too.

'It's all fine,' James answered, though they both knew that was far from being the case. 'I went in on my way here. I've handed the reins to Linda for now. For as long as necessary. While I'm looking after you.' He delved into the hold-all again, holding its contents up in front of Borja one by one as though they were rabbits pulled from a hat. Then he laid them on the over-bed table or else stuffed them away in the drawers of the locker beside the bed. 'There's one last thing,' James said, looking around the room to check for watching eyes before he produced the final rabbit: a quarter-bottle of Rioja and a sturdy glass tumbler to drink it from. 'For later,' he said, stowing both glass and bottle in the top locker drawer. 'After I'm gone. Whether you're allowed it or not.'

The following two days brought no real change. Andy and Nick came to see Borja and told James afterwards how good he looked, but talk of his imminent discharge seemed to have lapsed. The doctors had been reassuringly upbeat about the survivable nature of heart attacks that were experienced by men in their fifties, but James couldn't help noticing that they'd stopped saying it at some point. He told himself that once everyone had said that to him there was probably no need for them to repeat themselves and that there was nothing alarming to be inferred. On the other hand, the question of whether Borja would be able to captain a 737 again was avoided carefully: neither James nor Borja nor any of the doctors was ready to approach that one yet.

Borja told James repeatedly that he felt comfortable, though James noticed how very weak he seemed – and changed somehow by his experience. There was a flat look about the expression on his face, even when he smiled, though James was pleased to see he often did that.

On the third day Borja admitted to James that he'd started to feel pains everywhere. In arms and legs and lower back. He'd told the night staff this and they'd given him pain-killers and a sedative. This morning the pains had gone away. James said he was glad of that.

As he was leaving the ward, and saying polite good-nights as he passed the nurses' station, one of the doctors who was leaning over a desk there straightened up and asked if he could have a word with him. It was a young male doctor, one of the most upbeat ones, and one whom

James thought looked rather nice. They stood together beside a little alcove where chairs were stacked and the doctor told James that Borja would need to be kept under observation a little longer. It was possible that the heart attack was not the only thing Borja's body was dealing with. That might have been triggered by something else.

'Something caused by the plane crash?' James said, finding he could scarcely command enough breath to get the words out. He had suffered that stab of panic that most people feel when they hear a doctor use the words: something else.

'It's possible,' the doctor said, and went on to explain that they were still waiting for the results of one or two more recent tests. Shaken, James went back to Borja's bedside, only to find the place being cleaned up by auxiliary staff. Borja had thrown back his tea.

News travelled, who knew how. James thought someone should write a thesis on this, then thought that probably someone already had. Stuart the gardener had been the first to know that Borja was in hospital, because of James's phoning him about the cat. But he hadn't told Peter Masters at the farm. Nevertheless Peter had come to the door with good wishes for Borja and the offer, from him and his wife and young family, to help out in any way they could. As for the pub, even people James had never spoken to were coming out with words of support. In the city, theatregoers who could only have known James by sight stopped him in the street.

The news osmosis process had its limitations though. James put nothing on Facebook. It seemed to him that Facebook was where people posted good news only, even when the reality was very different, and that to announce any negative development via that medium would have been regarded as ill-bred and in poor taste. Borja's airline had to be telephoned. James did that on the first day. He also phoned Charlie around the same time. Charlie offered to come back up to Sevenscore if James wanted that. James did want that, but was afraid Borja might not, so he told Charlie: not for the time being. He'd thought about calling Borja's brothers in Salamanca, or one of them at least, but had decided to wait a day or two, till Borja was clearly out of danger. For the same reason he didn't contact his own brother. Both his parents, like both of Borja's, were dead.

Now things were different. On his way back from the hospital James went straight to the pub. There was no sign of Andy in, or behind any of the bars, so he went through into the big kitchen where Nick, in his whites, was supervising preparations for service. Nick had only to glance at James's face – though his appearance in the kitchen was unusual enough – to suspend all other thoughts. 'Come upstairs,' he said.

Sitting on one of the sofas in the sitting-room, facing Nick, who sat on the other one, James outlined the new development. He finished, 'It's not the things I know that scare me. It's the things I don't.'

Nick said, 'Like Rumsfelt. Known unknowns and unknown knowns.'

'Something like that,' James said, without bothering to ask himself whether he remembered the quote.

Andy came into the room, and was brought up to date very quickly by Nick. Who then got up and said to James, 'Sorry. Have to go. Come and find me again before you leave the pub.' He grinned unexpectedly, mischievously, and added, 'If you do leave, that is.'

James felt wonderfully relieved suddenly to have the company, the support, of his two best friends, like wings bearing him up. A moment later he was struck with guilt at the realisation that Borja did not. He was going to his child-early bedtime alone in a hospital five miles away, without Nick and Andy's company, without his. 'Can we phone him, do you think?' There was a fiendishly complicated and expensive machine that pulled out on folding arms from the wall beside Borja's bed and which did all sorts of things: it provided TV and radio and a direct-line phone, but most patients in their fragile states found it too daunting actually to use.

James dialled the number anyway and was relieved when Borja picked up. He was watching the TV news, he said. James nearly told him, that doesn't come on till ten, but let it go. He stood and handed his phone to Andy on the opposite sofa. Andy spoke briefly, brightly, and James heard Borja doing the same at the other end. Little sparklers of conversation that burned brightly but eventually fizzled out into dark. James took the phone back and said a few more words, while Andy crossed the room and opened a cupboard. James watched him uncork a bottle of wine, with guilty relief.

The doctor spoke to James and Borja together. They followed the stages of his announcement as if in a trance, fingering the key words and phrases as if they were rosary beads. Not good news. Tests have shown. Serious. Lesions. Cancer. They held hands at that point, the remorseless rosary beads seeming to pass between their thumbs. Spread. Aggressive. Treatment. Palliative care. Borja brought up most of his breakfast at that point and the interview was suspended.

When things were calmer and James and Borja could talk to each other alone James found Borja fiercely determined to focus on the practicalities of the situation. James had a sense that his lover's innermost thoughts had retreated like snails into their shells, into a place where, for the first time ever they were beyond James's reach. Especially upsetting, James discovered, was Borja's anxiety about how his brothers and sisters were to be told the news without upsetting them too much – as if it were some misdemeanour he'd been caught out in, like a sexual indiscretion or tax fraud.

Andy arrived during the afternoon. He spent some time with the two of them and then James let him have a little time with Borja alone. The fact that, long ago, Andy and Borja had almost had a fling together now seemed to James, curiously, a matter for rejoicing. James was glad that Borja had someone like Andy close to him now. The same could be said of Nick of course. Nick would be coming in during the evening.

James took advantage of the few minutes during which he'd left Andy and Borja together to do two things. First he telephoned Charlie. Then he went in search of one of the doctors. He found the youngish one who had given the bad news earlier. The one whose looks James found appealing. Again they stood next to the curtain that shielded stacks of chairs from the public gaze. 'Could the spread of the cancer have been hastened by the plane crash?' James asked.

The young doctor, whom James now knew as Timothy, screwed up his face a little. 'It's possible,' he said, the words coming slowly and carefully. 'It's even a likely scenario. But of course the cancer wasn't caused by the crash. The condition was obviously well advanced before that. If the crash hurried things along a bit...' Timothy made a gesture of weighing things on scales and let out an audible breath. He looked James very firmly, very kindly, in the eye and said, 'It would be a very difficult thing to prove. In case you were thinking of trying to. You could spend an awful lot of money on lawyers, I imagine, and not get very far.'

'Lawyers,' James said with a snort, and Timothy gave him a collusive half-smile. James thought, damn lawyers. Damn Pippa in particular. But damn them all, the long, short and tall. Damn the lot of them.

'I'm very sorry,' Timothy said, and James was surprised to see a hint of tears in the doctor's eyes, and deeply touched.

Everybody has a boss. James's was the chairman of the theatre board, a forty-something man called David Parkes. He wore large-rimmed glasses, extremely smart suits and, though quite seriously bald on top, allowed a remarkable mane of nearly golden hair to flow down the sides, over the earpieces of his spectacle-frames and to scroll to a halt over his impeccable collar. His appearance was thus a badge of suitability for the office he held, it spoke more eloquently of artistic credentials, and less time-wastingly, than any words of his could possibly have done. Looking in at the theatre following his hospital trip James found a message from David awaiting him. He called him back.

'I know how bad a time this is for you and you've other things to think about,' David's voice told him when they'd made contact. 'I just wanted you to know how hard we'll all be batting for the Regent at the meeting tonight.'

It had slipped James's mind that tonight would be held the city council meeting at which the future of James's theatre, and therefore of his career, would be decided. 'We all' meant the councillors who wanted the Regent to retain its independence, an issue over which the council was split. It was arguable whether the city could continue to support two major arts venues, the Regent Theatre and the Barraclough Centre, run by two separate managements, at a time of major economic stress. Although the Regent was by some hundred and twenty years the senior of the two institutions, in terms of size and financial importance it was decidedly the less important in the city council's eyes. 'Would you like me to come along?' James asked. 'Speak up alongside you?

A witness from the coal-face so to speak. If it would help, you know...'

'No James,' David said smoothly, 'there really isn't any need. With Borja now you've bigger fish to fry. You must give him my seriously good wishes. Keep fighting. That's what you and he have got to do. We'll look after the theatre end of things. Tom and Joanna and I have everything sewn up. We've done our canvassing and the votes are pretty well in the bag. We'll win the day. Depend on it. Talk again tomorrow.' David rang off.

David had spoken confidently, James thought as he put the phone down and looked around the big office, empty for just that moment of anyone but him. Always reassuring, always smooth. Yet sometimes James found himself wishing for the old chairman, with his gimlet eyes and trenchant criticisms and spades that were really spades. He was long retired now, but with him James had at least known where he was.

Arriving at the hospital the next morning James found arrangements already under way for Borja's transfer to the brighter and more comfortable environment of the hospice which shared the hospital's extensive grounds. Amongst more detailed concerns about packing clothes and scarily redundant-looking shoes, Borja found a moment to say seriously, 'Last night's meeting: how did that go? The theatre's safe, no?'

'I'm sure it is,' James answered breezily. 'I haven't been into the office yet so I can't say for certain. But David was more than confident when we spoke yesterday. Last night's council meeting! You remembered that!'

'We'll wait and see,' said Borja, sinking back into the pillows a bit, un-persuaded by James's bright tone. And both of them thought, though they didn't exchange the thought, that had the news been good then David would have phoned James, either late last night or first thing this morning, on his mobile or at home.

James's intuition about Borja's deeper thoughts had been correct. They had indeed crept into hiding, like snails in a drought, leaving his mind free to deal with the detailed concerns of the present, which all too often revolved around the needs to piss and shit, and the complicated logistical arrangements, involving other people, that had to be negotiated in either case. There was also the question of the next meal, of what it would be, and of whether he could hold it down. Then there was the question of James's job... It was only at night that the deep dark snails crawled from their shells and freely ranged Borja's brain. James again. What would happen to him when he was gone? Who would take care of him then? He wasn't very good at ironing shirts. It was hard to imagine someone else's future from the position Borja was now in, but in the wakeful half-light of the hospital night Borja found himself doing just that. There was his own future to stare into also. He'd been there before though, staring death in the face in the chapel of the Charity Hospital in Seville. *Domus Pauperum et Scala Coeli.* Then the face was a skeleton's, one whose bony fingers were snuffing a candle out, above a heap of church finery and vestments. *In Ictu Oculi* was written around the vanished flame. In the Blink of an Eye. Now there was not even a darkened candle, and no finery left. Only a vast black hole that was bigger than the cosmic kind, bigger than the universe itself. When he'd ridden on the back of his snail-shelled steeds to the brink of this abyss, usually around the time the first light crept into the sky Borja would find in himself an odd resilience, an odd calm.

Because he didn't get into his office till midday, where a phone message from David did indeed await him, and because he'd bought the local newspaper as he was leaving the hospital, James read the news of his own redundancy in a report of the city council meeting on an inside page. He read it after getting into his car, then folded the paper, put it on the seat beside him and stoically drove off. But he hadn't gone a hundred yards before the most dreadful thing happened inside him and he had to pull over to the side of the road, beating the steering-wheel with his fists and for the first time in his life hearing a grown man howl.

David's phone message was full of apology and included an invitation to lunch in a day or two. When James rang him back he was glad for once to find his boss's phone switched to voice-mail. He was able calmly to thank David for his efforts and to suggest that lunch could be delayed until the following week. Then he phoned Charlie, ostensibly to check that he was still planning, as he had promised, to drive up in two days' time. Really, he just wanted to hear Charlie's voice.

When James returned to Borja in the afternoon the move to the hospice had already taken place. He found his partner in a bright and spacious single room, with a seriously big armchair, whose altitude and heading, pitch, roll and yaw could be controlled by the push of a button as easily as in any flight-simulator. On a roll-around kind of stand was an impressively big television. There was a French window that occupied most of one wall, outside it a raised terrace, plank-surfaced, surrounded by a wooden balustrade. Beyond the balustrade lawns rolled down to a line of trees, from which squirrels were emerging to forage on the acorns that were beginning to drop on the grass. It was a pleasing view, James thought, that might almost have been planned as a miniature representation of the view from the front of the Court House.

Borja seemed a little dazed after his short journey in the ambulance. James was dismayed to find that, when they walked out onto the terrace together, Borja needed a stick in one hand, while he clung on to James with the other. The stick, a handsome black metal affair that folded up when you weren't using it, had materialised from somewhere, like the hospital dressing-gown.

James reminded Borja that the next day was his birthday. Borja said he hadn't forgotten that, and shot James an impish little smile. He didn't mention the theatre, James noticed, but he knew that Borja had not forgotten that either, desirable though such a memory lapse might be.

James woke next morning to a sort of vision of Borja. He appeared to him, sitting in his flight-simulator armchair, in front of the French window that overlooked the hospice grounds, bathed in sunshine and welcoming James with a pain-free radiant smile. And when James went in to see him later in the morning – his hands full of birthday cards that had arrived at the Court House, plus his own, and a bottle of aftershave and another of wine – that was exactly the sight that presented itself: a smiling Borja, sitting back comfortably in his chair, fully dressed and haloed with the autumn sun. 'Happy Birthday, darling,' James said, although he'd already said it over the phone. Then he told Borja how he'd seen him in his mind, as he awoke. 'It's good to see you looking better again,' he said. 'Just like in my vision of you.'

Borja continued to smile at him, though now with a slightly puzzled look as well. 'Why are you crying?' he asked.

'I'm not,' James said. He laid the gifts he was carrying down on the bed and moved forward with a kiss that might obliterate his un-admitted tears.

But in the afternoon, when James went back to him again, Borja was still sitting in the same chair, having had some lunch, but doing nothing except waiting for James to return, and looking terribly alone. 'You should have gone to bed for a nap,' he said, his joy of that morning turned to bleak misery.

'I might have missed your visit,' Borja said, apparently seriously.

'I'd have woken you up. I wouldn't have gone away. After today you rest in bed after lunch. Got that? I'll wake you when I arrive. Now let's see what the telly's got to offer this fine afternoon, and we'll uncork that bottle of wine.'

'I've got a surprise for you tomorrow,' James told him later, when he was leaving. (A process that was becoming more difficult by the day.) 'Charlie's coming up tomorrow for a few days.'

Borja was visible cheered by this. He grinned broadly. Rioja and morphine together did wonders for his morale. 'That's loverly,' he said, pronouncing the word in the charming three-syllabled way he had done when James first knew him. 'I'll look forward to that.' Then, 'Can you bring me a notebook?' he added unexpectedly. 'An empty one. You know. To write things in.'

NINE

Lunch was more than the sandwich and glass of wine that Karsten had expected; it was a full-blown white tablecloth affair in the Brasserie restaurant. 'You are our guest,' Jo reassured him as the waiter presented them all with leather-bound menu books as big as the largest laptops, and her husband George, who was wearing a suit and tie, wrinkled his nose and snuffled like a porcupine as he opened his menu up, as if making it quietly clear exactly whose guest Karsten was going to be. George looked nearly twice as old as his wife, which confirmed Karsten's intuition, and he had a physiognomy that seemed to be made up of scrolls. His hair, grey streaked with black, scrolled up and back from the dome of his forehead, then scrolled up again after it had fallen to his collar. The profile of his nose was another double curve, and the same went for those famous tin ears. Even his eyebrows and drooping eyelids did something of the sort.

As the waiter delivered bread rolls with tongs so long that he might have been serving supper at the devil's, Jo asked Karsten what had brought him to Spain, and from there to the sea beyond its coasts. He replied with a carefully filleted account of his career, to which George in particular listened very attentively, nodding and wrinkling his nose. Politely, although he was interested as well, Karsten asked Jo and George why they were crossing the sea. 'We have a small place in Portugal,' Jo said, with a little tremor of pride. 'Near Coimbra, on the coast.' Karsten had been to Coimbra when a priest. It was a place where miracles had occurred, miracles that he'd persuaded himself to believe in for a time. He told them that he knew Coimbra, but not why.

Then Jo came to the point of the meeting. 'I have a little agency in London. I send musicians of all sorts all over Europe and beyond, matching the right artist with the right venues, clients and dates. Forgive me if I'm getting ahead of myself but it did strike me that you might be someone who was looking for work of that kind. Perhaps I'm wrong about that.' She gave Karsten a smile that was quite coquettish, yet which touched his heart. Did she really want to send him to the furthest corners of Europe, or did she have another end in view? Karsten allowed himself the luxury of considering that.

'You may be right,' Karsten said. 'I mentioned that I was going to try and find an old friend in England, someone I lost touch with. When I've done that I shall certainly look for work. What kind of work … I haven't really thought.' A starter of avocado with anchovies arrived in front of him. 'As I told you, I was a school teacher for many years.'

Jo didn't react to that. She said, 'If you are interested, and if you have the time, would you care to come and talk to me in my London office in a few days' time? We could have a serious chat. Thank you,' she said to the waiter, just then delivering a small salad topped with a roundel of toasted goat's cheese. 'I mean,' she spoke to Karsten again, 'a businesslike chat, in more businesslike surroundings.'

'That would be good,' Karsten said. 'I mean, actually, that's most kind. In three days we dock in Portsmouth and we stop there for two whole days. It's a sort of mid-week weekend. After that I'm supposed to do one more trip to Santander. But I could travel from Portsmouth easily to London, I think.' He thought through the days of the week in his head. 'I could come on Thursday. Would that be OK?'

Jo thought Thursday would be fine. 'Say twelve thirty? Then you can get up to town from Portsmouth without too horribly early a start. You won't need to bring your guitar. I already know what you can do.'

'That's good,' said Karsten. Then he gave Jo a twinkling smile that was almost as good as one of her own. 'Will I need to wear a suit?'

The tide was massively high as they entered Portsmouth harbour and, because the ship he was travelling on was immensely big, Karsten had the impression as it passed the ancient fort that guarded the sheltered waters and Portsmouth's old town, that he was arriving in Lilliput. From the promenade deck he looked down upon the homely red-tiled roofs of Spice Island and on ant-like figures that fished with rod and line from the sea wall. The experience was disconcerting: it reminded Karsten of scenes he'd watched on TV of liners arriving in Venice and gliding surreally up the Grand Canal, towering above the Doge's palace and the previously lofty churchscapes of Palladio. By the time his ferry had rounded the corner of the fort and he was looking down even at the zinc sheeting of the cathedral roof and its green-capped tower Karsten was beginning to feel the situation not just disconcerting but verging on the sacrilegious.

There was a two-hour turnaround, in which Karsten played no part, but took a siesta instead, before they set sail again in the late afternoon. They were heading for Bilbao, sixty kilometres east of their port of departure the previous day. This was because the company's ferries sailed at regular times, while the distances between the ports of southern England and northern Spain were not exactly the same, not tidily arranged with a precise twenty-two hour sailing time between them, so that a complicated but economically efficient system of criss-crossing routes had grown up. His siesta over, and watching their departure now from the deck, Karsten was pleased to notice that the tide had fallen sharply and that they were sailing past the ancient buildings at a more respectful height. He had parted in a very friendly manner from Jo at the end of lunch – they had exchanged a little kiss – and was wondering a little at himself for entertaining the ideas he now had. He was unsure if he'd read the signals he'd been getting from Jo aright. But if he was, then he found himself contemplating with complete equanimity the possibility that his first real dalliance with a woman might involve a specimen who was already married to another man. He thought that, since being a priest just a few weeks previously, a position from which he'd denounced such liaisons with the full might of the Church's teaching at his back, he had come a long way rather fast. He went below again to run through the pieces for his evening slots. Mercifully the passengers would all be new; the programmes could remain the same as yesterday's. And so on throughout the week.

In the morning the sound of the sea's swish had grown to something like a roar, the ship's rocking-chair motion more like a fairground ride. Around the topmost deck, where the rigging sang with a deep-throated hum, Karsten saw a score or more of small birds hopping about and in occasional flight. He realised they must be autumn migrants heading south: they had descended in the night, attracted by the lights of a convenient floating mass that was heading in the same direction as themselves. They were chaffinches and pipits, and wagtails and a robin, a starling or two, and other species that he couldn't name. Others were hopping among the tables outside the passengers' breakfast room. A woman opened a door with some difficulty against the wind and went out to them. She carried a croissant, from which she broke off crumbs to throw. She did this a bit self-consciously as though she feared a reprimand from the waiters. But with no shame at all the birds hopped and fluttered, and pecked at the crumbs from between the decking slats.

The following morning, as they headed north again, Karsten surfaced to find a major clean-up and salvage operation going on. He had apparently made his third crossing of the Bay of Biscay in a Force Twelve but had slept through the whole thing. The storm was behind them now (they were once again, he thought, presumably abreast of Brest) but whole sections of the public areas were cordoned off as breakages were swept from floors, furniture righted and liquid spillages mopped up. Mike was restoring order to the children's play area, though to Karsten's eyes it looked no more despoiled than it had done at close of play the previous night. 'Survived another night, then,' Mike said on seeing him. He looked at him for tell-tale signs of *mal de mer*. 'And not been sick.' Karsten assured him he had not. 'Good,' said Mike. Although the subject had been avoided until now, a tendency not to be seasick was looked on with approval by anyone who employed the likes of Karsten in his current job. 'Well,' Mike said as Karsten went over to him and took the other end of a play-house that he was trying to set the right way up, 'if you fancy any more weeks at sea we'd be happy to have you back. You've done us proud the last few days.'

'I'll think about that,' Karsten said. 'It's good to be asked. I've got an appointment tomorrow in London with… Remember the lady who came and spoke to us that first morning out on deck? I think she's some kind of agent or … I don't know the word in English... anyway, something like that.'

Mike gave him a look, in which Karsten could have read any of several meanings if he'd wanted to. 'Well, good luck,' he said. 'I hope that goes well for you – in whatever sense. But if it doesn't, you know where we are.' Karsten thanked Mike for that, and went off to look for breakfast. He found he had quite an appetite.

It was easy to get to London. You took the bus to the station, asked for a ticket, got on the first train and there you were. Although Karsten hadn't actually been in London since he was a teenager he had the feeling that he knew the place well. It was on the news quite often, after all, and appeared in films quite scenically, and in books. Arriving at Waterloo and walking across the bridge to the north side of the Thames, he felt quite at home. The Houses of Parliament appeared before him across the grey water, and their clock most reassuringly showed him the time. Even the lions in Trafalgar Square and the man on top of the obelisk there – for a moment Karsten couldn't quite remember who he was – had the air of old friends about them. It wasn't until he turned left out of the Charing Cross Road and found himself in Old Compton Street that it dawned on him that London might actually have changed quite a bit.

But he was buoyed by the feeling, as he turned into Wardour Street where Jo's office was, that he was setting off on a new venture, or adventure, and that this day might open new doors for him, either of the professional or of the personal kind. The feeling stayed with him while he gave his name to the secretary or receptionist through the buzzer at the street door and, a minute later, was conducted by her into the presence of Jo herself. He found her looking a little prettier in her many-coloured jacket and scarf than an ordinary business meeting might have called for. She greeted him with real enthusiasm, rising from her chair and coming round the desk to meet him with a kiss which he returned unguardedly, like a boy thirty years younger than himself. It was three days since they'd had lunch together, four days since she had heard him play, but her memories of the experiences clearly remained sharp. Knowledgeably she praised his phrasing in a certain fantasy by Bach, and asked him why he preferred a particular étude by Villa-Lobos to another one. With an odd little smile and eyelids momentarily lowered she told him that her husband had sent his regards.

Coffee arrived. It hadn't been offered, and Karsten hadn't said he wanted it, but the lady receptionist or secretary brought it anyway. Jo and he sat, away from the desk, in armchairs at the less businessy end of the room. Jo filled Karsten in with details of what it was that she did. She was not an agent exactly nor – Karsten had struggled to find the exact words in English for this – a concert promoter. She explained that her role was to manage the concerts of her performers – publicity, public relations, hospitality and so forth – for an up-front fee. She looked at Karsten very directly as she came out with this.

It was not quite what he had been expecting to hear and he looked sideways at other things in the room as he tried to look at the positive aspects of this. If he were to find himself giving large-scale concerts of course...

'I can see you're thinking hard about this,' Jo cut in smoothly on his thoughts. 'The way it works is this. The individual artist or his or her agent actually finds the concert dates and negotiates the terms. Where I really come in is in helping to get the right people *to* the concert. The people who can help build the career and take things to the next stage.'

Again Karsten glanced sideways, hoping it wasn't too obvious what he was looking at. It was something he'd seen on his way in but had not really noticed or thought about. It was a nineteenth century Ottoman sofa. It looked slightly out of place in a room that was furnished in an otherwise thoroughly modern way. It was occupied by two stuffed toys or dolls. Karsten thought they might represent a pair of Beatrix Potter characters (one of them had very long ears) though their names didn't spring to Karsten's mind either in German or in English. He returned his gaze and his attention to Jo, whose smile now looked less coquettish and more businesslike. He said, 'May I check that I have understood? The artist finds the dates and your job is to – is this the right expression? – to ice the cake.'

Jo moved back in her chair a little way with a rustle of sleeves and gave a tiny laugh. 'I think that's exactly the right expression. But I could put it more positively than that. It's not just about icing the cake but about making the cake a bigger one. About adding value to an event. Adding value to an artist's prospects, to his or her whole career in fact.' These sentences about adding value turned out to be the beginning of quite a long speech. Karsten found himself failing to listen to it. It struck him quite suddenly that he had travelled in a few days to an extraordinary place and back again: it was a journey far more amazing than any trip across the Bay of Biscay and through the English Channel and back. A few days ago he wasn't thinking of himself as someone who would be giving guitar recitals on a ship. But that had happened, and he was still doing it. He certainly hadn't imagined himself as a concert artist who might perform in prestigious venues around Europe. The first thing had come about by the most extraordinary chance. Being in the right place at the right time, he had managed to make a major success of his role as a ship's entertainer for a few days. Being in the right place a second time had allowed him to meet Jo, and brought the prestigious faraway places that he hadn't even dreamed about suddenly into his imaginary reach. He had spent three days building up an idea of a possible future, in which a handsome and powerful woman would take a hand in building him up. Building him up in some way, though his imagination had been a bit hazy, or lazy, about that. Maybe he had imagined her building his career up. Maybe he'd thought of her as building him up, him personally, into a sexually active, emotionally functioning, human being for the first time in his life. And because the first of the two things had come about so easily and so unexpectedly he had allowed himself to imagine that the second would materialise in a similar way. Philosophy had a word for that particular fallacy, but Karsten couldn't remember just then what the word was. He tried to refocus his mind on Jo's words but found he could only refocus his eyes on her face. It was really a lovely face. He had to admit that. He'd fancied her. He had to admit that too. And perhaps she'd fancied him; he hoped so at least; but that was all there had been; there was nothing else, and nothing of any of it was left.

He stood up. 'I'm very sorry,' he said, bringing Jo's speech abruptly to a stop. 'I'm sorry,' he said again, as she too rose to her feet. 'I think I misunderstood something. I made a mistake.' What a fool she must think him. He bowed slightly to her. 'I seem to have wasted your time.' Though he still had the mental strength to be conscious, without saying so, that she had also wasted his. 'It was good to meet.' You always said that. He was genuinely unsure whether he meant it or not. He didn't try to listen, to check whether she wanted to say something or was perhaps already trying to get words out. He turned quickly towards the door, opened it for himself and went through it, closing it behind him, and marched swiftly down the stairs.

He went ashore that evening with Mike. That was Mike's idea. He hadn't needed to ask Karsten, when he first ran into him after his return from London, how the interview had gone: the answer was spelled out in advance upon Karsten's face. They went to two traditional Spice Island pubs, and by the time they reached the second one the whole story of Karsten's disappointment with Jo had come out. 'It was a detour anyway,' Karsten was able to say, philosophical after two pints. 'I mean, a detour on the journey I am on.' Mike frowned at that. 'I am actually looking, in England, for a man I used to know. A Spanish man I shared a flat with once.'

'I thought women were your thing, not men,' said Mike, genuinely surprised, as for him it was the other way round and he had not seen in Karsten any signs of a fellow traveller along his path. He was usually good at recognising those.

'I didn't mean I was looking for him like that,' said Karsten. 'Though he is gay. But I am not.'

'You're free all day tomorrow,' Mike reminded him. 'Free till we sail the next day at eleven o'clock. You could track him down tomorrow, I suppose.'

'I don't know quite where he lives,' said Karsten. 'It may take me some time to find out. And it's a journey I'm on. In a way the journey itself is the destination. That's what we say in Germany anyway. Do you know the poem Ithaca?' Mike did not. ''If you sail off to Ithaca',' he quoted approximately, ''may your voyage be long'. My friend has survived quite well without me for many years. I think he will be able to wait while I go one last time to Santander and back. Especially as he is not expecting me at all. I am thinking actually I could go tomorrow to the Isle of Wight. It looks interesting when you are coming in on the ship.' Mike looked doubtful for a moment but then was kind enough to make an encouraging face.

Karsten changed the subject. 'Do we say *on* Spice Island, or *in* Spice Island. Because it isn't really an island, is it? Not like the Isle of Wight. And I learnt that you say *on* the Isle of Wight.' Mike didn't know the answer to that. Between them they asked one or two local-looking lads who were sitting near them. The question totally flummoxed them and, though the opinions of two older people were canvassed after that, no-one seemed able to give an unequivocal answer. Which confirmed Karsten in an opinion that he already held about the British and their approach to life.

TEN

'For God's sake,' Charlie said, 'forget about his brothers and sisters and put yourself first for once.'

'He can't be dragged to the registry office now: it's far too late for that,' James said firmly, the way people who are driving a car tend to speak. They had left Charlie's car at the Court House as soon as he had arrived, and gone to see Borja at once. Now they were on their way back, Charlie in a state of near shock. He said,

'Then let the registry office come to him.'

'What? Like priests delivering the Last Rites? Not that he'd want that, of course.'

'There are ways to find out,' Charlie said. 'They're called the telephone and the internet. And, OK, if you'll let me – though actually even if you won't – I'll do it for you. Find out, I mean. You've got enough to think about.'

'You're supposed to give fifteen days' notice,' James objected again. 'That's what happened when Nick and Andy got hitched. He hasn't got that.'

'They'd waive that, surely. I mean, they must.'

James swung right, into the car park of the Rose and Castle. Nick or Andy, whichever of them was there, would want an update. And they would want to see Charlie again.

James's days had a routine now that had developed quickly but equally quickly had become as fixed as the courses of the stars. The routine began with a phone-call to Borja around nine o'clock. Borja had his mobile beside his bed. He was no longer at the mercy of the money-gobbling apparatus, phone and TV system combined, that the hospital had provided. From the way Borja spoke to him James would understand whether he had had a comfortable night, and that he could still hold a rational conversation. Then James would assure him that he'd be along in person at about eleven o'clock. When he arrived at that time Borja would be washed and shaved and sitting out of bed, dressed to some extent, in his armchair. James would unpack from his bag whatever Borja had requested, discovering or deciding his needs day by day. It might be mouthwash, or a banana, or clean clothes. Or a photo of the cat. Or James would produce a surprise: garden flowers, perhaps, or something in the post.

At twelve James would leave Borja while he sipped his complimentary sherry and waited for his lunch. He'd then drive to the theatre – a place that occupied less of his time and thought with every day that passed – and deal with any outstanding matters there. If he could, he'd get home for a very brief nap before setting out for the hospice again a little after three. By then Borja would be emerging from his own morphine and sherry induced nap. Borja complained often that he wished they could have their siesta snuggled up together as they would have done at home. James's heart ached, because he would have liked that too – would have given his gold tooth for it actually – but thought there might be a rule against it. There was no point trying to find out though. It clearly could not be done. Not in a single bed with high, cot-like sides; with an array of buttons to press for raising and lowering the whole high-tech contraption in three semi-autonomous parts. Plus the plastic tube that augmented Borja's oxygen supply via an attachment that clipped on, like a toy moustache for a child, just inside his nose.

As an alternative to the impossible intimate nap, they would watch afternoon TV together, once Borja was properly awake and had been helped by James to cross the room and get into his chair. There was usually a re-run of a Lewis or a Morse to see, and they would watch those, speaking little but tightly clasping hands. The more private parts of their bodies that had been their shared playgrounds for more than half of both their lives were suddenly, unexpectedly, out of bounds – since just a week or two ago. In the blink of an eye, this had happened. *In Ictu Oculi.*

This afternoon routine seemed to both of them a fixture so immutable that it felt as though it had been going on for years. It also felt as if it always would. They began to feel that they had never so much enjoyed the time they spent together. Never had the other meant more to each of them than now. Never had they been more profoundly in love.

James had told Borja about his phone-call to Charlie in inviting him to come up. He didn't tell him about the email he had sent him at around the same time.

Charlie

This is mainly about dreams. I could perhaps share this with any of half a dozen friends, women as well as men, with whom I go back thirty or more years. Or with my lovely friends Nick and Andy, who listen to me, when we get slightly pissed some evenings, with unsentimental understanding. But for some reason – I don't know why – I feel that at the moment I can only write this to you.

Just before my mother died a few years ago, I had vivid dreams about her which hurt a lot. Each time I had Borja's arms and voice to soothe me on waking. Now my dreams are about him, of course, and I can't expect his consolation over these.

Back in the summer Sancho Panza got into a fight with one of the farmyard toms. Screams woke us in the night, and for the next few days Sancho's forehead was a mess of scabs – which we treated with antiseptic powder and which he persistently scratched off. Since then he's been under curfew – the cat-flap locked at night. (And his face looks lovely once more.)

The night after Borja's cancer was diagnosed I dreamed Sancho had been in a fight again, his face a mess of blood, one back paw hanging half off, the bones showing. I cleaned him up a bit but he insisted on going out in the garden again, and when I called to him he just looked back over his shoulder, meaning, 'I've got to face things myself, my own way.' I was able to tell Borja about that dream, but not what I understood from it: that the dream was about him, not just the cat. But I think he somehow knew.

Another night I saw him vividly as I dropped off to sleep, sitting in his hospital chair, cadaverous and with tubes everywhere. When I saw him in real life next day he didn't look quite so bad. Another night I saw him equally clearly, as he'd looked when much younger, in shorts, hunky and bronze-thighed, with his thick dark hair and impish smile.

I dreamed he was crossing a road while trying to eat some soup that everyone (incl me) had said he must try to finish. He was terribly sick all over himself. I woke up, brushing the dream away from me like a filthy cobweb. But when I saw him that morning he wasn't smiling. 'I've been sick again,' he said. For the second morning, it seemed, he'd thrown his breakfast up. I hadn't known.

Two days ago he was so sleepy when I went back in the afternoon (he'd been given an extra morphine shot) that I went for a walk and came back an hour later. Sometimes in the mornings I climb the grass bank outside his window and stand outside the fence that rails his terrace, trying to catch his eye through the window. I did this now, though it was getting dark, because I'd seen his light was on. I saw him now – he was just waking up – and had been put in his chair. He was looking through the bits and pieces on the over-chair table in front of him. He picked up the last card you'd sent him and re-read the words inside. I drummed on the fence with my fists and called his name but he couldn't hear through the plate glass. I started to climb the fence, a very young man in love, wearing jeans and a backpack, but some staff began to open another window onto the terrace and I backed down (literally) and went round by the proper way. When I got to him he asked me, to my astonishment, if I'd been cottaging!

When I got back home that evening there was no sign of Sancho. Until I went back into the kitchen a few minutes later and heard his piteous crying outside. By mistake I'd locked the cat-flap instead of the door before leaving the house earlier. I scooped Sancho up and cuddled him until he felt safe again and began to purr. Then it seemed that Borja and the cat were one and the same, and that it was Borja I'd shut out. It was only with an effort that I managed not to howl.

Happily Nick came in later and we shared a bottle of Cava and most of a bottle of Bergerac. I was able to tell him about the cat-flap mistake, though not the last part – though I think he sort of knew.

Now Sancho spends every night with me, curled up alongside, in the small of my back. When I wake up in the night I can reach out and touch him and make him purr.

I wish there could be a happy end to this missive, but there can't. Thank you, Charlie, for being my friend at this bad time.

It was hardly surprising, after this, that when James phoned Charlie to invite him up to Sevenscore, he had come at once.

Whether the registrar would arrive before Borja's brother Javier's plane landed at Luton in the afternoon was anybody's guess, though it was James's solemn hope that she would. Charlie's promise to sort out the matter of the civil partnership had not been an empty one.

While still at the Rose and Castle that first afternoon he had contacted the registry office with a little help from Nick, had emailed them the relevant details and received the assurance that the ceremony could take place at the hospice: a registrar would arrive there either at nine-thirty in the morning or at four pm. They would know for certain which of those times it was to be at eight o'clock next day. Unless Borja's condition deteriorated in the meantime. Then there was a special number to ring.

It all went very smoothly in the end. The registrar arrived a little before nine-thirty and within a few minutes, with Charlie and Nick as witnesses, the two men became an item in the eyes of the law for the first time in their thirty-three years of living together as partners in love. When the ceremony was finished, Borja turned to Charlie and said, 'Have you made any progress with your documentary about the crash yet?'

'It's on hold for the moment,' said Charlie, sounding astonished, though he also felt honoured, that Borja was thinking about that. Two hours later Charlie drove off down the motorway to Luton, to pick Javier up. He didn't need to be told that the civil ceremony was not to be a subject for discussion in the car on the way back.

When Charlie returned to the hospice in mid-afternoon, with Javier, James was surprised to find Borja taking his brother's visit as very much a matter of course. It was as though he understood Javier to be passing through the city by chance, on his way to be somewhere else. It was not until they took their leave later in the evening that Borja began to behave as if the visit were anything other than routine. He asked his brother to kiss him, which Javier did very tenderly. Then James kissed him too. After which Borja said, 'Eskimos,' and the newly legal couple rubbed noses for ten seconds or so. They both said, 'Christmases and birthdays,' and then James followed the other two men out of the room. As he parted from Borja he felt as though an elastic thread of something were being pulled to its limit as the distance between them grew from inches to a couple of yards. He imagined a strand of honey perhaps, or melted cheese. He was unable to imagine – his brain would not allow him to imagine – the moment at which it actually broke. His last look back at Borja showed his lover to be asleep.

Next morning Borja didn't answer James's nine o'clock call. That didn't alarm James unduly, but he did phone the nurses' room immediately afterwards. He was told that Borja had had some discomfort in the night but was sleeping peacefully now. He'd almost certainly be awake again by the time James arrived at eleven, with Javier.

Borja was awake, though still in bed. He smiled with pleasure to see James. 'How are you?' James said.

Borja answered, 'The night has been unruly: where we lay, our chimneys were blown down.' His last ever quote from Shakespeare, though gloomy, could not have been more apposite. But after that, when he spoke to James, either in answer to a question or off his own bat, it was a bit of a toss-up as to whether the words would come out in English or in Spanish. Also whether they would make much sense. The staff could not tell, of course, whether his Spanish utterances were coherent. Even James was sometimes unsure. It was a matter on which Javier proved his worth as expert judge.

Borja was uninterested in his lunch. The staff let James attempt to feed him a spoon of soup or two. But that was, more than anything, to give James something to do. Meanwhile Borja drifted in and out of sleep, hardly seeming to recognise the forlorn duo beside his bed. Later, Charlie arrived, with Andy and Nick.

Around five o'clock Borja came back to life again, focused his eyes on James and asked him in Spanish to give him a kiss. A moment after James had leant down and done that, Borja's eyes filled with a terror that James had never seen in them before. He called out twice, 'Mamma,' and writhed as if trying to get away from something, or someone. Javier tried to take his hand and comfort him, but Borja was beyond recognising his brother now and fought him off, and groaned in protest through clenched teeth. A nurse arrived and, negotiating his protesting limbs, slid a shot of morphine into an upper arm. 'I want you to drift off for a bit,' she said to him, quite matter-of-factly. 'Think of your last holiday, lying on a beach...'

'The Alhambra gardens,' James found himself interrupting her. 'The Generalife. The Alcázar in Seville. Streams, fountains, golden orioles among the trees...' His voice had given out before he got to the golden orioles but he was rewarded with the sight of Borja's face relaxing into a smile as sweet as any he had ever seen there, as his consciousness sailed out of its home port for the last time.

Borja slept peacefully for two days. Then came the phone-call in the night, like a thief. James scrambled into clothes, woke Charlie and Javier, and they drove along dark roads, then empty streets, pressed the buzzer at the hospice's night door and were let in. They had missed his final departure by ten minutes. He looked like a small rag-doll, lying on his back in pyjamas between tidy sheets. Eyes shut. A doll with beautiful long dark eyelashes. A mortal angel crumpled to earth. James took his right hand, limp for the first time since he'd first held it, and kissed his warm lips. He was conscious of the lack of breath between them, an absence more awful than the silence of the room. Words came into James's mind as if put there by someone else. *This is the first day of the rest of my life*. The thought made him shake with terror. The sun and the moon had been gouged from his sky as irrevocably as if they'd been his eyes, and the rest of his life lay dark as night in front of him. 'Goodnight, sweet prince,' he said to Borja, surprised to hear the words coming out in an even tone, 'and flights of angels sing thee to thy rest.'

Javier had moved to the long French window and unbolted it. Neither James nor Charlie bothered to ask him why. He pushed it open slowly, without drama or fuss. The long gauze curtains stirred in the cool night air.

In the evening Javier invited James and Charlie to dinner at the Rose and Castle. James thought this a good time and place to tell Javier about the civil partnership. He had not been looking forward to telling his partner's closest blood relation that Borja's worldly possessions would now belong to himself. He explained the situation in the mixture of Spanish and English that they had been using during the last few days for Charlie's sake, feeling slightly ashamed that he'd chosen to enlighten Javier in the safety of Charlie's company and the presence of a dozen other diners at tables within arm's reach.

Javier drew his dark eyebrows together as he listened but took the news without any sign of displeasure or surprise. Perhaps he had already guessed. A man much bigger and taller than Borja, and someone whom James had previously met only twice, he had a sunny temperament: it had only been a little dimmed by his brother's death. Also, he had been quite unfazed on arriving at Sevenscore to find another man, Charlie, in residence with James at the Court House. James had found himself glad, for the moment, of the size of his home. With Charlie in the red room, near the kitchen at the back, and Javier in the Chinese room at the opposite end from James along the front, and with a separate if not very up-to-date bathroom each, they had not been getting in one another's way at all; after a whisky nightcap they could all withdraw gracefully to their distant, private parts of the house.

The next day Charlie drove Javier to Luton to catch his flight back to Madrid. Although he needed to return to London, and work out of Gatwick, the day after, he returned to Sevenscore to spend one last night. It was the first time he and James had been alone together since Javier's arrival five days before. Five days in which James's life had been turned upside down like a shoebox full of personal treasures, and all the treasures emptied out. That evening, when bedtime approached, Charlie dealt with the situation as simply and matter-of-factly as anyone ever could. Returning from his private bathroom to the big fire-lit room where James still sat he announced baldly, 'I've forgotten to do my fly back up.' James got up from his armchair, embraced Charlie's shoulder loosely with one arm only, while reaching out with his spare hand into the obvious place. Charlie didn't return to the red room or use his own bathroom again that night.

Andy and Nick had offered to have James come and stay with them at the pub for as long as he might want. He said no, citing his obligation to Sancho Panza as the reason. In truth, going beyond Sancho, there was his knowledge that he now had to live alone and the sooner he got into practice the better. But he welcomed the alternative offer: that on his first night after Charlie's departure Andy would drive up and spend some time with him and that on the second night it would be Nick.

Of course he had spent many nights at Sevenscore alone. Being a pilot's partner inevitably involved that. But when he'd slept alone before in the big house, he'd done so as the representative of a massive powerful structure more solid and stable than any house: the unshakeable entity that had been Borja-and-James. Now

James was less than even a small piece of what he'd been before. All that remained among the ruins was a lonely middle-aged man who owned a cat.

The company of Andy that first evening brought him great solace. He managed to articulate a few of his thoughts. 'I've had the most wonderful adventure for the last thirty-three years,' he was able to state without a tremor in his voice. 'And I really resent that it's had to stop. But somehow I want us to go on together. Like the two larks in the Four Last Songs of Strauss. Onward and upward, pursuing a joint dream together.'

Andy nodded and took a sip of Cava, which was what they happened to be drinking that night. 'I don't know the Strauss,' he said, 'but I know what you mean. It's what I'd feel if anything happened to Nick.'

'It will,' James said, more grimly than he'd meant. 'Assuming you stay together, one of you will go first. That's the logic of it. Unless you both go in one big plane crash.'

'Well, thanks for that,' said Andy, a bit displeased, but forgiving his friend because of where he knew James was. Meanwhile a memory punched violently into James's mind. The first time Borja had called him darling in English – probably pronouncing the word aloud for the first time in his life. They'd been scrambling across a street in Seville in torrential rain. He remembered the frisson of the moment; it would live with him for ever, embedded in his system like a benevolent virus that could never be destroyed. He wanted to share this thought with Andy now but he knew – at any rate his voice knew – that he could not.

He relished Andy's departing hug and goodnight kiss – things he'd taken rather for granted over the years – with a newly awoken desire to hang on to someone: a desire that, assuaged though it had been by a night in Charlie's arms that had ended only twelve hours earlier (and he did not tell Andy about that) had seemed to grow, not lessen as the intervening hours had passed.

But some magic had remained after Andy had taken his leave, his concern for James engraved across his face. The dreams that James had feared would come to him that first night alone had in fact not. Instead he'd found himself in a bus that drove through flooded streets, pushing the water in front of it into a travelling hillock as it went. Red leaves floated on the water, making it a crimson wave. A torn-up plant came floating past, the right way up. It was some sort of spiky pampas grass, the long sharp leaves pointing up and outward to form a sunburst.

The daytimes were less good. James felt his reduced scale quite physically. When he woke up he found himself, or thought he found himself, reduced to Borja's physical size. Borja had been four inches shorter and, even in the best circumstances, a good stone lighter than James. As he moved around the house these autumn mornings, feeding Sancho, putting on the kettle for a coffee for himself, he felt himself occupying that much less physical space, carrying that much less body-weight. Once he had the impression of himself as shrunk to the proportions – and physical attractiveness – of the cricket that lived behind the fireplace in the big living-room.

Mentally there was something else. People talked of their partners, spouses or whatever as their 'other half'. What an understatement of the case that was! That other person was your eleven twelfths or some such fraction, your other ninety-six percent. James felt that by far the greater part of him had been torn out by the root, and that very little of himself remained. It was like having a tooth pulled out and discovering that you had been the tooth: that what remained of you now was simply the cavity that had been left.

He was astonished at the way that Sancho Panza, who had been something of a bit-player in his life up to this time, now moved centre-stage. He had never before considered what the two of them might have in common. Now he found himself giving a lot of thought to this. The first and biggest thing that united them was the fact that they both missed Borja. Secondly, that they seemed equally puzzled by his disappearance. That shouldn't have been so, James thought. Unlike Sancho, who had so recently been *their* cat but was now simply *his* cat, James had the knowledge that was unique to his species, that all living things must die. He knew, at least from the outside, what had happened to Borja. That didn't seem to make it any easier to deal with, though. He found himself as flummoxed by the new situation as Sancho Panza was.

They discovered a new desire to be as close to each other as possible whenever they could. They would share an armchair in the evenings, side by side, James with an arm around Sancho, while the cat purred his satisfaction with the arrangement and James drank a glass of wine. He occasionally offered a glass to Sancho, out of politeness only, since he knew in advance what the cat's reaction would be: a tentative but curiosity-driven approach to the glass, followed by a fastidious recoil, nose-led, in disgust.

They took to sleeping together. Sometimes James would go first, then hear the light padding of Sancho's journey across the floor of the living-room, through the half-open bedroom door, the pause and spring and then the sound and feel of his new companion kneading and purring before settling in behind the crook of his knee. Sometimes Sancho would get there first, then James would discover him when he switched the bedroom light on, enthroned where the duvet and the pillow met. He would reposition the duvet, cat and all, so that Sancho thought he was riding on a magic carpet, before climbing into bed, when he would arrange the bedclothes and their purring figurehead around him for the night.

The difficult thing was explaining to Sancho what had happened. 'You have to understand,' he said, cradling the wide-eyed animal in his arms. 'I know we both want Borja back. But he can't come back. He's dead. He's died. Just as you will one day. Just as I will. He's died but he's in Heaven.' James didn't actually believe the last bit. He was just saying it for the sake of the cat. 'He's happier now than you or I are.' It was only after he had explained this to Sancho, with the greatest tenderness, that James found himself letting go of the tears that for the last few days had been surprisingly unready to flow.

David, who was James's boss, had sent a card of condolence at once. But it was not until three days after Borja's death that James spent a full day at the office, and that day David came to call on him. This happened rarely and when it did James would vacate his desk and sit with his visitor at the big table in the middle of the room where heads of department meetings were held on Fridays and on which drinks and canapés were set out on first nights.

'I hardly know what to say,' David began once he was seated. 'I'm sorry that everything has to be happening at such a bad time.'

'When troubles come, they come not single spies but in battalions,' James said matter-of-factly. He registered David's expression, which managed somehow to be goggle-eyed yet at the same time windowless, and added, in order to be helpful, 'Hamlet.'

'We have to talk about the next few months,' David said. 'We're on course up to the pantomime, and the musical after that. Current season, current brochure. No change there.'

'And when do we actually...?' That was a question that James had to ask. Even if he couldn't bring himself to utter the final words.

'There'll be a spring season, as we've already begun to discuss. Two shows most probably, to take us up to early May.'

'And then?'

'A summer of refurbishment seems to be the order of the day.' James and David eye-balled each other rather hard at this point. Neither of them was going to spell out what would happen next, although James, who had not stopped reading the local newspapers since Borja's death, knew as well as David did. James's job would cease to exist on the last night of the final production. So would the company that ran the place: Regent Repertory Players Ltd. would be wound up. And David's unpaid but prestigious post as chairman of the board would also go. When the building reopened later in the year it would come within the remit of the city council's department of recreation and arts. The city council owned the site anyway: Regent Repertory Players had leased the building for a nominal rent. But now a new management entity would be set up, one that would manage both the Regent Theatre and the Barraclough Centre on behalf of the department of recreation and arts. The head of this new structure, which was to be called Barraclough Regent, would be David, the man seated across the table from him now. He would draw a salary twice the size of James's current one. James felt that he ought to find some polite words of congratulation for David on the way that things had turned out for him, but no formula presented itself.

On the other hand, faced with the termination of his contract and of his association with the theatre – a building that had stood, hosting plays, concerts and variety shows of every kind during its chequered history of a century and a half – James was surprised to find that he didn't care an awful lot. He had been part of the Regent's history for about one sixth of that time. First as front of house manager, later as general manager and now, more grandly, as artistic director. He was surprised to find himself feeling so detached from this place that had been such a big part of him and whose concerns had preoccupied him for more than half his life.

He was more concerned, he discovered, about the other person who had been in the room when David had arrived, but who had left her desk and the room in the last few minutes, presumably because she was needed somewhere else. That was Linda the general manager who, during Borja's illness, had been doing most of James's job in addition to her own. Linda had worked with James for more than twenty years. She had been his administrative assistant when James had been general manager and the artistic director the late lamented Guy Levinson. When James had moved across the office and taken over Guy's desk, Linda had made a similar hop of a yard or two and taken over his. Looking up to check that the door was not just then opening to readmit her, he asked, 'What's going to happen to Linda?'

David smiled in a relaxed sort of way. Clearly he had already thought out the answer to this. 'She's older than you are, remember. Next year she'll be sixty, if I'm not mistaken, and due for retirement anyway. If it's a matter of a month or two, one way or the other, we'll make it right with her. You needn't worry there.'

That was all right then. James had no need to worry about Linda, although he would. In principle at least, he would need to worry only about himself. He was beginning to realise that what he had at first thought of as Borja's own private plane crash had now become his own very public plane crash too.

The internal phone rang on Linda's desk. With an excuse-me to David, James got up and crossed the room to answer it. It was the box office, one floor directly below. The voice belonged to a young woman called Toni who was on duty there. 'I've got someone at the window, James. He's asking for Borja. I'm not quite sure what to say. I thought I should tell you.'

'Thank you,' James said. 'I'll be right down. Does this person have a name?'

'Carson Baker, I think he said.'

'Carson Baker?' James couldn't place the name. 'Sounds like a firm of accountants.' This drew a collusive chuckle from David, still sitting at the table but unable not to overhear James's end of the conversation. 'Tell him I'm coming to see him. Whoever he is.'

ELEVEN

It was good to have someone else in the house again. Even two nights on his own seemed in retrospect to have been rather a lot. James might have preferred the company of Charlie and a repeat of the comforting experience that he had shared with him. But that happy little event had had *one-off* tattooed all over it; anyway, you were never going to get everything you might want.

It was strange to be sharing the house with Karsten of all people: someone James hadn't given a thought to recently and who had spent most of the three decades in which they'd been out of contact being a priest. The fact that he no longer was one didn't make James feel any less uncomfortable with the thought.

When you hadn't had anything to do with someone for such a long period of time you had to dredge the silted channels of your memory for reminders of what they had been like. In addition, on such a time-scale people did actually change a bit. Karsten turned out to be an intensely practical person – a fact which James now remembered, but would not automatically have expected from someone who had been a priest.

'Did he wear glasses? Spectacles?' Karsten used both words, like a lawyer who doesn't want to leave anything to chance.

'No,' James said. 'He was beginning to think he might have to before long, but in the event he didn't get as far as needing them even for sewing.'

Karsten was nonplussed for a moment, wondering whether he'd understood the word sewing correctly in the context. At its most straightforward it meant something he hadn't thought a pilot would have to bother with, but then realised that a gay or un-womanned pilot would. Then he laughed. 'That's good, then. Because glasses are some of the things you need to get rid of quickly. Having them lying around still, peering at you, can hurt. The next thing is shoes.' He looked James up and down. 'I don't think you had the same size of feet.'

'His were a size smaller.'

'Then they're next to go, if you haven't already...'

'I haven't.'

'Socks? Unless some were special in some way.'

'None of his socks were special. Some were quite unspecial in fact.'

'Then underwear, I think. Unless...'

'Definitely no unless.'

'Shirts and pullovers might be a different thing, all the same,' Karsten went on in a businesslike way.

James agreed. 'We often wore each other's shirts. Actually, the sudden doubling of my stock of them is about the only good thing to have come out of all this.'

Then Karsten actually did the work of going through Borja's shoes and garments, sorting the discards into bags for, respectively, the charity shop and the dump, while James cooked pasta for them both.

After they had eaten they sat and talked. James's wine supply had given out, but there was a stack of canned beer in the kitchen and they laid into that. Karsten still couldn't say exactly why he had come looking for Borja; it wasn't just to escape the clutches of a too grateful grief-stricken family in Seville – he had to take James through all of that. 'But at last I find I am too late to find Borja. I find you instead. In some kind of need. In the past I would have said that was engineered by God. But these things are not ordained by God, I now believe. Or by fate. It is pure chance only. But I find it interesting still.'

A can of beer later he said, a bit ponderously, 'Perhaps it is good I failed to be in time for Borja's death.'

'How?' asked James, not particularly pleased by the remark.

'I might have felt obliged to give him the Last Rites. And as he didn't believe in that any more – and neither do I since last month – it might have made a difficult moment for us both.'

'But you did it for that girl who died in Calle Santander,' James said.

'It was different. People were shouting in the street for a priest. And because in the eyes of the Church my own belief in the validity of the sacraments is irrelevant, I am still a … conduct? Is that the word? ... for God's grace and forgiveness even when I don't believe in them myself.'

'A conduit, I think,' offered James. He took a gulp from his can. 'I have to say, you do seem to be a bit of a theological yo-yo. Or weathercock. You'd stopped believing in all that when we knew you in Seville. Then surviving the plane crash that Rafael died in made you believe it all again. So much so that you went and got trained up as a priest. Now, thirty years on, you're saying you've lost it all once more.'

Karsten shrugged. 'These things happen.' Then he looked James very directly in the eye and said, 'Actually, although I do not compare my situation to your situation at present, there is in one way a similarity. When a priest loses his faith that is a bereavement in a sense. His faith has been the biggest thing in his life. No wife, no girlfriend, partner or close friend. Only God. Who has been enough. But then suddenly you lose all that.' He smiled. 'Or you could be cynical and say it's like a kid who stops believing in his *…imaginärer Freund.* How do you say that in English?'

'Imaginary friend,' James said. Sometimes German could be easier than you thought. 'I see. I hadn't thought of all of that.' He altered the conversation's heading by a degree or two. 'Sometimes, although I don't believe in an afterlife, I have a powerful urge to know where he's gone to – and go there too, of course.'

'You won't be surprised to hear me tell you,' Karsten said gently, 'that I've heard many many people say that.'

'Then you've probably heard the next thing also. I'd rather have him back again, the way he was in those last few days, confused and uncomfortable, than not have him at all. I'd rather have him lying on the ground beside me in the pain and terror of his heart attack than not have him...'

'Stop now,' said Karsten, who had heard James's voice threaten to crack. 'Yes, I have heard that before. It's what everybody feels.'

'I had never understood,' James resumed, his voice under control once more, 'why people so desperately wanted to believe in an afterlife. For thousands of years. Even when my parents died the penny didn't drop. But now it has. It's what people must want. They have to want it, can't help wanting it. It's like a desperate thirst. They want it because there's nothing else.'

Karsten took a quick gulp of beer. The remainder of it then fell back within the can with an echoing plop. 'For a time,' he said.

Nick was concentrating hard on the Schumann. Only gradually did he become aware that someone had come in through the open door of the ballroom and had sat down in one of the chairs just inside the door, at the other end of the long room. When Nick reached the end of the series of pieces he swivelled round on the piano stool and looked at his visitor.

The man on the chair, who was also looking directly at Nick, was a trim and wiry individual of roughly Andy's or James's age with pepper and salt hair and a neat little pepper and salt beard to go with it. He got up from his chair and crossed the carpet towards Nick. 'I'm Karsten,' he said. 'A friend of James. And of Borja. I arrived last night.'

'Nick.' The younger man got up and shook Karsten's hand.

'I know. James has told me about you.' Which put Nick at a disadvantage, as he knew nothing about Karsten at all: didn't even recognise the name. 'The Schumann Kinderscenen, you play them very well,' Karsten was now saying to him and then, more surprisingly, 'You know Alexa, I think.'

A few minutes later they were sitting outside on a bench with the low October sum shining into their eyes and causing them to screw them up. 'I have heard of you,' Nick was able to reassure his visitor after a few more sentences of explanation had been exchanged. 'You're the German guy who shared their flat. I'd pictured you as younger, that's all.'

'I was younger,' Karsten said with a straight face.

'So what are your plans now? Having come to find Borja and found he's ... dead. Sorry. That didn't sound very good.'

'Look for a job, I think,' said Karsten. 'Which won't be easy, either back in Germany or over here. It won't be playing the guitar, I think.' He told Nick about the job he'd done on the ferry and the woman called Jo he'd met and in whom he'd rashly placed too many hopes. He left Nick to infer that those hopes had touched on the professional sphere only; he left the more personal ones unvoiced. 'So something manual, I imagine. I don't think I'm qualified for much else.' He paused a second, wondering whether to say the next thing or not. He decided he would. 'It went through my mind last night to ask James if there could be any work at his theatre. Moving the scenes or something like that. But I learned that his time there is coming to an end.'

'You could always still ask, I suppose.' Nick turned sideways and looked at Karsten carefully. 'Backstage does tend to be a young man's job. I did it – worked for James at the Regent – nearly twenty years ago. That's how we met.' Karsten already knew that. 'Borja did it for a time.' Karsten had not known this. 'Even in his mid-thirties he found it a bit hard taking orders from people he thought of as kids. I remember him losing his rag when a new stage manager ordered us all to move a piano downstairs in a building with no lights.'

'I can understand that,' said Karsten. He had never heard the expression losing his rag before but had no difficulty in sorting out what it meant. 'But why was Borja doing that?'

'He was grounded after an incident. He had time on his hands.' At that moment they heard the faint sound of a propeller-plane accelerating along a runway a couple of miles away, but hidden by the trees. Nick cocked his ears and listened, like a dog hearing the approach of his owner's car. A minute later the plane became visible above the treetops, heading south into the wind. Behind it streamed a tow-line with a gull-white glider on the other end. As they watched, the tow-rope was loosed by the glider pilot, a tiny parachute attached to it opening like a flower. The glider then pitched upwards – you could feel the excitement of its new freedom – and began to soar. The tug plane continued on its course a few seconds longer, then unhurriedly began to turn away, to disappear again beyond the trees. Nick jerked his head in the direction of the fading drone. 'Andy,' he said. 'My man.'

It was only a matter of time – less than half an hour actually – before Karsten found himself escorted down the old carriage drive towards the pub. The poplars in their two long lines were all yellow now; everyone said this year was one of the brightest displays of autumn colour they'd ever seen. Distant sycamores glowed as if they were alight, their crowns flamed gold, copper and pink, while their black branches showed through like a bonfire's charcoal sticks.

The Rose and Castle was the sort of pub Karsten had imagined might exist in the English countryside but hadn't quite dared to hope for: stone walls and mullioned windows and thatch, low beams inside and a small fire in the grate. His conversation with Nick now had gaps in it, since Nick was officially at work: the bar counter separated them, and from time to time there were other early customers to serve. Between the gaps they talked about Andy, and about Alexa, and even about customers of the pub who hadn't arrived yet. Nick was something of a gossip, Karsten found. He'd spent most of his life believing gossip to be a terrible thing but in recent years had begun to swing towards the opposite and more popular view. He decided he liked Nick.

'Your friend Borja and my Andy nearly had a fling once,' Nick took the opportunity to tell him. It probably was the right moment, as Andy wouldn't be back till later and James was safely away in the theatre, at work. 'Of course, because it was Borja it always did turn out to be *nearly*. Since I've known him anyway – but of course, only as far as I know. They met on a stopover at Casablanca. The time I was telling you about when Borja came to work backstage... It was after that. They'd both been grounded.'

'They were grounded for having sex? For nearly having it?'

'No,' Nick clarified. 'They'd flown to Casablanca by mistake. They were supposed to be landing at Rabat. That was the incident. They got grounded for that. Well, they'd kind of fallen for each other on the way out while flying over Seville. Borja pointed out the house he'd lived in ... your house, I suppose, now I think about it.

Anyway, nothing happened in the end. Andy was a free agent at the time, it was only after that that we met. But Borja and James of course...'

'Were together already,' Karsten helped him finish. 'Interesting,' He would be curious to meet Andy now, which five minutes earlier hadn't particularly been the case.

'I didn't want to tell you that in front of James,' Nick finished a bit superfluously, then had to walk away to pull someone a pint of Pedigree.

'Does Alexa know that Borja's dead?' Karsten asked him when he came back.

'I telephoned her in Seville.' Nick wiped a wet patch on the bar in front of him with a cloth, probably unaware he was even doing it. 'Andy and I phoned a lot of people that day. On James's behalf.'

'She still lives in Seville?' Karsten hadn't expected that. He hadn't got around to talking about Alexa with James the previous night. There had been too much other stuff.

'She and Mark.'

'Not the half-American, half-Spanish Mark? He used to...'

'That's the one. He used to be Pippa's boyfriend, wasn't he? Or Philippa, as we now see she's called. On TV all the time. The ubiquitous Philippa Brookes.'

'Pippa is Philippa Brookes?' Karsten remembered seeing her face on the TV screen in his old flat, viewed from the Bodegón across the street. 'I thought she looked familiar somehow, but it didn't... How do you say...?'

'It didn't click,' said Nick. 'Or,' he thought for a moment, 'or, the euro didn't drop.'

Karsten asked, 'Does she know Borja's dead?'

Nick shook his head. 'There was never any contact between them after Pippa left Spain, whenever that was.

Twenty years ago. Thirty... Anyway, there was a time when she seemed to be on our TV screens almost every night, berating the government for everything it tried to do – no matter what government it was. Borja used to say she defended the indefensible and dispensed with the indispensable – he could be a bit convoluted in English sometimes. But I don't think James would want to contact her particularly, or have her at the funeral, if that was what you were thinking about. Borja had his heart attack a few minutes after shouting at her on the TV screen and I think both he and James afterwards sort of held her partly responsible for it... However unjust that was.'

'Ye-es,' said Karsten. Then, carefully, 'I can understand how that might have made them feel. But Borja didn't die of his heart attack, he died of cancer, and whatever faults Pippa may or may not have, she can not possibly be held responsible for that.' A silence fell between the two of them for a moment and Nick rearranged the pile of food order pads on the bar top.

Karsten broke the silence after a bit. 'Alexa, though.' In the end he was more interested in her than in Philippa, or Pippa, Brookes. 'You worked with her for the memorial trust for her old piano teacher. Is that what you said?'

Nick made an uncomfortable face. 'Somebody ran off with the money. The treasurer. It was wound up.'

'Her old piano teacher was Eulogio Pérez. I met him once.'

'I heard him play in London once,' Nick said. 'I was only a kid.'

'I played the piano to him in his villa outside Seville,' Karsten went on without acknowledging Nick's rival claim to acquaintanceship.

'You played to him?' Nick was disproportionately impressed.

'A bit of Mozart. It didn't go very well. I'm not that much of a pianist.' It was Karsten's turn to make an uncomfortable face. 'But I played the guitar in front of him and that went better. He was nice about that.' He smiled a bit vaguely. Then a line appeared on his forehead. 'Did she – Alexa – ever mention me?'

'Of course she did,' said Nick. 'She often did.'

Karsten looked up at him a bit shyly. 'If you have her phone number...'

'Of course,' said Nick.

TWELVE

There were a few minutes before Inés would return from school. Alexa clicked on 'News'. And there she was again. Philippa Brookes. Pippa. Alexa wondered what Mark's thoughts were when Pippa popped up on the news from time to time, more often in recent months than previously. He never volunteered those thoughts and Alexa never asked him for them. Had Pippa had children? she wondered. She had once or twice found herself looking to see if there was a ring on her finger but it was never quite in shot. Did Mark feel envious of her success? Would he admit it, even to himself, if he did? Few women would, Alexa knew that. She suspected the number would be even fewer among men.

Were TV appearances the measure of success in life? Alexa hoped not, but realised that those TV appearances were the only things about Pippa that she now knew. She didn't know if her high profile career was making her rich. She hazarded a guess that it made her marginally richer than she and Mark were. But seriously wealthy? She doubted that. As for whether her high-flying job in Europe and the public exposure that came with it made her happy, not even the highest definition television screen could show you that.

The clattering of the *reja*, the iron grille that served as main entrance to their house, announced the return from school of Inés. One minute you weren't a parent and could never imagine yourself in that foreign-language role, the next you were suddenly playing it and discovering that the role had been waiting for you and, like an insurance policy that had been set up for you without your knowledge by generous relatives, had suddenly reached its maturation date, and had been yours all along.

Alexa never gave concerts now. The startlingly red-haired twenty-something human dynamo whose solo performances on the classical guitar had charmed audiences throughout Spain and beyond existed only in the memory of her sometime audiences and herself. There survived a few recordings, a few photographs. Life today revolved around school. Three schools in fact. There was Inés's school... Alexa called out loudly as she heard her footsteps on the stairs, 'Darling, there's strawberry yoghurt in the fridge.' There was no answer, nor did Inés come into the room to see her mother, but could be heard opening her bedroom door instead. Alexa's face tensed for a second, then relaxed. She supposed all sixteen-year-old daughters were like that.

There was Mark's school, where he taught English to an inexhaustible supply of young Spaniards, South Americans and – these days – Asians and Eastern Europeans as well. They came along, year following year, as though on a conveyor belt. Then there was the school she herself worked at, though not full time, teaching guitar and piano to yet more youngsters, children whose imaginations could only dimly perceive the brightness of the career that she had once had.

Those things happened. One year your work was wanted everywhere, the next the public taste had changed, or there had come along a generation of classical babes with redder hair even than your own. The call for her work had disappeared as irrevocably as the cuckoo's call in July.

Her phone rang. The call came from a number she didn't recognise but she answered anyway. A voice spoke in Spanish though the accent it spoke in was not. 'Alexa, I'm Karsten Bäcker. Back from the grave, if you like.' Which wasn't too tasteful he at once realised, but it was too late.

'Karsten, where are you?'

'I'm with James in England. You know that Borja died, I think.'

'You're at Sevenscore?' The image of the house, the gardens and pavilions came vividly to her mind.

'The funeral is on Friday. Will you come to that?'

'Karsten, I don't know.' Alexa was a bit dismayed by his directness, though she'd admired it once. 'I'd have to talk about it with...' A sudden anxiety popped into her head. 'You do know I married Mark?'

'I do, of course.'

That reduced the anxiety somewhat but didn't dispel it altogether. 'The thing is, it's term-time – we've got a daughter – we both teach. It really wouldn't be easy... But tell me a moment... About yourself...'

They talked for half an hour. Mark came home another half an hour after that. Alexa told him, 'I've had Karsten on the phone. Karsten from Seville, who became a priest. Talking about Borja. We have to find a way to get to his funeral at the end of the week.'

To save Karsten agonising over whether or not to ask James about work possibilities at the Regent, Nick asked James himself. He did this when James called in at the pub on his way home from work that evening. He would not have been surprised to find Karsten there, though he did not; but he was not at all surprised to learn that he'd been there earlier in the day. Nick told James that Karsten had gone off to the village shop before walking back to the Court House and was planning to cook a meal for him later.

'It's certainly nice to see him,' James said. 'A bit of a bolt from the blue. It'll be good to have some company up at Sevenscore between now and the funeral, if he's staying that long.'

'I think he will be,' Nick said, pulling James a pint. He told him that Karsten had said he was looking for a job, and had mentioned the theatre in the same breath.

'I'd be happy to give him some temporary work,' James said, 'but at the moment there's nothing to give. 'If it was panto time... well... Maybe, if he's still here in another month. Meanwhile, it's going to be a bit awkward, him here without a car.'

'He wasn't to know you lived up a lane, two miles from the nearest bus stop. At least the pub's nearer than that. Anyway,' Nick continued, 'I lived with you for half a year without a car and managed all right.'

'You bought a motor-bike.'

'Perhaps Karsten could do that.'

'Now you sound as if he's going to become a fixture,' complained James.

'You can't have it both ways,' said Nick.

When he thought about it later, after Karsten and he had gnawed their way through a rather tough schnitzel of pork chop and had worked through the cans of beer that Karsten had brought up from the village in his backpack, as well as one or two of those that still remained in the kitchen stock-pile, James realised why Karsten needed to work. It was the same for him. That bereavement thing. He knew that going to work was necessary. He knew that dealing with the constant stream of people that work brought him in contact with was good for him, even as they asked him endlessly, tactfully, how he was. He needed that. But his work was no longer something into which he could throw himself. Though this had less to do with the loss of Borja than with the impending disappearance of the job itself.

The following day began as the previous one had. James drove off to work in the morning, Karsten was going to come into the city later on the bus, to join him for lunch. Before that Karsten would see Nick again when he came up to do his practice. But Nick turned up sooner than expected. Not in person, but on the telephone – the Court House phone startled Karsten by ringing at nine o'clock, and Karsten gingerly picked it up.

Nick had already suggested to Karsten that he would be the ideal person to conduct his oldest friend's funeral service. But Karsten had told him there was a difference between offering a sacrament to a person in extremis, when no-one else was on hand, and conducting a routine funeral service that could be planned days in advance. James had decided anyway, to ask the local Church of England rector to lead a not too religious, non-denominational service at the crematorium on the edge of town. There would be no role for himself, Karsten said. Well, he was wrong about that as it turned out, but he hadn't known that then.

He made the discovery now. Nick, on the phone, was asking him, 'Are you still looking for a job?'

One of the lunchtime staff had dislocated a shoulder, falling out of bed the previous night, Nick explained, and would be off work for about two weeks. Ten minutes later Karsten was making his way down the old driveway across the fields. Sancho Panza accompanied him a little way along the double line of poplar trees but then turned back, as if alert suddenly to the possibility that he too might be roped in and asked to work.

Karsten had done bar work when a student, though that had been a long time ago and everything, including the arithmetic, had been done in German. He hoped his English would be up to the task. It was. When his first shift came to an end, and he was hot and sweating slightly, he felt pleased with himself, announcing that he was probably unique in the world: a German ex-priest who had worked most of his life in Spain, now pulling lunchtime pints and making small-talk behind the bar of an English country pub.

James said to Karsten one evening, when the fire was lit and conversation had reached the philosophical stage, 'I don't know what Borja's feelings about dying were. In the Seville days and before, he used to have some sort of visions of death. And he'd go along to the Charity Hospital and look at the Valdés Leal Death paintings. It was a bit morbid, I used to think. But he grew out of that. I don't know how he felt about dying when he was actually confronted with it. He never volunteered his thoughts and at that stage I didn't have the gall to ask. And it was odd that he nearly died twice – in a plane crash and of a heart attack – before the cancer got him a week or two afterwards. Like that story of the Baghdad merchant. Know the one? The merchant sees Death in the market place, and Death has a startled look on his face. The merchant rides like a bat out of hell to another city seventy miles away to escape, but when he gets there he runs into Death among the crowd. Death says to him, 'If I looked surprised to see you in Baghdad yesterday it was because I had an appointment with you here today.''

Karsten nodded but made no comment on the story. He went back to James's previous drift. 'Borja's feelings about dying... Well, what are your feelings about dying, come to that? Since you know you've also got to do it some day.'

James grimaced. 'Not very positive, I suppose. It's hard to say.'

'Then I guess it's reasonable to imagine that Borja felt much the same.'

Charlie came back. The presence of Karsten in the house rather scuppered the chances of a repeat of what had happened on Charlie's last night there. James didn't think Karsten would feel comfortable about his sleeping with someone so soon after Borja's death, and even he had mixed feelings about it now. But even without the physical contact it was good to have Charlie around again. His presence provided a welcome counterbalance to Karsten. James was delighted, awed almost, that chance or fate had blown Karsten along to help him hold his life together just when it was falling apart. But Karsten did have rather a habit of laying down the law on how things should be done. Charlie responded to events more flexibly. With a *what if* or a *maybe*: expressions that sometimes seemed absent from Karsten's vocabulary and mindset. Rather to his surprise, after an initial period of wariness, Karsten and Charlie took to each other and would even collaborate on cooking operations, filling the kitchen with laughter. James realised that in having the two of them at his side, propping him up like lion and unicorn, he had in a way got the best of both worlds, even as he found himself in a new world that didn't actually have a best.

Charlie asked James what he planned to do immediately after the funeral was over. He understood from other people's experience that it was a particularly hard period to go through. 'I thought I might take myself off somewhere for a few days. Just go.' Charlie was glad to hear that. 'I thought of going to Bruges. It's somewhere I've never been. Everyone says it's beautiful, and it's got no Borja memories.'

Charlie made a thoughtful face. 'Yeah, but... Think of the time of year. There's rain forecast for next week.' Like Borja and Andy and, James guessed, other airline workers too, Charlie always seemed to have the long-term weather forecast at his fingertips. 'Think of yourself traipsing through wet North European streets on your own. In your position I'd look at somewhere warm. Italy. Spain...'

'I'd rather not go to Seville,' James said. 'At least, not just yet.'

'Madeira, then,' suggested Charlie. 'It's not Spanish, it's part of Portugal. Weather's good at this time of year and it's nice. Like the Canaries but with more trees and houses. Been there lots of times. With Borja sometimes.'

'He said it was pretty,' said James. 'Never been myself.' He thought of Borja and Charlie being there together and for a moment felt insanely, absurdly, jealous. 'Maybe that's the place to go. I'll Google it. Hey...' He had a sudden, equally mad thought. 'Want to come with me?'

Charlie said, with what sounded like real regret in his voice, 'I can't. I've got to go to work.'

James stepped out of the funeral directors' limousine after Karsten, Charlie, and Borja's brother and sister. He was startled to see Alexa and Mark among the little crowd that had already gathered at the crematorium. 'You should have said you were coming,' he told them almost crossly as his eyes focused on the greying hair of both his old friends, and the new lines on their faces. He hadn't seen either of them for over ten years. He was sure his own face wasn't getting as lined as that. 'You could have stayed at Sevenscore.'

'It looks as if you've quite a full house already,' Alexa said, her eyes darting towards the others. She hadn't identified Karsten yet. 'We're at the Three Feathers. Just last night and tonight. It's perfectly fine. Inés is staying with a friend's parents in Seville.'

'And at a very reasonable price,' Mark said, leaning into the conversation, and meaning the Three Feathers rather than his daughter's temporary billet back home. His wife looked as though she thought he hadn't needed to mention the price.

How odd it was, meeting people at funerals. Especially if you hadn't seen them for a long time. How different they were from the people you remembered. Greying hair had something to do with it. Though if you thought about it it was obvious that people would wear grey hair to funerals: it was usually older people who had died; their close friends and family would naturally be of similar age. For a moment James had an impression of Alexa and Mark as two grey statues, like the lichen-covered angels in the cemetery that surrounded them. He looked quickly around the sober gathering and saw that everyone else was looking like that too. Faces were grim and pinched; smiles, though warm, were a bit tight. That was why you had drinks afterwards, he realised. And thank goodness for that.

You might go to a number of funerals in your life, and the frequency of them would only increase if you lived long enough. But you would never get much practice in attending the cremation of the love of your life. James hoped he would not make a tearful exhibition of himself but could not be sure until it was all over that that would not be the case. In the chapel pew he was buttressed by his own brother, who had driven up from London that morning and, on the other side, Conchita, whom he hadn't met before the previous night. Then the whole improbably assorted household had eaten at the Rose and Castle, a sensible idea when few of them knew each other and nobody felt like cooking for five; the procedure would be repeated tonight. For the moment James remained unsure whether his emotions would trip him up, and he wondered about them as he alternately stood for prayers and sat while various friends, Charlie among them, paid short tributes to the Borja they knew and loved. But it seemed that the tenderest and most soft-shelled of his feelings had gone into hiding, for today at least.

A fleet of cars drove back to the Rose and Castle, where wine glasses already filled with red and white stood on the tables of the 'new' bar alongside high-piled plates of canapés cold and hot. Charlie, who had been on his phone several times that morning, James couldn't guess why, now came up to him. 'I've wangled something,' he said. 'For Madeira.' James had already arranged a six-night stay for himself there: he'd be flying the next morning. 'I've got a couple of days free in the middle of your stay there. I can come out and join you if you like. Actually work my passage, so at no cost.' It felt to James as though the sun had just come out.

Karsten found himself alone with Andy in the pub kitchen for a minute as they re-stocked plates. 'Everybody fell in love with Borja, you know,' Andy said, peering very earnestly into Karsten's face. 'Me for one, of course.' Andy smiled, self-deprecatingly. 'I expect Nick's told you that. He's told every-bloody-body else. And of course Nick fell for him too. He may or may not have told you that.'

Karsten said, 'Nick also fell for James, don't forget. Even I fell a little bit under Borja's spell at one time, and I'm not even gay.' Another memory came to him. 'I suppose you know who Rafael was?'

Andy nodded. 'The first conversation we ever had... Borja talked about Rafael then.' He shook his head. 'Sorry. You were in the same plane crash...'

'And what about Charlie? Was he in love with Borja too?' Karsten said He wanted to steer away from plane crashes.

Andy's blond eyebrows rose up. 'Maybe, maybe. I hadn't thought of that. I only saw them together a few times. Just in the last few weeks. Here, and at the hospice...' He thought for a moment. 'Most important of all, Borja died while they were still madly in love.' He had to stop then because Nick came into the kitchen. But Karsten didn't need to be particularly clever to realise that Andy was also talking about Nick and himself.

Mark and Alexa couldn't refuse the offer from Nick of a lift up to Sevenscore to see the place again before they left.

'It hasn't changed at all!' Alexa said, thinking back to her first and only visit there nearly twenty years ago. Stepping down into the living-room she touched the bow front of an old marquetry chest with a finger-tip.

'Don't forget,' said Mark, whose recall of such things was impressive, 'they call that forest we drove through the time-warp wood.'

They, Alexa thought. The place was going to be awfully big for James on his own, and was he going to stay on up here or move somewhere else?

'Even the bathrooms are unchanged,' said Nick, with a snicker of a laugh, 'although they've had a few licks of paint.' He was acting as host for the moment, while James and the others changed their clothes and perhaps availed themselves of the ancient plumbing.

'And the piano?' Mark asked.

'Still the same. I come up most mornings and do my practice here.'

Alexa smiled at him. 'That's good to hear. Keep him company. After Karsten's gone. And – what's his name again?'

'Charlie. He's nice. He's going to join him in Madeira for a couple of days while he's there.'

Alexa gave him a searching look. 'Is that good?'

Nick looked faintly puzzled. 'I think so. Why not?'

The three of them walked out through the garden door, Nick picking up the ballroom key from the hall table as they went, then crossed the lawn, still dewy from the previous night. They walked down the central steps between the colonnades, around the stone-edged *bassin* where the carp hid now beneath decaying water-lilies. They stood for a moment by the balustrade, looking out across the fields that began a few feet below them and unrolled in front of their eyes towards the canal, the River Tove and, miles further off, the tree-hidden outskirts of Stony Stratford and Milton Keynes. Beyond the unseen M1 a church spire spiked the horizon just left of the centre of the view as if placed there by Constable with a single masterly stroke of the brush.

They turned together, retraced their steps up to the colonnade and past its border of hellebore and acanthus plants. Nick let them into the pavilion with the key. As the door opened their group reflection appeared in the various mirrors around the walls and behind the piano at the other end. Alexa led the way towards the piano and began to examine the books of music that Nick kept on the top of the lid. 'Beethoven still,' she said. 'That's good. Late Schubert too. Sonatas... Is that a new departure, Nick?'

'I'm looking at the late B-flat,' Nick said a bit diffidently, as if expecting to be told he wasn't old enough, or good enough, for that. But Alexa gave an approving grunt.

She looked around her and up. 'November, and it's still not cold in here.' She looked back at Nick. 'Don't stop coming up here when the winter comes. Please Nick. Even if it's too cold to play in here, just come up and have a coffee with him if he's on his own. Promise me that.'

Nick did.

THIRTEEN

It was almost like disappearing on your honeymoon, leaving your guests still at the party. Though James didn't leave till the day after the funeral, and departed in convoy with Simón and Conchita and Charlie. They all drove along together until the hustle of the motorway shook their cars apart, as they headed respectively for Luton airport, central London and Gatwick. The other difference between James's journey and the typical honeymoon was that, whereas when you go on honeymoon you travel as a couple, James was now the residue of a couple, single for the first time in thirty-three years. It was good that Charlie would be joining him in two days' time, but that wasn't quite the same. Of the party, if that was the right word, only Karsten would remain at the Court House, feeding Sancho Panza and working at the pub. James felt a bit bad about leaving Sancho in the care of someone the cat hardly knew. Sancho was feeling the pain and puzzlement of missing Borja, just as James was. He hoped that having the familiar gardens to roam, the hedges full of shrews and mice, would help to take the cat's mind off things and soften the bewilderment he would feel at James's disappearance – Sancho couldn't know it was only temporary – following so soon after the more final disappearance of Borja himself.

Borja had talked often to James about Madeira and the high-adrenalin adventure that the pilot's approach to Funchal airport involved. The runway was cut into a mountainside, and both ends jutted out over the sea: into a tightly curved, high-sided bay that was fanged with unwelcoming rocks. But Borja had spent nights there and had commented favourably on its balmy climate, mountain scenery and its capital's graceful flower-filled streets.

As his plane took its heart-stopping turn around the Bay of Santa Cruz the starboard wing-tip became a compass pin that skewered the sea, while the rest of the machine revolved around its axis like a giant hand. James had a sudden sensation of Borja's nearness – of Borja who had flown this exacting, virtuosic turn so many times, though never with James in the back. The sensation was so powerful it made him gasp. The island, its tree-quilted mountain coast an arc that spun slowly in his port-hole's upper edge, and the homely orange roof-tops that were beginning to come into sight, took on for a moment the character of a place where Borja somehow still was, even as James's intelligence told him the idea was nonsense, in no uncertain terms.

He had booked into a hotel that stood on the cliff a little way outside the centre of Funchal, towards the west. A walk around the town his first evening, as sunset was followed by dusk and then the dark, gave him a good feeling about the place and made him glad he'd chosen it – or that Charlie had. For the evening darkness of Funchal's centre was lit by soft copper-coloured lighting in the streets and by the lamp-pricked panoramas of the hillsides above. The favourable impression was heightened by a good meal and a number of glasses of wine at the outdoor tables of several bars.

The next morning the sun shone brightly and, although James was not sure once breakfast was over how he would spend the day, he knew that a layer of sun-cream would be appropriate for whatever he did. He was sitting on the edge of his bed applying the stuff and trying not to slop it onto the carpet (something which always seemed to happen no matter what precautions you took) when he heard Borja speaking to him. The voice he heard was not quite as he remembered it – he'd last heard it less than two weeks ago – it had a muffled quality, as if it were speaking through a flannel. It came from just behind his right shoulder, a foot or two away. He heard it quite calmly, felt no urge to spin round and look in that direction; he knew he would see no-one there, but he knew without any doubt to whom the voice belonged. What Borja's voice said was, 'Washing-up liquid.' And James found himself quite matter-of-factly thinking that this was interesting because, yes, the supply of detergent in the kitchen at the Court House was getting low. Karsten wouldn't think to replenish it, he might not know what to ask for in English. The reminder was timely, then. James didn't attribute it to anything supernatural but put it down to a small malfunction of the brain that was perhaps quite common in the recently bereaved. Was that a scientific fact? James had no idea. He went on quietly spreading the sun-cream around.

The following day Charlie arrived by taxi around midday. James had prepared for his arrival by arranging with the hotel management to turn his single-occupied room into a double one for two nights. He thought stumping up the extra money would be preferable to smuggling Charlie onto the premises like a rent-boy and having him in his room for two days as a stowaway: the deciding factor was the embarrassing possibility of getting caught. The duty manager looked into James's face carefully. Would he prefer to change to a room with a double bed? James said no. His room, which had a glorious view of the mountains behind the town, was furnished with two generously proportioned single beds which were butted up against each other. The manager cleared his throat and asked if James would like the two beds pushed a little way apart. James said no to that too; the arrangement of the furniture was perfectly fine as it was. And apparently Charlie thought so too, as he made no mention of it when James showed him the room a few hours later.

Although James had had a two-day start on Charlie when it came to finding his way around the town he quickly realised that Charlie knew the place better than he. He reminded James that he'd paid the place several short visits in the course of his work. Some of those visits had been made with Borja, James remembered uncomfortably, though he didn't voice that thought. Charlie led the way up narrow, near vertical, streets where blue-tiled churches with towers like minarets were tucked away, and there were grand *quintas* with tree-shaded gardens, orchid-filled, that you could explore. They walked round a corner and found a tiny square with a view over a parapet down to the sea, to the harbour and the cruise ships that were docked far below. Sitting there for a minute beneath a broad-leaved tree, James told Charlie about his impression that Borja had been speaking to him about washing-up liquid the morning before. Charlie showed no inclination to laugh, nor even surprise at this, about which James was glad. 'It was just the way he used to speak when I was writing a shopping list and he was remembering something that ought to go on it. That tone of voice.' He turned towards Charlie with an earnest face. 'Do you think I'm going mad?'

'No, not at all,' said Charlie, starting suddenly at the arrival of a humming-bird hawk moth almost at his elbow, among the geraniums that were arranged in tubs by the parapet they sat alongside. 'I think your emotions have taken a battering, that's all. It's a sign of the stress they're under.'

'Well, it happened again this morning,' James said, and drew a breath.

'What did he say this time?' Charlie asked, but in a serious tone.

'He said...' and this time James had difficulty getting the words out, 'I...love...you.'

Charlie reached out a hand and placed it over James's for a second. James found himself noticing that Charlie's hand was quite a bit smaller than his own. Startled by the movement the long-tongued hawk moth skittered away. 'Well, nothing could be better than that,' Charlie said.

They brought themselves down to earth with a tour of the Blandy wine lodge, filing round the darkly atmospheric former monastery that was suffused with a sort of Christmas pudding and brandy smell, and tasting the gold and raisin-coloured products that shared the island's name.

'A man got into conversation with me at breakfast,' James said. 'He was comparing hotel holidays to going on a cruise. Something I've never done. I suggested perhaps unwisely that one of the advantages of a hotel was that you could go out to bars late at night. He said the trouble with late bars abroad was that they were frequented by people who were not at all like oneself. I couldn't help thinking – though I didn't waste time by contradicting him – that I thought the opposite was the case.'

'I'm with you on that one,' Charlie said. 'So where are you taking me tonight?'

James took Charlie to a place he'd discovered the previous evening and which Charlie didn't know. It was the town's handsome theatre: a little jewel-box designed along the same Italian opera-house lines as the one James had come to think of as his own. Although a little smaller, it boasted one feature that the Regent didn't: a large open-air bar along one side of the building. A sloping, stepped courtyard, it was planted with trees and shrubs among the tables. High overhead a translucent awning, like a tent, kept the worst of the weather out, and the awning was pierced with holes through which a couple of trees poked their branches and raised their crowns. One wall was painted with trompe-l'oeuil bookcases so that you got the surreal impression of sitting among palm trees inside a London gentlemen's club. Over a beer, James told Charlie about another feature of the place. 'The men's toilet – well, you'll see it. The urinal – immensely wide for one – a bit intimate for two – is made of the shiniest reflective metal sheeting. It gives you a view of yourself... Well, you know the triple portrait of Charles I by Van Dyck?' Charlie nodded. 'Well, it's like that, but as if the painter had decided not to paint the king's head but to concentrate on his dick.'

Charlie guffawed, and James did too. But when James had to make use of the facility after that, he found Charlie popping up beside him a few seconds later, nudging at his shoulder and saying, 'Budge over, there.' After they had chuckled loudly at their double reflections, and crossed swords a bit, James found himself in very little doubt about how this evening was going to end.

They used only one of the beds for the first half of the night. Later, when Charlie had slid sideways into his own, James asked him a question that had been on his mind – one of those questions that can really only be asked and answered when both of you are tucked up and the lights are out. 'When you were here with Borja...' He didn't complete the sentence, but Charlie had no doubt about where it was leading, as he showed by continuing, though not completing, the thought himself.

'Did we...? No we didn't, as a matter of fact. I wanted to, don't get me wrong. And actually,' he said this a bit assertively, 'he wanted to too. But he was attached – to you – and that meant, no deal.'

'But you knew he was attached,' James said. 'Maybe you...'

'Shouldn't have tried? OK, but I didn't know *you*. For me, the fact he had a partner was an abstract one. People are attached in different ways to their partners. In different degrees, by different understandings and agreements between them. People aren't all the same. Anyway, he was grown up. It was his responsibility to protect his virtue, to honour his commitment, not mine.'

'No, you're right,' James conceded. He'd let himself be guided by the same principle in the past from time to time. He slid an arm out and under Charlie's duvet and for a moment grasped his hand.

They explored the island's interior by bus, corkscrewing up to the cattle-grazed mountain plateau in the centre, then down again by dizzy-making turns and twists through eucalyptus forest to small towns on the north coast where waves smashed themselves to bits on rocks, only to rear up again, phoenix-like, as the massive white ghosts of their former selves, high as mansion blocks. At one remote spot, a former whaling base, the only café offered a short list of sandwiches that ran like this: *Ham, Cheese, Ham and Cheese, Tuna, Octopus*. Neither of them had eaten an octopus sandwich before. They found them surprisingly good.

With Charlie around, James felt wonderfully un-alone. His presence was an anaesthetic that numbed his pain. Back in Funchal, its bay an oasis of warm calm weather after the bracing shock of the north coast, they sat outside the Golden Gate, the graceful café and bar with its wickerwork chairs on the pavement and views along four streets. The street-corner of the world, as it proudly announced it had been called in a nineteenth-century book. They watched the world in miniature as it sauntered by.

That night, after rather gentle and non-adventurous sex – James refused to allow himself to think of it as making love – Charlie stayed in James's bed, and in and out of James's arms, all night. Had Charlie gone back to his own bed, James thought, there was a particular speech that he would probably have made. But it didn't materialise and James was relieved and pleased about that. At any rate for the rest of that night. But Charlie delivered the speech in the end, as James knew he would.

It came at the airport, where James insisted on going with Charlie on the bus. 'It's been great these last two days,' Charlie said, after he'd checked in and they were walking across the wide polished floor towards the arrowed departures sign at the foot of some stairs. 'Nice place, nice you. Had a good time with you. We'll do it again some day – maybe.' He looked closely into James's eyes and gave him a smile that was more cautious than his usual one. 'But I'm not going to be around for keeps. I'm not really like that. Not like you and Borja, or Nick and Andy, wanting one particular person for their whole life.' He turned away and looked out through the vast plate-glass wall. They both did. Outside, beyond the airport approach road, the vast Atlantic began at once, about a hundred feet below them. It was punctured by the jagged chain of rocks that formed St Laurence Point towards the north and, in the other direction and further off, by the three Desertas Islands, which rose like flint axeheads from a surface of polished jade. The ocean appeared infinite in extent. Charlie looked back at James. 'You got to swim in the sea,' he said.

Nobody swam off Madeira's near vertical, volcano-side coast. Not even Charlie, who had been a schools' swimming champion for West London once. But James didn't think the advice was meant to be taken at face value. They hugged each other tightly for a moment, then Charlie turned and went up the escalator to the security scanners. James couldn't help watching him ride all the way to the top.

Before returning to the airport the following day, James took a solitary farewell stroll around the streets of the Old Town, between the market hall and the cable car. His attention was caught by the sight of two men, younger than himself, who were setting out chairs on the pavement outside a bar. From the look of them James guessed that they were Brits, and he made the two further assumptions that they were gay and owned the bar. He said a cheerful good morning to them, which they both returned with smiles. As he passed on he regretted for a moment that he was leaving that day. He would have liked to call in at their establishment in the evening and to make their acquaintance properly over a few drinks. Perhaps next time. If he ever came here again.

He thought about those two men later, when he was on the plane. The younger one had had strikingly red hair. He'd looked about thirty. He also had the rather red face that red-haired people who move to sunny climes tend to acquire – especially those who have moved abroad to run a bar and are fond of their own wares. Despite the red face he was remarkably good looking. He must have been a stunner a few years ago, and his mid-fortyish other half must still consider him quite a catch. Not that the older man, shorter and stockier, was bad-looking either, in a Matt Damon sort of way. The pair reminded James of Andy and Nick, of Andy and Nick a dozen or so years ago, settling into life together, settling for each other and for running a pub together rather than for doing the more ambitious things they might have done separately. The condition of both couples now seemed painfully enviable. He wondered whether there would one day be a younger man in his own life. If one did materialise, he would most happily give up everything, up sticks and go off to run a bar with him in Madeira, Timbuctoo, or anywhere else. With Charlie, for instance... He stopped himself there. Charlie had warned him not to dream of that. He peered out of the porthole and at the Bay of Biscay far beneath. Swim in the sea. Plenty more fish. Moving to Timbuctoo... Taking Sancho Panza with him of course.

He wondered if Sancho Panza had felt depressed in his absence. He'd spoken to Karsten a couple of times on the phone and Karsten had told him Sancho was doing fine. Though he couldn't know how the animal felt. Even in the age of mobile phones you couldn't call a cat to tell him you were on your way back. He'd be with Sancho tonight and make everything all right with him...

And he did. Sancho spent the entire night curled up on James's duvet, making himself a cradle out of the angle behind James's knee. He wasn't Borja, or even Charlie, but he wasn't a bad third best.

Karsten had looked after Sancho Panza as well as anyone entrusted with the stewardship of a cat might be expected to. And he had given the Court House a good clean-up: something that had been neglected, if understandably so, during the period of Borja's illness and death. James was very grateful for that. He checked the plastic bottle of washing-up liquid that stood beside the kitchen sink. There was still a good week's supply inside, so Borja's reminder had been a bit premature, though he didn't mind that. He noticed that Karsten had got the sink itself cleaner and shinier than it had ever been before. But Karsten had also done something else. He had written a letter – an old-fashioned affair of paper and envelope and ink – to his parents in Germany, explaining that he was no longer in Gijón and no longer a priest. They had replied, or at least his mother had, by telephone. They accepted the change in his status, even if they would never understand the reasons for it. Now they wanted to see him again, back in Düsseldorf. His mother knew someone who she thought could find him work teaching guitar not far from their home. Karsten had accepted the invitation, or summons, whichever it was. In any case the injured member of staff at the Rose and Castle would soon be returning to work. Karsten would be leaving the Rose and Castle, and Sevenscore, in a couple of days' time.

It meant another farewell. 'I'm not sure I was able to be much help to you,' Karsten said. 'In your time of necessity.' (Hour of need was the expression he was looking for.) They were in the car. James was driving into town and dropping Karsten off at the station on his way to work. 'I think perhaps it was the company of Charlie that did you more good.'

Did Karsten know the form that some of that doing him good had taken? He didn't think that Charlie would have told him. Did it show from the outside? Had Karsten simply guessed? 'I needed all of you,' James told him sincerely. 'You as well as Charlie. Nick and Andy. Borja's brothers and his sister too. It was like there were lines between you all that made a kind of … I don't know … a net of safety, or comfort if you like, holding me up.'

'I'm glad,' said Karsten. 'And it's strange, because I originally came because I wanted to see Borja. In some way I felt I needed to see him, and needed him, but it didn't work out like that. And the reason why I needed him, if I ever knew it, has rather got lost.'

'Do you know a poem called Ithaca?' James asked. 'It's about... it's the journey, not the arriving that counts. Something like that.'

'Yes,' said Karsten, thinking about the next stage of his journey that was just beginning, as they turned in to the station yard. 'I know it. It is something like that.'

James pulled up outside the plate-glass entrance to the station. He heard the click as Karsten undid his seat-belt before getting out.

On his own again at the Court House James found himself stepping every morning into a new day of a life he had never imagined experiencing and would certainly never have wanted to. He felt himself putting one foot in front of the other – in the most literal sense as he got up in the morning, walked to the bathroom and made himself tea – as if on a plank bridge of which only one end was supported – the end that lay behind him, grounded, cemented into, his past with Borja, the only life he could remember having ever had. Each day the plank bridge extended a little further behind him, but little of it was visible ahead; there was no sign of an opposite bank or shore; beneath lay no visible means of support.

How strange we grow when we're alone, and how unlike the selves that meet and talk and blow the candles out and say goodnight. Siegfried Sassoon's lines danced in James's head. There were moments when everything seemed in free fall: James was sliding through the floor; his legs were giving way; the flesh was falling from his bones; he was falling from an aeroplane, impossibly high; he was sky-diving without a parachute; his head spun and he wanted to be sick. He heard himself howling like an animal facing death.

Those moments didn't happen every day, thank God. Twice it was music, as if coming round a corner unexpectedly, that brought the symptoms on. He still listened to Radio 3 while getting up, usually without ill-effect. But Beethoven's cello and piano variations on See the Conquering Hero Comes surprised him one morning and broke him up. The second time was worse. Stephanie Shirley, president of Autistica – James had heard neither of the person nor the charity up till then – talked in an interview of hearing Dido's Lament, sung by Janet Baker, on her car radio. In the voice and in the words she imagined herself hearing the never before heard voice of her dead son, who had lost the little power of speech he'd had at the age of two and a half. Of course that very recording then came over the airwaves. *When I am laid in earth, remember me, remember me, remember me, but ah! forget my fate.* Dame Janet's voice, unearthly in its beauty, seemed to come from the deepest part of what being human means. And like a fist delivering an upper-cut it laid James out.

The attacks only occurred when he was quite alone. The cure lay in catching sight of another human being. Once, from the car, he had focused his eyes on a woman pushing a pram. On Madeira, before Charlie arrived, feeling vertiginous and the pavement beneath him giving way, he'd saved himself by staring at two Japanese women opening up a shop. Back at Sevenscore he'd stepped outside and seen Stuart the gardener at work – hadn't needed to go and speak to him – or, walking a little way down the track, made contact with his farmer neighbour Peter who was arguing with his son beside the tractor in the yard.

Sancho Panza was also finding Borja's disappearance difficult to deal with, and there was some solace for James in sharing his loss with the cat. Sancho found all kinds of things difficult: things that presented no problem to James. The appearance of the mower, powerful and noisy, on his private patch of grass –

known to everyone else as the front lawn – sent him running in panic, his little heart pounding in his chest. The sight of anyone lifting an armchair from one part of a room to another, or beating a doormat against a wall, put pressures on his mental capacity that threatened to overheat his brain and make the circuit-breakers pop. As for the washing line... When James or Borja hung clothes to dry on the line that was rigged up across the back yard Sancho would sit back on his haunches and scrutinise the row of garments, towels and sheets, with his eyes narrowed, like a midshipman attempting to decipher the language of flags run up by an enemy ship. *If I could just crack this,* his body language seemed to say, *I might have the key to the meaning of life itself.* Sancho was not unique among mortals in harbouring delusions of that sort.

And yet Sancho had coping mechanisms inbuilt. He didn't die of fright every time the grass got cut. He quickly made friends again with James after he'd put down a heavy chair. Eventually he'd even given up trying to read the secrets of the universe from the washing-line. In time he would learn to manage the chilling fact that Borja was no longer about. If there was a lesson for James in that, then with due humility James would try to learn it from the cat.

Several weeks passed before James could bring himself to open the notebook that Borja had asked for, and presumably then written in, during his last days. He saw that Borja had begun, like a schoolboy, by writing his name and address. Then his birthday, then James's. He had gone on in diary form. It was a diary whose entries were of the briefest kind, as if not only the action of writing but even the effort of marshalling his thoughts exhausted him. One day's entry might read: *James came. TV. Soup. Peaches and cream.* His handwriting, previously neat and tidy, had become difficult to read. It had also become very small – James's mind jumped to the mouse's last note at the end of The Tailor of Gloucester: *no more twist.*

James's whole frame shook when he came across his lover's final Shakespeare quote – the lines of Mercutio's in Romeo and Juliet that foretold his death. *Romeo, good night: I'll to my truckle-bed; this field-bed is too hard for me to sleep.* Shakespeare had written *too cold for me to sleep.* But at least the hospice had never been cold, and Borja had never shirked from improving on Shakespeare when he thought he could.

The only times Borja had added anything about his feelings it was to praise James. *'James wonderful'. 'James a tower of strength'.* After a while the compliments were expressed in Spanish rather than English, as Borja's original first language reclaimed what was left of his thoughts. Now James became Jaime, and sometimes even Sancho Panza by mistake. James found himself overwhelmed by Borja's fixation on James's good qualities during his final days. Memories came sheepishly to him of his occasional infidelities to Borja. The one big one, with William thirty years before, which Borja knew about. The three or four minor ones that he didn't. He hoped that Borja too would have regarded them as minor if he'd known. Had Borja carried secrets of his own to his grave? Charlie had said that nothing had happened between them. But people always said that. James found he didn't care a fig. He closed the notebook at the point where it petered out: Borja recorded being visited by Sancho Panzo – he'd meant James – then it became indecipherable and then the twist ran out.

James found that tears were running down his face. But they were not accompanied by the anguished howling of recent weeks. There was something of relief in them, perhaps, and something else. Someone on the planet had once managed to love him so much that even as he lay dying he had been able, in his own scrambled jottings, to weave a thread of joy into the mesh of James's grief.

Part Two

Spring 2013

Anthony McDonald

FOURTEEN

Karsten had got his first teaching work in Düsseldorf organised within a day of arriving at his parents' house. Finding himself back in that domestic situation after so many years was, he discovered, a very powerful incentive for getting out and getting a job. His mother's promise of a useful contact turned out to be less than helpful: the contact was a retired music teacher who no longer had contacts of her own in the field. Instead, Karsten took a bus to the school he had attended as a child and asked for the name of the head of music there. And the name they gave him – Michaela – was that of someone who had actually been a fellow pupil of his all that time ago. Two days later they met in a café over a drink.

Michaela listened with astonishment to the story of Karsten's recent past, as well as to a very brief account of the earlier part of his life. She'd remembered him vaguely as a happy-go-lucky teenager who played in a rock band and smoked and drank a bit too much. He no longer looked or sounded the same person, though once she'd peered attentively into his blue eyes she saw that essentially he was. She had good news for him. One of the local guitar teachers was about to take time off to have a baby and would be out of circulation for several months. She had already asked Michaela if she knew anyone who could take over during that time. Now Michaela promised she would put the two of them in touch. 'It seems I'm becoming a matchmaker,' she said, and then, 'You and I must keep in touch.' Only after they had parted did Karsten realise he'd forgotten to find out if Michaela was married or not.

A day later he went to the house of the young woman who was expecting the baby. She certainly was married;

her husband sat with them the whole time as they talked in the living-room, while Karsten's very first glance at her, as she opened the door to him, had told him that if the meeting went well he could expect to start work very soon indeed.

'They're a nice lot,' the expectant mother said encouragingly. She clearly wanted Karsten to like the package he was being offered. 'The adults and the kids. Even the parents are OK, mostly.' She paused a second as if a shadow had flitted across the thought. 'One's a bit difficult perhaps. Francesca. She's actually Spanish. Divorced and bringing a kid up on her own, and she can be a bit temperamental. Mind you, that's with me. As you're a man you'll probably have her eating out of your hand. And you've lived in Spain.' She smiled a bit roguishly. 'You must have had a lot of experience with Spanish women.' Her hand went to her mouth as she realised what she'd just said, but she saw Karsten begin to laugh and relaxed into a laugh herself. Her young husband, next to her on the sofa, smiled a bit distantly. 'That didn't come out quite right,' she said a moment later. 'You did tell us you used to be a priest.'

There were twelve pupils. The logistics of travelling between them using public transport were already sorted, the system being up and running already. Karsten thought he could just about live on the proceeds, provided he didn't start to smoke again and limited his intake of drink. He could use his spare time to hunt down more pupils of his own or even, armed with his recent experience at the Rose and Castle, work part time in a bar. In due course he thought he could put down a deposit on a small studio flat and get himself out of his ageing parents' house.

The students were nice enough, as Karsten had been promised: adults and children alike were polite and a pleasure to teach. Even the parents of those too young to pay their own fees gave him no trouble and let him get on with the job. Even Francesca. She turned out to be attractive and intelligent, and the two of them indulged each other and themselves by speaking in Spanish whenever they met.

Karsten started this off on the occasion of their first encounter. His experience of Spain and his fluency in the language would not have been evident, unlike Francesca's, unless he brought the subjects up. Which he did. After his second weekly lesson with her son Bruno she made him a coffee and they sat and drank it in the end-of-autumn sunshine in her glazed conservatory patio. Francesca gave him a brief account of how she came to be living in Düsseldorf. She had first arrived in Düsseldorf as a teenager, as an au pair. She had kept in touch with the family, and some years later had come back, to work with the travel agency they owned. Married a man who worked for the railway company Deutsche Bahn. But after fifteen years the marriage had come to an end, leaving her with Bruno to bring up on her own.

Karsten's story was a more unusual one; he was reminded of its novelty value by the look on Francesca's face as he recounted it. But both of them, she in her early forties, he fifteen years further on, now found themselves contemplating an uncertain future – even if in her case she could expect to share the immediate part of it with her son.

A week after that first cup of coffee, when the time for Bruno's next lesson was approaching, Karsten realised that he was looking forward to seeing Francesca again.

Over the months that followed, coffee in the conservatory after Bruno's lesson became a regular feature of the week. Then one day in February Karsten arrived at the house to find the boy absent and his mother explaining that she'd forgotten he had extra football practice that day. What happened next didn't surprise Karsten very much. If anything did surprise him, it was simply his own readiness for a situation that lay outside all his previous experience of life.

For the first time Francesca joined Karsten on the sofa when they had gone into the conservatory with their coffee cups, instead of sitting in the armchair that stood a little way apart from it. Karsten's memories of kissing girls had faded to a blur as a result of being buried years before and never dug up for inspection since. So he found himself pondering afterwards, as if for the first time in his life, one of life's most ancient mysteries: did she start it or was that me? More immediately and more importantly though, when Francesca began to touch him in places where no woman had touched him seriously before, he was startled, though thoroughly pleasantly so, to find himself responding as promptly and vigorously as he would have expected to when he'd been a much younger man. On the way up the stairs he told her, 'I have to warn you, I've done nothing quite like this before.'

Francesca pulled even tighter against him as they climbed together, half embracing, half stumbling on the treads. 'And I haven't for a very long time. We can be beginners together, or beginners again.'

Karsten arrived at the house for Bruno's lesson a week later, his feelings at the mercy of some pretty rough cross-currents. The least complicated thing was his new pride in his sexual prowess and appetite. He had thoroughly enjoyed his first time, late in his life though it had presented itself, and knew that he had given pleasure to Francesca too. It was just every other aspect of the thing that seemed problematic. As a priest he had plenty of exposure to the sex that other people had – although he had viewed it only from the outside. He had counselled women who'd been raped or had experiences that came close to it. He'd dealt as best he could with the concerns of parents whose daughters had fallen pregnant in circumstances they considered less than ideal. He was well aware that sex could create havoc in people's lives. That was why he had officiated at countless marriage ceremonies: the Church was among the many institutions in the world's history that thought the official union of one male and one female was the only box in which sex could safely be confined without its doing too much harm.

Karsten wasn't sure yet whether he was looking for a relationship with a woman, or simply for sex. If the former, did he want a relationship with Francesca, a woman with a thirteen-year-old kid? He wouldn't have the luxury of mulling this over and reaching a conclusion all by himself. He was acutely conscious as the time of his next lesson with Bruno drew near, that Francesca would have opinions about the matter as well.

He arrived for that next lesson neither early nor late but with an exquisite punctuality that would have impressed even the Swiss. He was braced for the possibility that young Bruno might be having a further suddenly arranged football practice. He was relieved in the main – though a small piece of him was disappointed – to discover that was not the case. Francesca greeted Karsten with a smile that was no different from her usual one: it was neither wary nor intimate. She ushered him straight into the room where Bruno awaited him and left them. When the lesson was finished, and before his mother entered the room, Bruno said, 'Mutti is in a better mood this week than she's been in for a long time. Don't know what's brought that about.' Karsten wasn't sure how to read the look the boy gave him just after he said it.

It was one of those February days that fool even the mature and experienced into thinking that spring has arrived early. The sun was warm and the windless air caressed the exposed skin of hands and face. 'We could have coffee outside on the terrace,' Francesca said, once she had come back into the room and Bruno had run off to do something else. 'If you have time, that is.'

'Yes, I have time,' he answered, smiling his relief. He had taken in the implication of coffee on the terrace in the time it took Francesca to utter the words – or perhaps even more smartly than that. Neighbours might appear in their gardens at any moment on such a fine day, or glance out of windows from any side. Karsten took the invitation as a signal that while some sort of friendship was still ongoing, the previous week's adventure was not. And in fact no reference was made by either of them to what had taken place.

Several more weeks passed and winter, as always, came back with snow and ice, then retreated again at last. Bruno's regular teacher would soon be back at work, and Karsten had a few new prospective pupils lined up. After Karsten's last lesson with Bruno Francesca said, 'I'm glad we didn't repeat our experiment of a month or two back.' Then she smiled and added, 'But I'm not too sorry it happened.' For once Karsten found he had no words of his own to add and could only nod. As he left Francesca's house that day he found himself thinking that he had got off more lightly in the circumstances than he could possibly have foreseen, let alone deserved to. But he surmised that he was not the first male in history to have had that thought.

He also guessed he was not the first person who, while dealing with feelings of relief at his escape, had found himself also wondering where, when and how the next opportunity of a similar nature was going to present itself – and what he could do to bring this about.

Karsten had continued to be in touch with James by email and phone, solicitously checking that he was surviving the novelty of his new existence as well as he could be expected to. He told James about his teaching work, and about the day-to-day tragi-comedies of living with elderly parents when you were not so young yourself, with a view to keeping James entertained and cheered up. But he volunteered nothing about the Francesca episode or the development of his own emotional life. He did not suppose James would have told him if anything of the kind had happened for him. But Karsten was beginning to mull over something else: an idea was beginning to form in his mind that would involve James quite a lot. He would not tell James about this either. At least, not for the moment. There were other people he would need to discuss it with first.

FIFTEEN

At the very moment when you'd stopped having children – just when they'd stopped being children, had completed university or whatever else and were beginning to make their own way in the world – you discovered that you'd got parents. In your thirties and forties the parent was you. You were a parent and, however high-arcing your career path might be, there was nothing you could do about that. Then in your fifties, ready to sigh with relief that your duties in that area had been discharged at last, you were clobbered with a new set of realities as you were reminded, usually brutally, that you had parents of your own.

Those thoughts were running through Pippa's mind as she put the phone down. She didn't mind too much that her mother had taken to phoning her at work, even though it could be extremely inconvenient at times. What she resented was her own time-wasting uselessness when she found herself confronted by the many-headed monster of the ageing process, especially when it manifested itself among the tribulations of those whom she held most dear.

Pippa was anything but useless in the situations that she faced in her professional life. Within the last year she had almost single-handedly secured the release from custody of two innocent men whom the government, the police and the press all believed were hell-bent on perpetrating some hideous atrocity. That near-universal certainty of the two men's guilt lay alongside the fact that no shred of evidence for an atrocity in preparation had been unearthed.

Her efforts had made a major contribution to the success of an extradition process that had led to four Eastern Europeans standing trial on war crime charges at The Hague. And, long before that, her spearheading of a campaign to lobby MPs of all parties had secured the defeat of a Private Member's Bill that sought to reduce prisoners' pension rights. All this she could do, all this she had done, yet she found herself helpless now in the face of her mother's plight.

'He's cut off all the flower stalks on the tomato plants,' she had just told Pippa in a voice that brimmed with distress. 'I mean, instead of pinching the side-shoots out.'

'Well, couldn't you have supervised him a bit?' Pippa had gently reproved. 'Watched while he did the first few, or done a couple yourself to remind him how?'

'I did,' her mother replied. 'And he started out fine, getting rid of all those little buds in the angles between the leaves and the stalks... Oh what are those little corners called?'

Pippa found herself floundering through a muddy torrent of knowledge acquired over the years, all the way back to O-level biology. 'The axis, isn't it?' she had suggested in vague hope.

'But when I left him... Well, you know. Now there are no flowers left at all.'

'Won't they flower again higher up?' Pippa asked, willing this to be the case.

'In time, perhaps,' her mother said doubtfully. 'But then they'd have to grow so tall. Tomato plants eight feet high... Think of the watering they'd take.'

'Then I really don't know what to suggest. Maybe start all over? Get new plants...?'

'Oh, I don't know. He insists on the early varieties and it's getting late in the spring for those. The nurseries'll have...'

'Well, you could take him down and look, at least,' Pippa gamely urged. 'Persuade him to go for a later variety for a change. Give him something to get out of the house for. You know. A purpose... Look, I'll have to get on with work. You can phone me tonight if you like.'

Pippa, who could arm-wrestle a government and cause an international human rights organisation to pronounce more boldly than, without her, it would have ever dared, had found herself powerless to restore fruitfulness to wrongfully deflowered tomato plants. She tried not to begrudge the time and energy she was being obliged to divert towards her parents' needs. Clearly her father was in the early stages of dementia, though no-one had yet dared to point this out. While her mother was suffering from a variety of obscure but debilitating ailments of her own – psychosomatic was another of those taboo words, one that even Pippa had not dared to utter yet – and was having what remained of her health undermined by worrying over her husband and the need to watch him like a hawk.

It seemed unfair to Pippa that she had to be alone with all this. Her elder brother Richard had stayed out of their parents' way for years now, and stayed out of Pippa's as well, she'd noticed. Not that he'd be much help. Ineffectual was the word that sprang to mind when she thought about his grip on the practical things in life. Jeffrey, the husband who might have supported her on her way along a difficult road, was long gone: their marriage had been fed through the fine-grade mincer of the divorce court. Her daughter Gina was far away at medical school in Nottingham and too busy on the wards now to lend an ear to her mother's family concerns. And too young actually to be able to offer much in the way of practical advice. Simon, her big disappointment, was driving lorries to the continent and back at all hours of day and night, throwing away a good degree in maths. She supposed it was all done to spite her, though he'd vehemently denied this when he'd been asked. Perhaps he was doing it subconsciously then, she thought. Though the money he was making was quite enough to impress anyone, she had to admit.

People thought that lawyers made a lot of money. Well, some of them did. But Pippa wasn't one of those. A high profile she might have. But people didn't pay you well for taking the Home Secretary to court, or for taking on Legal Aid cases – which was mostly what she did – or for lobbying members of parliament... If it wasn't for her two days a fortnight at the Court of Human Rights in Strasbourg she knew she'd have a thin time of it indeed.

Five years at most remained of Pippa's working life. Why now did she have to be distracted by her parents needs, needs that it seemed must be addressed by her in the absence of anybody else or otherwise go unmet? So much remained to be done in the field of human rights, and in the day-to-day business of defending society's weakest. That there were other people doing this Pippa did not deny, but she hadn't been able to help noticing, though without feeling any need to boast about the fact or letting it go to her head, that nobody else – nobody else in the United Kingdom at least – was being as effective as she was: nobody else was getting her results. Here in her busy chambers on the Marylebone Road, and in Strasbourg, was where she knew she belonged. She knew that quite simply because she knew that it was in these two places that she could do most good. Not dealing on the telephone with the problems of a greenhouse in a London suburb twenty miles away to the south.

Just for a moment Pippa allowed her attention to stray to the curtains that hung, floor-length, in front of the windows that overlooked the street. They were worthy and excellent curtains, in a sort of hard-wearing green tweed. They had hung there certainly since Pippa had joined the chambers in 1986. In the succeeding years the offices had been repainted twice, and the computers and telephone systems updated on a regular basis. But none of the partners, nor the manager of chambers, had ever dared to raise the possibility of replacing the curtains in all that time. It would have looked frivolous in the extreme if anyone had. Just for a second Pippa found herself wishing that one day someone would. A nice fresh oatmeal would make a pleasing change. She imagined her lungs expanding as she walked into the room and felt the difference that would make. She returned to work.

While talking to her mother, she soon discovered, she had missed an important incoming call. It was from the Leader of Her Majesty's Opposition, all of whose calls were important, and she had to get her secretary to call him back. Pippa did not do flustered and apologetic but on this occasion she came quite close to it. All the time she was listening to the LO her eyes, which she was no longer allowing to gaze at the curtains, kept wandering to a report which had been sitting on her desk for two days and which was rapidly approaching its read-by date.

There was no chance of her finding time to read it here, yet it was marked Highly Confidential and she was terrified of taking it on the tube to Euston and then on the train to Hemel Hempstead to read at home. Not a year went by without some highly placed official who had too many ingredients in his pressure-cooker life leaving vital government or security information on public transport only to see it gleefully aired on the TV news when he got home – thanks to public-spirited people who felt their duty in that moment lay towards the media rather than the official into whose keeping the abandoned documents had been placed.

When the phone-call came to an end Pippa dived across the desk at the report and grabbed it firmly, as if it might have been liable to slip away of its own accord. She opened it and began to read, making notes in the margin as she did so, the first page and then the next. Then the phone rang again.

The secretary's voice said, 'A Ms Alexa Soares. She says you'll know her and that she'd like a brief word. Will you take it?'

Pippa felt dizzy for a second. There couldn't be another Alexa Soares. Yet why would this one, whom she hadn't seen or spoken to in thirty years, want to phone her after all this time? She realised it could only be to tell her Mark was dead. Mark who was Alexa's husband but who had been Pippa's boyfriend then fiancé back in Seville. 'I'll take the call,' she said, and heard her voice sounding quite breathless with surprise, with the dismay, the shock of it all.

Alexa's voice was suddenly in her ear. 'I hope you'll remember who I am,' she began, but her confident, authoritative tone made it clear that she didn't really have any doubt about that.

'Of course I remember you,' Pippa said, sounding impatient, wanting to spur the conversation on. She did just that. 'It's Mark, isn't it?'

'What's Mark?' Alexa's voice was puzzled.

'I'm sorry. Sorry, Alexa. Please go on...'

'Borja died.'

'Borja? James-and-Borja Borja?'

'Yes.'

'That plane crash last year. But I thought...'

'He survived the crash. He died of cancer a few weeks after that.'

'In that short a time?' Pippa found it difficult to take all this in. These names from the past exploding around her as she sat in her office like bangers flicked through the letterbox. And one of those names now dead. She'd seen him on TV in the news footage captured minutes after the crash, standing in front of the plane awaiting transport... Dead so soon after appearing on TV... I appear on TV, Pippa thought.

Alexa's voice cut in. 'Look, I'm sorry to be phoning you at work. So very out of the blue. But I didn't want to do it with an email, cold, or a letter. Could you give me your home number and I'll call you back tonight? The thing is that Karsten wants to arrange a get-together of all Borja's oldest friends. In Seville.'

'Karsten?' Another half-forgotten name exploded and made her jump. 'Alexa, I don't normally give out...'

'Oh for heaven's sake, Pippa!' Alexa didn't hide her annoyance. 'How long have the two of us...?'

'I'm sorry, Alexa.' This was the second time Pippa had said that. Sorry wasn't a word she normally used more than once a week. 'Force of habit. Please forget it. But I do happen to be in the middle of a whole lot of things this afternoon.' She recited her home number and said, 'Yes, please do call. But after nine. No, after eight: that's nine your time. Actually phone any time. I've really got to go.'

Pippa stayed clasping the phone for several seconds after the call was finished, as if she thought it might suddenly decide to say something more. She felt unexpectedly overwhelmed by things.

When the weather was good Pippa liked to walk to Euston from her chambers at the Lisson Grove end of the Marylebone Road. If she had time she would make the small detour involved and walk along the southern edge of Regent's Park. But most days, despite her better intentions, Pippa simply took the underground, cutting through the dark subsoil beneath the street, to Euston Square, where she would disembark and walk across the road and the tree-grown square to the terminus. She did so this evening, as she had her briefcase with the report in it to take care of, and she focused her mind on it with an almost fanatical determination that it should not get lost, almost wishing, rather fantastically, that it could have been handcuffed to her wrist. On the semi-fast train to Hemel Hempstead she still clutched it tightly as it lay on her lap. There was no question of her using the half-hour journey to continue reading it. Anybody who took from their bag a document marked Highly Confidential while on an overcrowded commuter train would have to be naïve to imagine people averting their eyes while she opened and perused the contents of the report. She would not have blamed her fellow human beings for doing that. Deprived of the opportunity to work for a short time, she looked out of the window and thought about Borja instead.

He had materialised suddenly on the TV in front of her a few months ago. It must have been early autumn. There he'd been, in front of her, in front of the eyes of the world, and in front of the wreck of a plane that had spectacularly and photogenically belly-flopped just short of the runway at Gatwick. The footage had been shot from a distance; there had been no interview with him or anything like that, yet the news-hounds had somehow already got hold of his name and fitted it to the brief shot of him, when he'd appeared against a background of downed plane and other crew members milling about, talking on their phones. He was still recognizable, unmistakeably himself after all the years that had passed.

Several times since the crash Pippa had thought of getting in touch with him. That always happened when someone you'd known years ago turned up on the news, and it always happened that you did nothing about it in the end. In this instance there had also raced through her mind the unworthy thought that Borja might at some point require the aid of a legal professional in connection with what had happened. It was a litigious age. She had quite quickly managed to banish that particular thought to the darkness it deserved, but the idea of making some attempt to contact him continued to enter her head from time to time, though at less frequent intervals as the months passed. But now death had come calling and had made her unformed plan already obsolete.

Harrow appeared: the low hill crowned with trees and its church-spire spike crossed the window in the distance as the train began its broad curve towards the north... Pippa remembered the strangeness of her first encounter with Borja and his partner James, just an hour after she'd landed for the first time in Seville. Two men passing by on the pavement as she was stepping out of a taxi, or climbing into one, she couldn't remember which. One taller than the other and blond, the smaller of the two dark-haired and Spanish. Both aged about twenty-two. Kids, she thought now, looking back. She'd been ready – at twenty herself – to fall in love with either of them, or both. She'd heard the taller one – the one she would learn was called James, when he was introduced to her less than twenty-four hours later – say the most extraordinary thing to his Spanish friend. 'How could you lose a window?' Still ready to fall in love with either of them when, astonishingly, she met them both in the Bodegón Torre del Oro the following night, she had then met Mark a few minutes later and fallen in love with him instead.

Had it really been as simple as that? she wondered. It did seem so, looking back. Chess pieces moving of their own accord into place. Had things been otherwise... Had she not met and fallen for Mark... Had James and Borja not been a couple, not been gay... But those were ridiculous tracks for the thoughts of a woman her age to be travelling along. She was past Watford now, the Ovaltine factory at King's Langley sliding into sight, the sprawl of London giving way to open countryside beyond... But the memory hadn't done with her just yet. She'd been more attracted to James at first. He was blondish, biggish, British and butch. The charms of Borja had been subtler. Dark and neat-featured, he had also been a good-looking young man. Or boy, he now seemed in hindsight, especially as she hadn't seen him for so long, and as he was now dead. He grew on people, with his earnest appreciation of the arts and books. With his strange preoccupation with death. Didn't someone tell her, James probably, that he had visions of death sometimes in the street? That he'd stand staring at the Valdés Leal Death paintings in the chapel of the Charity Hospital? Well, he was beyond worrying about that grinning monster now, he'd come to his own arrangement with death. Just as – Pippa thought grimly as the train began to slow – in the end everybody did. Or would have to. Including herself.

Was Borja religious? She tried to remember as she started to stand up. She rather thought, or thought she remembered, that he was not, but had been in his youth. Unlike Karsten, whose memory popped back into her mind at just that moment. With him it had been precisely the other way round. Squeezing herself among the other Hemel Hempstead passengers who were beginning to fill the gangway, she clutched tightly at the briefcase that contained the report. At least she'd got it this far without mishap.

She laid the report down, open at page fourteen, on the polished coffee table when Alexa phoned at five past eight. Even at home Pippa automatically looked at her watch to note the time at which a phone-call started; it was one of those lawyer habits that she simply could not break. Within a few minutes Pippa learned that Alexa and Mark had a teenage daughter who was 'difficult', and she only just managed not to say, welcome to the club. About Alexa herself she was surprised to learn that she'd had a successful concert career as a guitarist; she was less surprised to learn that that career, like a meteor, had burnt itself out. Of course she had to ask about Mark.

He had run a small language school in Seville for a time. It hadn't done well, and he had gone back to the British Institute, where he'd worked many years earlier, as a rank and file teacher once again. Pippa thought that trajectory was probably inevitable for someone as lacking in ambition as Mark had always been, and that all those years ago she'd had a lucky escape. Of course she didn't tell Alexa this. 'And what about his poetry?' Pippa couldn't not ask.

Alexa answered slowly, her voice measured and grave. Mark had written nothing for over twenty years. As for what he'd written up to that time, he'd burnt the lot. He'd used the barbecue that stood in the patio-garden. One afternoon when Alexa had been out. Pippa felt herself turn hot, then cold on hearing this. She thought, if this news was having such an effect on her now, what had it done to Alexa at the time? What had it done to Mark?

They talked of Karsten next. Pippa had last heard of him going to train for the priesthood in Valladollid. He was no longer a priest, Alexa told her, but was living with his parents in Düsseldorf and eking out a living giving guitar lessons to kids. It made Pippa feel physically dizzy sometimes – it did now – when she was forced to think about the menial and humdrum jobs to which some of her most gifted friends and contemporaries had had to turn their hands.

'And whose idea is it to have everybody meet up again in Seville?' Pippa finally asked. Although she dismissed the scheme as impractical and not something she would be able to find the time for in any event, the idea did have an appeal, almost a frisson, that she couldn't deny to herself. 'James's idea, I guess.'

'Apparently not,' Alexa said. 'Karsten told me the idea was his. I believed him. He may have stopped being a priest but I wouldn't expect him to lie about something like that.' For the first time each heard the other's wisp of a laugh at the other end of the line.

'And when's it supposed to be?' Pippa asked, adding, 'Not that there's the smallest chance I'd be able to come along.'

'A shame if you couldn't,' Alexa said smoothly. 'Karsten's idea was to do it a couple of months from now. Say late May or early June.'

Back in those far off Seville days May seen from March would have been an aeon of time ahead. So many things would happen in the intervening weeks, so many things would change: relationships would be entered into or would fall apart; work opportunities would be gained or lost. It would have seemed absurd to talk in detail about something that might be going to happen so far ahead. But life was different now. As the years passed so time telescoped itself. And unlike an actual telescope, which could only be reduced to a certain minimum length, life would telescope down to absolute zero and nothing of it would be left.

'What Karsten suggested,' Alexa hustled Pippa out of this negative train of thought, 'was that we all rented an apartment together or, if we couldn't bear the thought of all that proximity, took rooms in a hotel. Our house, mine and Mark's, wouldn't be...'

Pippa hastened to interrupt her friend before she voiced the admission that she didn't have a very big house. 'No, of course not. Nobody would expect you to... Anyway, what would the idea be? What would people do when they got there?'

'It would be a sort of long weekend, I think. Karsten talked about revisiting places we used to know... ' Alexa's voice sounded less confident as she said this. 'Perhaps taking a trip to Córdoba or Granada...' Alexa was silent for a second. 'Does that sound awfully tacky to you? Mawkish perhaps? I did wonder, when Karsten suggested...'

'No, no,' said Pippa. 'I mean, yes, it might appear mawkish, tasteless even, to go so clumpingly literally down memory lane. But in a way I wouldn't care.' She was surprised to hear herself saying this. She adjusted it. 'I mean, if I was able to join you. If it went ahead.'

'So you think you might come?' Alexa's voice had brightened. Pippa was conscious that there were moments during this conversation when they seemed to have returned to the days when they had last talked as close friends, yet at others they were the solid and mature women they had since become. She now heard the grown-up Alexa say, 'I'm sure James would be ever so glad.' Alexa didn't know that James had told Karsten he blamed Pippa for Borja's heart attack. Karsten might not have turned into a liar but he had chosen not to share that particular piece of knowledge with his old friend. 'Of course, we'd try to arrange the dates around your schedule,' Alexa went on accommodatingly. 'You're the only one of us with an international profile and the full diary that goes with that.'

'Well, perhaps we could talk again nearer the time,' Pippa said. In spite of herself she was oddly, untypically, attracted by the idea of spending a few days in a southern city with a group of people she hadn't seen in what amounted to her whole adult life. The two women exchanged email addresses. Then instinctively Pippa looked at her watch as she ended the call.

She ploughed on with the report she was reading. Although it was the kind of task she normally carried out with relentless concentration she found herself distracted again and again by memories of Seville. She'd been in her third year at Leicester University, studying Spanish and French. An integral part of her course was the year abroad, getting to know one of those languages better, on the ground. Her French had been quite fluent already, thanks to family holidays and exchange visits with other families during her teens and so she'd opted to go to Spain. A contact between a member of the university staff and a rather scruffy language school had resulted in her getting a job teaching English – a subject which she was not studying at university at all. But that was the way these things worked out.

For much of her life Pippa had regretted her choice of university course. She should have studied law right from the start. The year in Spain had begun well: she'd met and fallen in love with Mark; they'd got engaged. But Mark had wanted to stay on in Spain when it was time for Pippa to go back. They'd rowed about that and split up. There hadn't been anything between Mark and Alexa then; that had started afterwards. Although Mark and Alexa had liked each other to some degree right from the start... Pippa had returned to England empty-handed. Minus an engagement ring.

But Pippa couldn't regret Seville itself. She hadn't known in advance what Seville would be like. It had been simply the name of a Spanish town, which might have been drawn from a hat. It might have been north, it might have been south. It might have been Bilbao on the Biscay coast. It might have been Huelva among the mosquito-ridden marshes on the Gulf of Cádiz. But it hadn't been. Pippa had found herself living in a city whose beauty took the breath away and whose atmosphere had changed her – in some way that she had not cared to remember for some time perhaps. Perhaps it changed everyone who went there. Provided they were young enough.

Not until she was in bed, some time after finishing her appraisal of the confidential report and listening to her mother, on the telephone a second time about tomato plants, did it occur to her that she perhaps ought to write James a letter of condolence on his loss. She hadn't thought to ask Alexa for a contact address.

SIXTEEN

It was the middle of March already. For a while it had seemed to James that time had ended for good at that moment, that *Stunde Null*, when he found himself contemplating Borja, cosy in pyjamas, an abandoned rag-doll, a dead angel, in a hospice bed. But time hadn't ended. It had gone on inexorably, the sand running through the hourglass in the same slow way, or fast way, have it your own way, as before. March, by coincidence, was a good word for the month. Left: crocus out today. Right: primroses. Left: lords and ladies under the hedge. Right: chiff-chaff arrives from Africa on the fifteenth. The onward tread of spring, that not even death could hurry or delay.

'What is it with time?' James asked. They were sitting, Andy, Nick and he, in the garden of the Rose and Castle, in the somnolent bit of a pub Sunday afternoon when the lunchtime service has ended and the customers from far afield have dispersed, but the small gaggle of local regulars have yet to arrive for the evening drinking shift. Sitting on the heavy oak benches that furnished the small lawn – plastic furniture would have been cheaper, and easier to move out of the lawn-mower's path, but would have tempted passers-by to take it away – they were discussing the oddness of outward-bound morning journeys seeming to take longer than the evening's return.

'I used to notice that on medium-length flights,' Andy said, stretching out his legs and crossing them at the ankles, the way people do when they are confident with what they are talking about. 'When I did that sort of flying. If I had a day going somewhere like Cairo or Crete – or the Canaries – it used to seem an age getting there. But you used to hop back in no time. Or so it felt.'

James, his hand wrapped round the stem of his wine-glass as if distrustful that gravity alone would keep it on the table, said, 'Isn't that the same as the two-week holiday thing, though? You know – we all must have noticed it as kids – the first week goes on for ever and the second one's gone in a flash.'

'I think I can explain that,' said Nick, who was still in his chef's whites, but suddenly sounded rather serious for a Sunday afternoon.

James looked at Andy and raised his eyebrows deliberately. 'Out of the mouths of babes and sucklings,' he said. Since Borja had died there was no-one to call Nick the kid – or *El Kid*, but that didn't mean the other two had stopped thinking it.

'So what's the explanation?' Andy asked, curiosity and amusement waging equally in him.

'It's down to maths,' Nick said, with a hint of the smugness that he could never help feeling when he suddenly captured the attention of the two older men. He leaned forward across the table. 'When you complete your flight down to Cairo or wherever in the morning you look back on it as the total of all your travelling that day. But when you've flown back again in the afternoon and you look back on that flight... Well, you see it as only half of your travelling for the day. With a two-week holiday it's just the same.'

'I see,' said Andy thoughtfully. 'I'm impressed.'

'Yes,' said James, 'that's quite a point. But why doesn't it work with a one-week holiday, then?'

'I think,' Nick began slowly, 'I think it may be that nobody clearly calculates the mid-point. Too difficult. Three and a half days? Nobody ever really thinks about it – especially on holiday. Nobody tries to work it out.'

Andy and James looked at each other, both pairs of eyebrows now raised in an ironic expression of a feeling towards Nick that they shared for real but could hardly talk about.

'I'll give you another example,' Nick went on, emboldened by the effect he'd produced. 'An even clearer one.' He took a slurp of the white wine in his glass. 'Imagine it's your fourth birthday. No, imagine it's your fifth. It's easier for me to do the arithmetic in my head. OK. You look back at the past year and it seems a really, really long time. Yep?' The others nodded. 'Well, that's because it is. It's a whole fifth of the life you've led up to that point.'

'Yeah...' James began to object.

Nick forestalled him before he could get to the *but*. 'Don't complicate things by thinking about the bit in the womb. I want to do this without having to go in and get a calculator. All right?' He grinned at the other two.

'There's one on my phone,' Andy teased him but Nick pretended he hadn't heard that.

'When you reach ten and you're looking back on the year since your ninth birthday, well, that year's only a tenth of your life. Well, OK, it's still quite a big bit of it, so you don't really notice much difference. But by the time you're fifty and you look back at being forty-nine you're only looking at two percent of the life you've lived. As for when you're seventy-five ... well, you can only imagine. But that's why older people are always telling you the years seem to be rushing by, each one quicker than the last...'

James felt a chill of disquiet as he heard this. It was not an idea that had ever crossed his mind and he saw a momentary look of angst on Andy's face that told him Nick's thesis was equally new and unwelcome to him. To dispel the momentary frisson James said to Andy, 'When did you first realise you'd married a genius?'

Andy replied smoothly, 'When I found him naked in a bathroom that had two entrance doors.' At which everyone's mind went back to the night when the unusual layout of the Court House had so serendipitously led to Nick's spending the night in Andy's bed on the second ever occasion that they'd met. That memory now led to a three-way smirk that bubbled into a three-way laugh.

James spent as much time as he reasonably could with Andy and Nick, while trying to be careful not to impose on them too much. The single person was always placed in this situation in his or her relationship with any couple. This was a fact of which James had been blissfully ignorant throughout his adult life: it had been brought to his notice only now, and by the most brutal of means. For their part, Andy and Nick had been more than sensitive to James's needs since Borja's death. They had had him for Christmas Day and New Year's Night. If one of them had an evening off from the pub they would spend it at Sevenscore with him, and the evenings when both guv'nors were working often found James in their bar, chatting to them between the calls that duty made on their time. It was during one of those evenings in the bar that Andy told James, 'We had a call from Karsten earlier.' He glanced along the counter at Nick, but Nick was talking to someone else and didn't notice, so he turned back to James. 'He thinks Nick and I should be at the Seville thing he's planning. It surprised us a bit. We thought it should be something specially for the people who knew Borja in Seville. When you were all young together.'

James corrected him. 'We still are young, together or apart. You mean, when we were very young together.'

Andy smiled. 'Of course. That's what I meant. Anyway, we thought it was for you to decide who you wanted to be there with you. Not Karsten.'

'He seems to have been doing all the deciding up till now,' James said.

Nick, having finished his chat with the other customer, tuned into the conversation that Andy was having with James across the bar and came and stood beside his partner. 'Apparently he's got Alexa to try and get Pippa to come.'

'Pippa?' Andy queried.

Nick gave James a raised-eyebrow look then turned to Andy. 'The one who's always on TV. The one we think caused Borja's heart attack.'

'Ni-ick...' James turned the name into two syllables of gentle reproof, then went back to the last remark but five. 'Actually I'd really like it if you two could come to Seville. I know you'd have to find someone to run the pub. But, selfishly, it would save me from being the only gay in the village. And, look, the three of us go back a pretty long way too.'

'Thanks,' said Andy. 'That's very nice of...'

Nick came in over the top of him a bit less gently. 'Trouble is, you'd still be the only single gay in the village, even then.'

'Well, that's how things are,' James replied in a similar call-a-spade-a-spade tone. 'I just have to get used to that. And that's exactly the reason why anyone's even thinking about going to Seville in the first place. Because of Borja, and of what's happened to him.'

But what had happened to Borja? James asked himself later, returning alone to the Court House rather late. And what had happened to Sancho Panza, come to that? He had given up waiting for dinner, it seemed, and gone out. Usually the return of James's car would trigger the cat's own unhurried return through the flap a minute or two afterwards. That didn't happen tonight. When it was time for James to go to bed there was still no sign of Sancho. In sudden distress James ran outside the house, calling the cat's name loudly into the darkness in dread that

Sancho would not reappear, and that another terrible darkness would compound his lover's death.

James went to bed, his heart weighing in him like a stone. When Sancho awoke him at three in the morning with the flump of his leap and landing on the bed, James clasped the startled animal to his chest, and would have wept for relief into his fur, had the tears been ready to come. But they were not. It is only children and lovers who have the luxury of weeping easily, for they alone have someone to catch the tears before they hit the ground. Crying is hard for everyone else.

A few days after that, as James was leaving the Rose and Castle and crossing the car-park towards his car, Nick emerged from the kitchen door and called out, 'James.' Nick didn't normally begin speaking to his old friend by calling his name, so he knew at once that Nick had something to say to him that he'd already thought carefully about. He turned and walked towards the kitchen door outside which Nick stood.

There was something about that moment. James thought later of the meeting in Crime and Punishment between Raskolnikov and Razumikhin under the lamp. But in that scene the lamp had lit both men's faces and revealed Raskolnikov's dark secret in his. Whereas in the moment that was now unfolding the light from the door left Nick's face and the whole of his tall spare figure in unrevealing silhouette. 'I had a thought,' Nick said, and for once James could find no clue in his face as to what the thought was. But the melodramatic inscrutability of Nick's black shape was belied by one almost comic, almost surreal touch. His ears were not in silhouette at all: instead the light from the door behind him shone straight through them and made them blaze bright crimson, as though they were hazard warnings, or navigation aids, or Christmas lights.

'What?' James asked, too startled by this odd new appearance of Nick, which was something that Nick himself could not have guessed at, to say anything more affectionate.

'I was thinking about Seville,' Nick said. 'I was thinking ... I mean ... what about asking Charlie along?'

'Charlie?' James hadn't thought of that. Although he'd kept in touch with Charlie. They'd phoned occasionally, and exchanged emails. Charlie had even started off by texting James, though had given that up when he discovered James's lack of enthusiasm and talent for the medium. For his part, James brooded on the thought that texting had been invented by and for people whose fingers were younger and more dexterous than his. 'Charlie...'

'I know you don't know him that well ... and I mean, nor do I ... but he was very close to Borja ... if you don't mind me saying that. I just thought, well, you said yourself, you'd be the only single gay man there. I just wondered if it might be nice if there were two of you... Just a thought anyway.'

This struck James at once as a blatant bit of matchmaking and the thought, together with the knowledge – not shared by Nick and Andy – of what had happened with Charlie at the Court House and in Madeira, made him smile. Clearly Nick and Andy had discussed this together. He could imagine them going on to argue about which of them should raise the matter with him. Now he would have been willing to bet that Nick was blushing: something that couldn't be seen on his dark-side-of-the-moon face. But his ears appeared to shine even more brightly, as when rear lights brighten when a driver brakes, which seemed to confirm James's guess. He said, 'I think that's a very good idea. If you like to ask him. But I think I'd rather you got onto him about it. Not me. You understand that?'

Nick said yes, of course he understood that, and they exchanged a goodnight hug. Then James turned and walked towards his car. As he drove away up the hill his inner eye retained the residual image of Nick's ears, like glowing crimson petals in the dark.

Lapwings were doing aerial cartwheels and looping the loop above the fields, making their spring music: it sounded like the bubbling of brooks over pebbles, but coming from the blue air overhead. James and Andy were doing something they didn't often do together: taking a walk through the meadows that flanked the River Tove. From half a mile away came the sound of Nick's piano playing, floating out of the West Pavilion's open windows and making its way downhill towards them, past occasional trees.

'Are you applying for other jobs?' Andy asked, striding along beside James.

James made an ashamed-of-himself sort of grimace. 'I should be, I know.'

Andy cut him off. 'No, you shouldn't be. You shouldn't be doing anything. And I shouldn't have said that. Everything in its own time. Time... Well, all things will fall into place, given time.' He broke into a different thought. 'What is that piece Nick's doing? I know I know it...'

'Beethoven again,' James said. 'His last sonata but one. The Opus 110. Nick explained it to me. He wrote it after a near-death experience – syphilis or typhoid, one of those things composers used to get. There's a final fugue...' He stopped and listened a second. '...No, he hasn't got to it yet ... the tune goes away, reappears all upside-down and scrambled up, then returns properly in triumph. Nick said it was supposed to be death and resurrection. He told me that years ago. He hasn't mentioned it since...'

'No, of course,' Andy came in hastily. 'I was going to say though, I mean about new jobs, I'm the last person who'd want you moving away from here, taking up a job in Sheffield or London, say. Selfishly, Nick and I both want you here.'

The very thought of moving to Sheffield or London all alone in pursuit of a job produced a moment of physical terror in James. He fought it down. 'I don't want to move away from you two either,' he said. 'You bet I don't.' Another thought cropped up, which he didn't share with Andy. That if he moved away from the Court House Nick would have no grand piano to play on. There was no room to install one at the pub. They'd have to build an extension, a special room... In such untidy ways were all people's lives tangled up. 'But the new job thing...' He wrenched his thoughts back. 'It's not just because of, you know, that tendency to inaction they say affects everybody...'

'I know what you're saying,' Andy said gently.

The sound of a small plane arose behind a distant copse. 'That's not you today, then,' James said facetiously, pleased by the opportunity to lighten things.

'Chap called Eddie,' Andy said. 'He's on all this week. You've met him in the pub.'

'It simply wouldn't be easy for me to get a job in another theatre,' James continued. 'Not as a number one. Artistic Director, Administrative Director, whatever they like to call the post. Strictly speaking, I'm not qualified for the job I do. I've never directed a play myself, never worked as an actor. I simply grew into the different jobs because of changing situations at the Regent. I couldn't easily transplant my skills into another theatre.'

'Yes,' said Andy, 'but what about directing plays freelance, like the people you employ to do exactly that? You must have watched how they go about things often enough.'

'It's not quite the same,' James argued. 'I've never watched directors directing, with a view to learning to do it myself. It's like – well, like Charlie, who told me he's watched pilots landing planes lots of times from the jump-seat. But you wouldn't say that qualifies him to drive the thing himself. You wouldn't let him loose on a 737 and a hundred passengers, would you?'

'Take your point,' said Andy, a bit squashed by James's demolition of his kind thought.

'The other thing is...' James stopped walking and turned to look Andy very directly in the eye, which made Andy do the same to him. Two pairs of blue eyes that had seen bluer days peered into each other. 'We're the same age, you and I. We both know how it is. Other theatres all over the country have thirty-somethings or forty-somethings at the helm. By the time you're fifty you need to be sitting pretty tight somewhere, because the music is about to stop.' It was not necessary for him to point out in how many ways, in his case, the music had already stopped and how painful the silence was. For a moment an actual silence fell between the two men.

Andy said, 'I need to pee. Just a sec.' He turned modestly aside, while James walked on a few paces more, thinking, Andy too knew about the music stopping. Airline captain transferred to cargo... Made redundant from that... Now a part-time tug-pilot who ran a pub... But who ran a pub with the man he loved.

Andy trotted up to where Nick stood waiting, smiling and still doing himself up.

'You run a pub with the man you love,' James said to him, and Andy grinned and nodded, as though the remark had not come out of the blue and he had been following James's train of thought the whole way along.

They passed through a line of scraggy blackthorn trees that must once have been a hedge. On the other side a row of small cattle stood facing them, like a reception committee or an interview panel, swishing their tails. 'Oh fuck,' said Andy. 'They're all bulls. Look between their legs.'

James bent his head and looked. 'You're right.'

'Ought we to be afraid or something?' Andy said. 'Didn't know they put bulls in groups. They're usually solo in a field of cows. Make a run for it?' He didn't sound alarmed though. Expressing a modicum of Scottish prudence was nearer the mark.

'They're very young bulls,' said James. 'Just big calves, really.' He thought, Borja would have known exactly what tactics to adopt. Borja the farm boy, and Spanish to boot. Borja who'd slept with a bullfighter once. Ex-bullfighter, at least. Rafael... 'I think we just walk calmly through the middle of them,' James said. That was what he supposed Borja would have said.

So they continued to walk forward, side by side, passing between the nearest pair of animals, which stood still, only turning their heads to watch them pass. Then the whole herd turned and followed them slowly, about ten yards behind them, all the way to the end of the field, where their progress was halted by the fence, while Andy and James, with some relief, climbed over the gate.

'I've got the directors for the last two productions lined up,' James announced once that little test of their sang-froid was behind them. When the spring season had been planned the closure of the Regent had been a looming possibility but by no means a fact. Now that things were definite James looked with a rueful kind of satisfaction on the choices he had made concerning the final two shows. Last but one would be Rattigan's In Praise of Love. Out of fashion for a generation or more, the poise and balance of Rattigan's writing was being rediscovered by a new audience, one that was unused to the display of fine-tuned, nuanced feelings on screen or stage. Then to finish... 'Of course, I got a bit of stick for wanting to do another Shakespeare,' James said, as the distance between Andy and him and the bulls watching them steadfastly from beyond the fence slowly increased. ''That's two in six months,' one of the board objected. Councillor Stackpole of course. I just said, 'Well, let's just do it for once,' and that seemed to do the trick.'

'And it's quite different from Romeo and Juliet, surely,' Andy said. He already knew that James's swan song was to be A Midsummer Night's Dream. 'The Dream,' he said, demonstrating that after so many years of knowing James and Nick he was quite capable of talking the way theatre insiders talked. He would always refer to Macbeth as 'the Scottish play', and to the character Hamlet as 'the Dane'.

'Mary Warren's directing the Rattigan,' James said. 'She was here last year – you met her. She did a good job. And I'm getting someone new for the Shakespeare. Someone I've never met. He's called Freddie Jay. I've seen his work at Stratford and on the South Bank. I'm meeting him in London next week.'

'Freddie,' Andy echoed, stopping and looking at James with a crooked smile. 'Is he younger than we are and quite good-looking, by any chance?'

'I suppose you could say that. I've googled him and seen a photograph. Though that's not...'

'Only joking,' said Andy. A lapwing wheeled and bubbled overhead.

James went to London on the train. In years gone by he had driven down, but since congestion charging had come into force he had taken to the rails. He looked out of the window as they raced through Hemel Hempstead, saw the still bare chestnut trees, a hundred or more along the canal there, and imagined them as they'd look in two months' time in waxy candle flower, light green and creamy white. After the trees came brick houses: well cared for, with gardens trim and neat. What people lived there? he wondered idly as he passed.

He met Freddie in Covent Garden, at Carluccio's. Freddie, arriving through the door a minute after James, spotted him at once, seated at the table he'd been shown to and apparently admiring a selection of bread sticks. Evidently it was not only James who'd used the internet to find out what the other looked like. James spotted Freddie a second later and beckoned him across.

Freddie was about thirty-five, James surmised, and had chestnut hair and nice brown eyes. He looked as good as his picture on Facebook, which not everybody did. More importantly, they were going to get along well together, James realised right from the start. James paid him the compliment of telling him how much he'd enjoyed the two productions of his that he'd seen so far, while Freddie managed to dredge up the names of one or two actors who'd worked at the Regent and come back with good reports. They broke off to order a dish of pasta each when the waiter arrived, and then, just as James was launching into the question of how Freddie would approach A Midsummer Night's Dream were he offered the task of directing it, the younger man surprised him by stopping him in mid-sentence. 'May I just say something before we go on?'

'Of course,' James said, because you always had to say that, although it was unusual to be interrupted in mid-flow by someone to whom you were just about to offer a job.

'It's just that I know about your double whammy. About the theatre having to go, right on top of losing Borja. I just wanted to say... Well, you know.'

'Thank you,' James said, a bit startled, a bit taken aback. 'How did you know about Borja? How did you know his name?'

Freddie looked awkward, even abashed for a second, though for no longer than that. 'I got in touch with David Parkes. Just as a matter of routine, because I know he's going to be running the Regent building after you've gone. Sorry – does that sound dreadfully calculating? It's just that... well, it's one of those things we all have to...'

'I suppose it is,' said James, wanting to put Freddie at his ease, though sounding a bit distant when the words came out. It wasn't the sort of thing James had ever done, nor did he think he'd be very good at it if he tried. Perhaps that had been his Achilles heel throughout his life. His lack of talent for schmoozing was certainly going to prove a handicap when May was out, he thought.

As if James had said all this out loud Freddie asked, 'But you? Do you have somewhere to go on to? I mean, obviously I'm talking about work.' He had the grace to realise at once that he'd been talking out of turn and suddenly turned boyishly pink. 'I'm sorry. I'd no business to...'

'It's OK,' said James, warming to Freddie suddenly because of that blush. 'No, I haven't started looking yet. Well, for obvious reasons. I've been a bit...' He looked down and fidgeted for a second with his serviette. He looked up again and eyeballed Freddie. 'Perhaps we should talk about The Dream for a bit.' He smiled at him. 'Perhaps later we can come back to that.'

They settled into a businesslike discussion of the subject they had met to talk about. It was soon obvious that Freddie wasn't going to say no to James's offer, even when he mentioned the fee the Regent would be offering, which James knew could not measure up to what Freddie received at Stratford and on the South

Bank. It was equally obvious that James was more than happy to offer Freddie the job.

When all that was done and the pasta was being followed, against their better judgements, by a dessert each of tiramisu, Freddie said, 'And do you never direct, yourself?'

'No,' James answered baldly. 'No qualifications to be doing that.'

Freddie answered, looking thoughtful, 'I'm not sure if any of us have the qualifications in any deep sense. Maybe all we have is a kind of … vision, and a hell of a bloody cheek.'

'I've never even been an actor,' James said, 'and I'm not going to start now. Though I've worked in the theatre most of my life. Backstage as well as front of house.'

Well,' said Freddie, shifting in his chair slightly, 'if you're interested, you'd be more than welcome to sit in on rehearsals when I'm working on The Dream. Whatever else you've got to do – closing down a theatre, I suppose – may not be a very cheerful way of spending your time.' He stopped and for a second time looked embarrassed. 'Now I'm out of order again. And making it sound like I could teach you something. What I really meant was that you'd probably discover you didn't have very much to learn.'

Either way, James was again astonished at being spoken to in this way by someone he'd only just met. He found he didn't mind it in the least. He had already taken care to look at Freddie's ring finger and seen no ring there. But that proved nothing. In the UK many married men didn't wear a gold band. He'd given nothing away as to what his sexual orientation might be: not in what he said, or the way he said it, or the way he looked. But why should he? He was at a job interview, not out on a date. James might ask around his contacts in due course.

Google him again more carefully. Have another look at Facebook.

The phone in James's pocket rang. 'Oh, I'm sorry,' he said, fishing it out. 'I thought I'd switched it off.' But he answered it anyway. He listened in silence for nearly a minute before speaking himself. 'I'm really sorry,' Freddie heard him say. 'I'm still in a meeting. I'll call him as soon as I can.' He ended the call but kept the phone in his hand. He looked across at Freddie with a face that was a mask, or the face of someone else. He became aware that his hands were trembling. 'I'm sorry, Freddie. That was bad news. Of the personal sort.'

SEVENTEEN

Pippa was startled when her secretary, on the office phone, asked if she would take a call from her father. For years parental calls had come from her mother, who would then do the talking for her husband as well as for herself. But when this morning's call was put through to her she heard her father's tremulous voice saying, 'Your mother appears to have had a stroke.'

'Oh Dad! Have you called an ambulance?'

'I called the doctors' surgery. They called an ambulance from there.'

'And where's Mum now?'

'The ambulance men are here. She's on a stretcher. They're taking her outside.'

Thank God for that, Pippa thought. 'Where will they take her? St George's or Kingston?'

'St George's,' her father said firmly. At least he was clear about that.

'And are you going with them?'

'I don't know. Do you think I should?'

'Most certainly you should. Have you called Richard?'

'No,' said her father, then again, 'Do you think I should?'

Why was it always the daughter who was expected to act in these situations? Why never the elder son? Richard lived only ten miles from their parents. Unlike Pippa who had the whole of London and its suburbs in between. Richard was a partner in an accounting firm and, ten years Pippa's senior, was due to retire in a month or two. He could much more easily be spared from his desk than could Pippa.. The Ben-Shar case was coming up in Strasbourg the following week and Pippa really needed every minute between now and then to prepare for it. 'Call Richard now,' she said. 'Take the mobile with you to the hospital. The mobile phone. Get it now. Don't forget. I'll call you a bit later and I'll get down to St George's as quickly as I can.' She ended the call. If she hadn't heard from her brother in ten minutes as a result of their father's phoning him she would call him herself.

But she did hear from him in ten minutes, by which time she was walking towards Marylebone tube station. Brother and sister met, after what seemed to Pippa an achingly slow journey by underground to Tooting, at their mother's bedside in the short-stay stroke ward. Their father sat looking at his wife and intermittently holding her hand. Richard had arrived shortly before Pippa and was standing, taking small steps this way and that across the narrow space available, then wheeling rather dramatically and taking the same small steps back again. He looked relieved to see his sister arrive. Pippa thought that her mother, comfortable raised on pillows and wearing a rose-embroidered bed-jacket, looked the most composed and emotionally stable of the four of them.

It was their father's state that Pippa and Richard found themselves discussing first, when they went out into the corridor, having assured themselves their mother would not drop dead in front of them.

'He can't look after her at home,' Pippa said at once.

'I know,' Richard said. 'We've talked about it with the staff here. There's a number for you to ring. Something called Social Care Direct...'

'For me to ring?' Pippa interrupted. 'Why does it have to be me?' Why were men so feeble when it came down to knotty family problems? She thought of her ex-husband and then, perhaps because she'd recently been talking to Alexa, of Mark. Both of them had been exactly the same in that respect.

Richard dealt with Pippa's objection by pretending he hadn't heard it. 'They talked of respite care. That means going into a care home, just on a temporary...'

'Respite from what?' Pippa asked, in cross-examination mode. 'Which one of them? Both? Respite from whom? Each other?'

'Give us a chance... Yes, more or less. But the idea is they'd go together. To the same place, I mean. That happens these days. It's a question of finding a place that's got space at the right time.'

'And of someone finding the money.'

'There would be that, of course,' said Richard, his head nodding slightly.

'Look,' Pippa said, stuffing her hands into the pockets of her coat. 'I'll phone this social care thing. But I'm talking about the first time. Second time it's your turn. We're in this together. OK? Starting now.'

An hour later the two of them were sitting in the hospital cafeteria, drinking coffee and eating croissants. Their father had chosen not to join them but stayed at his wife's side instead. Sister and brother were discussing the question of how and where their parents were going to live in the longer term. 'The thing is,' Richard said, with an awkward look in his eyes, 'that I've got Amanda and the kids to deal with. You're on your own.'

Pippa could have pointed out frostily that Richard and Amanda's 'kids' were twenty-eight and twenty-six, no longer lived at their parents' address, and managed their own lives without needing much help. She did not. 'That is *so* unfair,' she said, startled out of lawyer mode and into being nothing more than a kid sister again. 'That's like saying that because of my parents I have to stay single all my life.'

Richard looked at his kid sister, took in the square set of the jaw that her career had given her, and the extraordinary fringe that she'd cultivated since her divorce and which gave her something of the look of a highland bull. At the same moment his mind gave him a fleeting picture of her youthful prettiness, and he felt an unexpected pang of regret. He stopped himself from saying the first thing that came into his head. 'I suppose,' he said instead.

Returning to the ward they were told that their mother would be kept in hospital for observation for two nights. Later that day it fell somehow to Pippa, not to Richard, to take her father home by taxi to New Malden, to cook him an evening meal and make up a bed for herself in what, impossibly long ago, had been her own room. She arranged with her chambers to take the next day off as well. For once there were no court appearances scheduled, and her next trip to Strasbourg was not until two days after that. She had the documents for the Ben-Shar case scanned and emailed to her iPad. Exceptional times required exceptional steps.

Later in the evening Richard phoned. She was pleasantly surprised by what he said. A respite arrangement in a care home had been made by the social service people. Richard had just been over to see the place, and pronounced it good. The double room would be available on her mother's discharge from hospital the day after next.

'Brill,' said Pippa, once again surprised into talking to her brother the way she would have done when a child. Though that didn't last. 'That still leaves tomorrow night. I can't possibly stay in New Malden another night. I've Strasbourg in the morning and I must get to chambers, and to Hemel, to get my stuff. You'll have to come over and stay with him yourself.'

'Surely he'd be all right for just one night on his own,' said Richard in a hopeful tone of voice.

'No he would not,' Pippa said firmly. 'And the next day he'll need to be taken, with a bag packed – and another one for Mum, don't forget – who will also need collecting from hospital – and both of them delivered to the care home, wherever it is.'

'I can't do all that,' her brother protested.

'Well you can, Richard, because you must. Get Amanda in on the act.'

'But... what would I cook for him tomorrow night?'

'Oh for God's sake. Ask Amanda. Ring up for a takeaway if you have to. Do whatever you must.' She added, very firmly indeed, 'See you at the hospital tomorrow afternoon,' and ended the call before Richard could say anything else.

It was just after ten. With her father dozing in his armchair alongside her, Pippa switched on the television news. The screen immediately filled with the tangled, red and white painted, wreck of a smallish plane. The pilot had been killed. The scene was a small airfield somewhere in the Midlands. Pippa listened attentively. She always paid attention to news of air crashes now. Ever since she'd been astonished by the appearance of Borja in front of the cameras at Gatwick. The more so since she'd learned he'd been mown down by cancer just a few weeks after surviving his crash.

The details of this accident, as far as Pippa could make out, were these. A plane towing a glider into the air had crashed on take-off. The glider had become airborne, just about, but had then crash-landed in a nearby field. Its pilot had been taken to hospital with minor injuries. (Hospital, thought Pippa. How all life seemed to revolve around those places now.) There had been no hospital for the pilot of the towing plane. He had been found dead at the scene. Names had not yet been released.

Pippa did a mental roll-call of friends and acquaintances. None of them, as far as she knew, had gone in for gliding as a pastime. Certainly none made a living from getting gliders aloft.

Her mind returned to Borja. A friend of his had died in that air-crash in Valencia, while Karsten's survival had led directly to his becoming a priest. Which for some reason he no longer was. She might discover that if she went to the bizarre reunion that was being planned. It was becoming less and less likely that she would be able to. Especially with her parents' new troubles. She glanced across the room at her father, still upright in his chair but now soundly asleep. Work seemed to be piling up in front of her like the sea in front of an advancing ship; her case-load at the Court of Human Rights was growing exponentially. Though she had no regrets about that.

After his meeting with Freddie James had phoned Nick directly, and Nick had given him the details without being asked. A glider being towed by Andy's plane had got airborne too soon, for whatever reason, and the still attached tow-rope rising behind the towing plane had tipped it nose-down into the ground a second or two before it would have taken off. The single engine had exploded, abruptly ending Andy's life. Returned from London James drove from the station directly to the pub. By the time he was out of his car Nick was crossing the car-park towards him. When they were close enough James stretched out a hand and touched Nick's shoulder. 'Oh mate...'

Nick jerked away from the touch as if from an electric shock. 'Don't,' he said, his voice almost cracking under the weight of tears he couldn't afford to shed. He turned his head aside, allowing James only his profile to wonder at.

'I'm sorry,' James said. The rebuff had hurt him, though he knew that small hurt was just a whispered echo of the pain that was raging through Nick. He followed Nick into the pub.

Nick led the way upstairs, through the bar, oddly empty at five in the afternoon. James found a half second in which to suppose that the pub was closed for the day … or for longer.

The living-room looked as it always did, yet was changed for ever. Nick turned to face James. 'Scotch OK?' There was a bottle, open and three-quarters full, on the coffee-table. There were also two used glasses, the sight of which cheered James. Someone else had been here already, to try and comfort Nick. He hadn't had to chug the quarter of a bottle on his own. Unless he'd poured two glasses, one for Andy perhaps, as well as himself, and drunk from them both... James hoped not and shook the thought away. Meanwhile Nick was getting two fresh ones from the sideboard.

'Scotch is fine,' James said. At such a moment no-one would say anything else.

'What a ropey old way to die,' Nick said, sitting on one of the sofas and pouring from the bottle. And James, taking his cue, and a seat on the sofa opposite, discovered with a shock that he was facing a completely new Nick. For twenty years Nick had been the kid; now here he was, a suddenly mature man, in mid-life, competent and, for the moment at least, completely in charge of things. 'He was an airline captain, for Christ's sake,' Nick was saying. 'Now people will just remember him as a tin-pot tug pilot, eking out his days running a pub.'

How anger works. It throws you up in the air the way a bull chucks a matador or a cat tosses a mouse, then sends you running in all the wrong directions when you fall to earth. 'No, they fucking won't!' James said in a voice more suitable for rebutting an aspersion cast on his dead mother. He went on, not caring how brutal or insensitive he might seem, 'People die in old folks' homes every day of the year. Do people remember them as just the inmates of those places? No, of course they don't. It's the whole person people remember, not just where they were at at the moment the music stopped.' Though even as the words speared out James found himself fearing that he might be wrong, that perhaps the exact opposite was true.

Nick looked across at James with an unreadable expression on his face. It was no longer the boy's face that James knew and took for granted, but the face of a very grown-up man. Of someone more grown-up now, since this morning, than even James.

A new thought clutched at James. About Andy. About dead, beautiful Andy. James had never slept with Andy, although Borja had. James and Andy had never exchanged more than a chaste kiss and a butch hug. All right, sometimes a quite high-charged kiss and hug. But they'd never explored each other's body and heart, never gone to sleep trustful in their intimacy and woken to find the other's head on the pillow, the other's cock pressed against his own, in the morning's grey light. Just four days ago James and Andy had walked in the squelching meadows by the river in the spring sun, while lapwings tumbled overhead. Andy had turned aside to take his dick out and piss. Why had James not seized that moment, seized that cock, pulled Andy's jeans down and brought him off right there where they stood? Looking back, his decorum, his sense of responsibility to Andy's relationship with Nick, his respect for Nick even, seemed pitifully misplaced, his failure to seize that absolutely final chance a wicked waste.

It was not a thought he could possibly share with Nick. Nick continued to look at him with an unfathomable expression on his face. James returned him a stare of a similar sort. As a reflex they each took a sip of whisky. Neither knew whose turn it was to speak or what, when one of them eventually did, he could possibly say next.

Borja had slept with Andy. James knew that. Or rather they'd spent a night in the same bed. So Borja had told him. The Casablanca night. Although it had been very intimate, they hadn't had sex, and they'd hardly slept. They'd simply held each other, comforted each other after a day of shared turmoil and stress, after nearly crashing on take-off from Gatwick when Andy got stung by a wasp, then landing at the wrong Moroccan airport. They'd been in deep trouble with just about everyone, from their own bosses to the Moroccan airports authority and the powers that be, or were, at Air France. They'd been in trouble with James also. James who'd got himself in deep trouble that same night, almost spending the night in bed with Nick. James's head shook involuntarily. 'Are you all right?' Nick asked.

'Of course I'm not,' James said roughly. Then more gently, 'I'm sorry. That came out wrong. It's you I'm trying to focus on. But other things keep getting in the way.' He found himself unable to say more. Unable to speak. He didn't imagine that Nick felt any more competent, right now, in that respect. He stood up, walked – flailed would perhaps better describe it – around the coffee table on which their glasses, plus the other pair of empty ones and the whisky bottle, stood and as Nick rose from the other sofa, said – begged would perhaps better describe it – 'Nick, give me a hug.'

It was just a letter arriving by special courier. It might have been a letter-bomb for the effect it had. It was from the European Court of Human Rights. When Pippa had expertly sifted the lawyerly phrases and elegant locutions she was left with the core message that, because of the nature of some of the casework she had been undertaking in the UK, a potential conflict of interest had been perceived. She would no longer be able to work with the ECHR after the end of the following month.

She would miss the money of course. Everybody misses money. But that wasn't the painful thing. The Court of Human Rights was where Pippa belonged. If ever an institution had been created that exactly matched her capabilities and her goals in life the ECHR was it. Working there was by a long way the highest point of her career. And there still remained so much there for her to achieve. There were battles still to be won that she alone would be able to fight. Nobody better understood what the Court was capable of, how it could be developed and made to grow in scope. Nobody was better equipped to take it onward towards its greater destiny. Britain might be the mother of parliaments: the ECHR would become the mother of human rights institutions around the globe, its destiny and Pippa's career inextricably bound together. But now... Pippa read the letter carefully, three or four times, while she drank a mug of coffee. She had instructed the secretary to put no calls through to her during this time. The memory of that most famous of Edwardian Punch cartoons, Dropping the Pilot, came into her head. That unforgettable image of Bismarck walking down the gangplank from the deck of a battleship while an inscrutable, be-whiskered Kaiser Wilhelm watches from above. Now she understood precisely how Bismarck must have felt.

That evening an email came to Pippa. She read it at home.

Dear Pippa (Like most people of fifty or more Alexa topped and tailed her emails exactly as, nearly half a century earlier, she had been taught to write a letter.)

Sad news, I'm afraid. One of the people who should have been coming to Seville, but whom you don't know, has died in an air crash. His name was Andy, the partner of a younger man I worked with – on something that's neither here nor there right now... She went on to explain that Nick and Andy, and Borja and James, had been very close, and where they all lived, and how the accident had occurred. Then,

Impossible to know yet if Nick will still want to go to Seville. He did very much want to go with Andy. And impossible to know even if the reunion will happen at all. Needless to say, if it does go ahead, Mark and I, and Karsten, all hope very much that you'll be able to join us. Perhaps even more now.

Pippa didn't write a reply to that email. She phoned instead.

The hug that James had given Nick – or rather, had demanded that Nick give him – was brief. James offered to stay the night at the pub with Nick, or to have Nick up to Sevenscore to spend the night with him. Nick said a polite no to both. At that moment they heard the bar and kitchen staff arriving to start preparations for the evening. Nick had decided it would be business as usual as from seven o'clock. He told James he'd be fine with the support and company of his staff, and that after locking up he'd award himself a stiff whisky (for gallantry in the face of enemy action, James thought) and go straight to bed. James left him just after the pub opened at seven o'clock, promising to phone him first thing next morning.

He had barely taken his coat off after returning to the Court House from the pub when Charlie phoned. 'I want you to know before anyone else, the report on the Gatwick crash'll be published in two days,' Charlie began. 'Too late for Borja, of course, but better than

227

never. It exonerates Borja from any blame and gives him a posthumous commendation for...'

James's heart started to pound and his thoughts raced, but he had to interrupt. 'Charlie, you must know – do you know? – Andy's dead.'

'Holy shit,' said Charlie. 'How...?'

'It was on the news. Glider crash.'

'I haven't heard the news,' Charlie said. 'I just got back from Stockholm minutes ago. Still at Luton. Somebody said a light plane had crashed. They didn't say where. I didn't think... Look. Like I said, I'm at Luton. Just down the road. I've got the car. Do you want me to come up?'

When they were finished James phoned Nick at once to tell him Charlie was on his way, but the line was engaged. Charlie had obviously got there first: that was confirmed when, five minutes later, James did get through to Nick. 'I've told him to call in on his way,' Nick told him. 'If you want to drop down...'

'Well of course I do,' James said, unable to keep the pique out of his voice. He looked at his watch. Charlie would be at the pub in forty minutes, assuming he'd left Luton promptly and the traffic wasn't bad. 'I just need to grab something to eat.' He immediately regretted that. To someone who'd been bereaved more recently than he'd breakfasted, the question of whether James had had a bite of supper or not could hardly matter very much. James felt himself wrong-footed at every step he took.

'You can both have something here,' Nick said, so that James felt wrong-footed once again.

James killed a little time by checking his emails, finding among them a sweetly phrased message of sympathy from Freddie. Then he took a walk around the garden, where daffodils glowed dimly, like emergency lighting, in the dusk. He tried to put his thoughts about this extraordinary day into some kind of order in his head but without much success. Then he gave Sancho a very large helping of dinner and picked the cat up, cuddling him till he purred. He didn't know what time he'd be back.

EIGHTEEN

The light was out but they were still awake. 'Nobody else is going to have the bad taste to say this,' said Charlie, 'so I'll say it myself.'

'Say what?' James asked. They were lying side by side under the duvet on Nick's spare-room bed. They were wearing most of their day clothes still: the bed hadn't been slept in all winter and had that season's chill on it.

'That Andy's death leaves Nick... Hell, this is actually more difficult to put into words than I thought... I mean, that in the new circumstances, you and Nick...'

'You're right,' said James. 'That's in extremely bad taste.'

'It would really be in bad taste only if I said it to Nick,' Charlie countered, 'and I'm certainly not going to do that.' They were both speaking in low whispers because Nick was in his own bed just the other side of the wall, though whether, after the day he'd been through, he was asleep or awake was anybody's guess. But since Nick and Charlie had plied him with quantities of alcohol throughout the evening, there was a good chance that Morpheus was giving him a hug.

Nick's proximity and his newly bereft state had an impact on another thing: on something that actually didn't happen but which, had it done so, might also have been thought in bad taste. James and Charlie were making no attempt at sexual contact despite finding themselves unexpectedly sharing a bed. There were some other reasons why there was no sex that night. One was the coldness of the bed and bedclothes and the resulting necessity they both discovered of remaining nearly fully dressed. There might have been other things on Charlie's side, of course, that James didn't know about and would never ask. Although Charlie had been ready to have sex with James during the fortnight or so after Borja's death, he had told James quite candidly at Madeira airport not to expect that to go on being the case. If that was how Charlie felt then so be it, James thought.

And then there was another reason on James's side and he wasn't going to share *this* with his bed-mate. He felt oddly annoyed with Charlie, though he had the grace to realise that this was his own and not Charlie's fault. It was no fault of Charlie's that Nick had earlier refused James's offer of company during the evening and overnight, yet when the offer had come an hour or two later from Charlie's lips, Nick had accepted gratefully and with a genuine smile of pleasure on his face. James felt ashamed of himself for harbouring resentment about this. Nevertheless it did play some part in his decision not to fondle Charlie under the bed-covers, Though presumably it played no part in Charlie's decision not to fondle James.

In the morning James phoned his office, explained to Linda what had happened and told her he wouldn't be in till mid-afternoon. Charlie would also have to leave around that time: he had a flight out of Gatwick the next morning; it was a matter of pure chance that he wasn't flying today. This gave the pair of them a morning at least to help Nick manage what James termed the bureaucracy of death. It was a morning spent between Sevenscore, the pub, the airfield and the centre of town. A morning of emails, phone-calls and texts. Again it was Charlie who said what most people wouldn't have dared to: that his own recent experience had made James the ideally qualified person to be helping Nick with all of this. And in the middle of the morning there was a moment to make sure that Sancho Panza, who had always liked Andy and who James thought would no doubt miss him, got petted and fed.

The post arrived at Sevenscore around midday and coincidentally James and Charlie were there when it did. A letter with a first class stamp and a hand-addressed cream envelope caught James's attention and he opened it first, in the kitchen, in the presence of Charlie and the cat. 'Good God,' he said, after reading the opening, then rustling the two pages over to the signature to see whose it was. 'It's from Pippa. Philippa Brookes. The lawyer woman.'

'The one Borja didn't like.'

'Well, I don't want to say... But yeah, OK, you've got the one.' He read through the letter, giving Charlie the gist as he went along, while they both stood on the kitchen's brick floor, and Sancho slipped away to deal with something somewhere else. 'It's condolences on Borja's death. Good heavens. I wonder where she got the address... And sorry about the death of Andy. She's quick off the mark. She can't have known he existed till yesterday... *Please accept my sympathies over what must be a horrible second blow. Alexa told me...* Oh, OK, yeah, she's been in touch with Alexa – who you met... Oh, this is weird... *Alexa told me that a reunion was being planned in Borja's honour in Seville. This will sound very presumptuous of me in the present circumstances, but may I express the hope that...* Charlie, we've hardly discussed this... It's only just come up...'

'I know about it,' said Charlie, his head nodding involuntarily at the surprise of all this. 'Andy phoned me just two days before he died and said they ... and you ... wanted me to come along. Then there was the trip to

Stockholm, and now ... this.' He waved his hands around vaguely. 'It went out of my head.'

James still had his nose buried in the letter. 'She hopes the trip will go ahead, she says, though she understands that it may well not. And she wants to come along. She says both Alexa and Karsten asked her...'

'Wow,' said Charlie. 'But would you want her to? Anyway, with Nick now...'

'I think we'd better say that all plans are on hold,' James said. He looked up from the letter and met Charlie's gaze with his own. 'It's not something Nick'll want to discuss. I'll find a moment to email Pippa – steel myself – and tell her that.' He shook the letter in his hand rather roughly and said, 'What a day for this to arrive!' but then, as though changing his mind about everything, folded it almost reverently and stowed it carefully back in its envelope.

By the time James had seen Nick off, had done some work in his office at the theatre and returned in the evening to the Rose and Castle, Andy's parents had already arrived there from Edinburgh. James spent a little time with them and Nick, and then left early. Andy's parents would be staying the next two nights at the pub. As he left them to it and drove away up the hill James consoled himself with the thought that at least he'd played his part in airing the spare room bed.

Two days later the report was out. Somebody from the airline phoned James to tell him that a copy would be sent to him in the post. But before that could happen there was a brief mention of the enquiry's findings on the TV news and anyway, tipped off by a phone-call from Charlie who told him where to look, James had read the whole thing on the internet. The main thing was, the great thing was, that Borja was in the clear. So was Ryan the co-pilot. And although it was recorded as a matter of fact that Charlie had been in breach of company regulations by videoing the approach and landing from the flight deck, there was no suggestion that this had had any impact on the way events unfolded, either before and during the crash, or in its aftermath. Instead Charlie was commended for his handling of the evacuation of the cabin, just as Borja and Ryan were for their calm and professional response to events. Particular mention was made of Borja's inspired adjustment during the last few seconds to the angle of the wing-flaps.

The blame landed fair and square on George. He was a more multi-faceted personality these days than he had been in earlier times. He consisted not only of the autopilot but of the auto-throttles system, which was separate. Of all the altimeters aboard the plane only one was used to convey its information to the auto-throttles: the radio altimeter on the captain's side of the cockpit. Not a lot of people – not even pilots – had known that before the publication of this report; certainly Borja and Ryan had not. But by unfortunate chance that was the instrument that had intermittently been giving faulty readings on the way over to Greece and back.

Receiving from the faulty altimeter the information that the plane was already on the ground the auto-throttles had gone into retard-flare mode: that meant the rapid reduction of power that normally takes place on touchdown. On Borja's final approach to Gatwick this had happened at precisely the same time as the engines were being throttled back quite normally in response to another situation: it happened during those very seconds when the plane was dropping rapidly onto the glide-slope from above and decelerating in order to do this. That coincidence prevented the pilots from spotting what was really happening until a moment later – when the plane failed to capture the glide-slope but continued to fall below it – its engines unexpectedly not powering up.

Well, thought James, mystery solved. It was just a pity that Borja was no longer around to appreciate the news, and nor was Andy, who would have been delighted on behalf of his pilot friend. At least James could share the news with Nick. He did, immediately, and the two of them managed in spite of everything to be pleased on behalf of those they'd subsequently lost.

In the days that followed Andy's death Nick had began to be more relaxed in the company of James – as opposed to the apparently easier company of Charlie. It was a development that gave James new heart. 'They want a Church of Scotland service up in Dalkeith,' Nick had told him with a morose look on his face. They, of course, meant Andy's parents. Nick and James were talking in the living-room of the Court House. Nick had driven up to talk to James within minutes of his in-laws' departure towards the north. This evident desire of Nick's for his older friend's company at this moment gladdened James a lot.

'It's not their say-so,' James reminded Nick gently. 'You're the civil partner. What happens is going to be what you want.'

'I know,' said Nick. 'But he was their only child...' James saw Nick's lip tremble as he spoke.

'Yes, but he was *your* only...' James couldn't decide which word to plump for. He decided to leave the sentence as it was. 'Look, Andy lived and worked here for years. In London before that. Everybody who knew him... Well, people from the pub... They can't all travel to Scotland. But a few family members coming south...'

'The religious thing, though,' Nick said.

'There must be some compromise available,' James said. 'His parents didn't seem as uncompromising as all that. Hardly the John Knox type. Can't we rope in some local Church of Scotland minister and negotiate with

Father Potter to let him take the service in the village church?'

'I suppose we could,' Nick said, with a lighter look on his face. It was a scenario that he obviously hadn't had time yet to conjure up himself. 'Pity we haven't got Karsten here this time. He'd soon sort everybody out.'

'He won't be able to make it over,' James said. 'Did he tell you that? I can't remember who's told who what. Alexa says – not that this has anything to do with him not being able to make it – he's got his own flat now in Düsseldorf. And he's got involved with a woman.' James saw a goggle-eyed look appear on Nick's face, then an incredulous smile. He knew that if he went on the smile would turn into a laugh. He went on. 'He's actually knocking off someone else's wife.'

Nick guffawed. Probably, though James, for the first time since Andy's crash.

'Didn't Alexa tell you that?' James asked him, poker-faced.

'Of course she didn't,' Nick answered, the remains of his laughter still twitching at the corners of his mouth. 'It's not the sort of thing people put in condolence letters. Though maybe you would...'

When Nick had his back to him, James realised, he showed his age. He now had the thicker neck, the broader shoulders and flatter buttock cheeks of the forty-year-old he was. Well, all right, a couple of years on from forty, but James, living in a glassier glass house than that, wanted to be nice. But when Nick was facing you, all that went. It was the power of the eyes, James decided. When he looked directly at James, Nick was still the twentyish youth he'd been when they'd first met. It was like the actor's power to convince you he or she was someone other than the person they really were – or else a younger version. Make-up and voice could do some of the work in the actor's case, but most of it was down to the eyes – and the will. Nick's eyes, bespectacled and brown, still worked their magic, whether he knew about it, whether there was any will involved, or not. They still looked a bit like Borja's eyes of course, as James had noticed all that time ago, almost at once. But that was not the point. Nick, turning to face you directly, still looked exactly the way he'd done when James first knew him. The same went, it was true, for other people James had known for a long time. He hoped it also went for himself.

He thought often of what Charlie had said, or tried to say, till James had stopped him, under the duvet the other night. The tidy logic of the situation was not lost on him. A friend with whom he'd nearly had a fling – or had not even nearly had a fling, depending how you looked at it – had lost his partner within half a year of James losing his. Any computer algorithm would have predicted the next simple step. But humans don't work like that. There was no next simple step.

In the days after Borja's death, or even in the days just before, James had gone through his address book and made a list of those friends and acquaintances with whom he could conceivably imagine spending the second half of his life. He found that he was obliged to write the words 'spoken for' or 'straight' after every single name. In several cases both. That was before even toying with the thought that the people on the list would probably not want to spend the rest of their lives with him.

Mercifully James had forgotten about the list. But the day before Andy's funeral he was forced to confront it again. He found it staring up at him from inside a pile of papers that he was riffling through in search of something else. He felt himself go hot with shame. For the first name on the list had been Andy's.

They'd been the best of friends for twenty years. There was a deep emotional bond between them, a romantic edge to their coming together. James had been prepared to dislike Andy when Borja had proposed inviting him to Sevenscore to meet Nick. Because Andy and Borja had almost got it together that fateful night in Casablanca when James and Nick had nearly got it together a thousand miles to the north. But on his arrival Andy had slashed through the whole tangle – by falling in love with Nick on the spot. It had added piquancy to their friendship ever since.

Andy had been the same height as Borja – five foot seven – and shared the same trim build. Andy had been blond and fair-skinned while Borja was olive-toned and raven-haired. But the appeal of a familiar body size was often overlooked, James thought, and wondered if anyone had done a thesis on that.

Against the name of Andy had been written 'spoken for'. Well, Andy was now unavailable for more unalterable reasons than that. But the second name on the list, also with 'spoken for' written beside it, was Nick's.

In his case too the 'spoken for' no longer applied, even though that had been so for little more than a week. But James refused to let his thoughts stray in that direction, let alone – the very idea gave him goose-bumps of horror – raise the subject with Nick. There was another thing though, and that was the matter of sex. Twenty years ago the idea of sex with Nick had seemed so desirable and uncomplicated that James had pretty well jumped on him when Nick had been naked, sitting on his bed in the Chinese room at the Court House. Nick had responded with the unmistakeable body language of a no thank you, even though he'd been as flirtatious as anyone could be during the evening that led up to that moment – and while he'd still been fully dressed.

With hindsight James realised that Nick's reaction had saved the night. And James. It had led them all, after a few circuits and bumps, onto the fairly level flight-path of the intervening years. James and Borja. Andy and Nick.

And yet, the point was that sex between Nick and himself, disastrous though its consequences might have been, had at least been easy for them both to envisage. Then. But now it no longer was. Where that aspect of the matter was concerned Andy, the same age as both James and Borja, would have been – if you excused a very dodgy metaphor – a more comfortable fit.

He went on looking for the document he was trying to find in the desk drawer. But before doing that he tore up the list.

James was pleased that Nick had taken up his suggestion about the funeral and negotiated with Andy's parents the compromise it involved. In fact he was so pleased, relieved that everyone wouldn't have to travel to Edinburgh, that he handed over all his spare bedrooms to those members of Andy's family – including his parents – who were obliged to travel south. Nick was putting up his own parents at the pub. James felt a bit sorry for him, having to deal with them as house guests at such a time. Over the years he had known Nick's parents he'd come to understand that they accepted their only son's gayness and his partnership with Andy in the spirit with which most of us accept a bright frosty morning. That, though it has its positive side (at least it isn't raining) our principal response is to take a deep breath and tell ourselves it's good for the soul, and then be proud of our fortitude in surviving it. But it could have been worse for Nick. The situation would be even more claustrophobic if he lived in a private, as opposed to a public, house.

The day of the funeral was not frosty, though it was bright and, in between momentary shocks of wind, quite warm for March. And the village church was situated in the best possible place. That is, as in all cosily traditional villages, just across the winding little road from the pub. Against the churchyard wall was the field gate that opened onto the bottom end of the old carriage drive up to Sevenscore. There was a bigger turnout than for Borja, James couldn't help noticing, but told himself not to dwell on that, and that in any case Borja had not been the landlord of the local pub.

Charlie drove up for the day from Croydon. He made it clear to James – perhaps insisting on the point a bit too much – that he would not be staying the night. But during the day he made sure to stick very close to James, and the two of them stuck very close to Nick. This led to a moment of comedy when Charlie and James muscled their way so assertively into the pew alongside him that Andy's father was temporarily bounced out at the other end, flailing like a penguin in the aisle for a second before climbing back.

James managed to make up for that little accident afterwards, as they were all walking through the graveyard and across the road towards the Rose and Castle. The sky was an unblemished blue and away to the north-west two aircraft trails had crossed, to create the Saltire in the sky. James quickened his pace a second till he was in reach of Andy's mother, walking a little way ahead. He clasped her hand from behind, and she turned to him in surprise. 'Look.' He pointed away to the left. 'In the sky. For your son Andrew. St Andrew's Cross.' Then he was surprised in his turn as she embraced him briefly in a fierce hug. He recognised himself in that hug as the proxy for her lost son. The prop of his parents' old age had been kicked from beneath them. James's imagination couldn't stretch to comprehending the grief of parents who'd lost an only child, even if the child were fifty-odd. A dead lover could, at least in theory, one day be replaced.

Later, after people had eaten and drunk something and conversation was beginning to flow more easily, people feeling free at last to talk of subjects other than the deceased, Charlie found a moment to tell James and Nick, 'I think I've got a TV company interested in my film of the Gatwick incident.' James noticed Charlie's care not to use the word crash.

'And the company are letting you do it?' Nick asked.

'No,' said Charlie, drawing himself up to his not very tall full height. 'I didn't ask them. They didn't confiscate the camera or what was on it, so it's still all mine, to do as I want with, as far as I'm concerned. If they kick up a stink afterwards – well, I'll handle the fallout then.'

'What Borja called the outfall,' James reminded the others. There were tight little smiles.

Charlie went on. 'But provided the programme shows the company and its pilots in a good light...'

'It'll have to show somebody in a bad light, though,' Nick said. 'The people who devised the altimeter-auto-throttle link perhaps.'

'Yes,' said Charlie, 'but whoever they are, I don't work for them.' He grinned impishly for a moment but then his face became serious again. 'Actually the people I'm concerned about aren't the company or anybody else. Just you two. Because … well, obviously Borja appears in the film, though mainly his right arm and the back of his head... And because...' He looked at Nick. 'It might be just as sensitive for you. If either of you have any objection or doubt about it then I won't go ahead.' He attempted a Russian accent. 'Simples.'

James and Nick looked at each other. 'I don't think I have a problem with it,' Nick said cautiously.

'Nor me,' said James, quite robustly now that Nick had spoken first.

'Well I'm glad we've got that out of the way then,' Nick said. He looked brightly at the other two in turn. 'So tell me then... Nobody's dared to bring the subject up with me this week... How are plans for Seville shaping up?'

NINETEEN

Alexa had spoken to Nick on the phone several times in the days after Andy's death. She'd asked if he would mind terribly if she and Mark didn't make the thousand mile journey to the funeral – the second one in six months. Repeatedly Nick had assured her that of course he would not. The projected trip to Seville was not mentioned during those phone calls, and neither was it when Alexa phoned James to ask if he thought Nick was really OK about her not showing up or if he was just saying so, and James told her that, yes, Nick really was OK about it and not just being polite.

But once Nick had unlocked the subject by bringing it up at the funeral wake, plans for Seville began quite quickly to come together. Strange how a project that no-one except Karsten had really thought was a good idea could snowball into one whose realisation was assuming great importance. A well-known phenomenon in business and politics, it now seemed to be happening with the Seville trip. James found himself in regular contact with Charlie and Karsten, discussing dates and arrangements, as well as with Alexa and Mark. The days that everyone was now pencilling into their diaries coincided, not entirely by accident, with the end of the Regent Theatre season and the end of James's job.

And yet, thought James, you had only to imagine taking the six people you liked best in the world and putting them all together for a long weekend to see the potential consequences: the opportunities for splits and breakages that would present themselves. Stir in the fact that those six people would certainly not all like one another as much as you liked them and you had the recipe – as Jean-Paul Sartre had argued – for hell on earth.

Arrangements somehow tumbled into place. Pippa would definitely be coming, she told Alexa, who told James. Her parents were back at home together now and their son had received enough tongue-lashings from his sister by this time to know that he was expected to keep an eye on them with frequent visits to their house. Pippa's workload had practically halved, now that she no longer worked at the Court of Human Rights, and when she told the other partners at her chambers that she would be absent for a few days in the middle of May nobody seemed to mind too much. Which took her somewhat aback. She asked Alexa to recommend a hotel in Seville and Alexa suggested the Hotel Simón, where her parents had stayed once. It had a splendid staircase, Alexa remembered, with mirrors descending on both sides of it, so that you could watch yourself from an infinity of angles as you walked grandly down.

James, Nick and Charlie, *the three boys* as Alexa had started to call them, were going to fly out together. They'd found a hotel on the internet, which stood near the Plaza de la Encarnación, at the other end of the grid of main shopping streets from the Hotel Simón. As for Karsten, Mark and Alexa had invited him to be their guest in their apartment on the Avenida Cruz del Campo. Alexa now had the task of imparting this news to Inés...

Inés returned from school in a worse frame of mind with every day that passed. Her lips would be firmly pressed together as if to avoid any possible greeting to her parents escaping them, in the event that either or both of them would be in. She would scutter up the stairs, firmly closing – not quite slamming – the door behind her. Even without an actual slam, the signal remained as unmistakeable as the closing of the oak by an Oxbridge undergrad: she was not available for conversation or other contact of any kind. She would then transport herself through one of the technological wormholes that were at the disposal of twenty-first century teenagers into a different reality from the earthbound one inhabited by her twentieth-century parents: the worlds of Twitter, Facebook and Whatsapp. They were worlds in which she felt herself at home and womb-safe, but around which her parents could only tiptoe apprehensively, fearful of every kind of danger that might assail their daughter within.

Inés would only emerge from her lair when it was time to eat with her parents, or dash out to meet friends: whichever was scheduled for the earlier hour. If she ate with her parents then it was rather as if a cat had joined them at the table. There might be a little purring but very little in the way of actual conversation. The encounter was purely functional; eating a biological necessity.

At least she ate now. She had gone through an anorexic phase a year or two ago. More recently though, and almost as worrying, was her habit of wallowing in long baths, excoriating every square inch of her skin with a pumice stone, as if attempting to remove that skin altogether. Her preferred option, it had seemed, was to grow one that was entirely new.

Sometimes Inés did speak to her parents without being provoked. On these occasions she spoke only in Spanish, in order to highlight the fact that, unlike them, she was Spanish through and through. Mark was only Spanish on his mother's side, while Alexa, despite having lived in Spain for over thirty years, was entirely English and not Spanish at all. That this latter fact made Inés only a quarter Spanish by blood – and thus less Spanish than her father – did not enter her calculations, and would not have weighed heavily even if it had. Mark actually spoke better Spanish than Inés – it was his mother-tongue, literally, which was not the case for Inés. But Inés spoke Spanish better than Alexa did, and had no qualms, when it suited her, about letting this be obvious.

Alexa chose a moment when she was alone in the kitchen with Inés to tell her about the reunion of friends that was going to take place in a few weeks, and to let her know that one of those friends would be staying with them for a few nights. Inés gave a nod to indicate that she'd heard at least, but made no comment. A couple of days later, though, Inés confronted her mother on the stairs. Inés was coming down, her mother coming up: that gave Inés the higher ground and the confidence to look directly down into Alexa's eyes. 'I'm thinking about your friends coming to stay,' she said. 'I don't want them here.'

'You needn't worry about *them*,' Alexa told her in English, refusing to argue with her daughter on the un-level playing field of Spanish. '*They* are not coming here. Only one person is. As I told you. My very old friend Karsten.'

'Well I don't want him. He's German. True? No? Everybody says the Germans are ruining our country. Making the economy go down so they can take over. They want to take over Europe.'

Alexa took a firm grip of the handrail. 'Even if that were true, you could not blame Karsten. You know very well he's lived all his life in Spain. He's about as Spanish as we all are.' She knew this would annoy her daughter and could see that it did. She didn't allow Inés time to explode but went straight on, 'And for most of that time he was a priest, living selflessly and in poverty in Gijón, a place where you wouldn't want to work even if they paid you a hundred thousand euros.'

Inés ignored that. 'A priest, yes, but he's stopped being a priest. True? That always means they interfered with young girls – or boys.'

'Inés, stop this. You know that in Karsten's case that isn't true.'

'How do I know?'

'Because I've told you. And I know because I know him very well. He was my boyfriend once. You knew that. If he'd had the slightest tendency in that direction – well, first, I'd have known about it and then he wouldn't have been my boyfriend for very long.' Alexa knew this was a feeble line of argument. She'd exaggerated the closeness of their relationship – they'd been friends rather than boyfriend and girlfriend. It had been a very long time ago and, anyway, how well did anyone really know anyone else? Karsten had astonished her a few weeks ago by declaring in an email, in very bald English, that he was currently having an affair with another man's wife. Perhaps if he'd written it in Spanish it would have sounded less startling and abrupt. She wasn't going to share this with Inés just now. But she wasn't surprised that Inés came back with,

'Ex-boyfriend. That was years ago. People do change.'

'In that case I suggest you ask him why he left the priesthood yourself.' Alexa was now holding the hand-rail on one side of her and the wall on the other, giving her daughter no opportunity to escape down the stairs unless she were physically to struggle past. 'You ask him whether he's interested in little boys or little girls. You'll have the opportunity to do that when he's here. You'll get an honest answer and a civil one. You can depend on that.'

'I don't want...'

'Inés,' her mother cut her off, speaking loudly now. 'He is coming to stay with us whether you like it or not. Look around you. Whose house are we living in? Who owns these stairs? This plaster, this wood?' She banged the flats of her hands on the materials as she named them. 'It isn't you just yet. So when he comes here you will please behave towards him in a civilised manner and keep your thoughts about not wanting him around the place to yourself. It's either that or going and staying somewhere else. Stay with friends. Or in a *pension*, perhaps, at your own expense.' Alexa had forgotten by now what she had been heading upstairs to go and do. 'I'm now going to prepare a meal for the three of us,' she said. 'When it's ready you're welcome to join your father and me – or not, if you prefer.' Abruptly Alexa turned away from her daughter and went back down the stairs towards the kitchen.

Alexa told Mark about this conversation later that evening. Inés had condescended to join them at the table, where she'd been a silent presence, and had then gone out. 'Are they all like that?' she asked her husband as she stacked the dishwasher and he scraped plates, 'or are we just unlucky with Inés? That's the trouble with having only the one. You can't make any comforting comparisons.'

'Even if you have more than one, you can't make comparisons until the second one comes along,' Mark said. 'By which time you've formed your judgement of the first, I would think.' His quiet reasonableness was one of the things Alexa loved him for. It could also be extremely irritating.

But as the time for the Seville reunion drew near, Inés seemed to become more accepting of the idea that her parents could invite whomever they wanted into their own house. Then she chose the moment, one morning, the moment when things are most pressured, when things are being got ready for school, and there is no need to keep an eye on the clock because its seconds are ticking away anyway in everybody's head, to say, 'They're all gay, no?'

'Who?' her mother asked, perplexed, not really caring, this precise second, to know who Inés was talking about.

'Your old friends who're coming here.'

'No, they're not. James is. Borja, his partner who died, was. You knew that. But Pippa isn't and Karsten

certainly isn't.' The memory of his extraordinary
announcement by email still fresh in her head, she was
more than ever certain of that. 'Nick, who used to do
some work for me, well, he is, of course. I told you his
boyfriend died a few weeks ago. Someone else is
coming, called Charlie. I met him at Borja's funeral last
year. I don't know if he is or isn't. Perhaps we can find
out when he arrives next month.'

'How shall we do that?' Inés asked in a challenging
tone of voice.

Why did she feel the need to use a challenging tone?
Alexa thought, biting back the impulse to put her
irritated thought into words. Even when the situation
involved no challenge from either side. 'Probably ask
him,' Alexa said instead, poker-faced.

'Oh you can't!' Inés's hand went to her mouth; Alexa
had shocked her for a second into being a little girl
again. But she quickly recovered, whipped the hand
away from her face and did her best to look sophisticated
once more. She said, more thoughtfully, 'Do any of them
have children?'

'Pippa does,' Alexa said. 'She has two but they're both
in their twenties.' She knew better than to say they were
both grown up. 'Not everyone embarks on kids as late as
Dad and I did.'

'But the others haven't embarked on children at all,'
Inés said, seizing on Alexa's English verb and using the
Spanish form of it.

'Well, you wouldn't expect Karsten to have kids. More
than twenty years a priest. And if he does have, he
shouldn't do.' Alexa twinkled a smile at her daughter.
The kind of smile they'd shared until a year or so ago.
She was delighted now to see that Inés half-twinkled
back. 'As for this Charlie character, who I was only
introduced to very briefly, that's another thing we won't

know until we meet him properly. That can be something for you to ask.'

Inés remained stubbornly attached to her previous thought. 'It's still quite a high proportion of people not procreating,' she said. 'Mustn't it seem like their lives are a bit of a dead end?'

'I wonder,' Alexa answered thoughtfully. 'If you hadn't come along, would our lives have seemed a dead end? I don't know. It's clearly not necessary for absolutely everyone to reproduce. Only that a reasonable number of people do. The human race goes on and those other people contribute to it in other ways.'

'Like...?'

'Well...' A reassuringly easy example came to Alexa's aid. 'Beethoven. Take Beethoven. He never had children. Nor did Schubert, or Chopin...'

'But Bach had enough to make up for all of them,' said Inés triumphantly.

'Exactly,' said her mother even more triumphantly. 'You've exactly made my point.' Then her glance strayed upward to the kitchen wall clock. She said, 'Inés! Oh my God!'

By mid-April it could have been said of James's tenure at the Regent Theatre that – as George V's doctor famously told the press when the king lay dying – its life was drawing peacefully to a close. There was one little ceremony to be performed first. Despite there being no real evidence that Shakespeare was born on St George's day the tradition was so widely accepted that it caused no controversy that the Regent chose to celebrate the dramatist's anniversary on April 23, just as it had done every year since 1884.

The celebration was simple, low-key and short. Fifteen minutes before the half-hour call at six fifty-five the company and staff – actors, electricians, usherettes and everybody else – assembled in the circle corridor, where in an alcove was displayed a bust of the familiar bearded head. For this one day only it was garlanded with a necklace of flowers, while a ritual glass of sherry was poured for everyone who stood crammed into the long, narrow, curved space.

James was careful about the choice of sherry. He regretted the dowdy image the wine had acquired in Britain during his lifetime and since arriving at the theatre had insisted each year on choosing the bottles himself. Often it was a bone-dry Tio Pepe, the colour of sun-bleached hay and with a tang of fresh yeast. This year it was a dark dry Oloroso, with a nose suggestive of raisins and toasted almonds and Christmas cake. As he poured from the bottles James would tell anyone who looked as though they might even half-listen to him that he had once done a morning's work for one of the sherry companies in Jerez. He never went on to say that he'd had a passionate affair with a young man who worked there full-time. Or that the young man, William, had been taken off him after eight months by his much older employer Paco. Paco Ybarra had actually done him a favour, James realised only now, as his predatory move on William had set James scurrying back to Borja, with whom he'd happily spent the following thirty years.

'It looks sweet, but it isn't,' James said as he filled Freddie's glass. Freddie had given the offering a suspicious initial frown. He didn't need to explain this to Nick, the only outsider present. Nick, whom James had made a special point of asking along, knew his ports and sherries as well as most other Old-World wines.

The front of house manager, already in his evening uniform of dinner jacket and bow-tie, now cleared his throat and asked for all glasses to be raised. 'Ladies and gentlemen,' he said, 'I give you Mr W. S.' Commendably brief.

'Mr W. S.' said the assembled group. The actors among the party said this pretty loudly, experimentally revving voices that would need full power in forty minutes' time. 'And now,' he half turned towards a small thin young man at his side, 'Mr Duncan Lloyd-Evans.'

Many of the company now cleared their own throats on Duncan's behalf. As the youngest member of the current acting company – he was playing Joey in In Praise of Love – it fell to him, as the tradition dictated every year, to deliver a Sonnet of his own choice. Every year found a new young woman or man shouldering the rather awesome responsibility of declaiming a favourite Sonnet in front of a company of older and more experienced actors.

Duncan was a wiry blond Welsh boy; his hair, which he'd allowed to grow into the style appropriate for Rattigan's 1973 setting, a mop. He looked nervous and very small as he stepped forward and the front of house manager stepped back, neatly exchanging places in the cramped space. But his voice was strong and authoritative as he announced, 'Sonnet number seventy-three.'

At that moment James and everybody else noticed that he carried no book or sheet of paper from which to read the text. Duncan, unlike most of his hundred and thirty predecessors, had chosen to memorise the piece. He looked very directly at his audience, opened his mouth, and James suddenly found himself listening to someone who looked and sounded a mere boy delivering Shakespeare's famous lines about growing old as if he'd just composed them himself.

'That time of year thou mayst in me behold
When yellow leaves, or none, or few, do hang
Upon those boughs which shake against the cold,
Bare ruin'd choirs, where late the sweet birds sang.

In me thou see'st the twilight of such day
As after sunset fadeth in the west;
Which by and by black night doth take away,
Death's second self, that seals up all in rest.
In me thou see'st the glowing of such fire,
That on the ashes of his youth doth lie,
As the death-bed whereon it must expire
Consum'd with that which it was nourished by.
This thou perceiv'st, which makes thy love more strong,
To love that well which thou must leave ere long.'

The applause was not just polite. James saw the actress playing Lydia brush with a quick finger at her eye. And then young Duncan startled everyone by stopping the clapping with an upraised hand. 'It's like a hologram, isn't it?' he said in an excited voice. 'Meanings in layer on layer. Bare ruined choirs the leafless winter trees … and the poet's no longer productive head, his hair receding or gone grey... And the monasteries, of course, emptied of their choir-monks and ruined when Shakespeare was a tiny kid...' He spoke in the adrenalin fuelled way of someone in the aftermath of pulling off a dangerous feat.

There was some shuffling among his standing hearers. It was nearly the half: time to down the last swallow of sherry and get to work. It was not part of the deal that the youngest member of the cast, having done his number, should detain everyone with his ideas about what Shakespeare meant. '...And that death and night are like comfort-bringing twins,' Duncan was going on, high on his own enthusiasm. 'The fire going out, choked by the ash of the fuel that has given it life... And if you love someone older than yourself you must bloody well love him a lot, because you know what's coming to you before long...' He stopped himself and suddenly looked sheepish. 'Sorry folks,' he said more quietly. 'I didn't mean to say all that. It just sort of tumbled out.'

The shuffling stopped and smiles broke out. 'Let's hear it for the Welsh,' said someone, and there was a bit of a cheer, then a lot of clapping and a crescendo of stamping feet. Re-emboldened by this, Duncan found he had one final announcement to make. 'I'm sorry the Regent has to close.' He reached for his untouched glass of Oloroso, which one of the stage crew had been holding for him in his spare hand. 'To the Regent,' he said, and drained the glass.

James looked across at Nick, and saw that he was looking intently at the young actor during that last second before the party broke up.

The group divided neatly. Actors and stage management went off towards the pass door on stage left, front of house staff trooped towards the foyer, stage right. James was left with Freddie and Nick, the only three people who had no work to go to just then. 'Circle bar?' he asked them, though it wasn't really a question. 'Grab a tray of empty glasses each?' There was some sherry left in the last bottle, James was pleased to notice. He grabbed that too.

As the three of them threaded corridors and stairways James thought about the sonnet and about Nick. He'd been relieved that, unlike most of his predecessors Duncan hadn't chosen Shall I compare thee to a summer's day – Borja's favourite and James's own, but now inextricably tied to Borja's heart attack and death. But Duncan's choice – even if he'd been thinking of the coming demise of the Regent, which was touching enough – must have affected Nick deeply, especially as Duncan had gone on to rub his nose in the idea of the love of a young man for an older one. James wondered what Nick was now thinking about. Perhaps simply concentrating on carrying a loaded tray round awkward corners on the stairs, but James doubted that. Nick had thrown in his lot with an older man, and must have known what to expect, even if he would hardly have expected it to happen so soon. Were Nick to start looking for a new partner one day, when he felt ready to, it came to James in a bleak flash of insight, he'd look for someone of his own age. He wouldn't want to travel the same road twice. He might even look for a younger one next time. Vividly James saw Nick as he'd seen him when he'd glanced at him a minute ago. In profile. Looking with great concentration at Duncan.

Nick had lost everything in losing Andy. James knew that, because in losing Borja James had lost everything too. Neither of them was a religious man. James wondered if being religious helped you in that situation. But he'd seen how religious people reacted in similar circumstances – most recently he'd seen Andy's parents at close quarters at the funeral of their son – and he strongly doubted it. A few days ago Nick had told him a story that his mother had told him. About an old aunt of hers, now long dead. Throughout her long widowhood Auntie Flossie had gone to church every Sunday with a pork chop wrapped in paper inside her handbag. This was in the hope that someone would invite her to eat a midday meal with them that day. But throughout all the years no-one ever did. Nick had rounded off the story by telling James, 'Got to be careful I don't turn into Auntie Flossie now. Now I'm on my own.' *Oh Nick,* James had wanted to say to him from his position of knowledge five months down the line, *darling Nick, little do you know how close you'll come to that, and how soon.* He hadn't said it, of course. He'd tweaked Nick's shoulder and given him a smile instead.

They reached the circle bar, that cosy womb-like space with its striped wallpaper and Victorian chandelier. *To love that well that thou must leave ere long.* James would be leaving this place for ever in a month's time.

There was another apposite quote from Shakespeare – Borja would have supplied it now if he'd been around. *The cloud-capp'd towers, the gorgeous palaces, the solemn temples, the great globe itself, Yea, all which it inherit, shall dissolve... Leave not a rack behind.*

For a few minutes they would have the bar to themselves, while Thomas the barman – seventy-six last birthday – clattered with ice-trays and soft-drink crates. James stacked the trays of empty sherry glasses under the counter, promising Thomas he'd wash them up himself when the curtain had gone up, at which both Freddie and Nick protested that of course they would help.

'Sherry OK still?' James said once he'd joined the others on the customer side again, and waving the half-full bottle in Freddie's face. Freddie grinned and said, could he have a beer please?, while Nick nodded and said that when the sherry was as good as this one he could stretch a point.

It made James happy that Freddie had taken a shine to him. This was the more gratifying for the fact that the good-looking young director of the next and final production wasn't gay. (James had gone to some trouble to check this out.) And because James, his career at its end, was unlikely to be of any use to the upwardly mobile Freddie in the future he could see no sign of a self-interested motive. It seemed that Freddie quite simply liked him.

'We're not doing a read-through,' Freddie had told him when he'd first arrived to start work, and they'd met over a Sunday evening drink in the Mail Coach, the stage-door pub. 'Everyone knows the story of The Dream, more or less. It'd take far too long, and everyone gets self-conscious about the way they read Shakespeare's verse. They've already had notice of the cuts I want to make. Save them wasting their time learning thickets of unused text.' He'd gone on to explain that, as the playwright had conveniently divided the play into five acts of two scenes each, it fitted very nicely with a five-day working week of mornings and afternoons. During the three and a bit weeks of rehearsal the whole thing could be worked through three times. Right now they were at the start of the third week. Technical and dress rehearsals would occupy next Monday and Tuesday; The Dream would open a week tonight. Back on that Sunday evening two weeks ago Freddie had said to James, 'Do you want to join me in rehearsals sometimes? Like I suggested when we first met?' He'd given him a rather sideways look. James hadn't wanted to sound too keen, or to muscle in on Freddie's big first day. He'd suggested turning up on the Tuesday instead. 'Great,' Freddie had said. 'Fairies in the forest all day. Act the Two-th.'

'And how's he shaping up?' James heard Nick asking Freddie, as though he'd been a party to James's digression of thought.

'Coming along a treat,' Freddie answered with a laugh.

'It's doing me good,' James said, though he didn't elaborate. Actually he was more than pleased with the way things were going, enjoying his new position sitting next to Freddie in rehearsals, with Freddie asking him his opinion of what the director and actors were creating between them moment by moment as they went along. By now, in the last full week of rehearsals, he had the feeling that if Freddie were off sick one day he would be able to hold the fort quite competently himself – till lunchtime anyway. But alongside that feeling he also had the more prosaic knowledge that it was the stage manager's job to do this if it came to it and that the present one, a young woman called Lizzie, would make a far better fist of it than James could, and with far less fuss.

'I worked backstage here,' Nick told Freddie. 'That's how James and I first met.' He recounted the story of how he and Borja, working a show together had been practising waltz steps behind the scenery, only to find themselves caught out by a scene change and suddenly in the audience's full view. Centre of attention in fact. James had been furious with both of them. But twenty years on, and especially now that one of the dancers was dead, the incident had become a treasured anecdote, frequently retold, and the occasion for fond and nostalgic laughter every time it was dragged out. Of course Freddie laughed fondly at it now. Those big jealous moments, those falls from professional grace, those grounds for sackings or divorce, how they too dissolved with time, left not a rack behind, when viewed from now, that place of relative safety from the past.

'You know,' said Nick, changing the subject suddenly, 'when Duncan was talking about that sonnet just now – that little bit of an outburst, which was actually very nice – he said 'he'.'

'He said...?' Freddie gave Nick a quizzical look, trying to make sense of this.

'He was talking about losing someone older than yourself. He said – if you love someone older than yourself you must bloody well love him a lot. Love him. Not her, not them.'

'He said that,' Freddie offered helpfully, 'because the sonnet was one of those dedicated to the young man of the sonnets, Mr W. H. So...'

'I know all that,' Nick said a bit abruptly, shaking Freddie's cold-water bath of fact off him almost physically, and turning to James instead. 'This Duncan guy. He gay, d'you know?' Three early arrivals for the show came into the room and Thomas bobbed up from under the counter, moving along to serve them, with a grunt.

'I don't know,' said James. 'Mary directed In Praise more or less *in camera*. I didn't get to sit in.' He gave Freddie a friendly nod, as if to make up for Nick's cold shoulder of a second before. 'And I've only been to the Mail Coach with the In Praise company about twice. His parents have been up to see the show – he introduced me to them – but I haven't seen any sign of a significant other of either sex.' He turned to Freddie again. 'Anything to add?'

'No idea at all. I've only spoken to him twice. I think he's lovely in In Praise, though. I'll use him myself one day when the right thing comes along.'

It was not surprising that Nick should be interested in Duncan, James thought, or that his imagination should be exercised by the discovery of him. Like James, Nick had had all his eggs in one basket. Now the basket had been kicked over, the eggs all dashed. 'It's like having a tooth pulled,' Nick had told him not long ago, in one of his moments of candour that were not as common as James might have liked. This had exactly coincided with James's feeling about his own experience of losing Borja. But by now he had come to feel the tooth analogy was on the small side. He had begun to imagine a massive uprooted tree. But when it came to similes of bereavement, it was each to his own, he thought.

As for hankering after a younger sapling to replant in the empty space, James had had more time to pursue that idea than had Nick. He'd spent many recent evenings at the Rose and Castle, each one ending with a hug outside the doorway and a perfunctory kiss. Then, as James drove off up the hill would come the urgent replay on his retina of Nick's face in enigmatic silhouette, and his ears glowing red, unknown to himself, back-lit by the light that streamed out of the door and the flood-lamp that lit the sign above. James was beginning to wonder, with a sinking, crushing feeling in the empty pit of himself, if he was moving in one seamless swoop from the pang of loss to the pain of unrequited love. He wanted to think, when spending time with his younger friend, that Nick needed his company and benefited from it more than from that of anybody else. But it was more than possible that this wasn't true, that it was the other way round: the case quite simply being that James needed Nick.

He heard Nick saying, 'I might be interested in Duncan, of course. He's certainly cute. But he's only, what, twenty-one? Twenty-two?' He gave James a look that James couldn't quite read. It might have been unconscious or it might have been meant as a warning shot. 'Anyway, there's no point thinking about someone that much younger than yourself.'

'All of us are in the dark' Alexa admitted to her husband. They were sitting on their plant-filled patio in the warm dusk. 'Parents with teenagers. Always have been. Though it seems worse today. The technology thing. Their brains are growing up differently from ours. Sometimes it seems there's no point of contact at all.'

Mark didn't answer that. At least not in words. He breathed in the scent of the plants around him that the sun had warmed and flavoured earlier in the day. His head moved slightly, which might have meant, 'I quite agree,' or else, 'I heard what you said and need to think before I reply,' or simply, 'I heard you.' You didn't always know with Mark until a very long time later. Sometimes years.

'The other thing,' said Alexa, 'which makes it more difficult, is that I never was a teenager. Other people's parents say, well, we were all like that ourselves once. But I never was. Being a classical musician, if that's what you're set on, you have to work at it in an adult way from the age of twelve or you never get there. For a piano-player the eye-hand-brain channels have to be carved out in the early teens otherwise it's way too late. Somehow I knew that, without knowing it. That's why I accepted a life of keyboard practice, hours every day, or auditions and scholarships – all that adult seriousness about an adult world that most kids don't have to confront until they're … well, adults themselves.'

Mark did reply at that point. 'I can't say I was much of a typical teenager either. Living half in Spain, half in the States...'

'You had a more normal existence than I did,' said his wife. 'Falling in love with Spain to the extent of dancing a whole night away during the Feria with a girl you were in love with but whose name you never asked... Fairly typical teenage boy, I'd say.'

'I'd forgotten you knew that story,' Mark said.

'Oh, it comes out every Feria. You probably don't remember.' Alexa fixed him with a roguish smile. 'It's always quite late on in the proceedings when you bring it up.'

Walking home from work the next day, Mark bumped into Inés in the Murillo Gardens. Their routes from their respective schools crossed at this point, but because of their different timetables they seldom actually met. Mark had last seen his daughter that morning, flouncing out of the kitchen, flinging her school-bag on her shoulder as she went. 'Dad, what are you doing here?' Inés asked. She was in the company of three school-friends.

He laughed at her and said, 'I'm walking home. Same as you are. Care to tag along?'

Inés almost said no, quite rudely. Mark could see the word forming in her face. He looked at the three friends, who knew him by sight at least, and saw them realise that he wanted a minute with his daughter alone. He was grateful to them now for promptly walking on ahead, giving Inés waves over their shoulders as they went.

The palm-shaded oases of the Jardines de Murillo were set about with stone benches of blue and yellow tile. Mark walked towards the nearest one. It was only three paces away, fortunately. He was aware that the fragile thread of intimacy he was spinning between his daughter and himself at that moment might have snapped had the distance been greater. Say five paces or even four. He said, 'Sit with me a moment,' and because Inés was caught off guard momentarily, and because her cohort of friends had vanished at the silent bidding of her father, and she couldn't think of any real alternative – were she to walk or run away her father would catch her up – she did.

'Your mother seems to think something's troubling you right now,' Mark said, staring ahead of him at the people and their pushchairs strolling the sandy walks. Without anything further in the way of a lead-up he said, 'I'm wondering if it's boy problems you've got.'

'It isn't a boy,' Inés announced with heat.

'No, I didn't think it was,' Mark said calmly. He didn't turn towards his daughter even now, but continued to gaze ahead of him. In the distance, along the far edge of the park, were tall columns with sculpted tops and beyond them the busy boulevard Melendez Pelayo, which later they would have to cross. 'No, to be honest, I wasn't really wondering that,' he said gently. There was silence between them for a second or two. When Mark broke it, it was to ask his daughter even more gently, 'Can you tell me her name? Or is that a secret too?'

TWENTY

They let Nick have his choice of seat. They were both conscious that he hadn't been in an aeroplane since his partner had been killed in one. James, whose partner hadn't died in an air crash, had flown to Madeira and back within the past few months, while Charlie, sensibly adopting the 'get back on your horse' principle, had been jetting around Europe ever since his own brush with disaster, right here at Gatwick. Nick chose the window seat. For whatever reason. They didn't ask.

James sat in the middle, between the two other men. He tried not to see portentous metaphors in that. But focusing instead on the moment at hand brought something else into unwelcome close-up. As they taxied at a jolly trotting pace towards the airfield's eastern edge James realised that their imminent right turn onto the runway would bring them in sight of the spot – James thought they might actually trundle right over it – where Borja's 737, sister plane of the one they now sat in, had finished its slide along the ground. He couldn't help looking out over Nick's shoulder when the moment came and the plane swung round onto the centre line of 26L, feeling his heart sink suddenly and, making some connection he couldn't explain, wondering for a moment whether the whole idea of revisiting Seville was not a ghastly mistake.

Expecting to see a great gash through grass and topsoil James saw instead that a winter-full of snow and rain, and the new spring growth of grass, had made the scar invisible. Nick, who had also been peering through the window, now turned back and looked at James. Clearly he had been having the same thought. He said, 'Hmmm,' without parting his lips, then they both looked interrogatively at Charlie. He was the only one of them who had actually been involved, sliding down an escape chute to land with a bump at almost this exact spot. But he had rolled over the spot on dozens of take-offs and landings in the intervening months. James and Nick saw that he was engrossed in the in-flight magazine: something he perhaps didn't have time to look at in the normal course of his work. It appeared that, for him, repeated revisits had damped the resonance of the place.

As they floated into the air some forty seconds later and James found himself half looking at clouds and fields and villages all beginning to tangle up, Sancho Panza came into his mind. Sancho would be looked after during the next few days by Stuart the gardener and his wife. They'd come in and feed and water him. But would Sancho be lonely at night? In Borja's lifetime, if they'd gone on holiday and left the cat in Stuart's charge, they'd never given a thought to that.

When he wasn't happy, Sancho's purr dimmed and died like Tinkerbell's light. It took a little time to rekindle it after that, but with caresses and soothing words – James likened it to blowing on the dull ashes of a fire – the purr would begin to spark up. So softly at first that you could hardly hear it, then little by little returning to full strength. Then it did wonders for the heart. Not only for James's but also, he suspected, for Sancho's too.

'Where's that?' Nick was pointing out to a stretch of the English south coast that looked like the edge of a jigsaw puzzle with alternate pieces missing. The question surprised James. He was used to sitting beside Borja on flights, and Borja always knew exactly where he was. Even above the featureless water of the Bay of Biscay or the Med he knew how far they'd got. James was almost startled by the realisation that he'd never before flown with Nick. Fortunately Borja had taught James well. 'Thorney Island, Hayling Island, Portsmouth Island and harbour,' he was able to tell Nick. 'The pointed bit is Bembridge Point: the beginning of the Isle of Wight.'

Nick was sitting so close to him that they were almost rubbing shoulders, their hands were just inches apart. And the same went for Charlie on the other side. Economy was the source of this intimate proximity. Charlie had got them seats from the airline he worked for at a preferential price, but he'd been unable to wangle a transfer to Business Class. Moving his head a fraction from side to side James stole a quick look at each of his two friends in turn. Their two heads were as close to him as if they'd been in bed. It wasn't who you went to bed with, James thought suddenly: it was who you woke up with in the morning that made the difference between being happy and not. He thought that he would be happy to find either of those two heads on the pillow beside him when he woke up. Morning after morning. For the rest of his life.

'Southampton,' Charlie announced authoritatively, without taking his nose out of his reading matter, not needing to glance towards the window to check as the plane banked steeply and took a very noticeable turn to the left. 'On the way to the sun, boys. Now heading south.'

Boys. Boyee... One of James's pet names for Borja in the past. There were other words left over from his time with Borja: vocabulary stranded high and dry now that the tide had gone out. Words like darling, baby, heartface, and the rest. Phrases like 'I love you', and private messages such as, 'Christmases and Birthdays', and 'Eskimos', now useless and redundant unless some other tide would re-float them one day. James wondered if Nick had the same thoughts. He couldn't possibly ask. Nor could he tell him of his discovery, ordinary and biological, hormonal and procreational in origin that it was, that those powerful magnetic waves that emanated from him and had anchored him to Borja for years and years were now being redirected, by some law of nature too powerful for him to do anything about, towards Nick. OK, and a little bit towards Charlie too. But Charlie had already raised a protective shield against them on Madeira, at the airport there, by warning him not to expect too much. As for Nick, there was no reason to suppose that his emotional energies, no longer able to home in on Andy, would be redirected towards James. No reason to suppose that James would be drawn into the vacuum in Nick's life in the way that Nick – or the idea of Nick – was getting sucked into the empty space in James.

Brittany, the plunging Biscay swells, the Cantabrian coast. Passing Madrid. At last descending from some point above the Sierra Morena, and watching Andalucía take shape. They crossed the winding course of the Guadalquivir, its bridges and eucalyptus groves, under the high hot sun of the southern afternoon. It looked ideal, as most rural landscapes do from five thousand feet. Then they bumped gently onto the tarmac, whose reflected light made them screw their eyes up when, a few minutes later, they climbed out and down the steps into the May heat.

Pippa hadn't noticed the mirrors on her way up to her room in the Hotel Simón, she had taken the lift. But, re-emerging after a short rest and a tidy-up, she was enticed by the sight of the elegant staircase. She walked down it, feeling absurdly as though she was in a forties film. She glanced at her reflections to left and right – in front of her as she turned the angles – though she tried not to do so too obviously, just in case someone (Celia Johnson, perhaps?) should be looking up at her from the lobby. She hadn't scrutinised herself in a mirror like this for years, having eschewed vanity quite deliberately when she'd taken up the sacerdotal calling of human rights law. She didn't even scrutinise her performances on TV. She took advantage of the rare moments when she happened to catch sight of herself by chance to leave the room and do something more productive, even if it was only to pour herself a glass of mineral water. After all, she always knew what her on-screen image was going to say. Examining that image now on the stairs she experienced a momentary feeling of disquiet, though she couldn't pinpoint its cause. Anyway, the moment passed and she forgot about it as soon as she emerged into the sun-washed street.

They had arranged to meet, the seven of them, for a drink at eight o'clock and to go on for dinner after that. At least Karsten had arranged it. So Spanish of him, Pippa thought. Like Mark and Alexa he'd lived most of his life in Spain. Pippa had not lived here since the age of twenty-one and now found herself in the position of most northern Europeans who visit Spanish friends. What did you do with yourself during that period of early evening which was going-home time, and feeding-yourself time according to your body-clock, but a time during which most Spanish people were still at work?

The answer was simple and obvious, and not at all unpleasant. Pippa would take a walk among the streets. They were streets she knew, or at least remembered, even if not always correctly. Like the long buried streets of civilisations from the past, her memories had got cracked and fragmented by the weight of what had been laid down since and piled on top. Twisted out of shape and nudged out of position. Sometimes the buildings told her where she was. More often, simply the names of the streets.

She turned right, up Calle Vinuesa, away from the river, towards the cathedral. She passed a bar she remembered, or thought she did. Casa Morales was its name. Then the cathedral filled the view in front of her, monumentally unchanged. But the busy street that crossed in front of it, the Avenida de la Constitución was shockingly empty now of all but pedestrians and silver-grey trams. As she walked, disconcerting dislocations were, one after another, followed by reassuring, recognizable things. There was the tourist office where Borja had worked, its huge plate-glass window so familiar that you imagined you could cup your hands against it, peer in and see him still at his desk after all these years. She stood by the Moors' keyhole arch in the cathedral wall that was the Gate of Pardon, and peered in at the orange trees, in scented blossom now, that filled the patio within. Then she crossed the road and took an alleyway that led away behind the line of tourist cafés, because she remembered its name. Argote de Molina. It was the start of the labyrinth-like route that led to what had once been home.

She didn't remember it at all. Hotels sparkled in buildings that had once been grim *hostales* and *pensiones*. Yellow and white paintwork brightened the cracked rubble walls she remembered and that, back then, hadn't been rendered or whitewashed in years. But she followed the street names that woke echoes in her head. Corral del Rey, Almirante Hoyos. Then Virgenes, Aguilas (Eagles), Plaza de Pilatos, and San Esteban. Even here on her one-time doorstep Pippa was surprised to find smart cafés, with tables set out on the pavement outside, in an area she remembered as verging on the condition of a slum.

She stepped quickly into the alleyway called Virgen de la Luz before she had time to hesitate and change her mind. The alley branched into yet narrower culs de sac. Pippa pushed on, into what was now effectively other people's front yards, with washing stretched across, three floors above. And then she was looking at the building in which she'd fallen in love, and then lived, with Mark. Looking high up she saw that there was glass in the kitchen and bathroom windows now, where only iron bars had been before. But the building and its neighbours still wore a decrepit, unwashed look.

Pippa felt that she was walking through a stage set, where the walls might prove to be made of canvas and wood, and would wobble if touched. An important piece of her past was here – absorbed into the walls as if into blotting-paper. And yet it was gossamer-fragile. Your past had really happened, yes, really. And yet when you were confronted by the frame and setting of it you had to think, yes, it happened: but only just.

She touched the walls, and the paintwork of the old front door, with wondering fingers. Was she touching the same molecules of paint and stone? No, they would have worn off with time. They shed themselves every few years... No, that was the cells of the human skin. Pippa was getting things mixed up. How long had Mark gone on living here? she wondered. Had he lived here with Alexa? She expected that someone would come out at any moment and ask her what she was doing, fingering the dark paintwork of their front door. Old dark windows with small and grimy panes gave no clue as to what lay behind them now. The door into that past was closed. Pippa turned and walked swiftly away, back into the sunlight and Calle San Esteban, where people sat, sipping coffee under sunshades in the late afternoon. She didn't dare look back.

Inés behaved very graciously towards Karsten when he arrived from the airport with her parents, who had gone to meet him with the car. She asked him if he'd had a good flight. He answered that he'd had two good flights. Plus a good long underground journey between them – there was a big distance between the two terminals at

Barajas airport, Madrid, where he'd changed, after flying out from Düsseldorf, onto an internal flight. Inés did not go on to interrogate him as to whether he preferred little boys to little girls. She made coffee for him and for her parents instead. She didn't stay to drink the coffee with them, though. She was going out; she would be staying the next few nights at her friend's house. The name of her friend was Conchita, both her parents now knew.

Parking in the historic centre of Seville was a nightmare; that was something that hadn't changed; it had been a nightmare thirty years ago. So to keep their appointment with the others they took the tram, up and running for just a few years. Its outer terminus was a short walk from Mark and Alexa's house, its stop by the Archive of the Indies just five minutes from the Bodegón Torre del Oro where they'd arranged to meet. It was a brief tram ride but a bright one. Past the vast baroque tobacco factory that had been the setting of Carmen, past the flowery gardens of the Hotel Alfonso XIII, and then the blazing blue plumes of the jacaranda trees that filled the sky and dazed the eye around the Puerto de Jerez. Alexa leaned across to Karsten just as they were standing up for their stop. 'This woman of yours,' she said close to his ear. 'The married one...'

The Bodegón wasn't the same. Karsten had warned James about this. He'd had his surprise there back in the autumn, watching Pippa on TV through the window of his old flat – before death on a bicycle had summoned him into the street. They had agreed to meet there for the simple practical reason that they all knew where it was and couldn't get lost.

There was nothing to disappoint Charlie or Nick, though. Nick had been to Seville but didn't know the Bodegón, while Charlie, except for forty-minute turnarounds at the airport, had never been to Seville at all. James had led them from their hotel along Calle Sierpes – Serpent Street – then past the flat on the corner of the Plaza del Salvador that he had shared with Borja for two years. The town hall – richly ornamented baroque, carved out of golden stone – and the gigantic mass of darker stone that was the cathedral then flanked their way along the Avenida de la Constitución. They turned into Calle Santander and soon found themselves outside the Bodegón's familiar long frontage, where James pulled open an unfamiliar new door. And there they were.

Except they weren't. James was disoriented not only by the different interior space in which he found himself but by the oddness, the uniqueness of the moment. People from his present life coming face with the geography of his past. Borja's past. He had to remember that. This reunion was not about him, or even about Borja and him, but about Borja simply. In this spot... Now all of James's thoughts came swarming like fishes around that idea. Standing exactly here – he thought – he had thrown himself on the mercy of Mark and Pippa when he had nowhere to live after William had gone off with Paco, and had been granted the mercy of the sofa in their flat in Virgen de la Luz. Pippa, arriving moments after Mark had made his kind offer, had been presented with a *fait accompli*. James would be meeting her again in a few minutes. He wondered if she still resented the fact that he'd been underfoot, in their flat, at the time of their breakup.

In this spot he and Borja had been reconciled a few weeks later. Borja had taken him in his arms – the first time he'd done such an audacious thing in a public place – in Catholic, only just post-Franco, Spain in 1978... He had cried – James had cried, that is – and Borja had said simply, 'Let's go home.' In this spot...

Yet where was this spot exactly? The Bodegón's interior was only half its old size. It was as if Doctor Who's Tardis had gone wrong: it looked huge on the outside but was greatly diminished within. The bar was on the left now, where white-clothed tables laid for tourist groups had once been. The pillared space where the old bar had been, that cavernous space where mounted bulls' heads had glowered down from the vaults above, and the bar counter had seemed a half mile long, had vanished behind a wall. The past, his and Borja's past, had been closed off for ever by a barrier that was immoveable. More fixed and more eternal, actually, than any wall.

'We followed you down the street,' a voice said in English. Mark's voice. The three men turned back towards the door. 'We called to you but you didn't hear.' Alexa followed Mark in; she was wearing what struck James as an uncharacteristically nervous smile. Karsten entered third. The expression on his face suggested that he was ready to apologise for the altered state of the place he'd summoned them to. As if it was all his fault. This, and all the other changes wrought by time in the previous thirty years.

In this spot... Karsten remembered that he had stood talking to Mark late at night, both of them getting quite drunk, on the night that Mark and Pippa had broken off their engagement and then within the hour, Borja and James had staged their reconciliation. They had left for home, in the building opposite, which had also been Karsten's home at the time. The particularity of that moment had precluded Karsten's returning there for a little while. He'd stayed talking to Mark – and found he was talking to someone who needed his company just then. That had strengthened his resolve, just a few days old at the time, to become a priest.

James was asking what everyone wanted to drink, and relaying the orders to a waiter who had stepped forward from behind the bar. And then the door opened again and Pippa was with them. Seeing her in the flesh, rather than on TV, James was struck by the thought that Pippa, when she was twenty, had been beautiful.

They took taxis to the place where Mark had decided they would eat: the bar Las Dueñas. Coincidentally the three English boys had discovered it in the afternoon. It was just around the corner from their hotel. It was the kind of ordinary bar-restaurant where Sevillanos rather than tourists ordinarily ate – at Sevillian rather than tourist times. Which meant quite late. The staff pushed small tables together to accommodate the seven of them, just as would have happened at the Bodegón in the old days. The menu was chalked on boards high on the wall. All kinds of crisp-fried fish, bread-crumbed prawns, bull's tail, pork and chick-pea stew...

Threads of conversation became tangled up. You heard interesting bits from time to time that were not meant for you. James heard Pippa say to Karsten, 'Of course, the Bodegón was where I first met Mark,' but he missed the next words because Mark was talking to him about something else. Then Alexa was saying to Charlie, 'I've never played electric guitar. Well, picked it up and tried it, I suppose, like pot and cigarettes, but never actually...' Karsten again. 'One morning, as we were approaching the Spanish coast, an egret arrived and circled the ship. Although we were still way out of sight of land. It was like Noah's dove, but three times the size. Another day it was a humming-bird moth, that buzzed around the passengers' faces as they sat on deck...'

A little later Alexa was talking to Charlie again, though more quietly. 'This thing about Nick. What makes you think...?' But her words, intriguing though they were to James – not to say slightly worrying – were drowned out by the noise and energy of Karsten's rising to his feet, scraping back his chair and calling out quite loudly, 'Eduardo!' Everyone turned and looked at three people who had just come in and were settling themselves at a table nearby. A wealthy-looking couple in middle age and an older man with silver hair. They were familiar to nobody – except to Karsten, it appeared. But James's heart gave a funny knocking movement as he recognised the older man. James had taught him English. In return he'd taken William away from him. The man's name was Paco.

TWENTY-ONE

They sat outdoors, breakfasting on coffee in glasses that were finger-burningly hot, and man-sized plates of *churros* – sausage-shaped pieces of sweet batter, fried to a crisp in olive oil and feather light. A little way away a single stall was set up. Behind it sat a woman in red slippers and grey woollen tights, a short black coat, and a dress that was grey but spotted with pink roses all over it. Her face displayed a darker weather-tan and more wrinkles than you would have thought achievable in a single lifetime. Another woman stood in front of her, keeping up an apparently endless monologue, though the distance and the bustle of the square made her words inaudible to the three breakfasting men. The sitting woman was holding a stick, which she repeatedly waved in the other's face, and looked ready to strike her with it. Meanwhile, beside the stall an old man stood imperturbably tying twigs of bay-leaves into bundles. Selling these, it appeared, was the main business of the day.

'You handled your reunion with Paco very well, I thought,' said Nick to James. 'And he seemed OK, really. I mean you didn't show any awkwardness on either side.'

'Well,' said James, and took a sip of coffee while he marshalled his thoughts. 'The thing is, I'd realised only recently that I bore him no ill-will. When William left me for Paco... OK, I was hurt. But it was my vanity that got hurt, not my heart. Didn't know that at the time. Now I do.' He gave Nick, and then Charlie, a mischievous look. 'Funny, that.' He looked down at his coffee and the plateful of *churros*, which seemed to heave slightly as he looked. He went on, 'I didn't love William, actually. I thought I did. It was just that he looked like me, and spoke like me, and we could talk about things in – if you like – an English sort of way. It made a change from Borja, I suppose. A change from someone so Spanish.'

'You met William again,' Nick reminded him.

'What *is* that woman doing with the stick?' Charlie asked absently, looking across the corner of the square.

'Here in Seville,' James answered Nick. 'And quite by chance. It was just after I met you actually, and I came over for the first meeting of Alexa's memorial trust for Eulogio. But twelve years had passed and we no longer looked or sounded alike. We had a friendly enough chat – I think we both knew it would be the last – and realised then that we had little in common and had never been in love. But it was a shock to learn he's dead.' James looked at the faces of the other two and decided he could risk the following. 'He did have a very beautiful cock.'

'Well, if he looked like you, of course he did,' said Charlie.

Last night they had slept in three separate bedrooms, one in each. Charlie's jokey remark hinted at the fact that he'd had sex with James. Who now wondered if Charlie had told Nick that already, or was deliberately letting him in on that secret now. James thought back to the days after Borja died, and the trip to Madeira. It all seemed a long time ago.

Now Nick said, in reply to Charlie, 'I don't think I'll add anything to that.'

James chose to raise the tone of the discussion a notch. 'With Borja – we weren't obviously alike. Not in looks, not in temperament. Though we both had a thing about Shakespeare of course. But we had things in common. At a very deep level we were so much alike that we were one person, not two.

'What things, exactly?' Charlie asked. 'Especially, I mean.'

'I don't know how to explain it,' James said, not looking at either of the others. 'We had things in common that lay so deep within us – perhaps every couple discovers this – that there are no words to express them. Not in English or Spanish at any rate. Perhaps not in any language. Deeper than being gay or straight. I used to think that was the deepest thing you could have in common with anyone. But I was wrong. It's inseparable from who we are, I do admit, but only in the way that blue or brown eyes are. Other things go deeper and unite us more strongly than that. Love is one of them. Other things too, though, but no-one's found names for them yet.'

Nick and Charlie exchanged a glance that James did not see. He was staring at the gypsy woman, if that was what she was, who was now standing up and beating the stick on the table in front of her. The other woman had revealed herself as a customer, plain and simple, if an exceptionally talkative one, and had gone away with a big plastic bag stuffed with some sort of green leaves. The man continued impassively to tie up bundles of bay twigs.

They finished their breakfast. *Churros* were a good hangover cure, James remembered. Of the kill or cure variety though. For the moment his stomach was still undecided as to which it was to be. They walked the few metres to the bay-twig stall, curious about what other produce might be on display. Quickly they realised that the main attraction was a box of writhing live snails. They were dainty translucent creatures, with long big-pupilled horns. Their small shells were striped black and white like mint humbugs. What the old woman was doing with the stick was sweeping back into the box those intrepid wanderers who had climbed up the inside of it and made it as far as the rim. She had not been banging it irately on the table after all, nor using it to defend herself against argumentative passers-by. As usual, things were not what they first seemed.

Also for sale were herbs of many kinds, and some sort of spinach. As well as a box of leafy vegetables that none of them recognised. They looked like dandelion plants of which snails had eaten the better part, leaving only the centre rib of each leaf. Though again, probably, things were not what you first thought.

The stall stood right outside the bar Alcázares, in which they had spent the final stage of the previous night. All ten of them: the seven friends of Borja, plus Paco and Eduardo and his wife. The three Englishmen had drunk too much, though Karsten had come quite close to matching them by the time Mark and Alexa took him home with them in a taxi. They took Pippa too: her hotel lay approximately along their route. Eduardo's party had departed a little earlier, arranging to meet the foreign contingent again in a couple of days' time. James, Charlie and Nick had gone on drinking till the small hours, until they could see one another's faces slipping out of focus and assuming strange shapes, and expressions that you could no longer read through the alcoholic mists, or even trust. It was a measure of a good friendship, James thought now, as he struggled for mastery of the *churros* he'd just consumed, that even in those disturbing circumstances, you remained good friends, and did not start to argue or fight.

Another thing that was not what it had first seemed was the story of Karsten's affair with a married woman. There had been an element of Chinese whispers about that, clearly, or something had got lost in translation. What had actually happened, they'd learnt last night, was that he'd had a brief fling, or a one-afternoon stand – Karsten's English was, forgivably, not as nuanced as that

– with the divorced mother of one of his guitar pupils. Though even that, now James examined the matter in the morning's sober though brilliant light, was startling enough, given that Karsten was Karsten, and until a mere eight months previously a celibate priest.

James shot a sideways look at Nick who was still staring as though hypnotised at the snails, clambering, tumbling, and squirming in a heap at the bottom of the box. Nick looked pretty dreadful this morning, James had to admit. The skin of his face was red and tightly drawn, his eyes had gone small. Yet he was still beautiful. For against this image of one morning, of one moment of one morning, weighed the balance of twenty years of images of Nick that had been projected onto James's retina and which were now stored as a sort of composite or montage in his brain. James hoped desperately that the same process was at work when Nick, these days, looked at the older James. Because when he'd looked at himself in his bathroom mirror an hour ago, he had by no means rejoiced at the sight.

They had agreed quite early during the previous evening that they would not spend the coming days trailing around Seville in a phalanx. They would do different things, in twos or threes, or independently, as the mood took them. But today, at any rate, they would meet for lunch, and then again for dinner. This morning, James was going to play tour guide to Nick and Charlie. And the three Englishmen each told themselves privately, without sharing the thought with the others, that today they would not get so drunk.

But although he knew the street plan like the back of his hand James realised that he no longer knew Seville. The place had escaped him somehow; he'd held it for thirty years on too loose a rein. People who had worked in shops when James was young here would now be dead, or retired at the very least. The streets were filled, like the streets of every city now, with youngsters who walked and talked with mobile phones. A moment of depression came at him like a wave and winded him as they walked once more through the Plaza del Salvador. New technologies, he decided in a sudden fit of irritation, made life flat. The computer and the mobile phone. Facebook. Twitter. The internet. There was no narrative any more. No crescendo, no diminuendo. No beginning, no middle, no end. All was a never-ending state of page one. Though there was the small print, which no-one read, or perhaps no longer could. Together, the flatness and the small print would entangle thought, stamp on what we'd thought was thought since the time of the Ancient Greeks. Even his two companions had, during the morning, occasionally taken out their phones and, absently almost, composed or received a short text. To or from God knew whom.

With a wave of a hand James indicated again the flat that had once been his. He'd told the story of the place yesterday when they'd first walked past. There was no need to go through it again. In this spot, where the Plaza del Salvador joined the Plaza de San Francisco, Borja had had the last of his youthful visions of death. Minutes later James took refuge from his moment of disquiet by showing his protégés into the place that must have changed less than any other building in Seville. The cathedral which, the biggest church in Spain and arguably in Europe, had hosted the wedding of the King of Spain's son since James had last set foot inside it. Yet it had changed in one way, which itself reflected the spirit of the new times. You now had to pay to go in.

As usual it was only after you'd returned to the sunshine outside that you had a fully rounded sense of the building's internal space, its dark vastness. On leaving the building behind James did what he'd done with other visitors in the past and took his friends into the tight alleys of the Barrio Santa Cruz. This old quarter, in the middle ages the Jewish part of town, worked as a good antidote to the cathedral's unyielding vaults of stone. Like coming out of a cold store into the warmth and light of day. You went through an archway in an ancient wall (how often you did this in Seville!) and the bustle of the big streets was behind you and spirited away. You were in an area of small quiet squares, lemon meringue coloured paintwork, miniature fountains and cascading flowers.

Or so it had used to be. By now a huge number of tourists had emulated the wide-eyed youthful James in discovering this gem of a place for themselves. There were crocodiles of them winding through the alleys, led by guides with parasols held aloft. There were shops selling an inexhaustible supply of blue, white and yellow glazed earthenware. These shops had popped up everywhere, in every corner. One was housed in a building that James remembered had been a private garage with a remotely controlled door. Everyone sitting outside the Casa Roman had had to get up and move their wooden tables and stools when its owner had driven his impractically large car around the tight corner of the Sacerdotes Venerables, poop-pooping like Mr Toad. James remembered that happening at least twice when he'd been sitting there with William, then was cross with himself for remembering that. It was memories of Borja they were celebrating today. But things never did go to plan. As a result of running into Paco the night before, memories of William were surfacing with indecent frequency and haste. Paco had certainly not been part of the plan. Indeed, had James been asked to compile a list of the people he'd hope not to bump into in Seville, Paco would probably have come near the top.

In the days after Borja's death Karsten had told James about Eduardo, the brother of the dying girl to whom he'd given the sacrament as she died. He didn't think he'd mentioned a gay uncle, and certainly not by name. The connection with Paco was an extraordinary fluke. But last night Karsten had gone on, rather tediously and drunkenly, about owing Paco money. It was clearly something that Paco didn't want to hear; he'd looked embarrassed every time Karsten had introduced the subject, and tried to wave it away. James was glad now that they'd arranged to meet the others at the end of the morning in a place that had no associations with William or Paco.

The Gitanilla, the azulejo-tiled gipsy bar, was the bar James had taken Borja to on his first night in Seville. James had waited in the street outside the tourist office for Borja to escape from his job interview within, then whisked him here through the quaint labyrinth of Santa Cruz. For though he was Spanish, Borja did not know Seville, and James had good reasons for wanting to impress him. 'I told him there was this little bar I knew, and he came along like a lamb. He had his overnight things in his old school sports-bag, which he wore slung over his shoulder. We spent the early evening here.' He pointed. 'Sitting there. Well, quite a lot of the evening actually. And the rest...' He tried to find an original end to the sentence but failed. 'The rest is history, as you all know.' He shrugged his shoulders, perhaps to indicate the full stop.

Karsten pointed to the deep and broad tiled windowsill on which he had used to sit playing, entertaining the customers, then collecting their coins on the back of his instrument. On one occasion Borja had sat on the windowsill beside him as he played, so that the audience half expected him to burst into *cante jondo,* flamenco song. Being a northerner from Castile, he naturally did not.

Karsten looked at Alexa. He had another memory he wanted to share, even if the others might think it ungallant of him to do so in the presence of the married Alexa and Mark. He hesitated for a second, reflected that the two of them had been married for a very long time, and then plunged in.

'At that table Alexa came and sat, the first time we met.' Karsten pointed the table out, just as James had done a few minutes before, although it was a different table, in a different part of the small room. 'I was playing. It was a Handel sonata, I think.'

Alexa shook her long hair and smiled, then corrected him. 'It was Scarlatti. Believe me. I do remember that.'

'All right,' Karsten conceded with a small smile of his own. 'It was Scarlatti then.'

'But is it the same table?' Pippa came in, her experience in Virgen de la Luz fresh in her mind from the day before. 'Is it the same chair? And even if it is the same, then it isn't the same exactly. Molecules have rubbed off the surfaces of things. Coats of varnish, of polish, layered on top...'

'I doubt the last bit,' Nick interrupted unexpectedly. 'From the look of them, and speaking as a pub landlord myself, I wouldn't think the furniture's been polished, let alone re-varnished, since Karsten and Alexa met.' Which made the others laugh, and caused James involuntarily to rumple Nick's hair, an action which James regretted at once. He'd been trying to keep his proprietorial feelings towards Nick under wraps.

Karsten wasn't ready to let go of the molecules just yet. 'The molecules are a detail, Pippa,' he said. 'If it's the same table it's the same table. The same substance. The same thing.'

'You were a priest too long,' Pippa told him. 'It's the Thomas Aquinas thing coming back to you. Trans-substantiation and all that.'

Karsten returned the shot sharply. 'I've put all that behind me. As this morning I told you...'

Mark faded their argument out. All morning Pippa and Karsten had been sparring together, sparking off each other like hammer and flint. They had walked through the María Luisa Park, the four of them, but those two had taken little notice of the beauty of the place, its pavilions, its palm trees, its sandy walks and spreads of green where white pigeons billed and cooed. They preferred, apparently, the business of scoring points off each other. Well, that was fine, Mark thought, if it was something they both enjoyed, but it wasn't his style at all. It was something he never did with Alexa and never had. He thought that if they had gone on like that their marriage would not have survived.

He looked again at Pippa. Had he passed her anonymously in the street he might not have guessed that this was the person who, when she was twenty, he had taken to bed with him in that romantically ramshackle flat in Virgen de la Luz. He hadn't been near the place for years. He wondered for a second what it might look like now, and who lived there. Then he refocused on the argument Pippa was having with Karsten. He heard Karsten say, 'You're just a romantic. You take your emotional baggage about socialism with you into mid-life because you don't want to grow up. In love with your youth...'

And Pippa, coming back with, 'That's the pot calling the kettle black. Just look at you with your guitar. Like a superannuated hippy...'

Mark felt himself shiver involuntarily. A thought came into his normally fastidiously chivalrous head. He decided that he had had a lucky escape.

TWENTY-TWO

The *pueblo* of Osuna lies some sixty miles east of
Seville. Like a North African town it first presents itself
to the traveller as a huddle of white houses coming into
sight across a rolling sea of unpeopled land. It is little
visited by tourists. Or perhaps, as an older generation of
guidebooks might have said, is visited by tourists of the
more discerning kind. The discerning party of Borja's
friends had decided to make a trip out to Osuna the
object of their second full day together.

They had agreed in advance to spend one day away
from the city centre of Seville, and over dinner on their
second evening discussed possible destinations. They
thought of Córdoba, where both Karsten and Alexa had
at different times studied the guitar. But Borja had no
particular connection with the place, and so the idea was
dropped. Granada was also mooted, but it was a long
way to travel to and get back from in a day. Borja had
loved the place, it was true, and had lived there for a
time with an aunt before moving to Seville and James.
But Borja and James together had a less happy
association with the place, which Karsten, Pippa and
Alexa didn't need reminding about. Borja had had to go
there to secure the release of James and William from
the police station after they had been apprehended
climbing a crane and trying to break into the Alhambra
late at night. It was not a comfortable memory for James,
and so Granada was also quietly dropped – to the
disappointment of Charlie, the one member of the group
who had never been there.

But Osuna was new and neutral territory for all of
them. Mark alone among them had visited the place
once, as a boy, and his recollections were positive – if

vague. That the place had no Borja connections seemed suddenly to present no obstacle. They had decided to go.

Mark and Alexa took Pippa and James in their car. Karsten shepherded the two younger Englishmen towards the station and they went by train. Approached by the twin spider-threads of the railway line, Osuna looked as isolated as an outpost of humankind set up on the moon. Or as Bethlehem might have appeared, two thousand years ago, to three wiser men than Karsten, Charlie and Nick. As the train drew near to the station there was nothing to be seen from its windows to indicate developments more recent than that time. A half kilometre of wasteland lay between them and the scruffy white wall that encircled the town. You could imagine that great doors in it would be shut when darkness fell, to keep marauding wolves out of the streets. Beyond the wall cinnamon coloured roofs made patterns with white walls as the town climbed towards the summit of a hill that was crowned with a couple of elaborate church belfries and what looked like a small castle or fort. Elsewhere a few tall towers were topped with the nests of storks, around which their owners, also brilliant white, flew stately laps.

They got off the train, but nobody else did, and then, staring along the straight and empty lane that led to the wall of the closed-in town, experienced the sinking feeling common to those who find themselves arrived at an unfamiliar and potentially hostile place. The train pulled out of the station, dwindled to a speck, and left them stranded – or so it felt – in one of the less welcoming, more frightening, centuries of the middle ages. Without speaking the three men began to walk up the gentle slope that led towards the town.

But once they reached the gate their mood lightened. Instead of the medieval slum that each was fearing – wild dogs scavenging?, ragged shoe-less children throwing stones? – they found themselves in an elegant enclave of the enlightenment, where the streets were well-maintained and lined with seventeenth-century mansions that were clean whitewashed except for their carved honey-coloured mullions and corner-stones. Twenty-first century signposts pointed towards the tourist office and the town's more up-market restaurants and hotels. They found their way up into the Plaza Mayor as arranged and there, with impeccable timing, happened upon Mark inching his car to and fro under the orange trees, shoe-horning it into a space that was, in theory at least, too small for it, while the other three stood on the pavement gesticulating and telling him how to do it.

By the time the manoeuvre was accomplished the five men were unanimous, whatever the wishes of the two women might be, in carrying the proposal that it was time for a beer.

'Café Tetuan,' said Mark authoritatively, taking the lead for the first time, and pointing along Calle Carrera.

He must have been looking on the internet, Pippa thought. He surely couldn't remember it from when he was a child. Pippa's mind went back to the way he had whisked her off on a tour of Seville during her first weekend there. He had seemed decisive and masterful then, but those qualities had faded in a steady diminuendo as their relationship had progressed. Pippa wondered suddenly whether some of that might have been her fault. To what extent were people responsible for what happened to the other people they came in contact with through life? For people whose rough corners they knocked off, or whose paintwork they scratched, like cars manoeuvring in the tight confines of a town square?

The men got their beer at last. Then they lunched on tapas: there was *cazuela* of pork intestine, tuna with olives and lettuce and Marie Rose sauce, slices of omelette and a dozen other things to try. Fino sherry to drink, and a view down Calle San Pedro with its elegant renaissance *palacios.*

During lunch James noticed that Nick and Charlie were busy once again with their phones, sending texts to persons unknown. He was mildly surprised by this again. They were both over forty. And then he wasn't surprised, struck by the sad realisation that over forty, when you yourself were over fifty, was still young. Then a few minutes later another thing dawned on him – the evidence lay in the nods and smiles the two younger men were exchanging from time to time across the table and the food – that they were actually texting each other. With a further sickening lurch he then stumbled over the knowledge that he was not the first of the party to become aware of this but the last.

In the afternoon Pippa and Karsten went off to explore together. So, inevitably, did Charlie and Nick. A disheartened James made no attempt to join them but tagged along instead with Alexa and Mark. As they climbed the hill towards the top edge of the town Alexa asked James, perhaps to take his mind off the unfolding story of his two younger friends, 'Tell us about the theatre closing. And what you're going to do now.'

'Interesting,' said James, equally glad to talk about something else. 'There's a young theatre director called Freddie. He seems quite keen – for what reason I don't know – to take my future career in hand. He seems to think I should be directing plays. He had me in on rehearsals for The Dream, in a very hands-on way. Not that I haven't done that before of course,' he added quickly. 'But he was trying to give me the confidence to do it off my own back.'

A warm feeling came over James as he talked about this. It was very welcome in the light of what he had discovered over lunch. He thought back to the last night of Freddie's production of A Midsummer Night's Dream, which had also been the last night of the Regent Theatre in its current incarnation, and the ringing down of the final curtain on his own job. It had been a jolly evening, in spite of everything, with big and serious promises to keep in touch, and vague optimistic assertions that the future was beginning, rather than the past ending. There had been champagne. Freddie, for all his heterosexual credentials, had given James a parting kiss.

Alexa broke in on this comforting reverie. 'So how would you go about getting a career as a freelance director?'

'I guess I'd ring round all the directors I've employed in the past and who now run venues of their own. I'd tell them I was now in the market for any freelance productions they wanted to chuck my way. That's how it normally works.' He paused, in a moment of self-doubt, or self-knowledge. 'I'm not sure if I could see myself doing that, though. A bit late in the day to be starting out on something so major.' He stopped again. 'You know I went abroad for a few days after Borja died. To Madeira.' He decided to throw in – might as well – couldn't do any harm now – 'Charlie joined me for a couple of days.' Then he wished he hadn't. It had come out tasting bitter. 'Anyway, I saw two men there – two gay men, I'm pretty sure – with what looked a very enviable lifestyle. They were putting out the tables and chairs in a back street, outside their own bar. A tough life, I can imagine, but a simple one.' James described the smaller, more thickset man who was in his forties, and the younger, taller, willowy one: the redhead with the sunny, rosy face.

Alexa said, 'That sounds like what Nick and Andy had. And what Nick still, has, of course.'

'The obvious question that follows,' Mark came in unexpectedly, 'is whether you're going to get it together with Nick.'

'Oh bloody hell!' James said, letting his annoyance be heard. 'I think you saw the answer to that at lunchtime. And anyway, I've never let myself think that.' He said that quite loudly too, as if doing so would turn a half-lie into sterling truth. He was in an almost physical state of anxiety that they would come across Nick and Charlie as they turned a corner on their climb to the town's summit: would see them arm in arm or, in the shade of an orange tree, in an embrace more intimate than that. 'Serves me right, of course,' he said a bit more quietly. 'I did go to bed with Charlie a couple of times,' he went on, not caring whether this was in bad taste or whether Mark and Alexa needed to hear it or not. 'Though I never have with Nick. In the case of Charlie, neither of us thought that gave us any sort of claim on the other, or prevented us seeing other people. If I *had* let myself think – after Andy's death – that 'other people' might include Nick...' James shook his head involuntarily, 'well, Charlie was entitled to the same thought.'

'Yes,' said Mark, 'but Charlie and Nick have only known each other a few months – and they've only been actually in each other's company for a few days. But you and Nick....'

'Darling,' his wife cut him off. 'I don't think James needs to be hearing this.'

They were emerging uphill into the square where the Colegiata church stands picturesquely, all Plateresque yellow stonework bathed in yellow sunlight. Mark pointed to a row of parked cars. 'Have you noticed the way they all knock into each other when they're parking?' He indicated the scuffed front and rear wings of several of the cars. 'I guess it's because they live in such wide open spaces round here.' He turned and pointed back the way they'd come. Over the roofs of the lower town the under-peopled plain could be seen rolling unimpeded towards the horizon twenty miles away. Mark gave the others a little smile, on which was stamped the memory of how neatly he had parked his own car in the Plaza Mayor an hour or two before. 'When they find themselves in the metropolis of Osuna they get a problem. Sometimes there's an advantage to being in practice with Seville.'

They were at the top of the town now. The building that crowned the slope, which they had taken for a fort, turned out to be the sixteenth-century university, an old stone box of a place, with minaret-like pencil-shaped towers at its corners. Behind it the town came to an abrupt stop, as walled cities do, with open fields beyond. They turned around and stared down over the parapet at the steep streets they had just wound up. Over the canal-tiled cinnamon roof-tops and the white walls. At the prairie undulating beyond, stretching away to the horizon to keep its appointment with the sky. An American-accented voice spoke from beside them. 'Quite a view we have today.'

They turned their heads, like swallows on a wire, to see the new arrivals who had come alongside them by the low wall. They made murmurs of polite agreement, the courteous exchange by strangers of banalities. But they were choked off by the surprised exclamations of recognition between Alexa and the second of the two men who were standing next to her.

'Alexa Soares!' The man, who sounded Spanish, pronounced the surname in the Spanish way. So-*ar*-es.

'Miguel!'

The five now came into a rough circle and, shaking hands, were introduced. James was astonished to hear Alexa present him as, 'a friend of Nick's.' That the name of Nick, the quiet bespectacled Nick who played the piano and ran a village pub, should have currency here in this remote Spanish *pueblo* came as an almost physical shock. The reason for this became apparent as introductions and explanations proceeded. Miguel had sat on the board of the Eulogio Pérez Cabrera Memorial Trust when Alexa had been its president. The ill-fated trust, whose treasurer had made off with the money, and for which Nick had done some secretarial work until that time. The man with him was an American business associate. He hadn't met Alexa, yet clearly knew who she was, for the next thing he said was, 'We were talking about you last night.'

Alexa said, 'Uh-huh?' and Mark and James rocked backwards and forwards on their feet by way of expressing their surprise.

'We're setting up a guitar school in Seville,' the American said. He was grey-haired and jowly; he didn't look like a fantasist.

'Flamenco and classical,' Miguel broke in, a bit excitedly. 'We've got someone lined up to head the Flamenco department. We need someone high profile to direct classical guitar studies – they'd also be principal of the whole establishment.'

'Which is how we came to be talking about you,' the American came back, in more measured tones. 'Miguel thought you'd fit the bill perfectly. If we could only get hold of you – we looked for a website, but you don't seem to have one – and, obviously, if you were interested, of course.'

Alexa looked quickly at Mark, who gave her an encouraging nod. She said, 'I'd need to talk to Mark properly before saying much. You've taken me a bit by surprise.'

'I can tell you that running into you here was an even bigger surprise for us,' said the American.

'I'd also need to talk to my daughter Inés, who isn't with us today...'

James said, 'Is there a café anywhere near here where we could go and sit?' He looked at Alexa. For a moment the vestiges of red hair that still remained among the grey seemed to take on new life as they glowed in the afternoon sun.

Karsten and Pippa were sitting outside the bar café on the north side of the Plaza Mayor. Pippa was enjoying a coffee, Karsten sipping a mid-afternoon San Miguel. In front of them the square was calm and bright. It was full of tiled benches on which a few people sat, beneath orange trees in flower. Theirs was the only table on the pavement outside the door to the bar. They were screened from view to the left by a large menu board shaped like the silhouette of a bottle of beer, propped beside them. Its presence also meant that passers-by emerged from behind it unexpectedly, popping out like jacks in the box. It was dawning on Pippa that the simple pleasure of this situation was something she hadn't allowed herself to enjoy for a very long time. She remembered keenly that it had been the most normal thing back in the old Seville days. It was a recollection that had faded with time, she realised now. She was even enjoying the conversation they were having, though for most people over the age of eighteen it might have seemed less interesting than the coffee and the afternoon sun that was slanting into her eyes and making her squint. 'Who are you to be making these decisions about what's in James's best interests?' she heard herself saying. With a bit of self-satisfaction she heard herself go on, 'It's this priest things again, isn't it?'

'Well, come to that,' Karsten answered, not at all abashed, 'if you go on about priests, who are you – a lawyer, lawyers collectively, all of you – to dictate to an elected government what it should and should not do? You, of course, with the backing of a supra-national organisation that hasn't been elected by anyone.'

'Some things have to be said.' Pippa's head sawed the air between them as she spoke. 'By somebody. The weak have to be protected. If the state doesn't see fit to do that in some cases, then someone has to intervene. Whatever the niceties of the democratic process.'

'Yes,' said Karsten, hissing the S a bit. 'But in Britain of all places. You have the luxury to live in a country where most public protest is focused on foreign policy. A major sign of civilisation, that. Try living in most other countries of the world and protest about foreign policy. See where that gets you. Borja...' He stopped. This whole trip was about Borja, but it seemed that every time the man's name was brought up something awkward or problematic surfaced alongside. 'It was Borja's feeling,' he went on in more conciliatory tone, 'and I'm only passing on what James told me, that you were kicking a very decent country, and its very decent democratic process in the teeth. He heard you on TV, supporting the introduction of Sharia law for communities in Britain in which Muslims outnumbered everybody else. I mean...'

'The Archbishop of Canterbury said it first,' Pippa objected. 'I merely made the comment that he had a point.'

'Don't forget,' Karsten went on as though the previous exchange between them had been wiped from the tape, 'that Borja grew up under General Franco.'

'I cannot believe I'm hearing this from someone who used to be a priest,' Pippa said, agitated enough to rattle her coffee cup against her saucer as she picked it up. 'The Catholic Church, one of the least democratic institutions in the history of the world. And in Spain of all places. A Church that supported Franco, right or wrong – and as we both know, mostly wrong – to the bitter end. The Spanish Catholic Church was the engine of tyranny and state repression, not just looking as far back as the Civil War but for centuries before that. Back to the Reconquest, back to Isabella and Ferdinand. You were a part of that, Karsten. If you say, well, now you're not...' Pippa sighed exaggeratedly, 'well, the time-scale has been very short.'

'I've changed,' said Karsten, poker-faced.

'In three short months?!' There was a pause, while Pippa waited for Karsten to riposte, but he did not. Pippa took another sip of her coffee, and Karsten a swallow of beer. Pippa changed the subject slightly. 'I have to say I've found James a little bit distant this last couple of days. I mean, I'd understand that, in view of his recent bereavement... It's only that he doesn't seem distant with the rest of you.'

'Well,' said Karsten, drawing a breath. He decided, or perhaps the San Miguel did, that it was time for a bit of Teutonic bluntness. 'Borja had actually developed some hostility towards you over the years.' He saw a bristly look appear on Pippa's face, and softened this a little. 'It was completely irrational, obviously. But that's what James told me.'

'But I hadn't met either of them for thirty years,' Pippa protested. 'I can't see how that could have come about.'

'You may not have seen them,' Karsten said, 'but they saw you. On their TV screens, quite regularly, I was told. Even I saw you on Spanish TV once or twice. The last time in the Bodegón of all places, looking out through the window into our old flat.' Pippa looked perplexed at hearing this. 'Though I couldn't quite remember who you were.' Which didn't improve things much. 'It was after seeing you on TV actually, a few days after the plane crash – and I'm only telling you what James told me – that Borja, who had been swearing at the screen apparently, had his heart attack.'

Pippa flushed, angry and red. 'That's dreadful, Karsten. I mean, it's dreadful of you. You should never have asked me to join this reunion, if you knew that.'

'I didn't ask you,' Karsten replied calmly. 'Alexa did.'

'But you asked her to. Did she know? Does she?'

'No, she didn't. And no, she does not.'

'Then it was very underhand of you,' Pippa said, half getting to her feet.

'Pragmatisch, perhaps,' Karsten said, for a rare moment mixing his languages up. 'Not underhand, though. Machiavellian, if you like. I did think,' he went on, fixing Pippa with a very blue-eyed look that made her sit back firmly on her wooden chair, 'that it would be good for you and James, the two of you, to meet. Better than let it fester for a lifetime in his mind.'

'Again, that's you being...' But Pippa was for once surprised into failing to finish a thought. From behind the bottle-shaped menu-board two men appeared suddenly. They were in profile for a mere instant, then in rear view, like passing cars. The taller of the pair put his arm lightly around the shoulder of the other for a second as they walked on. Neither Nick nor Charlie turned to spot the couple arguing contentedly behind the menu board. In another moment they were out of sight.

'What do you make of that?' Karsten asked, waving a hand towards the spot where they had disappeared.

'Why?' Pippa asked. 'Perhaps you had a different plan in mind – out of your concern for James. But things have a way of taking their own course.' She shrugged. But she found her mind going back to the scene she'd remembered a few weeks before. Her first ever evening in Seville. Two young men walking down the street, one taller than the other. She'd heard the taller one say, inexplicably, 'But how could you possibly lose a window?' They'd turned out to be James and Borja. How very young they'd been, Pippa thought in retrospect.

Back in Seville they regrouped for dinner at Las Dueñas. They had travelled back in different formations from the ones in which they'd set out. In a spirit of fairness the train travellers of the morning had given their return tickets to the other three, so that it was now Alexa, Pippa and James who rode the rails, while Mark drove Karsten, Charlie and Nick. There had been plenty to talk about: animated discussions had been a feature of both journeys. Frustrating for everyone was the fact that neither party could know what the other group had said. James in particular was dying to know what had gone on between Charlie and Nick, and was wondering if he could get either Mark or Karsten on their own and ask them to tell him, without sounding too desperately thirsty for the information, or too sad.

But one piece of information surfaced on its own. Charlie announced it to the table at large just after the first drinks arrived. 'Amazing thing happened on the way back.' They already knew that Mark had driven them by a back way, through Marchena and Carmona. 'We were near a place called El Alamo – not a name you'd forget – and the road was very rough, and not really made up. But nobody else seemed to know the road, at least that's how it was at first, as there was no traffic on it. There was a bit of a cutting at one point, with a double bend in it.'

James felt a small electric tingle on his skin at this point; he knew suddenly how the story was going to develop. He glanced towards Karsten, but Karsten was carefully not letting his eye be caught.

'It was a blind bend in fact, and the road very narrow at that point: really only the width of one car or truck. Then Nick suddenly calls out...' Charlie glanced across at Nick at that point – 'fondly' was the only word that came to James's mind that was descriptive of that glance. Nick was looking ahead of him and slightly down, the way people look when having to listen to someone who is praising them. 'Remember, he's sitting in the back, not the front... And he suddenly calls out, 'Car coming!' and Mark slams the anchors on, which is just as well. Hurtling round the bend towards us and taking up the whole road is this bloody great four by four, all spattered with mud. We stopped literally six inches from each other's bumper. The other guy was good enough to back up. But if Mark hadn't slowed... But I mean, there was no possible way Nick could have seen the thing coming. He'd have to be standing on the roof. It's like the guy's got radar or something.'

Again James tried to catch Karsten's elusive eye without success. Then Charlie spoke directly to James. 'I mean, have you ever known him do that before?' This appeal to him, the assumption it hinted at, that Nick belonged somehow to James, if only by virtue of his having known him the longer, warmed James momentarily, if uselessly – like having your hands warmed with a cigarette lighter outdoors on a snowy night.

'No,' said James in a very sober voice. 'I've never known him do that.' He'd known someone else who could pull off that particular trick. Nobody else present knew that, though, and James wasn't going to drop that extraordinary Borja thing into the conversation at this point. He let his face indicate that he had no more to say on the subject and let the others run after the ball that Charlie had tossed into their midst, with cries of, 'Well, how extraordinary,' and, 'There's theories about peripheral vision...' until the topic had run its course.

It was only the third time they'd been inside it but the Bar Alcázares was becoming a familiar hangout for the three Englishmen, after the others had made tracks for home and hotel, where they could enjoy a late night drink. They knew the barmen by name now, and were used to watching them showing off, at the very end of the night, throwing sugar sachets into the saucers laid out with the cups for coffee first thing next day, as if skimming stones. They knew by sight the other regular late night drinkers. In particular one lonely-looking elderly chap, who arrived on a wheelie walking frame around six each evening and stayed till some time after one. Whenever one of the ebony-skinned, white-toothed trinket sellers would walk in with his strings of watches and beads, this man would engage him in conversation, haggling without buying, but touching what he could, in his thirsty need for contact with someone young and beautiful. James wondered for a moment, with a chill on his heart, whether that old man's life would one day be his lot. Or if it already was.

There was a notice on the wall behind the bar, printed in Spanish and English, that made them smile as they deciphered it, with its unintended joke at the expense of the Spanish language's wordiness. *Este establicimiento dispone de un libro de hojas de reclamaciones a disposición de los clientes que lo soliciten.* The English underneath read, *This establishment has a complaints book.*

They talked of course, though not about the awkwardness of the situation that now existed between the three of them, preferring the easier course of discussing the members of their group who had already left.

'Will Accepta elect the job, do you think?' Nick asked, in one of those accidental drunken spoonerisms that seem better somehow than the correct version of things.

'Mark wants her to,' James said. 'Which is a good start. And I do, of course. And I'm sure you do too. She was too modest to say this at dinner, but it would involve occasional trips to America to give concerts there. The plan is to attract American guitarists to the institute as well as Spanish ones. The money behind it is American, and there's no shortage of it, apparently, so there's no appeal going to be made to Spanish public funds. No strumming while the Spanish economy burns. I think it would give her a new lease of life.'

'Didn't you tell me Mark was a poet, who'd burnt all his stuff?' Charlie asked. He addressed the beginning of the question to Nick but by the time he'd got to the end he was looking towards James. James thought that was a rather charming piece of last-second tact.

'That's right,' James said. 'In the car earlier Pippa tackled Alexa about that. A bit rudely, I thought. Still, I guess she was just being direct. That's always been her way. And she was his fiancée once, so I suppose she has the right. Alexa answered her very calmly. She said that Mark didn't need to be a poet. That he was a wonderful husband and father. She told us how wonderful he'd been in finding out about their daughter's sexual inclination and making her feel good about it. She said the daughter's a different person as a result. And that Mark didn't need to write poetry because he was the poem itself. The thing he thought he was trying to create turned out to be simply himself.'

James drained his glass of wine and ordered three more, almost as if he were challenging the other two to one more drink. Meanwhile the elderly man with the walking frame descended from his stool at the bar with a bit of an effort and made his slow way towards the door, a cloth bag of shopping and newspapers clutched awkwardly between hand and walking frame. He opened the door without help from anyone, and the counter staff, who had taken his money off him, smiling, since six o'clock that evening and every other night, watched him impassively as he went out into the lonely street without the blessing of a Goodnight. Nick and Charlie took up the gauntlet James had thrown down in the form of a glass of *vino tinto* each.

They were almost the last to leave the bar, but had only two street corners to walk round before they reached their hotel in Calle Jerónimo Hernández. James said goodnight to the other two in the little corridor with its chintzy sofas and striped wallpaper that served their three rooms and went into his room. But once in bed, tired and wine-hazy though he was, he couldn't sleep. After a time he heard the ever-so-soft sound of a door opening, then being closed again. A long half minute later the sounds were repeated as a second door opened and shut. He knew it was a different door because the pitch of the noise was not quite the same. But whose door was which, which the nearer one and which the further off, he couldn't guess.

There was nothing to be done about this, James told himself resignedly, as he lay awake wondering if the same thing had happened on the previous two nights after he'd gone to sleep. You don't own people, he told himself. He'd been to bed with Charlie in the aftermath of Borja's death, and he hadn't felt the need to ask Nick's permission for that. As for imagining, as he'd momentarily allowed himself to on the flight out here, that he was somehow in a position to choose between the two younger men as a partner for his future life... You fool, he told himself.

Yet he compounded his folly later in the night. The full moon woke him, prising open a chink in the thick curtains that lined his window. He got out of bed, pulled the curtain back and stared the moon full in the face. Aloud he said, 'I wish Nick will take care of me in my old age. I wish he'll come to need me as much as I need him.' He didn't voice the third wish out loud: the words simply went through his head. I wish I can get Nick to bed. A moment later, as he got back into that empty place it came to him that his requests to whatever deity might reside in the earth's satellite had been breathtakingly selfish: they took no account of what Nick's own wishes might be. And then he remembered that, anyway, it was the new moon you were supposed to wish on, not the full one. The full moon was associated only with the seriously insane.

TWENTY-THREE

Pippa woke the next morning unable to remember for the moment what plans had been made for the new day – their last full day in Seville. That was almost certainly the result, she realised with a feeling of pleasurable guilt, of drinking rather more during the last few days than she had drunk in a similar short space of time since she had lived in this city, aged twenty or twenty-one.

She remembered after a second or two. She was going to spend the morning with Alexa, visiting the Casa Pilatos, a glorious old palace very close to her old flat in Virgen de la Luz. All seven were then going to meet up in the grounds of the Alcázar, for a mid-day snack and a stroll around the gardens. In the evening, they would all have drinks with this Paco character, about whom she'd heard a lot back in those days but, until the other night, had never actually met.

Pippa got out of bed, she washed and dressed. The breakfasts at the Hotel Simón were excellent, and Pippa had found herself looking forward to that first meal of the day more with every morning that passed. Brightly she exited her room and walked to the top of the mirrored staircase. But the first glance she took at her many reflections there stopped her dead... It was her hair. That ruler-edged fringe across the front of her head. It reminded her suddenly, oddly, of the upper jaw of some kind of clamp. She realised now why she'd been vaguely disturbed by the appearance of her reflection on her first morning here. She looked an absolute fright.

Nick and Charlie went shopping together. At least, they went for a walk among the main shopping streets, in the vague expectation that they might see something among all the jewelled wonders on display that they would want, and could afford, to take back home. Leaving the Plaza de la Encarnación behind them, they dived down the narrow entry of Calle Cuna – Cradle Street. When they emerged from it they were back in the Plaza del Salvador, alongside the red west wall of the massive church. Nick, who had taken over the role of tour-guide from the absent James, now told Charlie a story that James had not. That someone had once stolen the front window from James and Borja's flat here by way of a joke. The joke had not been well received.

'Stolen a window?' Charlie asked, as everyone who heard the story did. 'How?'

'They jemmied it out, apparently,' Nick said. 'The whole frame. Just left a gaping hole in the masonry.'

'Must have made a fair bit of mess,' Charlie said.

'I guess it did. James said it took ages to put things right.' They had left the Plaza del Salvador and were in the adjacent Plaza de San Francisco. The ornate frontage of the Ayunamiento rose up on their right. 'Borja and James once went to an official dinner there, they told me. Something to do with the tourist office and the sherry company where Paco worked. Not quite sure of the details. Only that they had to have two separate invitations, and sat at different tables, with different groups. It wouldn't have been OK in those days for two gay men to be invited to an official function as a couple. Especially not in Spain.'

'Funny old world it must have been,' said Charlie. 'And was the window joke something against them because they happened to be gay?'

'I think James told me it was.'

By now they had left the shopping area well behind them, and were upon the tram tracks, curving out from behind the Ayunamiento and turning along the Avenida de la Constitución. A little way ahead the cathedral reared up on the left flank of the broad street. 'Oh,' said Charlie, 'We're back here already,' He came to a stop.

They turned in their tracks, headed back towards the shopping streets via Serpent Street, Calle Sierpes. Its shop windows were full of ceramics, of elaborate embroidered lace tablecloths and sheets, gem-like confectionery and cakes. There were a number of beggars about, walking up to people or sitting on an empty step.

Then it happened. It happened to Nick. He couldn't see the person who had arrived among them, arrived among the busy, shopping, beggar-sprinkled, throng, among the spenders and the spent. He couldn't see him, he would explain later when he told the tale to a very select number of friends; he just knew he was there: the very private thief that men call death. And all the people in the street around, though they continued to walk, talk and think about the money they were going to spend or had already spent, were at the same time somehow already their future dead selves. *The lilies of the field.* The words came unbidden into Nick's mind. *That bloom today and shall feed the furnaces tomorrow.*

Nick looked round for Charlie. He called his name in something like panic. But he had disappeared into a shop.

Pippa was the last to arrive. The others were hanging about the ticket office of the Alcázar palace. It was not a bad place to hang about. The south facing wall, tall and ancient, under which they stood was clad from bottom to top with summer jasmine along its length. It made the sunny corner, tucked behind the Archive of the Indies and the cathedral, smell like a perfume shop. A few yards away the walls of the cathedral and the Archive were protected with hanging swags of heavy iron chain, and in front of those stood patient lines of horses harnessed to little black and yellow open carts: an expensive but delightful alternative to taxis for tourists who wanted to see the sights. Then, picking her way over the cobble stones and among the horses and rows of orange trees, Pippa came. Something was different, they all noticed, one by one, but nobody commented. Especially not Alexa. For it was Alexa who, after some quite intimate and serious conversation at the Casa de Pilatos, had taken Pippa to the salon she used herself and introduced her to the patroness. Eventually, when Pippa had joined the group, it was Karsten who spoke. 'Oh,' he said. 'You've changed your hair. I think it's nice.' Pippa grinned at him and the others grinned at her, but no more words were said. They turned and joined the little queue for the ticket window and the turnstile next to it.

The gardens of the Alcázar, one of the bigger and greener oases of the city, held a special place in the affections of all Borja's Seville friends. Alexa and Karsten had come here on the morning they'd first met, Karsten in the role of knowledgeable guide, Alexa the open-mouthed and wide-eyed newcomer. Against the wall of the little Pavilion of Carlos V, half-hidden by pomegranate and lemon trees, Karsten had played his guitar, and a little group of tourists had filtered out from the maze of myrtle bushes nearby to listen to him. He'd charged then for the privilege, of course, handing round his guitar as usual, when he'd finished, for them to deposit coins on its cherry-coloured back.

Mark had once spent a whole night in here. As a teenager he had been wandering around late one evening, his head full of poetic musings, and had failed to hear the shouted announcements that the gates were being shut. He had slept intermittently, out on the grass, looking up in half-wakeful moments through palm tree fronds at a full moon and the stars, while nightingales sang from the shadowy bushes by the battlements. He had woken in the morning to the knowledge that he was in love. In love with Spain, that was. It was a love that had persisted till today. He had also realised that he belonged here in Seville. He would never live anywhere else.

There were other memories too, for all the older members of the group; some concerned Borja, and those they all shared, but the private ones went unvoiced as the seven individuals walked among the flowering shrubs and along fountain-stopped, tree-lined paths. Then, as they rounded a corner to see water cascading down a shallow hill in steps, Nick announced to all, 'I came here with Andy once.'

The pain behind that bald statement cut James like a knife. These few days were all about Borja. In agreeing to come here, in wanting to join the group, Nick had seemed to want to sideline his more particular grief. James happened to be walking next to him at this point, on the other side from Charlie. He put an arm around Nick's shoulder and squeezed him against his side, in a gesture that he had neither planned nor wished, given the events of the last twenty-four hours, to make. Nick's body made no protest, though James expected, in that moment, that it would. James said quietly to him, 'I'm glad you said that.'

Then Nick turned to James and said very earnestly, looking into his eyes, 'Take me to that chapel Borja used to visit.'

Oh fuck, James thought. *You're looking at me out of Borja's own eyes, the way you did the first day when, in a dingy pub on the edge of town, we ever talked. Those brown eyes of yours. Those brown eyes of his.* He said, 'What chapel's that?' He genuinely didn't know what Nick was talking about.

'The one in the Charity Hospital. Will you take me there? Charlie too, if he wants to come.' Nick flicked him a glance.

'The Charity Hospital?' Still James couldn't place it.

'You saw it from your kitchen window,' Alexa reminded him. 'My kitchen window before that. Carved in the stone. *Domus Pauperum et Scala Coeli.*'

'Yes, of course,' James said.

'The House of the Poor and Ladder to Heaven,' Karsten said. 'We used to argue about that. Alexa and I. The idea that being poor is good for you... I mean...!' said Karsten.

'Borja used to go there sometimes,' Pippa broke in. 'He told me he liked to contemplate the Valdés Leal paintings of Death.' She snorted. 'Bit grim, I thought, that. Still, he was a Spanish boy. They do that.'

'The *In Ictu Oculi* painting,' Mark said. 'Seen it once. Don't mind if I never see it again.'

Karsten translated into his sometimes surprising English. 'In the Blink of a Fucking Eye.'

'Blessed are the poor, for they shall inherit the kingdom of heaven...' Charlie remembered from somewhere. He plonked himself down on the brick and tile bench they were all standing next to, and the others followed suit, brushing off a light accumulation of twigs and faded orange blossom before they sat.

'Anyway,' James said, talking only to Nick, but careful to have seated himself a virtuous six inches away from Nick's own hip, 'if that's what you want to do, I'll take you there. Though not very willingly. I've also only seen it once. Believe me, and believe Mark, it's not nice.'

They entered the chapel from a courtyard of whitewashed walls. James, Charlie and Nick. They mounted a steep flight of steps. The door opened into the chapel through the side wall, at the back. Organ pipes climbed the rear wall on your left. But directly ahead of you – the first thing you saw – your heart skipped a beat – there he was, facing you, above the door on the opposite side, looking out at you from a background as deep and dark as a void, from a dark-framed canvas that must have been seven feet in height. He was a skeleton, resembling your old headmaster, with one foot on the globe, and he was staring at you, at only you. The trappings of power: the papal tiara – it flashed into all their minds that it was only a matter of weeks since Benedict XVI had relinquished his – and an emperor's crown, lie abandoned and ridiculous at the skeleton's feet. Death, his hand of bones – phalanges, carpals, meta-carpals – is in the act of snuffing out a tall church candle. Actually the candle is already out. Above the dark and aching space left by the parted flame, where a modern cartoonist might have written *phut!*, the words *In Ictu Oculi* flicker against your own living eye.

Nick and James heard Charlie whisper, borrowing Karsten's words, 'In the blink of a fucking eye.'

'Turn right,' James told the younger two, taking charge. 'Have a look at the rest of the place. Give death a break.' They turned and walked up the central aisle of the nave. The word chapel was an under-description. The space was huge and high and grand, under a round-arched vault. Behind the high altar were gold barley-sugar columns and a sculpted reredos that depicted two turbanned Saracens entombing Christ, with a busy montage of characters surrounding them. Behind the three-dimensional figures was a painted background of empty crosses against which ladders leant. Above, the *trompe-l'oeuil* paintings on the inner wall of a vast dome led the eye towards paradise.

Half of you did indeed get caught up in this, so that you wondered whether, being poor and in this place, you really were on the rungs of the ladder that inclined heavenward. While the other half wondered if the money that had gone to the creation of all this grandeur and beauty – this eye-candy for the poor, for the suffering, for the destitute, might not have been better spent. This was what the inmates of the poorhouse could see around them when they came to chapel for daily Mass. You couldn't help wondering what life in the wards those people returned to afterwards, back in the seventeenth century, was really like. How much those artworks, Leal's and Murillo's, really helped. They, or any other art.

They turned back from the high altar, pausing at the six Murillo paintings that lined the way like Stations of the Cross, and retraced their steps towards the door. But above the door they'd entered through, opposite the *In Ictu Oculi* painting, they came face to face with the second of Leal's dark canvasses: the message's other half. In the centre of the picture a pair of scales weighs human entrails and hearts. The Spanish, *Ni mas ne menos*, is written on either side: neither more nor less. Below, in front of a background of skulls and frowning owls, lies the decaying body of a pope. Underneath is written the end of the sentence that is begun on the wall behind you: *In Ictu Oculi*. It is completed on a parchment scroll: *Finis. Gloriae Mundi. ...*In the blink of an eye end the glories of the world.

James found his knees shaking and going weak. He didn't doubt the others felt the same. Charlie had seemed to take the paintings in his stride, James assumed from occasional sideways glances at his face. He'd hardly dared to look at Nick. He wondered now, as they left the chapel and actually rather staggered down the steps, if the two boys ... he couldn't help thinking of them as the two boys ... if the two boys would take each other's hand for a second, or one touch the arm or shoulder of the other. They were walking close enough to each other's side. But neither of them did.

'Let's get back to the sunshine,' Nick said, the first to voice what all three of them felt, and a moment later they were there, spilling out onto the pavement of Calle Temprado, where the sun greeted them with unfeigned warmth. And so did someone else. Waiting for them on a bench that stood against the railings that guarded the chapel and the hospital from intruders, Pippa sat. At that moment Nick put his hand on Charlie's hair and ruffled it.

In the hours and days that followed Borja's death, James had found contact with even his oldest friends and acquaintances difficult. It was as if shards of glass had been inserted in him all over and that even a friendly squeeze of the hand, or a hug or a shoulder-pat would inflict new and further agony. He knew from his own bruising experience with Nick a few months later, that Nick had felt something similar after Andy had died. Yet in his own case James had discovered Andy and Nick to be the exceptions, perhaps because they'd both been so close to him in the few weeks that were the prelude to the event. At first James had felt comfortable with them and with no-one else. But as the days had turned to weeks, then months, the number of people with whom he felt comfortable and safe, as opposed to feeling as vulnerable as an un-shelled hermit-crab, had grown one by one. First there had been Charlie. Then Karsten. By now the number of people whose company he could share without flinching included Freddie, and Alexa and Mark. But despite the last three days of friendly proximity to her in Seville, James hadn't yet been able to include Pippa on that very short list. Now here she was, looking up at him strangely, though not unpleasantly, from a bench.

'Oh dear,' she said, looking at each of them in turn. 'You all look dreadfully upset.' She smiled a bit impishly, something she hadn't done before during the past few days. James was reminded of Pippa's old cousin Sophie, whom he hadn't seen in thirty years, hadn't thought about in twenty, and who must surely now be dead. Pippa added, 'As two of you know from recent experience, death does have that effect.' Nick smiled in spite of himself and Charlie found himself surprised into a laugh.

James warmed to Pippa suddenly. A surge of emotion convulsed his chest and he lifted her from the bench and gave her a tight hug. Just as quickly he let her go. 'I'm sorry,' he said, shaking his head a little. 'Don't know where that came from.'

Pippa ignored the apology. She smiled at James but then looked towards Nick. 'Don't take too much notice of death, if you – you two – can manage that. I know. I know he's all around us...'

'Well, yes,' said Nick, in a ruffled tone of voice, as if his experience in Calle Sierpes were being questioned, even though he'd given no-one, not even Charlie on his re-emergence from the shop, an account of it yet.

Pippa steam-rollered Nick's interruption just as she had done James's. She said, 'My father's close to death. I haven't shared that with any of you these last few days. We've had better things to talk about. He's in a home now. My father, is, I mean. My brother's being very good with him, even though Dad hardly knows who he is. Eventually – well, it's always like this, with everyone – I don't know how far our mother will be behind him when he's gone.' She looked mystified for a moment, as if a key witness had said something unplanned under examination on the stand. Her face went blank. 'Oh, why did this come up?' She regained control of her case. 'Yes. I wanted to say, there's no time in life when there's no future. I've only just learned this, from visiting Dad. Even in an old people's home, I've seen this first-hand now, we all spend our final minutes looking forward to teatime … even if that's a cup we'll never drink from, and a sandwich we'll never get to taste.'

Her composure deserted her for a moment and she sat back down on the bench, making an effort, the others could see, not to cry.

'I'm sorry, Pippa,' James said, sitting beside her and taking her hand, not caring whether she found this condescending or not. 'You should have told us.'

Pippa turned quite fiercely towards him, any battle with tears she might have been fighting conclusively won. 'Then even more, you should have told me about what Borja felt about me. Karsten did... And I felt, to be honest with you, quite broken apart. It felt...' she paused and took a breath. 'Well, it felt as though you'd been lying to me for the last three days.'

('What's all this about?' Charlie asked Nick quietly. They were both still standing up.

'You know. That TV thing,' Nick half-whispered back. 'Tell you later, if you've forgotten.' Now they sat down alongside James and Pippa on the bench.)

'I had nothing to say,' James explained. 'There was nothing that could be said, so I said nothing.'

'That's not a good reason for saying nothing,' Pippa came back. Then her eyes twinkled. 'Anyway, throughout history that's never stopped anyone else.'

'I couldn't say anything to you,' James reiterated his point. 'It's not as though there was any quarrel between us. Between you and me. There's nothing to patch up. There was no quarrel between Borja and you, come to that. He didn't die cursing you; don't think that. He had other preoccupations. My disappearing job, Charlie's video-film, my relationships with … with other friends.' His eyes flicked towards the other two, then quickly back to Pippa again. 'Look, these things grow and get out of proportion in people's minds when they don't...' But he couldn't think through to what it might be that people did or didn't do that caused friendships to turn sour or simply lapse, and he gave up the attempt. He looked at his watch. Like most people of his age he seldom thought to check the time on his phone. His phone wasn't something he was very conscious of. 'Half an hour before we meet Paco in Morales. Anyone fancy a stroll down to the river and back?'

The riverfront promenade looked its old self: there were the same palm trees, the same view across the bounding currents of the Guadalquivir to the handsome buildings of Triana opposite, towards the springing, satisfyingly recurring, arches of the San Telmo bridge. At the end of the view, down the avenue of palm trees. was the drum-like stone tower, the Torre del Oro, where, according to legend, prisoners had been sentenced endlessly to count the coin of New World wealth. The four of them watched for a few minutes the parade of young men jogging up and down the Paseo between the palm trunks and blue plumbago plants. They didn't say much to one another, all busy with their own particular thoughts.

'I think you'll like this place,' James said to Nick and Charlie as they opened the door into the Casa Morales. 'If it hasn't changed too much.' And reassuringly, it hadn't, even if an up-to-date cash register had replaced the old hand-guzzling monster. But there that old relic of the twenties still was, displayed against the wall behind the counter as a museum piece. Though the old man who had counted the copper coins in it night after night with fingerless gloves was no longer to be seen.

Paco had got there before them. He was standing near the bar, in conversation with Karsten, Alexa and Mark.

James experienced again the shock he'd felt on seeing him a few days before: Paco as a white-haired elderly man. But just as on that occasion the shock wore off at once. There was the same old Paco that he'd known. Like the bar they were entering, he was reassuringly unchanged. Then for a second James experienced a downward lurch of the spirit, as though the boat he sailed in was plunging suddenly into a trough. Bowing to Neptune, sailors called that first downward lurch as you hit the open sea on leaving port. It was the absence of Borja that did that of course. For Borja and James would meet here, delightedly, after work for an early evening drink. Yet, swim in the sea, Charlie had told James. Charlie who now stood beside him. James gathered himself and rose to meet the waves. He saw Karsten's eyes light on Pippa and say, 'Come and listen to this...' Paco turned to greet the new arrivals, turned back to offer Pippa a drink, but finding Karsten had got there first, turned back to the three Englishmen and offered them one instead.

They were talking about Spain's economic woes. Nick had spoken already of his surprise at seeing so little sign of them in Seville's streets. '*Alegria* is the word for that,' Mark said. 'It's a kind of joy, or light-heartedness, that Seville is famous for. People dancing and singing, and always cheerful, in the streets. But really it's skin-deep. A protective carapace built up over centuries to deal with the hardness of life.'

'Which over the last twenty years seemed to be going away at last,' Karsten said. 'Now it seems it's coming back. The protective carapace is necessary once again.'

'The hardship,' said Paco. 'Ah yes.' He looked around the room, to see whether other customers were listening or not. But whether they were or weren't didn't make any difference apparently. He said, rather self-importantly, 'I have a plan to deal with that.'

'You have a plan to deal with the economic crisis?' James said in surprise and, because it was Paco saying this, making an effort not to laugh.

But Paco turned directly to James with a completely different thought. He had been speaking Spanish but he said in English now, 'Do I owe you an apology, James?' It was evident even from that short question that twenty years of living with William had improved his English more than all his lessons with James ever had.

'Apology for what?' James asked, although he knew.

'For taking William away from you.'

'For sending me back to Borja, I think you mean.' James smiled. 'No, you don't need to apologise for that.' He reached out and touched the back of the older man's hand for a second.

'You know,' said Paco, reverting to Spanish, 'I've done very well in life. I mean in the financial sense. I've realised a bit late that none of that mattered. It was William that made everything worthwhile for years and years. I didn't appreciate that fully at the time.'

'I see,' said James, trying to get his head round the idea that William had managed to make someone's life worthwhile – that he was capable of making anyone's life worthwhile – when he'd so spectacularly created havoc with James's. Correction, though. It was James who had caused the havoc, beginning the moment he'd ill-advisedly run his finger down William's cheek as they lay shirtless on Chipiona beach. Remembering that with a pinch of humility James managed to say, 'Well, he was a bit special, no?'

Realising that they were listening to a rather intimate exchange, Nick and Charlie slipped past Paco to join the others who stood behind his back.

'So I'm planning to put something back as you say in English,' Paco continued to James alone, skipping effortlessly backwards to two thoughts ago. 'I want to set up a food distribution network, perhaps in association with the Red Cross or even with the Church. I don't know yet.' He waved his arms about in the way James remembered him always doing when words and ideas ran out. 'I haven't really thought it through. But it will be based here in Seville.'

'And you're going to organise that yourself?' James's experience of Paco's organisational capabilities did not give him much grounds for hope.

'James, you know me better than that,' Paco said, his arms now held expansively wide and with a smile to match. 'William might have been able to do that but me, not. No, I'm looking for someone, or better still, two people, to actually set it up. And then to manage it in the longer term. A couple would be best.'

Oh dear, James thought. He's going to suggest Charlie and Nick. Or worse still, Nick and me. Or Charlie and me... And embarrass all of us.

'I thought of Karsten of course,' Paco said. 'Eduardo's with me on this. A shame he couldn't be here this evening. He promised Karsten he'd offer him a job when he needed one. And now here Karsten is in Seville again by chance. And he is not alone, which makes things better. He has Pippa with him.'

James remembered that if there was a wrong end of a stick lying around the place, Paco could always be relied upon to pick it up. He tried to warn him, for old times' sake. 'Paco, they're not a couple...'

Paco raised his hands like a priest who is about to say the words *Let us pray*. 'They're not married, I realise that. But these days that is no obstacle.' He went into English again, this time a little startlingly. 'I am going to propose to them at once.' He turned away from James and into the group behind him at the bar. As he made his out of the blue job offer to the unattached pair James was able to read their looks of astonishment and incredulity over Paco's shoulder. But as Paco continued to explain things to them – things which included the use, rent-free, of one of his houses in Seville – James saw their expressions change from astonishment to wonderment. He noticed that the change happened simultaneously on Pippa's face and on Karsten's. Then he saw the two of them turn and look at each other. He wondered at that moment whether, by some freak accident, in picking up the stick by the wrong end, Paco had for once judged the situation exactly right.

Nick dreamt of Andy that night, or more exactly, the following morning just before he awoke. It was not the first time. Many dreams about his partner had come to him in the days that followed his death. This one came rather unexpectedly, after a gap of nearly two months. Nick was setting out on foot, it seemed, to go somewhere for an early evening rendezvous, leaving Andy somewhere else. At home perhaps. Nick felt a bit sad about this, vaguely regretting that they seemed to be leading more separate lives these days. Then he was a passenger in a car, the driver an old school-friend he hadn't thought about in years, and there, what joy! was Andy, dressed in a scarlet jacket, in a crowd of people outside in the street. Excitedly Nick banged on the car window with the flat of his hand. Hearing the banging Andy peered towards him but could not see in. The car turned the corner of the square, leaving Andy on the other side. Nick told his driver friend to wind the window down and call Andy's name. He didn't seem to understand, reacted too slowly, the moment was lost.

But not entirely. Andy had gone into some kind of shop or covered market and Nick (gone were car and driver) followed him inside, pushing his way through crowds among the stalls. He pushed his way through a curtain and there Andy was. Though there he wasn't.

There was just a pile of clothes, dumped in a wheelchair. Something protruded from the bundle of clothing; Nick didn't want to look too closely. The clothes shrank as he looked at them, while from under them came Andy's voice. It was faded and muffled, the words unintelligible, fading out.

Nick woke with a whimper that he imagined was a shout, then started to cry. That woke Charlie, who sat up, leaned over him and comforted him with a kiss and those words remembered from childhood, 'Just a dream.'

Nick was acutely conscious then of where he was. That James, if he'd heard the commotion, would have realised it came from the wrong room. 'Tell me, baby,' said Charlie. 'About the dream. If you want to. If you can.' Nick couldn't. He burst into renewed tears.

TWENTY-FOUR

James hadn't looked at his emails while he was away. They were waiting for him, about thirty of them, when he returned the next evening from Gatwick to the Court House. Among the offers of half-price office stationery and cheap flights two stood out, both provoking, for different reasons, an involuntary sharp intake of breath.

The first was from Linda, general manager of the Regent Theatre until a few days before, and James's assistant for years before that.

Hi James

Hope you had a gd time, if that's the rt thing to say about something so important to you.

Big news here. New body set up by DRA, to be called Barraclough Regent now, we're told, but in other words David, is going to open with an autumn season of plays – in the Regent! Exactly what we cd have done ourselves – and have always done – at lower cost. First show to be a musical. Carousel. But guess who's going to direct it. Freddie Jay! What a wily little fox. Freddie Fox from now on.

Give me a ring if / when you want to chat.

The second one was from a more surprising source: the chief executive of the city council. James didn't think that mighty potentate had contacted him before on his private email address.

I have tried to phone you but guess you are away. Not surprising in the circs. There might be a bit of work for you, on City Council business, if you're interested. Do give my office a call and arrange a time for an informal chat.

James phoned at nine the next morning. At eleven he was sitting opposite the chief executive at his desk in that office of his where everything was dove grey and pastel blue. Over the years James had sat in this seat opposite three or four successive chief executives, but not very many times. He had taken the trouble to put on a suit. The chief executive, a large bald man with a benign countenance and spectacles, was also wearing one. James had only met him twice before, although they'd emailed, exchanged letters and telephoned each other often enough in the normal course of work. Now he leaned forward across the desk to James and half smiled. 'A rare moment of peace and co-operation has occurred between us and our county council friends,' he said. 'We want to do a joint audit and inspection of all the arts organisations in receipt of city and county funds. It would involve about six weeks' work, including writing up the reports. In another rare moment of agreement between city and county, we all thought you a very suitably qualified person for the job. If you were interested, that is.'

'I thought the county arts officer did that sort of thing,' James said.

'Normally, yes.' The chief executive paused and gave a tight little laugh. 'She's having a baby. The job's being held open for her. But there's no official maternity cover; the cuts, you know; people are just pitching in as and when. And we actually want to push this through quite quickly.' He clasped his hands on the desk in front of him. 'And it wouldn't be a bad idea to have a fresh pair of eyes looking at things. Hannah ...' he was referring to the county arts officer, 'has got a bit embedded, if you know what I mean.'

'I think I see,' James said cautiously.

'It's everything from youth dance groups through to the annual music festival. It also includes – even though it's just starting up – the new body within the department of recreation and arts...'

James finished the sentence for him. '...that now runs the Regent and the Barraclough. Barraclough Regent, I hear they're calling it. You mean I'd be auditing David Parkes?'

'For a few days only,' said the chief executive. He smiled a little mischievously. 'I thought you might like that.'

James shifted in his chair a little. He found he'd unthinkingly crossed his legs. He unwound them now and, adopting a more macho posture, planted the soles of his feet firmly on the dove-grey carpet. 'I think I could well be interested,' he said. 'Could you tell me a little more, perhaps?'

After the meeting James headed straight for the Rose and Castle. He drove dangerously fast, in the manner of a very young man whose testosterone levels have kidded him into believing he's invincible and safe from all harm. He seemed to be sitting higher above the ground than usual – at the height usually favoured by drivers of buses and trucks. When he'd parked and got out he saw Nick a little way off, dead-heading things in the pub garden beyond the car-park. He made for him almost at a run. 'Hey, Nick!'

They hadn't contacted each other this morning. James hadn't alerted Nick to the surprising content of the chief executive's email even by text. They had parted almost awkwardly, late the previous night. They had been three on the Gatwick Express, but only as far as East Croydon. There Charlie had got out, James parting from him with a brief hug, then sitting down again and deliberately not watching too closely as Nick and Charlie had exchanged a farewell that was a little more intense. Nick and James had continued their journey together – train, tube, another train – finally sharing a taxi from the station to home. That had deposited Nick at the pub before taking James on up the hill to the Court House. 'Catch up tomorrow at some point,' Nick had said, getting out of the taxi after giving James a very minimal hug.

James made up for that now – or got his revenge for that – by embracing Nick very warmly as they came together in the sunshine. 'I've got a bit of work lined up,' he crowed in Nick's ear. Whether Nick had or had not just spent the morning on the phone to Charlie or texting him – a scenario that had dampened his spirits the previous night – James no longer gave a toss.

Nick extricated himself from James's arms, though not as hurriedly as all that, and grinned at James and said, 'That's something we ought to celebrate, then. I mean properly, tonight. A bottle of something fizzy, and seriously priced.' James would have quite liked to pop that cork now, but was mollified to hear Nick say next, 'I've got a hell of a lot on this afternoon or I'd open it right away. For now, would you settle for a quick half?'

In his small garden Nick had tried to achieve what generations of gardeners at Sevenscore had created in an area forty times as big. He hadn't done too badly, it had to be said. Red campion and half-wild geraniums craned tall from among seeding feather-grass at the edges of the mown area where customers sat. There were nods to Shakespeare too: eglantine and wild woodbine climbed the fence posts. Tall daisies stood in pied clumps. And deep mauve columbine flowers like tiny ballerinas appeared to curtsy in the wind at the top of their invisible stalks. Nick and James returned out here after Nick had pulled their Pedigree half pints, but as Nick had already made the point that he had things to do, they walked around admiring the vegetation rather than sitting down as they quaffed their brief drinks. It came suddenly into James's mind that here was a nicer spot to be setting tables out in than a Madeiran back street, as he again remembered the two men he'd seen there, doing that. On the other hand, the here and now was late May on a particularly good day. In January the situation would be reversed.

'There's a couple of things I want to ask you,' Nick said, a little diffidently. For years diffidence had been a quality James associated with Nick. It had been part of his charm in fact. But on Andy's death it had vanished with startling swiftness, to be replaced by a new assertiveness and self-assurance that had come from who knew where. But just for a moment now Nick the kid was back, and James warmed to that. 'But tonight, when there's time and we've got a proper bottle in front of us.'

Sometimes James felt there was no getting to know Nick. Every time, something different. But even that was rather nice. Every time you opened his book it was as though he'd started on a new draft.

'Happy to oblige,' James said and, prompted by Nick's doing so, drained his glass.

Nick had a busy afternoon ahead of him. Of course he had. Returning from four days' absence to a business he ran single-handed. It would have been the same for James in the past: the piles of letters, queries and enquiries, internal difficulties arisen that needed settling, that faced any manager or director going back to work. Only this time, the first time ever, there was none of this. All James had to do, until he began his new task for the city and county councils tomorrow, was to enjoy the gardens at Sevenscore in the sun. All he had... Good God, he thought, am I to complain at that?! With an evening with a good friend to look forward to at the end of the day?!

James's afternoon was enlivened, as it happened, by the arrival of an email from Karsten. He had not returned alone to Germany. Pippa had gone with him although, they had both made it clear, only to spend the weekend.

Hello James

I have some thoughts after Seville. One – though I thought this in the Bay of Biscay too. We travel through life like ships through the sea. Endlessly churning up the past behind us, nosing sharply into uncertainty, cleaving the waves ahead.

Two, I seem to have the relationship with Pippa that normally have teenagers between each other – best friends who begin to explore each other deeply. After so many years of knowing Pippa and not knowing her, I find this strange.

Three. Despite what all the philosophers said, there can be no a priori difference between friendship and love. It is only the presence or absence of sexual feeling that causes us mistakenly to see a difference where none exists. For though every relationship is different in its depth and detail, in essence love and friendship are the same.

Four. Do you sometimes think that the only purpose of life – after putting food in your belly, trying to keep warm, and scratching your cock, is trying to find out what the word love – which we throw about carelessly like a cheap ping-pong ball – actually means?

Four. Do you think some of these thoughts contradict each other?

I am very happy today and light-hearted. I hope your return to England was also good.

With love and friendship

Karsten

James spent the rest of the afternoon, out in the garden, wondering how to answer that.

An unusually warm end-of-May evening, and it would not be dark until late. James walked down the old carriage drive to the pub. The evening light cast shadows between the medieval field strips, and the poplar trees, in pairs, whispered over his head as he passed beneath. As he walked into the car-park Nick materialised at the kitchen door. A coincidence that, James thought. He would not allow the thought that Nick might have been looking out for him.

They sat in the garden, a bottle of Moët on the rustic table between them. 'I wanted to ask you,' Nick said as soon as they'd exchanged remarks about how nicely the birds were singing and how good the garden looked, 'if, after that time you heard Borja talking about washing-up liquid and telling you he loved you, you heard his voice again.'

'Well, it wasn't really his voice,' James said cautiously. He wanted to tread softly, in case he trod on some dreamlike Andy-experience of Nick's. 'I presume it came from the inside of my head. No, I haven't heard that voice again. Why, has Andy spoken to you?'

'No,' Nick said. 'Not yet. Except I sort of heard him speak in a dream. But it was... It was faint, and I couldn't make out actual words.' He then recounted the dream he'd had in Seville two nights before. He had some difficulty getting his own words out.

James sat quietly as he listened, not trying to catch Nick's eye, giving him a chance to get through to the end at his own pace. When Nick did finish, telling of how Andy had faded into a pile of empty clothes that had then faded into nothingness along with his voice, James wanted desperately to get up and walk round the table and to throw his arms around his friend. But prudence, or cowardice, overruled the urge. He was afraid, more deeply afraid than he could have imagined six months ago, that Nick would physically throw him off. As he had done once before, oh so many years ago, in the Chinese bedroom at the Court House.

Suddenly Nick was back in charge of his voice, the situation, and himself. He looked directly into James's eyes and said, 'What made it worse, you know, was being where I was.'

'In Charlie's bed, you mean,' James said, nodding broad-mindedly while wondering how he was managing to do this. Perhaps he had it in him to be an actor after all. Or a poker player. He was even more amazed at what he found himself saying next. 'Andy wouldn't have minded, you know. He'd want you to do anything to deaden the pain in the short term. And in the long term he'd want you to do whatever would make you happy.'

'Thank you for saying that,' Nick said, though in a rather formal tone of voice. 'But I actually didn't think that Andy would have minded. I was afraid that you might. I behaved very insensitively towards you in Seville.'

'Look,' James said, shifting slightly in his chair. 'These things...'

'It was just a holiday fling,' Nick said, sounding rather grimly certain about that. 'For both of us.'

'You don't know that.' James tried to feel generous.

Nick said, 'Did he tell you to swim in the sea?'

'Yes,' James said. A whole torrent of thoughts and feelings rushed into his mind and flooded it, as if someone had opened a sluice-gate. 'I didn't know that you...'

'I did know,' said Nick quite neutrally. 'Charlie told me.'

'The reason I didn't tell you myself... I was afraid you'd think it in bad taste, so soon after...'

'Don't be silly. Borja would have understood. And it was no skin off my nose, was it?'

That last little throwaway, meant to reassure and soothe, had precisely the opposite effect, but James wasn't going to point that out.

Nick leaned forward and topped up both their glasses. Then he changed the subject abruptly. 'How long is this audit thing you're going to do supposed to take?'

'Six weeks, I think,' James said. 'Should be over by mid-July.'

'Hmm,' said Nick. 'I was thinking, I'll need a bit of extra help over the summer. Holiday time on the canal.' He became El Kid again and looked up at James shyly. 'I guess you wouldn't be available to lend a pair of hands?'

'Who knows?' said James, again treading carefully, this time to avoid treading on himself. 'It's a bit of a way off still, but you never know.'

'Sure,' said Nick. 'Just thought I'd ask.'

A little later, when the champagne was finished, Nick said, 'You know what? I opened a bottle of burgundy earlier. I don't know if you'd...?'

They sat out, quaffing burgundy until it was nearly dark. A short distance away customers came and went through the main entrance of the pub, but few saw the two men sitting talking in the dusk. Eventually the burgundy was gone and James made his way back across the fields, lighting his way with a torch he'd been lent by Nick. A thought began to seep into his mind. He didn't want it there; it didn't make him feel comfortable; he couldn't acknowledge it. But there it was. Sitting out in the dusk among evening-scented flowers, with a good bottle of wine. With Nick. He'd felt happy again. This evening that had ended a few minutes ago with a brief chaste hug in the lane outside the pub had been as good as things ever got or could get. It was as simple, and as complicated, and as difficult to deal with, as that.

James spent the next three days darting, woodcock-like, between the offices of the chief executive at City Hall and the lair of Hannah the county arts officer, a few streets away. He told himself the walking kept him fit. He expected to run into David in one of the corridors at City Hall, and was looking forward to the encounter whenever it might happen. Inevitably it would at some point, but during those days it did not. He didn't see Nick again until the end of the third day, by which time he'd been given a particular reason to go and see him – in an email from Charlie, no less.

Hiyah

Nick told me your job news. The audit things. Sounds a good start to something. Congrats hahaha. New lad joined cabin crew this week. Lovely. Black. And everywhere, if you know what I mean. I hope Nick doesn't think I was taking advantage of his situation back in Seville. (Hope you didn't back last autumn ;-) I don't think he does, guessing from his emails and texts. Cd you just check though? Set my mind at rest...

But when James arrived at the pub in the early evening he found he didn't have its landlord to himself. Among the small number of people clustered in the top bar sat Freddie, to James's surprise, chatting to Nick across the counter. When he saw James come in Freddie turned to him with a smile and said, 'That's good. I hoped I might run into you here.'

'And how very nice to see you too,' James said with total insincerity and not caring whether that showed or not.

'Well,' said Freddie, 'you can probably guess what I've come about. I'm sure you know they're doing the first show of the season at the Regent, and that it's going to be Carousel...' He looked at James questioningly, wondering if he knew the next bit and, if so, whether he would volunteer the fact. James did not. Freddie went on, 'They've asked me to direct it. There's money in the budget they've given me for a production assistant. I just wondered if you might be interested. Thought I'd ask you before trying anyone else.'

James managed to maintain a smile. He didn't care if Freddie noticed how glacial it was. For a moment he wanted to hit the man but the desire quickly subsided. Probably because he had a better weapon at his disposal than a mere fist. 'Oh what a shame,' he said. 'Might have been fun, but I won't be able to. The city and county councils have asked me to do an inspection-cum-audit of all the arts organisations in the county. Including the Barraclough Regent management, of course. There'd be a bit of a conflict of interest if I was actually working for them at the time.'

'You're doing an inspection of the new management?' Freddie looked gob-smacked. 'But it's not even up and running yet.'

'I think the councils want to start as they mean to go on,' said James. 'And as I'm now technically independent from everyone, they thought I'd be the best person for the job.' Freddie drew breath but James didn't let him make use of it. 'And when that little task's finished, Nick...' Nick, half-listening behind the bar while pretending not to, now turned his full attention to James. 'Nick wants me to come and work for him here for a bit. After that, well, who knows?' He looked at Nick and was rewarded by the sight of something on his face that he couldn't think how to describe other than as a glow. He was so taken up with observing this that he didn't bother to check Freddie's face for his own reaction to the speech.

But he did turn to him a moment later to say, 'If you're staying overnight you're more than welcome to crash at Sevenscore if you want.'

'That's kind of you,' Freddie said. 'But I've already been invited to stay in town, with David and his wife.'

Unexpectedly, from behind the bar Nick said, looking at James, 'If you're looking for company up there for an hour or two I've got a bit of time off later. I'd bring a bottle. Might even volunteer to cook us something.'

When, an hour later, they got to the Court House – Sancho Panza greeted them in the kitchen with his tail up and in the shape of a question mark – an email from Pippa was waiting for James. Nick and he read it together.

Dear James

Will you be surprised by this or won't you? Karsten and I – having talked a lot in Germany, as you can imagine – though talked might perhaps not adequately describe things – have decided to throw in our lot together for what may remain of our lives. We're taking up Paco's job offer and moving back to Seville next month. We call it downsizing on my part and being upwardly mobile on his.

James thought that if he'd had to invent a joke that might have been laboriously put together by an English lawyer who was Pippa and a German priest who was Karsten he couldn't have done much better than that.

I've given notice to my partners in Chambers and there was quite a bally-hoo as you can imagine. But these things can't be helped. We have only one life to lead. When a chance comes to get things right I think you have to take it.

We're not going to get married. That seems unnecessary at our time of life. It's not as if we're going to have children, and at least that's a bit reassuring for my existing two. As for my parents, sadly they're rather beyond noticing details like their offspring's marital status now. And Karsten's parents have always been shocked by every decision he's made throughout his life, so there's nothing unexpected there.

I haven't asked anything about you in this email, and for the moment I won't. But I feel sure that somehow the right thing will happen for you too, if you give it time. Just be receptive, open – and remember our conversation in Seville outside the Charity Hospital. Don't take the man with the hourglass too seriously. Don't let thoughts of death, your own or someone else's, grind you down or alter your attitude to life. Death can't be avoided, it's like the rain, and just like the rain it's one of the necessary processes of life. Let life happen to you. Which it will. I'll leave it there for now...

For months James had wondered what to do with the notebook in which Borja had written his last thoughts. In handwriting that had got smaller and more spidery as his final days passed. He didn't want to throw it away; most of its pages were empty, and James hated waste. Yet the pathos of its incomplete state was hard to bear. Late one evening in the middle of June he had an inspiration, and having had it – as is the way with all good inspirations – saw its obviousness at once. He would write in it himself.

He was well into his inspection / audit work by now but this day – a rare one of bright sunshine and some heat in what was turning out to be a less than flaming month – he had a day off. There was still a pale wash of light across the sky as he sat down outside the open garden door of the Court House and on the page that followed Borja's last entry, in which he'd confused James rather charmingly with the cat, wrote this.

I am alone this morning but can hear Nick playing the piano in the pavilion. A little while later the music has stopped, the door opens and Nick stands there grinning like a gargoyle. He makes a swigging gesture. 'Still on for this evening?' he says. We have a provisional arrangement to meet at the pub. We meet either down there or up here most nights. Suddenly today he looks about 20 – looks like he did when I first knew him.

We meet as arranged. We look again at the photos he took in Seville. We talk about Pippa and Karsten, about Alexa, who at last has accepted the new job, about Charlie and his handsome new friend. Astonishingly Sancho Panza arrives. He's never done that before, crossing the fields, following me down – it must be a quarter mile.

A good bottle of red follows the now traditional Cava. We listen to owls in the dusk. We talk about gay marriage – a bit cagily, it has to be said – and about religion and the new Pope. I couldn't be more relaxed than I am with this man. Couldn't be happier. It's as good – now I'm saying it at last – as it was with B in the old days. Am I allowed to write, or even think such a thing? To write it in your diary of all places, Borja, my dearest love, my oldest friend? I do hope you're OK with me about that, because I just have.

I get up to go. I'm not invited to stay. I don't expect that. What will come will come, as Pippa said. Or not, as the case may be. Qué será será. As B would so often say.

We hug goodnight in the car-park. We talk a bit more. I hug him a second time, maybe the first time I've ever done that. I don't know. I say, 'Love you. Small L, but I do.' We laugh. It's light and low-key. He wishes me a safe journey home with a laugh still in his voice. I feel good, as I set off, walking up the old carriage drive, where Sancho Panza has gone ahead some minutes before. I might be wrong but actually I think Nick feels good too.

****

Woodcock Flight is the third book in the Seville Trilogy. The first book is **Orange Bitter, Orange Sweet** and the second is **Along the Stars**.

Anthony McDonald is the author of thirty-one books. He studied modern history at Durham University, then worked briefly as a musical instrument maker and as a farmhand before moving into the theatre, where he has worked in every capacity except director and electrician. He has also spent several years teaching English in Paris and London. He now lives in rural East Sussex.

Novels by Anthony McDonald

**TENERIFE
THE DOG IN THE CHAPEL
TOM & CHRISTOPHER AND THEIR KIND
DOG ROSES
THE RAVEN AND THE JACKDAW
SILVER CITY
IVOR'S GHOSTS
ADAM
BLUE SKY ADAM
GETTING ORLANDO
ORANGE BITTER, ORANGE SWEET
ALONG THE STARS
WOODCOCK FLIGHT**

Short stories

MATCHES IN THE DARK:
13 Tales of Gay Men

Diary

RALPH: DIARY OF A GAY TEEN

Comedy

THE GULLIVER MOB

Gay Romance Series:

**Sweet Nineteen
Gay Romance on Garda
Gay Romance in Majorca
Gay Tartan
Cocker and I
Cam Cox
The Paris Novel
The Van Gogh Window
Tibidabo
Spring Sonata
Touching Fifty
Romance on the Orient Express**

———

And, writing as 'Adam Wye'

**Boy Next Door
Love in Venice
Gay in Moscow**

All titles are available as Kindle ebooks and as paperbacks from Amazon.

www.anthonymcdonald.co.uk

Printed in Great Britain
by Amazon